Annie Darling lives in London in a tiny flat, which is bursting at the seams with teetering piles of books. Her two greatest passions in life are romance novels and Mr Mackenzie, her British Shorthair cat. *The Little Bookshop of Lonely Hearts* is her first novel.

THE LITTLE BOOKSHOP OF LONELY HEARTS

Once upon a time in a crumbling London bookshop, Posy Morland spent her life lost in the pages of her favourite romantic novels. So when Bookends' eccentric owner, Lavinia, dies and leaves the shop to Posy, she must put down her books and join the real world. Because Posy hasn't just inherited an ailing business, but also the unwelcome attentions of Lavinia's grandson, Sebastian, AKA The Rudest Man In London. Posy has a cunning plan to transform Bookends into the bookshop of her dreams, if only Sebastian would leave her alone to get on with it. As Posy and her friends fight to save their beloved bookshop, Posy's drawn into a battle of wills with Sebastian, about whom she's started to have some rather feverish fantasies . . .

ANNIE DARLING

THE LITTLE BOOKSHOP OF LONELY HEARTS

Complete and Unabridged

CHARNWOOD
Leicester

First published in Great Britain in 2016 by
Harper
HarperCollins*Publishers*
London

First Charnwood Edition
published 2018
by arrangement with
HarperCollins*Publishers*
London

The moral right of the author has been asserted

This novel is entirely a work of fiction. The names, characters and incidents portrayed in it are the work of the author's imagination. Any resemblance to actual persons, living or dead, events or localities is entirely coincidental.

A catalogue record for this book is available from the British Library.

ISBN 978–1–4448–3706–3

Published by
F. A. Thorpe (Publishing)
Anstey, Leicestershire

Set by Words & Graphics Ltd.
Anstey, Leicestershire
Printed and bound in Great Britain by
T. J. International Ltd., Padstow, Cornwall

This book is printed on acid-free paper

From the *London Gazette*

OBITUARY

Lavinia Thorndyke OBE, April 1, 1930
to February 14, 2015

Bookseller, mentor and tireless champion of literature, Lavinia Thorndyke has died aged 84. Lavinia Rosamund Melisande Thorndyke was born on 1 April 1930, the youngest child and only daughter of Sebastian Marjoribanks, the third Lord Drysdale and his wife Agatha, daughter of Viscount and Viscountess Cavanagh.

Lavinia's eldest brother, Percy, was killed fighting for the Loyalists in Spain in 1937. Twins, Edgar and Tom, both served with the RAF and died within a week of each other during the Battle of Britain. Lord Drysdale died in 1947 and his title and family estate in North Yorkshire passed to a cousin.

Lavinia and her mother made a home for themselves in Bloomsbury, just around the corner from Bookends, the shop gifted to Agatha on her twenty-first birthday in 1912 by her parents in the hope that it would prove a distraction from her work with the Suffragette movement.

In a column she wrote for *The Book-seller* in 1963, Lavinia recalled: 'My mother and I found solace among the shelves. To compensate for our lack of a family, we were happy to be adopted by the Bennets in *Pride and Prejudice*, the Mortmains in *I Capture the Castle*, the Marches in *Little Women*, the Pockets in *Great Expec-tations*. We found what we were searching for in the pages of our favourite books.'

Lavinia was educated at Camden School for Girls, then took up a degree in Philosophy at Oxford University where she met Peregrine Thorndyke, third and youngest son of the Duke and Duchess of Maltby.

They were married at St Paul's Church in Covent Garden on 17 May 1952 and started wedded life in the flat above Book-ends. On the death of Lavinia's mother Agatha in 1963, the Thorndykes moved into her house in Bloomsbury Square and many a young writer was mentored, nur-tured and nourished around their kitchen table.

Lavinia was awarded an OBE in 1982 for her services to bookselling.

Peregrine died in 2010 after a short battle with cancer.

Lavinia remained a familiar sight in Bloomsbury cycling from her home to Book-ends. A week ago, after a recent collision with another cyclist resulting in nothing more than scrapes and bruises, Lavinia died suddenly at her home.

She is survived by her only daughter, Mariana, Contessa di Reggio d'Este, and her grandson, Sebastian Castillo Thorndyke, a digital entrepreneur.

1

Lavinia Thorndyke's wake was held at a private members' club for ladies of a literary persuasion on Endell Street in Covent Garden, which she'd belonged to for over fifty years.

In a wood-panelled reception room on the second floor, its windows looking out on to the bustling streets below, people gathered to remember. Even though the mourners had come straight from Lavinia's funeral, there was a rainbow of colours on display. Women in floral summer frocks, men in white suits and crisp sherbet-coloured shirts, though one man was wearing an egg yolk yellow blazer as if it were his personal mission to make up for the lack of sun on this grey February day.

But then Lavinia's instructions had been quite clear in the letter she'd left detailing her funeral arrangements — 'Absolutely no black. Cheerful colours only' — and maybe that was why the atmosphere was less funeral and more garden party. A very raucous garden party.

Posy Morland was dressed in the same shade of pale pink as Lavinia's favourite roses. She'd unearthed the dress from the back of her wardrobe where it had hung limply for nearly a decade, hidden behind a leopard print fun fur that Posy hadn't worn since her student days.

Over the subsequent years, there'd been a lot of pizza, quite a bit of cake and huge amounts of

5

wine. No wonder the dress strained against her breasts and hips, but it was what Lavinia would have wanted, so Posy tugged ineffectually at the tight pink cotton and took another sip of the champagne, which had been another of Lavinia's express wishes.

With the champagne flowing, the conversation in the room had reached a deafening crescendo. 'Any fool can put on a production of *Midsummer Night's Dream* but it takes real guts to do it in togas,' she heard someone bray in a booming luvvie voice and Nina, who was sitting next to Posy, giggled, then tried to mask it with a delicate cough.

'It's all right, I think we're allowed to laugh,' Posy told her, because the two men in the corner behind them were guffawing so uproariously that one had to stop and clutch his knees. 'Lavinia always said that the best funerals turned into the best parties.'

Nina sighed. She'd matched her gingham dress with her hair, which was currently a vibrant Prussian blue. 'God, I'm going to miss her.'

'The shop won't be the same without Lavinia,' said Verity, who was sitting on Posy's other side and wearing grey because she'd argued that grey wasn't black and that she didn't have the complexion or the disposition to wear cheerful colours. 'I still expect her to come barrelling through the door all excited about a book she'd stayed up half the night reading.'

'And how she'd always refer to five on a Friday afternoon as champagne o'clock,' Tom said. 'Never had the heart to tell her I don't like champagne.'

6

The three women and Tom, who comprised the staff of Bookends, clinked their glasses together and Posy was sure that all of them were taking time to scroll through their favourite memories of Lavinia.

The breathless, girlish voice, her perfect 1930s English, like a character from a Nancy Mitford novel.

How she'd read everything, met everyone, but was still excited at the thought of new books, new people.

The roses in the same shade of pink as Posy's dress that she'd buy on Monday and Thursday mornings and arrange carelessly but so artfully in a chipped glass vase she'd bought from Woolworths in the 1960s.

The way she'd call each of them darling and how that 'darling' could sound affectionate, reproachful, teasing.

Oh, Lavinia. Sweet, funny Lavinia and the hundreds of tiny kindnesses she'd heaped on Posy. After Posy's parents had died in a car crash seven years ago, Lavinia had not only given Posy a job but let Posy and her little brother Sam stay on in the flat above Bookends that they'd always called home, and so she was sad that Lavinia was suddenly gone, she really was. It was the kind of sad that sat deep in Posy's bones and rested heavy in her heart.

But there was also worry. A gnawing anxiety that had taken hold of Posy's internal organs and kept tugging at them every few minutes or so. Now that Lavinia was gone, who knew what would happen to Bookends? It was highly unlikely, verging on impossible, that a new owner would let Posy and Sam live rent-free in the flat above the shop. It just wasn't good business sense.

On Posy's meagre bookseller's salary, they certainly couldn't afford to rent anywhere other than the tiniest of shoeboxes somewhere far, far away from Bloomsbury. Then Sam might have to change schools and, if money was too tight to stay in London, they might have to move to Wales, to Merthyr Dyfan, where Posy hadn't lived since she was a toddler, and camp out in their grandparents' two-up, two-down and Posy would have to try and get a job in one of the few local bookshops, if they hadn't all closed down.

So, yes, Posy was sad, desperately sad and aching from the loss of Lavinia, but also she was worried sick, hadn't even been able to choke down a piece of toast this morning, and then she felt guilty for being worried sick when all she should have been feeling was grief.

'Have you any idea what's going to happen to the shop, then?' Verity asked tentatively and Posy realised that the four of them had been sitting there silent and lost in their own thoughts for long, long minutes.

Posy shook her head. 'I'm sure we'll know something soon.' She tried to smile encouragingly but it felt more like a desperate grimace.

Verity grimaced back at her. 'I'd been unemployed for over a year before Lavinia gave me a job, and that was only because she said that Verity Love was the most splendid name she'd ever come across.' She leaned closer to hiss in

Posy's ear. 'I'm not a people person. I don't do well in interviews.'

'I've never even had a job interview,' Posy said, because she'd worked at Bookends forever. She'd spent twenty-five of her twenty-eight years on earth at Bookends where her father had been manager and her mother had taken over the tearoom attached to the shop. Posy had learned her alphabet as she was shelving books, and her numbers as she counted change. 'I don't have a CV and if I did, it wouldn't take up one sheet of paper.'

'Lavinia didn't bother to look at my CV — which was probably for the best, because I was fired from my last three jobs.' Nina held out her arms for their inspection. 'She just asked to look at my tattoos and that was that.'

On one arm, Nina had a trailing design of drooping rose petals and thorns that framed a quote from *Wuthering Heights*: 'Whatever our souls are made of, his and mine are the same.'

On the other arm, for a change of pace, Nina had a full sleeve depicting the Mad Hatter's tea party from *Alice in Wonderland*.

Then the three girls turned to look at Tom because it was his turn to confess his unsuitability for employment outside Bookends. 'I'm a PhD student,' he reminded them. 'I could easily pick up some more teaching or research work, but I don't want to. I want to work at Bookends. On Mondays, we have cake!'

'We have cake every day,' Posy pointed out. 'Look, none of us know what's going to happen so I suppose we'll simply carry on as normal until . . . um, we don't. Let's just take today to remember how much we loved Lavinia and — '

'Ah! There you all are! Lavinia's waifs and strays! Her merry band of misfits!' declared a voice. A deep, pleasant voice, which could have been described as attractive, if the things that were said in that voice weren't always sarcastic and cutting.

Posy looked up at Sebastian Thorndyke's face, which would have been a very attractive face if it wasn't always sneering and she forgot that she was meant to be remembering how much she'd loved Lavinia. 'Ah, Sebastian,' she snapped. 'The self-styled, so-called rudest man in London.'

'Not self-styled or so-called,' Sebastian said in the smug, self-satisfied high-handed way that he'd perfected by the age of ten and which always made Posy curl her fingers into fists. 'The *Daily Mail* said I was and the *Guardian* too, so it must be true.' He glanced down at Posy, eyes lingering over her breasts, which to be fair were testing the buttons of her dress to breaking point. Any sudden movements and she'd flash her M&S ditsy print bra to the room, which would be highly inappropriate at any time, but especially at a wake. Especially in front of Sebastian, but he'd now stopped gazing at her breasts and was looking around the room — probably to see if there was anyone present that he hadn't insulted yet.

You could never tell with Sebastian, Lavinia's only grandchild. Posy had fallen instantly in love with him when she'd arrived at Bookends at the age of three and first encountered the haughty

10

eight-year-old with a sweet smile and eyes as dark as the bitterest of chocolate. She'd stayed in love with Sebastian, following him around Bookends like a devoted and faithful puppy, until she was ten and he'd locked her in the dank coal-hole under the shop where spiders and beetles and rats and all manner of horrible, diseased, crawling creatures lived.

Then he'd denied all knowledge of her whereabouts and it was only when her frantic mother was about to call the police that he'd confessed.

Posy had got over the Coal-hole Affair in time — though to this day, she refused to so much as stick her head through the hatch — but Sebastian had remained her arch nemesis ever since. All through his sullen, sulky teen years, then his cocky twenties when he'd made a fortune developing horrible websites (Zinger or Minger? had been a particular low point, even for him) and now his dissolute thirties when he was never out of the papers, usually with a beautiful blonde model/actress/whatever clinging to his side.

He'd reached peak notoriety after his first and last appearance on BBC's *Question Time* when he'd told a red-faced MP, who was utterly furious about everything from immigrants to green taxes, that he needed a good shag and a cheeseburger. Then when a woman from the audience had embarked on a long, meandering speech about teachers' pay, Sebastian had drawled, 'God, I'm bored. I can't do this sober. Can I go home now?'

11

It was then that the papers had started to call him 'The Rudest Man in London' and Sebastian had been playing up to it ever since — not that he needed any encouragement to behave in an obnoxious and completely offensive manner. Posy suspected that the offensive gene made up at least seventy-five per cent of his DNA.

So, it was actually quite easy to hate Sebastian, but it was also very, very easy to appreciate his beauty.

When his lips weren't curled in derision, he still had a sweet smile, still had those dark, dark eyes inherited from his Spanish father (his mother, Mariana, had always had a weakness for Mediterranean men). His hair was just as dark, and coaxed into cherubic curls made for women to wind around their fingers.

Sebastian was long-limbed and lithe (six foot three, according to *Tatler*, who insisted, despite all evidence to the contrary, that he was one of the most eligible bachelors in the country) and he favoured bespoke suits that clung so lovingly to his body that they were approximately one centimetre away from being obscenely tight.

Today, in deference to Lavinia's last wishes, Sebastian's suit was French navy, his shirt red with white polka dots that matched his pocket square . . .

'Morland, stop staring at me. You're starting to drool,' he said and Posy's face flared as red as his shirt, and her mouth, which had been hanging open, snapped shut.

Then she opened it again. 'I'm not. I wouldn't. In your dreams!'

Her protest simply glanced off Sebastian's Teflon-coated hide. She was working up to saying something really crushing to him, as soon as she could think of something really crushing to say, when Nina nudged her. 'Posy, have a heart,' she said through gritted teeth. 'We've just come from his grandmother's funeral.'

They had. And Lavinia had always been the weak spot in Sebastian's bespoke caddish armour. 'Come on, Granny, I'm taking you to cocktails,' he'd announce as he swept into the shop. He never entered a room when he could sweep into one instead. 'How do you fancy a Martini bigger than your head?'

Lavinia had loved Sebastian, despite his many failings. 'One has to make allowances,' she was fond of saying when she caught Posy reading about his latest beastly act, whether it was an adulterous affair or his soulless dating app, HookUpp, which had made him millions. 'Mariana always over-indulged the poor boy.'

Earlier, in church, Sebastian had read a eulogy to Lavinia that had had everyone roaring with laughter in the pews. As most of the women, and some of the men, had craned their necks to get a better look at him, he sketched a vivid, vibrant picture of Lavinia as if she were standing there next to him. But then he'd finished with a quote from *Winnie the Pooh*, a book he'd said that Lavinia had read to him countless times when he was a child.

''How lucky I am to have something that makes saying goodbye so hard'',' Sebastian had said, and only someone who knew Sebastian as well as Posy could hear the break in his voice, a tiny, terrible fracture. He'd stared down at his notes, which he hadn't looked at once, then raised his head and smiled his brilliant and careless smile and the moment had passed.

Now Posy realised that, as much as she was hurting, Sebastian must be hurting more.

'I'm sorry,' she said. 'We're all so sorry for your loss, Sebastian. I know how much you'll miss her.'

'Thank you, that's very kind of you.' His voice caught again, his smile slipped, but then it was back in the time it took Posy to blink. '*Sorry for your loss.* God, it's such a clichéd sentiment. It doesn't really mean anything, does it? I hate clichés.'

'People only say that because it can be very hard to know what to say when someone's di — '

'You're being very earnest now, Posy. It's so boring. I much prefer it when you're being bitchy,' Sebastian said, and Verity, who hated anything that even faintly resembled a confrontation, covered her face with a napkin and Nina made another hissing noise and Tom looked expectantly at Posy, like he was waiting for her to cut Sebastian down with her rapier-like wit, in which case he'd have a very long wait.

'Rude. Very rude,' was what she did say. 'I would have thought that today of all days, you might have taken some time off from being as thoroughly obnoxious as you usually are. Shame on you!'

'Yeah, shame on me. And I would have thought that today of all days, you might have

14

brushed your hair.' Sebastian actually dared to lift up a piece of Posy's hair, before she swatted him away.

Posy longed for hair that could be described as tresses or locks or even a silken fall. The reality was brown with reddish tones, which she liked to think was auburn in a certain light, but which attracted knots like bees to honey. If she brushed her hair, it transformed into a gigantic frizzy puffball and if she combed it, it was an exercise in pain and futility as she encountered tangle after tangle, so she tended to scoop it up and secure it with whatever was to hand. Usually pencils, but today Posy had made a special effort and used hairclips, even if they were all different colours. She'd hoped the overall effect was eclectic and Bohemian, but apparently it was neither of those things. 'I don't have the kind of hair you can brush,' she said defensively.

'That's true,' Sebastian agreed. 'It's more the kind of hair that birds love to nest in. Now, come on, get up!'

His tone, as ever, was so peremptory that Posy prepared to launch herself off the chair then stopped as she realised that she didn't need to do anything of the sort. She was quite comfy where she was and besides, she'd already had two glasses of champagne on an empty stomach and her legs were doing a good impersonation of jelly.

'I'll stay where I am, if it's all the same to you . . . What *are* you doing?'

Sebastian was manhandling her, that's what he was doing. His hands were under her armpits and he was trying to heave Posy out of her chair, though as she was made of stronger, much denser stuff than the women he was usually seen with, she stayed exactly where she was, until his heaving and her struggling resulted in the inevitable: two of the buttons on the bodice of her dress gave up the good fight and suddenly, Posy was flashing her bra to anyone who cared to look in her direction.

As it was, most of the guests were staring at them because it wasn't often you saw two people almost come to blows at a funeral.

'Get off me!' Posy growled as Verity shoved a napkin at her so Posy could protect her modesty. The two offending buttons had been flung to the far corners of the room with the force of their trajectory. 'Look what you've done!'

She glanced up at Sebastian, who was looking at what he'd done, and not bothering to disguise his leer. 'If you'd got up when I asked you to — '

'You didn't ask. You ordered. You didn't even say please!'

'Anyway that dress was too tight, I'm not surprised your buttons made a bid for freedom after the ordeal you've put them through.'

Posy shut her eyes. 'Go away. I can *not* deal with you. Not today.'

Her words failed to register with Sebastian, who was tugging at her arm now. 'Don't be such a baby. The lawyer wants to see you. Come on. Chop, chop.'

The urge to put her hands on Sebastian so she could inflict grievous bodily harm upped and left, to be replaced with an unpleasant churning

16

in her guts so that Posy was suddenly pleased that she hadn't been able to eat anything.

'Now? He wants to see me now?'

Sebastian threw back his head and groaned. 'Yes! Jesus! Wars have been fought and won in less time than it takes to hoist you out of a chair.'

'But you didn't say. You just demanded and grappled.'

'I'm saying now. Honestly, Morland, I'm losing the will to live here.'

Posy shut her eyes again so she wouldn't have to see the anxious faces of the Bookends staff. 'Why does he want to see me? We're at Lavinia's wake. Can't it wait?'

'Apparently not.' It was Sebastian's turn to close his eyes and pinch the bridge of his elegant, aquiline nose. 'If you don't start moving, I will put you over my shoulder and God knows, I really could do without the hernia.'

That had Posy jumping to her feet. 'I don't weigh *that* much. Thank you!' she added to Nina, who'd produced a safety pin from the depths of her bag and was waving it in Posy's face.

Then, with Sebastian gripping her elbow, because he was incapable of keeping his hands to himself as Posy tried to reunite the two sides of her dress, she found herself hustled out of the room.

★ ★ ★

They walked — well, Sebastian strode and Posy scurried to keep up with him — down a long

17

corridor hung with portraits of the late, esteemed lady members of the club.

Then, just as they reached a door marked 'Private', it suddenly swung open and a small figure swathed in black appeared, paused for a second then threw herself at Posy.

'Oh, Posy! Isn't this awful?'

It was Mariana, Sebastian's mother, Lavinia's only child. Despite Lavinia's request, she was dressed in black from head to toe, her severe attire completed with a beautiful, full-length black lace mantilla, which was a touch of overkill, but then Mariana could never resist a dramatic gesture.

Posy closed her arms around the older woman, who clung to her as if she were the last lifebelt on the *Titanic*. 'It is awful,' Posy said with a sigh. 'I didn't get a chance to talk to you at the church but I'm so, so sorry for your loss.'

Mariana had nothing sarcastic to say about Posy trotting out that well-used phrase. Instead, she clutched Posy's hands tight as a tear trickled slowly down one baby-smooth cheek. She'd had some work done, but even some skilful and discreet fillers and a little Botox couldn't dim Mariana's fragile, delicate beauty.

She reminded Posy of a peony that had blossomed gloriously and was now one sunny day away from drooping gently and gracefully; its petals wilting ever so slightly under close scrutiny.

'What am I going to do without Mummy?' Mariana asked Posy mournfully. 'We spoke every day and she always used to remind me when it

18

was a rollover on EuroMillions so I could ask the butler to go out and buy a ticket.'

'*I'll* call you when it's a rollover on EuroMillions,' Posy said, even as Sebastian folded his arms and leaned back against the door with a put-upon sigh, as if he was about to be dragooned into EuroMillions servitude too.

People thought that Mariana was a silly woman because she cultivated an air of vague helplessness that had ensnared four husbands, each more rich and titled than the last, but she was also as kind as Lavinia had been. Sweeter too, because Lavinia had refused to suffer fools, whereas Mariana was so soft-hearted that she suffered along with anyone who was in pain.

When Posy's parents had died, Lavinia and her husband Peregrine had been two rocks of utter steadfastness but it had been Mariana who had jetted in from Monaco and had swept Posy and her brother, Sam, off to Regent Street. She'd taken Posy — still stunned by the knowledge that suddenly she was an orphan at twenty-one, as well as legal guardian to a devastated eight-year-old — to Jaeger to buy a coat and dress for the funeral. As Posy had mechanically undressed and then dressed in whatever she was handed, Mariana had come into the changing room, cupped Posy's face in her hands and said, 'I know you think I'm a silly, vain woman, but the funeral will be hard, probably the hardest day you'll ever have to get through, darling. A beautiful dress, a well-cut coat — they're armour. And they'll be two less things for you to worry about when I know you have the weight of the world on your poor, young shoulders.'

Once dress and coat had been purchased, Mariana had taken them to Hamleys Toy Shop and bought Sam a huge train set, which when assembled took over their entire living room and most of the hall.

Since then, every few months Mariana would send Posy beautiful designer clothes and Sam a huge box of toys. Although Mariana seemed to think that Posy could squeeze herself into an XS when she was an M at the least, and that Sam had remained eight for the last seven years, she had the best of intentions.

And on what had to be Mariana's hardest ever day, Posy wanted to do what she could to ease her burden. She squeezed Mariana's hands. 'Honestly, if there's anything I can do, anything you need, I'll try to help. I'm not just saying it because it's what people say in these sorts of situations, I really mean it.'

'Oh, Posy, no one can help me,' Mariana told her sorrowfully, and Posy tried to think of some other words of comfort, but she could feel her throat aching, eyes smarting, as if her own tears weren't far off. So she said nothing but stared down at the safety pin that was anchoring her dress together, until Mariana slipped her hands out of Posy's. 'I need to be alone with my thoughts.'

Sebastian and Posy watched Mariana glide down the corridor, until she turned a corner and was gone. 'I guarantee that she'll be bored rigid after three minutes alone with her thoughts,' he said to Posy. 'Five, tops.'

'Oh, I'm sure she won't,' Posy said, though she

too doubted Mariana's staying power. Someone who'd had that many husbands couldn't be expected to do that well under her own steam. 'This lawyer, then?'

'In here,' Sebastian said, opening the door and giving Posy a firm push, as if he suspected that she might bolt. She was certainly thinking about it. But Sebastian flexed his fingers against the small of her back and that was all she needed to propel herself forwards in an effort to get away from the burning brand of his touch through the cotton of her dress.

It was a small sitting room where the ubiquitous wood panelling had been ignored in favour of chintz. So much chintz; be-swagging and be-swathing everything from curtains and pelmets to the sofa and chairs. Posy stood uncertainly in the doorway as Sebastian sat down on the sofa and crossed his legs. His socks were the same shade of red as his shirt and pocket square. Even the laces of his highly polished black brogues were red.

Posy wondered if Sebastian had different coloured laces to match each of his shirts, and whether he spent five minutes every morning threading them through his shoes or if he had a minion to do it for him . . .

'Earth to Morland! Don't tell me you need to be alone with your thoughts too.'

She blinked. 'What? No! Your shoes.'

'*What?*' he echoed in an exasperated tone. 'I do think you might say hello to Mr Powell. And to think that you always accuse me of being rude.'

Posy tore her gaze away from Sebastian to see

that, sitting on the other side of the room, was a middle-aged man in a grey suit and half-moon spectacles. He waggled his fingers in a half-hearted greeting.

'Jeremy Powell, the late Mrs Thorndyke's solicitor,' he said. He looked down at the sheaf of papers on his lap. 'And you are Ms Morland?'

'Posy. Hello.' She took a deep breath and clutched her hands together. 'Is this about the shop? We've all wondered . . . but I didn't think we'd hear so soon. Are you selling it?'

They'd lost so much, she and Sam: their mother and father, Peregrine, then Lavinia and now Bookends, which was more than just a shop. It was their home. The place they always came back to. And now, they wouldn't even have that.

'Sit down, Morland, and stop hovering,' barked Sebastian, indicating the sofa. 'No one likes a hoverer.'

With a baleful glance at Sebastian, Posy skirted around the sofa and sat in the armchair opposite Mr Powell. Sebastian plucked a bottle of champagne out of the ice bucket placed next to him. He peeled off the foil, untwisted the cage then slowly eased the cork out with all the skill of a virtuoso, so it came free with a small but emphatic pop. Posy hadn't noticed the delicate glass coupes on the table, but Sebastian picked one up, poured some champagne into it and handed it to Posy.

'I shouldn't drink any more.' If bad news were imminent, then maybe brandy would be better. Or a cup of sweet tea.

'Lavinia's orders.' Sebastian looked at her, and

his scrutiny, combined with the knowledge that a savage remark was sure to follow, were too much for Posy. She looked away and although she had only been planning to take one sip, just to be polite, she ended up chugging the champagne down in one graceless gulp.

Then she had to concentrate very hard on not belching as Sebastian smiled smugly and gestured at the lawyer. 'Mr Powell, will you do the honours now?'

Posy feared the worst, but she hoped the worst would be brief: 'Please vacate the premises at your earliest convenience and don't let the door hit you in the arse on your way out,' Mr Powell would say, though he might be more polite than that. Instead he leaned forwards to hand Posy an envelope.

Smythson's Cream Wove Quarto. Lavinia had a box of them in the back office of the shop. Posy's name was written in Lavinia's beautiful cursive script in the navy blue ink she'd always favoured.

All of a sudden, Posy's hands didn't want to work. She was shaking so hard that she could hardly open the envelope.

'Let me do it, Morland!'

It turned out that Posy's hands were in full working order when it came to slapping away Sebastian, then she was easing a finger along the flap and pulling out two sheets of the same cream paper, closely covered in Lavinia's writing.

Dearest, dearest Posy,
I hope the funeral hasn't been too grim

and that they haven't stinted on the champagne. I always found that the best way to get through both funerals and weddings was to be slightly tipsy.

I also hope that you aren't too sad. I've had a good innings, as they say, and though even at this late stage in the proceedings I'm not sure that I believe in an afterlife, if there is one then I'm surrounded by the people I love that I've missed so dreadfully. Reunited with my parents, my beautiful brothers, all those fallen friends and, best of all, my darling Perry.

But where does that leave you and Sam, my lovely Posy? I'm sure that my death, my demise, my passing (no matter what word I choose, it still seems unthinkable, ludicrous, that I've shuffled off this old mortal coil) has stirred up memories of your parents. But then you'll remember what Perry and I told you on that awful night after the policeman had left.

That you weren't to worry. That Bookends was as much yours as it was ours and that you would always have a home there.

Posy, darling, that still stands. Bookends is yours. Lock, stock, and that copy of Men Are From Mars And Women Are From Venus that we haven't been able to sell for the past fifteen years.

I know that the shop hasn't been doing well. I've been so intractable and resistant to change since Perry died, but I have every faith that you'll turn the shop's fortunes around. Make it the success it used to be when your father and mother were running it. I'm sure you'll think of all sorts of exciting schemes to transform the old place. With you at the helm, Bookends will start a new chapter in its life and I know that I couldn't be leaving my beloved shop in better hands.

Because you, my dear, of all people know what a magical place a bookshop can be and that everyone needs a little magic in their lives.

I can't tell you how happy I am that Bookends will stay in the family, because I've always regarded you and Sam as family. Besides, you're the only person I truly trust to protect its legacy and keep it safe for future generations of booklovers. I'm counting on you, dear Posy, so don't let me down! It's so important to me — my dying wish, if you will — that Bookends will live on after me. However, if you feel that you don't want to be burdened with it or, I hate to say this, if it's not operating at a profit within two years, then ownership will revert to Sebastian. The last thing on earth I would want, darling Posy, is for you to be saddled with something that will grind you down into the ground, but I know it won't come to that.

Now, don't be afraid to ask Sebastian for help. I'm sure you'll be seeing lots more of him anyway as he'll inherit the rest of Rochester Mews, so you'll be neighbours and, I hope, friends. Time to put all that bitterness about the Coal-hole behind you. Yes, Sebastian can be a little obstreperous, but he really does mean well. That said, don't put up with any nonsense from him. I do think he'd benefit from a good clip around the ear from time to time,

So, goodbye, my darling girl. Be brave, be strong, be a success. Always remember to follow your heart and you won't go astray.

Much love,
Lavinia xxx

2

Bookends was situated at the northern tip of Bloomsbury. People walking from Holborn down Theobalds Road, towards the Gray's Inn Road, often missed the tiny cobbled Rochester Street on their right. If they did happen upon it and decide it was worth exploring, chances were they'd pause as soon as they came to the delicatessen to look at the cheeses and sausages and brightly coloured edibles in glass jars all lovingly displayed in the window.

They might browse the boutiques full of pretty dresses and soft and cheerful winter knits. Then the butcher's, the barber's, the stationery shop, until they came to the pub on the corner, the Midnight Bell, across the road from the fish and chip shop, There's No Plaice Like Home, and an old-fashioned sweet shop, which still weighed out pear drops and lemon sherbets, aniseed balls, winter nips, humbugs and liquorice allsorts and poured them into little candy-striped paper bags.

Just before the end of this delightful street, like something from a Dickens novel, was a small courtyard on the right: Rochester Mews.

Rochester Mews wasn't pretty or picturesque. There were weather-beaten wooden benches arranged in a circle at the centre of the courtyard, planter pots full of weeds . . . even the trees looked as though they'd seen better days.

On one side of the yard was a small row of five empty shops. From the peeling, faded signs, it would seem that in another life the premises housed a florist, a haberdasher's, a tea and coffee merchant, a stamp shop and an apothecary. On the other side of the yard was another, larger shop, though it looked like a collection of shops all joined together to make a jumbled whole. It had old-fashioned bow windows and a faded, black-and-white striped awning.

The sign above the door read Bookends, and on this particular day in February, with the afternoon sun already sinking and the shadows lengthening, a small, red sports car turned into the yard and came to a halt outside.

The door opened and a tall man in a dark suit and a shirt the same shade of red as his car unfolded himself from the driver's seat, complaining bitterly all the while that the cobbles were playing havoc with the suspension of his vintage Triumph.

He strode around to the passenger side, pulled open the door and said, 'Morland, I haven't got all day. I drove you home, I've done my good deed for the day, now can you shift your bloody arse?'

A young woman in a pink dress stumbled from the car, then stood there swaying slightly on unsteady legs as if she was still getting used to dry land after months spent at sea. In one hand she clutched a cream-coloured envelope.

'Morland!' The man snapped his fingers in the woman's face and she came to with a start.

'Rude!' she exclaimed. 'So rude.'

'Well, you're standing there like one o'clock half struck,' he said, then slouched against the wall as she rooted around in her bag and produced a bunch of keys.

'I won't come in now,' the man said. He gestured at the courtyard, neglected and unloved. 'What a dump. I suppose we'll have to chat this out quite soon. Can't do much with the mews with you as a sitting tenant in the shop, can I?'

The woman was still struggling to get the door open but she turned to look at him. Her face pale, eyes wide. 'But I'm not a sitting tenant, am I? I thought I was the owner. Well, for two years at least . . .'

'Not now, Morland. I'm a very busy man.' He was already walking back to his car. 'Laters!'

She watched him drive away with a crash of gears, then opened the door of the shop and stepped inside.

⋆ ⋆ ⋆

Posy had no memory of leaving the club with Sebastian, getting in his car, doing up her seat belt — none of it. It was as if there'd been some breach in the space-time continuum as soon as she folded up Lavinia's letter and placed it back in its envelope.

She was still clutching it now as she stood in the dark shop, the familiar shape of the shelves, the stacks of books, the comforting smell of paper and ink all around her. She was home and suddenly the world was back in focus, but still

29

Posy stood there, not sure that she was capable of walking, much less able to think of where her feet should carry her.

Then Posy heard the bell above the door tinkle. It made her jump and she turned around to see Sam, school bag slung over one shoulder, anorak undone despite the cold and the fact that she told him every morning to do it up.

'My God, you frightened the life out of me!' she exclaimed. It was completely dark now; she didn't know how long she'd been standing there. 'You're home late.'

'It's Tuesday. Football practice,' Sam said, moving past her, his face in shadow but his steps slightly crabbed, which made Posy's heart sink because it meant his shoes were getting too tight and he didn't want to tell her because she'd only just bought him new ones in the January sales.

This time last year he'd been the same height as her, but now he'd shot up by a good six inches; he was going to be as tall as their father. As Sam reached the counter and snapped on the lights, Posy caught sight of his grubby white socks, which meant he needed new school trousers too. She hadn't budgeted for either new school shoes or trousers this month. And then she looked down and saw Lavinia's letter still in her hand.

'Are you all right, Posy? Was it awful?' Sam leaned on the counter and frowned. 'Are you going to cry? Do you need some chocolate?'

'What? No. Yes. I mean, the funeral, it was hard. It was sad. Very, very sad.'

Sam peered at her from beneath his fringe,

which he refused to cut, despite Posy's threat to creep into his room with the kitchen scissors while he slept. 'I still think I should have come. Lavinia was my friend too.'

Posy moved then. Stretched out her arms and legs, which were stiff from being still for so long, and walked over to the counter so she could brush the hair back from Sam's eyes. They were the same blue as her own eyes, the same blue as their father's. Forget-me-not blue, her mother had always called it.

'Honestly, Sam, as you get older, you'll have plenty of funerals to go to,' she said softly. 'You'll be sick of funerals. And there'll be a memorial service later in the year. You can go to that, as long as it's not on a school day.'

'We might not even be in London by then,' Sam said, pulling his head back so his hair flopped over his face again. 'Has anyone said what's happening to the shop? Do you think they'll let us stay here until Easter? What's going to happen about school? I'll need to know quite soon. This is a very important academic year for me!'

His voice squeaked then broke on the last sentence. It sounded painful and Posy gulped in sympathy. 'Nobody's going to come in and take the shop out from under us,' she said. Saying it out loud didn't make it sound any less unbelievable. Or true, because Sebastian seemed to have plans for the mews that didn't involve Bookends or Posy. 'Lavinia's left the shop to me. I own the shop, so I suppose I own the flat above the shop too.'

'Why on earth would she leave you the shop?' Sam opened his mouth, probably to unleash a whole new volley of questions, then shut it. 'I mean, it's lovely of Lavinia to leave the shop to you, but you're not even allowed to cash up unsupervised at the end of the day.'

This was also true, after an incident involving a missing one hundred pounds, which hadn't been missing at all, it was just that the 0 key on the shop calculator was sticky because Posy had been eating a Twix while she cashed up. 'Lavinia was being kind, wanting to make sure that we'd be all right, but I wonder if this was the best way to go about it,' Posy admitted. 'Oh, Sam, I can't even think in whole sentences right now. Have you got any homework?'

'You want to talk about homework? *Now?*' Posy was sure that Sam was rolling his eyes. 'What's wrong with you?'

Where to start with that one? 'Mostly, I'm hungry. I haven't had anything to eat all day. Shall we have fish-finger sandwiches for dinner?' They always had fish-finger sandwiches for dinner when either one of them was feeling down. They'd had fish-finger sandwiches for dinner quite a lot recently.

'Crinkle chips and baked beans too,' Sam decided as he followed Posy through the back office and up the stairs to their flat. 'Also, for English I have to pick a rap song and rewrite it in the style of a Shakespeare sonnet, so can you help me with that?'

★   ★   ★

Later, after fish-finger sandwiches had been eaten and Sam's English homework had been accomplished with a glass of wine and only a small amount of flouncing and door slamming (mostly from Posy), she crept back downstairs to the shop.

Sam was meant to be getting ready for bed, but she could hear the faint but tinny sound of a computer game from his room. Posy didn't have the energy for another argument though; not after trying to rewrite Jay Z's '99 Problems' in iambic pentameter.

Posy only put on the sidelights so the shop was mostly in shadow then slowly walked around the main room. Shelves lined the walls from floor to ceiling; there was a big display table in the centre of the floor, flanked by three sofas in varying stages of decay. Open arches to the left and right led to a series of anterooms sectioned off by book cases. Posy suspected that the bookcases bred overnight. Sometimes she'd be poking around in one of the furthest reaches of the shop and would come across a bookcase that she swore she'd never seen before.

Her fingers trailed over the shelves, the spines of the books, as she did a silent inventory. The very last room on the right, accessed through a pair of glass doors, had once been a little tearoom. Now it was a curtained-off store room; its tables and chairs stacked to one side, the cake stands and china lovingly sourced from charity shops, antique fairs and car boot sales, packed away in boxes. If Posy closed her eyes, she could imagine it as it had once been. The smell of coffee and freshly baked cakes wafting through the shop, her mother weaving through the tables, her long blonde hair escaping from its ponytail, her cheeks pink, green eyes sparkling as she dispensed coffee and tea refills and took away empty plates.

In the shop, her father would have rolled up his shirt-sleeves — he always wore a shirt and waistcoat with his jeans — and could usually be found halfway up the rolling ladder as he selected a series of books for a customer waiting down below. 'If you liked that one, then you'll *love* these,' he would say. Lavinia had called him the King of Hand-Selling. As Posy reached the poetry section, her eyes immediately searched for the three volumes of poetry that her father had written, which they always kept in stock. 'I think, if Ian Morland hadn't been taken from us so cruelly, so suddenly,' Lavinia had written in his obituary, 'then he would have become one of our greatest English poets.'

There'd been no obituary written for her mother, but that hadn't meant she was missed any less. Far from it. As Posy retraced her steps to the main room again, she wasn't wandering through a shop, but through her home, memories of her mother and father alive with every step she took.

In the back office, one of the walls was covered with the signatures of visiting authors, everyone from Nancy Mitford and Truman Capote to Salman Rushdie and Enid Blyton. The notches on the doorjamb faithfully recorded the heights of the Bookends children, starting with Lavinia and her brothers and ending with Posy and Sam.

Outside in the courtyard, they'd have summer fetes and Christmas fairs. Posy remembered how the trees would be strung with fairy lights for launch parties and poetry readings al fresco. They'd once held a wedding reception out there after two customers had fallen instantly and madly in love over a copy of *The Unbearable Lightness of Being*.

Under the shelves in a corner by the counter was the cubbyhole where her father had built her a little reading nook. Posy's mother had made her four plump cushions to lounge on while she read.

It was in Bookends that Posy had met some of her best friends. Pauline, Petrova and Posy (whom she was named for) Fossil from *Ballet Shoes*, her mother's favourite book. Not to mention Milly-Molly-Mandy and little-friend-Susan, the girls of St Clare's and Malory Towers and the Chalet School. Scout and Jem Finch from *To Kill a Mockingbird*. The Bennet sisters. *Jane Eyre* and poor, mad Cathy 'mopped and mowed' about the moors as she searched for her Heathcliffe.

And it had been a night very much like this one, but far, far worse when she'd wandered around the darkened shop, still dressed in her funeral black, still seeing the two coffins slowly being lowered into the ground. That night, unable to sleep, determined not to cry because she knew that she'd howl and she didn't want to wake up Sam, she'd plucked a book, a random book, from the shelves and crawled into her cubbyhole.

It had been a Georgette Heyer novel, *Regency Buck*. A beautiful flighty girl, Judith Taverner, locks horns with the sardonic, dandified Julian St John Audley, her legal guardian. Judith launches herself on London society, has madcap adventures in Brighton, meets and charms Beau Brummel and the Prince Regent, and has many spirited disagreements with the arrogant Julian, until they're both compelled to admit their love.

It had pushed buttons that Posy didn't even know she had. The Heyer Regency romances weren't *quite* up there with *Pride and Prejudice*, which was the gold-star, triple-A standard of romance novels, but they came quite close.

Over the next few numb weeks when just getting through each day intact was a major triumph, Posy had read every single Regency romance Georgette Heyer had written. She'd begged Lavinia to order more and when she'd finished them all, Posy took to the internet to find other writers who were considered Heyer's successors: Clare Darcy, Elizabeth Mansfield, Patricia Veryan, Vanessa Gray — they couldn't match Heyer's exquisite attention to detail or her wit, but there were still flighty young heiresses and sardonic men trying to lord it over them until love prevailed.

Posy had taken over one room of the shop and filled it with novels by Julia Quinn, Stephanie Laurens, Eloisa James, Mary Balogh, Elizabeth Hoyt and others. And when Posy had read every Regency romance that she could find, there were other books, lots and lots of them, where the girl didn't just get the boy, she got the happy ever after that everyone deserved. Well, almost everyone. Serial killers and people who were cruel to animals and drunk drivers — especially drunk drivers, like the one who had careered over the central reservation of the M4 and ploughed into her parents' car — none of them deserved happy ever afters, but everybody else did.

It turned out that a lot of the women who worked in nearby shops and offices and browsed Bookends in their lunch-hour were also suckers for a well-written romance. Since no one was buying enough misery memoirs or stodgy books on military history to warrant the shelf space, Posy persuaded Lavinia to allow her to take over two more rooms of the shop.

But these days, people weren't buying enough books of any kind. Not from Bookends anyway. In her letter, Lavinia had seemed sure that Posy would immediately devise a bulletproof scheme to entice people back into the shop to buy books in great quantities, when nothing could be further from the truth.

Suddenly, Posy couldn't bear to be in the shop a moment longer. It had always been her happy place, her lodestar, a comfort blanket made of wood and paper, but now the shelves upon shelves of books taunted her. It was so much responsibility and Posy wasn't very good at responsibility.

She turned off the lights in the shop, shut the door that separated the shop from the stairs that led up to their flat, which was usually left open, then slowly climbed the stairs. She was about to open Sam's door without knocking, but remembered just in time the 'knock first' rule she'd instigated after Sam had barged into the bathroom and caught her in the shower, screeching 'Bohemian Rhapsody' into her shampoo-bottle microphone.

'Sam? Are you decent?' Dear God, don't let him be doing indecent things, because she wasn't ready for that. 'Can I come in?'

She heard an affirmative grunt, and tentatively pushed open the door. Sam was lying on his stomach on top of his duvet, staring at his laptop. 'What's up?'

Posy sat down on the edge of his bed and looked at his bony shoulders hunched over the computer screen. Even now, though he'd been in her life for fifteen years (their miracle baby, her parents had called Sam, though at the time thirteen-year-old Posy had been mortified at the prospect of what her parents had been doing to produce a miracle baby) she still sometimes had an overwhelming urge to squeeze Sam until he squeaked, such was the depth of her love for him. She settled for reaching out to ruffle his hair but he twisted away from her. 'Get off me! Have you been drinking?'

'No!' Posy settled for nudging him with her elbow. 'I need to talk to you.'

'But we've already talked about Lavinia and I already told you that I'm sad and everything about it sucks, but really, Pose, I can't take any more speeches about feelings and emotions.' He pulled a face. 'Can we just not?'

Posy was sick of making speeches about

38

feelings and emotions, so that worked out fine, but still, she was the big sister. The parental figure. The designated adult. The *responsible* one. 'But, you know, if you did want to talk, you can. You can tell me anything.'

'Yeah, I know.' Sam looked up from his screen and gave her a wan smile. 'Are we done now?'

'I wanted to talk to you about something else, actually.' It worked both ways. She was meant to be able to talk to Sam about anything — except her period, her weight, her love life or lack thereof (he'd drawn up a list) — but this was proving harder than expected. 'I know you haven't had much time to think about it, but how do you feel about me taking on the shop? I could make a go of it, right? After all, bookselling is in my blood. Like, if you cut me, I'd bleed words, so who better to take over Bookends than me?' Posy's shoulders slumped. 'Though I suppose, it would mean being very grown-up and responsible.'

'Hate to be the one to break it to you, Pose, but you're twenty-eight, so technically you are grown-up.' Sam hoisted himself up on his elbows so Posy could see the doubtful look on his face. She made a mental note not to come to Sam if she ever needed a character witness. 'And I suppose you are responsible . . . in your own way. I mean, you've been responsible for me for the last seven years and I'm still alive and I don't have rickets or anything.'

It wasn't quite the validation that Posy had been after. 'What about being responsible for the shop, though? I have two years to turn it round.

39

Make it into a viable business.'

'Less than two years really, because the shop isn't doing very well, is it? It hasn't made a profit for ages and it was only because Lavinia had family money that it's kept going as long as it has.' Sam shrugged. 'That's what Verity told Tom when he asked if he could have a pay rise.'

The problem with Sam was that he was too smart for his own good. The other problem was that he heard things that he shouldn't and then he worried about them when he didn't need to. It was Posy's job to worry for the both of them.

'We don't have to stay. I could give up the shop and then I guess we could move somewhere else and I could get another job — '

Sam's head shot up. 'What? No! I can't leave school, not with my GCSEs coming up! And where would we live? What kind of money would you be able to earn? Have you any idea how much the average London rent is?' He looked as if he might burst into tears. 'We'd have to move miles and miles away. To, like, *the suburbs*.'

Sam made it sound as if the suburbs were just a fancy way of saying a cesspit. 'Lots of people live in the suburbs, Sam. Or we could move to another big city but one that isn't as expensive as London. Say, Manchester or Cardiff. If we moved back to Wales, we'd be close to the grandparents.'

'But Manchester or Cardiff isn't here, is it? Why would anyone want to live anywhere else but here?' Sam asked with all the arrogance of someone lucky enough to have lived their entire life in Central London. Coram Fields was his back garden and the British Museum was his corner shop full of mummies and fossils and ancient weapons. In five minutes they could be in Soho or Oxford Street or Covent Garden. They could jump on a bus or a tube and the whole of London was theirs for the taking.

People who didn't know London thought it was a cold and unfeeling place, but their London wasn't at all like that. Posy and Sam knew all the shopkeepers along Rochester Street (Posy was even a member of the Rochester Street Traders' Association) and got mates' rates on everything from fish and chips to scented candles. They knew the names of their favourite assistants in the big Sainsbury's opposite Holborn tube station. Posy volunteered at Sam's old primary school, going in once a week for one-on-one sessions with reluctant readers, and Sam's best friends, Pants and Little Sophie, who worked in Bookends on Saturdays, lived just around the corner on the sprawling Housing Association estate.

It was like living in a village without the inconvenience of living in a village. When they went to stay with their Welsh grandparents, everything shut at six in the evening, one o'clock on Thursdays, *all day on Sundays*, so God help you if you'd forgotten to stock up on chocolate.

'So, you want to stay here, then?' Posy asked, because they were in this together, she and Sam. 'You reckon I could make a success of the shop?'

'Yeah. You have to try at least, don't you? It's what Lavinia wanted.' Sam looked at his laptop then sighed. 'The only thing is . . . I'm not saying that it will, but if it all goes horribly wrong, what's going to happen to us? We might end up owing money, instead of just being poor. And then what about tuition fees and things?'

The urge to squeeze Sam came over Posy again and she had to slide her hands under her thighs. 'You don't need to worry about that,' she said, swallowing hard. 'When they died, Mum and Dad . . . they had a life insurance policy. I haven't touched a penny of it because I've been saving it for your university fees. There's enough there to get you through a degree, maybe a postgraduate degree too, if you only eat Pot Noodles. So you don't have to stress about that, OK?'

'OK. Wow! I wasn't expecting that.' Sam let out a deep breath. 'I'd been worrying about how we were going to pay for the tuition fees. Though if you really need the money to, like, pay the staff wages, then maybe I could skip university and get a job.'

'You are going to university,' Posy stated forcefully. 'Are we clear about that?'

'We are,' Sam agreed, and Posy thought that maybe he was smiling, though his back was to her and neither of them had smiled much this week. 'And until then, we're staying here — which is good 'cause I hate it when things change.'

'Yeah, me too,' Posy said feelingly. 'They never seem to be good changes, do they?'

Sam rolled over and propped himself up on one elbow. 'About the shop . . . ' he said. 'You'll be fine. Better than fine. You'll be amazing. You'll be the best bookseller ever. You have to be, Posy, because otherwise we'll be homeless right when I'm meant to be doing A-levels. What more motivation do you need?'

'I think that's more than enough motivation,' Posy said, though rather than spurring her on, Sam's words had put the fear of God into her. 'Another half hour, then lights out.'

'You can kiss me if you like,' Sam offered magnanimously. 'On the cheek.'

Posy settled for ruffling his hair, which made Sam squawk in outrage as she knew it would. That was the only reason she was smiling as she closed his bedroom door.

3

Telling Sam that she was going to take over Bookends and do her utmost to turn it into a profitable business was a doddle, a breeze, a walk in the park, compared to having to tell the staff the latest developments.

'What happened to you yesterday?' Verity asked when she arrived for work the next morning, closely followed by Nina, then Tom. 'You disappeared with the dreaded Sebastian and that was the last we saw of you.'

Nina was in the little kitchen off the back office, but she stuck her head out of the door, kettle in hand and a grin on her face. 'Did he take liberties with you? Did you slap his face and storm off?'

'Liberties weren't taken but I did want to slap his face several times,' Posy said, as she turned on the till. 'It was touch and go at one point.'

'Didn't he drag you off to see Lavinia's lawyer?' Tom looked up from his breakfast panini. 'Oh God, it's bad news, isn't it? Are they selling the shop?'

All three of them wore matching expressions that could be summed up as 'The end of the world is nigh', when it wasn't nigh at all. At least Posy didn't think it was.

'No one's selling the shop.' Posy gripped the counter tight for moral support, felt the scarred, polished wood firm beneath her fingers.

'Lavinia's left the shop to me and I'm not going anywhere.'

Posy paused and waited. She wasn't sure exactly what she was waiting for; perhaps some heartfelt congratulations, maybe a 'You go, girl!' Instead she got silence and three perplexed faces staring back at her. Was there anyone, anywhere, who had even a tiny bit of faith in her? Apart from Lavinia, whose faith in Posy, it seemed, was entirely misguided.

Posy rubbed her hands together nervously. 'Not that it's going to be easy, but Sam and I are up for the challenge. Well, Sam's kind of up for it, anyway. Although I'm . . . we're . . . going to have . . . There will be changes but, um, good changes. Er, exciting changes.'

'You're in charge then? You're the boss of us?' It was impossible to know how Verity felt about that — in fact, it was impossible to tell how Verity felt about most things. She was very hard to read, for all that Posy had known her for four years and considered Verity one of her very best friends. Verity was also the assistant manager of Bookends, which meant she stayed in the back office doing the accounts, ordering stock and refusing to interact with anyone coming into the shop to buy a book. She'd been Lavinia's right-hand woman while Posy had drifted about colonising more space in the shop for her romance novels. Without Verity, Bookends would cease to function within days. Within hours.

'Boss is such a harsh word,' Posy said soothingly. 'Nothing will change. Well, some things will need to change, but I'm not going to turn into a despot and shout, 'It's my way or the highway!' whenever we have a disagreement. I'll still make tea and stock shelves and go out on a chocolate run.'

'So is my job safe?' It was easy to tell what Nina was thinking because Nina was biting her lip and frowning and generally looking as if Posy was about to issue her with her P45 — not that Posy would have had the first clue how to do such a thing. 'And Tom can still work part-time — or, to be more accurate, whenever he feels like gracing us with his presence? Or is it last in, first out? Which would mean me, because I've only been here two years. Though *technically*, I've worked more hours than Tom.'

'Shut up,' Tom hissed. 'Of course, Posy isn't sacking anyone because Posy's our friend as well as our new boss. Our sweet, kind, dear friend. And may I say that you're looking particularly lovely today, Posy.'

'You can but I'm writing you up for sexual harassment,' Posy said, and she pretended to write something in her notebook, which was a long-standing shop joke and Tom was always the punchline, so he pretended to scowl and Nina went back into the kitchen to put the kettle on. Only Verity remained standing there, hands on hips.

'I'm pleased for you, Posy — it would have been awful if you and Sam had been made homeless — but very soon we won't be able to afford *any* members of staff, full-time or part-time,' she added in a whisper, though Tom was more interested in his panini than their

46

conversation. 'These changes you mentioned, what are they?'

As of now, the changes hadn't made themselves known to Posy. She needed more time to research and ponder and possibly make some lists, maybe a pie chart too. Then, hopefully, she'd have a big idea, a grand scheme for Bookends, that Posy could present to Verity and the rest of the staff with such passion and conviction that they'd be completely on board too. What could be simpler?

It occurred to Posy, as she tried to avoid looking Verity in the eye, that she wasn't cut out to be a leader. She wasn't a follower either, or even a plodder. At least plodders got to their destination eventually. No, Posy was a floater, happy to do her own thing and be swept along with the tide and this was all a bit too much, a bit too soon when she was still reeling from Lavinia's absence.

'Like I said, good changes,' Posy murmured vaguely, though she could feel sweat breaking out on her forehead and her upper lip while at the same time her hands were icy cold. She also had a terrible taste in her mouth, like she'd been licking batteries. It was fear. Big, stinky fear. She pulled up the corners of her mouth in a pitiful excuse for a confident smile. 'Exciting changes. Very, very exciting. I'm going to need your help, I won't be able to do it without you.'

Verity nodded. 'As long as these changes aren't like the time when you wanted to have the books arranged by colour and not by alphabet,' she said.

47

'But it would have looked pretty,' Posy protested weakly.

'God help us.' Verity shook her head before scuttling off to the back office.

Telling her colleagues that they were now her employees had been more of an ordeal than Posy had anticipated and now she realised that she had their futures to worry about too. This wasn't only about her and Sam. She didn't want to be the person who was standing between the Bookends staff and unemployment, possibly destitution.

★ ★ ★

When she woke up the following morning, Posy felt galvanised into action. At the least, she should probably write a to-do list. Maybe pop to the fancy new Foyles on Charing Cross Road to scope out the competition.

Neither she nor Sam were morning people. They had a house rule that neither of them spoke at breakfast unless it was absolutely necessary. With her eyes half-closed, Posy made Sam toast and scrambled eggs, which he shovelled into his mouth while finishing his history homework. He should have finished it the night before but Posy didn't have the energy to tell him off about it, not when she was still halfway down her first cup of tea.

Sam dumped his plate and mug in the sink and left for school with a grunt that might have been 'goodbye', leaving Posy sitting there, drinking her tea and reading *The Pursuit of*

Love, even though she'd lost count of how many times she'd read it. It always reminded her of Lavinia and what her life might have been like before the war.

Posy cherished this hour when she was still in her pyjamas and befuddled with sleep. It was the one part of the day that was hers and hers alone.

It was a pity that no one had thought to mention it to the person banging on the shop door, ignoring the sign which spelled out very clearly, in the plainest English, that they didn't open until ten. They weren't expecting any deliveries either and anyway the drivers knew to come round the back and ring the bell.

Posy put down her cup and book and shuffled down the stairs in her slippers. The closer she got, the louder the banging was. Muttering under her breath, she moved through the shop and as she got nearer to the door, she saw who was responsible for breaching her peace.

'Stop making all that noise!' Posy banged on the glass to get his attention. 'I'm unlocking the door.'

'My breakfast meeting got cancelled,' Sebastian informed Posy as he shouldered his way past her. 'God, Morland, you're not even dressed yet!'

Technically, Posy was dressed; in pyjama bottoms adorned with Christmas puddings, an old Minecraft T-shirt of Sam's, and a threadbare cardigan. 'It's not even eight thirty, Sebastian. I wasn't exactly expecting callers.'

'Is that what you wear to bed?' He narrowed his eyes, which weren't puffy with sleep like hers. Posy was sure he could see through her layers to

49

her braless state. She folded her arms. 'What a thrill-killer.'

'Shut up! What are you doing here anyway?' Posy asked, but she was talking to Sebastian's back. He'd already done a complete circuit of the main room and was heading past the counter.

'Thought I'd have a proper look around before I make any decisions,' he called from the stairs. 'Come on! I haven't got all day.'

Posy took off after him. 'What kind of decisions?' she panted as she took the stairs far too fast for someone who hadn't finished their first pot of tea. 'This is my home, you can't just barge in here without asking.'

Sebastian was currently peering into Sam's room. 'Really? Why not? What unspeakable things do you get up to in here? Have you got a man on the premises?'

The last man on the premises had been Tom, when he'd come upstairs to mend a dripping tap. Though he hadn't mended it so much as looked at it, then at the screwdriver Posy had given him, with a quizzical expression, and shrugged. 'Just because I'm a man doesn't mean that I know how to do useful stuff,' he'd said and gone back downstairs.

The tap still dripped and Sebastian didn't seem like the sort of man who knew how to do anything useful either. His speciality subjects were being rude and having absolutely no respect for people's personal boundaries.

'It's none of your business what I get up to in my spare time,' she told him indignantly. 'I could

50

have a whole football team up here if I wanted.'

Sebastian pulled his head out of Sam's room, slammed the door and turned to her with a knowing look. 'Highly unlikely. I think footballers tend to prefer their women in something a little more alluring than sagging pyjama bottoms with turds on them. You really are an odd girl, Morland.'

'They're not turds! They're Christmas puddings! These are my Christmas pyjamas!' Posy tugged at the offending pyjamas even as she knew she'd never wear them again. First chance she had, she was going to burn them.

'But it's February,' Sebastian pointed out helpfully as he brushed past her into the living room. 'This place is a fire hazard. Why do you need so many books? Haven't you got enough of them downstairs?'

Posy followed him into the room. 'These are for my personal use,' she said primly, as if she had never, ever read a stock book very carefully so she didn't crease the spine, then placed it tenderly back on the shelf. 'Anyway, there's no such thing as too many books.'

'Oh, yes there is,' Sebastian assured her as he strode over to one of the bookshelves set into the alcoves on either side of the fireplace, where the books were triple stacked. 'I'd say you reached peak book several years ago. There are books everywhere!' he added in disgust as he made a sharp left turn and sent a pile of novels crashing to the ground. 'You must be personally responsible for the destruction of at least three rainforests.'

'I recycle a lot, so I'm sure it all evens out,' Posy said and as Sebastian was obviously intending to stay there for some time — he was currently switching the main light on and off, though she had no idea why — she decided to leave him to it and make a fresh pot of tea. Not wanting to be thought completely devoid of manners, she asked, 'Do you want a brew?'

'Coffee.' Sebastian stared down at the coffee table where last night's dinner plates still sat and his beautiful cupid's bow of a top lip curled. 'Sumatran beans, if you've got them. If not, I'll have Peruvian.'

'Does this look like a branch of Starbucks?'

'No, it doesn't. If this was a branch of Starbucks, it would have been closed down by Environmental Health months ago.'

'You can have instant coffee out of a jar — and it's your lucky day, sweetheart: the Douwe Egberts was on special offer,' Posy said and she swept out of the living room as grandly as anyone could when they were wearing Christmas pudding pyjamas and bunny face slippers.

She didn't want to leave Sebastian unattended but anything was better than having to see the sneer etched on his face and listen to him pass judgement on her soft furnishings and lifestyle choices.

Lavinia had had the roof replaced a few years ago after she'd ventured upstairs and seen the bowls and saucepans positioned to catch the various leaks, but the flat hadn't been redecorated in all the time Posy had lived there. Redecorating would mean having to pack up everything and put it into storage; it didn't bear thinking about, so Posy never thought about it.

She made a fresh pot of tea and poured Sebastian's coffee into a Penguin Books *The Invisible Man* mug — wishful thinking on her part, especially when she discovered that Sebastian wasn't in the living room any more. With sinking heart, she padded down the hall to find him in her room, lounging on her unmade bed and staring at the pile of clothes heaped on the pale blue Lloyd Loom chair. Or maybe he was staring at the pile of clothes heaped on the floor. Or the clothes spilling out of her open drawers. Or the teetering stacks of books by the bed and under her bedside table and next to her bookcases, which were straining under the weight of yet more books.

It was odd, a whole wide world of odd, to have Sebastian of all people stretched out on her candy-striped sheets in another impeccably cut, verging on obscenely tight suit — this one was light grey tweed, accessorised with sky blue shirt, pocket-square, socks and shoelaces. It had been a long time since she'd had a man on her bed, but it wasn't as if Sebastian had seduction on his mind, thank God. Not when his attention was riveted on the half-eaten Double Decker, a sticky and congealed tub of Vicks VapoRub and a balled up pair of socks on her bedside table. Posy might just as well have a sign above her bed that said, 'Abandon hope, all ye who enter here.'

'Not a word,' Posy warned him. 'Or you'll be wearing this coffee.'

Sebastian held up his hands in mock

surrender. 'Oh, Morland, there are no words.' He leaned back on his elbows and eyed yesterday's bra, which was hanging forlornly off one of the knobs of her old-fashioned headboard where Posy had thrown it when she'd got undressed the night before. 'That's twice in three days that I've seen one of your bras. People will start to talk.'

'My bras are no concern of yours.' Posy made a little shooing motion and slopped coffee over an upturned copy of *Valley of the Dolls*. 'Come out of here!'

Sebastian bounded off the bed, snatched the mug from her and was out of the room and all set to sweep into the room next door, when he came to a halt. A locked door would do that.

'What's in here?' he demanded.

'It's none of your business because you're not going in there,' Posy told him. She tried to look stern. 'Anyway, you can't just barge into my shop, my home, and start snooping about like you — '

'Is this where you bury the bodies?' He rattled the door handle again so forcefully that Posy feared for its safety. She insinuated herself between Sebastian and the door and then wished she hadn't because now they were nose to nose. Or rather, her nose was somewhere in the vicinity of Sebastian's chin and she could take great whiffs of him. He smelt heavenly; a heady mixture of mossy forests, warm leather chairs and smoky gentleman's clubs.

Not only was it quite overwhelming, but Sebastian was in a perfect position to look right down the gaping neckline of her T-shirt. As he

54

opened his mouth to make yet another sarcastic remark, Posy put one hand on the centre of his chest and pushed him back. He was so warm, all bone and muscle and —

'Careful, now. I think that counts as inappropriate touching,' he said kindly.

'You! You're inappropriate! This is my parents' room and you're not going in there.'

Sebastian frowned. 'Was. Not is. It was your parents' room. They've been dead, what? Five years.'

'Seven years, as a matter of fact.' Though actually it was six years, eight months, one week and three days, because the exact date of their . . . parting was etched on Posy's heart.

'Seven years and you've got some weird shrine going on in there? How mawkish.'

Posy took a deep breath and tried to exhale through gritted teeth. 'It's not mawkish and it's not a shrine and, again, it's none of your business.'

Maybe it was a shrine and maybe the shop was too and that was why she was determined to hang on to it for dear life, but she couldn't tell Sebastian that. He had the emotional intelligence of a goldfish. Not even a goldfish. Posy had heard tales of goldfish pining away after setting up home with another fish who'd then had the misfortune to die. No, Sebastian had the emotional intelligence of a gnat.

'It's not a shrine,' she repeated. 'I go in there. Vacuum, dust, that kind of thing.'

Sebastian's eyebrows shot up. 'Really?' Those two syllables dripped with scepticism. 'Are you telling me you possess a vacuum cleaner and, on occasion, actually use it? And you *dust*?' Then because he was so much taller and more annoying than her, he reached over Posy's head to run a finger along the top of the doorframe and held it out for inspection. 'Look at that! It's as black as my favourite Alexander McQueen suit.'

It was black. Black with years of accumulated grime and gunk, but who had time to run damp cloths along every nook and crevice? 'Didn't someone once say that after three years the dust doesn't get any worse?' Posy offered with a weak smile. 'Anyway, a bit of dirt never hurt anyone. In fact, it helps to build a healthy immune system.'

She was preaching to the choir — she certainly wasn't preaching to Sebastian, who had suddenly launched himself out of her orbit and was tearing down the stairs, shouting over his shoulder about estate agents and developers. ' . . . have to replace all the windows and I'm pretty sure your electrics are about to blow. Whole place is a death-trap. Not worth spending money to bring it up to code when you're only going to be here for another two years. Probably less than two years. Best you sign it over to me now and we'll put it on the market as a redevelopment site.'

Posy caught up with Sebastian in the back office and had no choice but to grab his sleeve and yank him back so hard that he shrieked. 'Not the suit! Don't ever touch the suit!'

'Sit down! Now!' It was a voice she never, ever had to use on Sam, because he was a paragon among teenage boys and wouldn't dream of doing anything so heinous that she needed to go all Wrath of God on his arse. She'd never used this voice on anyone in her entire life, but she was using it now and it seemed to work because Sebastian immediately dropped down on to the big leather swivel chair, though he swung this way and that with a grin on his face to show that he wasn't completely cowed.

'So stern. You remind me of a dominatrix, I once knew,' he remarked, then lowered his eyes demurely and took a sip of his coffee, though he couldn't quite hide a grimace as his lips made contact with a beverage that had started life as freeze-dried granules.

Posy shook her head. There was nothing for it but to tell Sebastian her plans for Bookends and do it quickly and, hopefully, painlessly. 'I'm not signing the shop over,' she said firmly. 'It's up to you what do you with the mews, but Lavinia left Bookends to me and I can manage perfectly well without your help. Did I say *help*? My mistake. What I meant was interference.'

'What are you going to do with Bookends then?' Sebastian asked. He gazed around the office, the one room in the building which was a model of efficiency and organisation — and that was down to Verity. 'I mean, why on *earth* would you want to take on a failing business?'

'It's not failing!'

Sebastian snorted, rather elegantly, into his coffee. 'I take it you haven't seen the books then? If you had, you'd know that it's losing money hand over fist.'

Those weren't the kind of books that Posy had any interest in, though now she made a mental note to ask Verity to go through them with her. Or rather, hit the horrible highlights for her. 'Obviously, I'm going to have to make some drastic changes, but Lavinia left me the shop because she knew what it meant to me and that I'd honour what it meant to her. It's Lavinia's legacy.'

'Do you know how many bookshops have closed in the last five years?' Sebastian pulled a phone out of an inner pocket of his jacket and held it aloft. 'Shall I google it? Or leave it to your imagination?'

Posy didn't have to leave it to her imagination. She already knew. Some people navigated their way around London via public toilets or branches of McDonald's, but for Posy, London was a collection of bookshops with streets attached to them. They were fast disappearing now and Posy always felt a flicker of fear and foreboding each time she passed a shop where she'd once whiled away many a happy hour browsing the shelves only to find that it was now a coffee shop or a nail bar.

But she also knew that the rise of e-readers and the recession hadn't killed off the printed word. People still loved to read. They still loved to lose themselves in a world forged from paper and ink. They still bought books and, with the right kind of plan and passion, they'd buy them from Bookends.

'I don't care,' Posy said to Sebastian, though she cared very much. 'Lavinia left the shop to me, I can do what I want with it.'

'Yes, but she made me her executor. That means I act in the best interests of the estate.' Posy wasn't sure about that. The lawyer — she couldn't remember his name — had said something about coming to his office to sign a few forms and then Bookends would belong to Posy. Was Sebastian going to contest the will, on the grounds that Lavinia was mentally diminished when she wrote it?

'Lavinia said I had two years to make a go of things. If you're determined to force me into giving up and handing over the shop to you, then you're going against her last wishes. Do you want that on your conscience?' Posy asked, though she wasn't entirely sure that appealing to Sebastian's conscience would work. In any case, Sebastian was on the move again, out of his chair and stalking back into the shop, pausing only to smile wolfishly at Verity as she came through the door.

Verity treated him to her patented dead-eyed stare, which she used to great effect on customers who assumed that because she worked in a bookshop she was there to help them with their bookish needs. Ditto, men who tried to compliment her, buy her a drink or engage her in small talk. It usually had the recipient backing away while apologising profusely, but Sebastian didn't seem at all fazed. He shrugged, smiled to himself as if to say, 'Well, you can't win them all,' then walked over to the centre table and stopped dead.

Traditionally, the large round table in the

middle of the main shop was where they displayed new releases, but yesterday, in her first act as owner, Posy had broken with tradition. She'd bought a bunch of Lavinia's favourite pale pink roses and placed them in Lavinia's treasured chipped vase from Woolworths, next to a framed photo of Lavinia and Peregrine standing behind the counter, taken shortly after they got married. Then she'd typed out a notice and printed it on fancy card:

In loving memory of Lavinia Thorndyke, a bookseller to her bones. On this table is a selection of Lavinia's favourite books; the ones that brought her the greatest joy, that were like old friends. We hope that you may find the same joy, the same friend-ship.

'If one cannot enjoy reading a
    book over and over again,
there is no use reading it at all.'
        Oscar Wilde

By some miracle, Sebastian at last fell silent. He traced the photograph, one long finger caressing the curve of Lavinia's cheek; a Lavinia frozen in black and white who'd always be young and gay and gazing up at Peregrine with a teasing, loving look.

'Oh . . . well, now . . . that's very . . . thought-ful.' He swallowed around the word, as though it had got stuck in his throat. 'Sometimes Perry used to tell Lavinia that she loved this shop more than she loved him. Then she'd laugh and say that they were on pretty equal pegging.'

'Lavinia did love this shop.' Posy clasped her hands together and tried to compose herself. She needed to be impassioned but in control; it wouldn't help her cause if she launched into some incoherent, garbled speech. 'This is more than a shop. It's part of your history, Sebastian. It was founded by your great-grandmother, Agatha. It survived the war. Everyone from Virginia Woolf to Marilyn Monroe to The Beatles has come through that door. But it's part of my history too. It's the only home I've ever known. It might not be making money right now, but it has done, it used to, it could again.' She wasn't clasping her hands together any more so much as wringing them, but she felt Verity pause to give her shoulder a squeeze as she brushed past the counter on her way back to the office. 'Is this because Lavinia left the shop to me? Are you angry about that?'

'Angry?' Sebastian dropped his usual look of sneering condescension in favour of letting his mouth hang open in disbelief. 'What? No! History, books, a place covered in dust. What would I want with that? I'm already rich beyond the dreams of avarice anyway.'

'I just thought . . . '

'Look, Posy, we're veering dangerously close to talking about our feelings. Messy things, feelings. Almost as messy as your flat. Let's go back to the bit where you explain why you want to commit financial suicide. You might as well

61

light a big bonfire in the yard outside and throw all your money on to it.' Sebastian cast his eyes to the heavens. It was a good look for him, showing off the lean, corded beauty of his throat.

Posy blinked and tried to pay attention to what Sebastian was saying, but given that he was hell-bent on ringing the death knell for Bookends she didn't know why she was bothering. ' . . . and you've got the London Review Bookshop and the big new Foyles around the corner. It's *huge*. Then there's the flagship Waterstones on Piccadilly. It beggars belief, really, why anyone would want to come here. Or buy a book at all. So much easier to download it straight on to an e-reader. Not so dusty either — you should try it, Morland.'

There was no point in explaining to Sebastian how lovely it was to crack open a new book and inhale that wonderful smell. Or the powdery, almost earthy smell of old books. To feel the comforting weight of a novel in your lap, or let the pages dampen and curl as you read in the bath. He wouldn't get it. She'd have to stick to the facts, lead with her business plan, which was nothing more than a to-do list in an old exercise book and with Verity earwigging from the back office.

'We can't compete with the big chain bookshops, I know that,' she said calmly, though that was about the only thing she did know for certain. 'But Bookends is about more than selling books, it's about the experience and expertise we can offer. We don't sell books like they're cans of baked beans or bars of soap. We *love* books, and that comes across in our bookselling.'

'Not that there's much selling going on here. Quite the contrary,' Sebastian said with a smug sniff, as if he knew anything about the subject. 'Maybe you love books too much, Morland, and that's why your sales are so shocking. People come in to buy a book and you scare them off by frothing at the mouth as you bang on and on about the new Dan Brown.'

'I do not froth — and certainly not about Dan Brown,' Posy said crossly. 'You don't know what you're talking about. And I do — know what I'm talking about, that is. Which is why Lavinia let me take over the three rooms on the right, to sell romantic fiction.' Posy didn't mean to, she was out and proud, but she whispered the last two words and blushed as Sebastian pulled an agonised face as though she'd made his instant coffee with curdled milk. 'It's been going really well because I'm passionate about romantic fiction. I doubt there's another bookseller in London who's read as many romance novels as I have, and it shows in my sales. I've been taking a lot of orders online too, even though our website is really basic. So, FYI our sales for romantic fiction are up by . . . a lot.'

Posy had wanted to wow Sebastian with percentages and profit margins, but she'd never concerned herself with that side of things. She was, however, an expert on romantic fiction. If she were to go on *Mastermind* with romantic fiction as her specialist subject, she'd get a clear round every time. OK, she'd come a cropper on the general knowledge, but whatever! The problem with knowledge was that it was too general, too wide, impossible to know everything and . . .

Oh goodness! Posy had to clutch on to a shelf because she was having an idea. A big idea. A grand scheme. A USP. She'd got it! By God, she'd got it!

'Are you having a funny turn, Morland?' Sebastian asked solicitously. 'I'm not surprised. I'm pretty sure you've been inhaling all kinds of poisonous spores from the mould in your flat.'

'We don't have mould,' Posy snapped; she wasn't about to let Sebastian distract her now. 'As I was saying *before I was so rudely interrupted:* instead of trying to do everything, compete with the big bookstores, which is a hopeless task, Bookends is going to specialise in one genre. Go niche or go home.' Posy paused for dramatic effect — and because she couldn't quite believe what she was going to say next. 'We're going to become the only bookshop in Britain, maybe even the world, which specialises in romantic literature. So, what do you think about that? Hey! Did you hear what I just said?'

Posy was talking to Sebastian's back again. He'd disappeared into the first room and Posy had no choice but to follow. She caught up with him as he began pulling a book from one of the shelves. It was a US import, which was why it had a cover that featured a long-haired piece of beefcake with a rippling six-pack, straddling a woman who was wearing a filmy negligee and showing a lot of leg, as befitted someone who was about to be *Seduced by a Scoundrel*. Sebastian stared at it in horror then thrust it back in the wrong place.

By the time Posy had restored it to its rightful place, Sebastian had moved on to the classics section of her little romance fiefdom and was waving a copy of *Pride and Prejudice* around. 'Boring!' he proclaimed, which was treason. High treason. Before Posy had time to react he'd moved on to *I Capture the Castle*. 'Banal!' And *Tender Is the Night*. 'Facile!'

'You're so predictable! You make all these assumptions about romance novels and I bet you've never even read one. The whole world revolves around people meeting and falling in love; if it didn't then, the human race would die out, you silly, ignor — Mpppfffhhhh!' She got no further because Sebastian had clapped his hand over her mouth.

How she longed to bite his hand. Maybe it would teach Sebastian a lesson about invading her personal space. Getting so close to her that she could feel the heat coming off him. 'Not another word!' His eyes flashed, not with anger but amusement, as if this was the most fun he'd had all morning. 'Stop banging on about romance novels and *lurve*. I swear I can feel my testicles shrivelling.'

Posy yanked his hand away. 'I think you can get a cream for that. Try Boots.'

'Good idea!' Sebastian was in forward motion again. He flung open the door of the shop, because he couldn't even open a door, without it turning into a big, dramatic gesture. 'I'll be in touch,' he said with an airy wave of his hand. Then he was gone.

Posy put a hand to her racing heart.

'Bloody hell! That was bracing.' Verity had decided it was finally safe to emerge from the back office.

'I feel like I've just run with the bulls at Pamplona.' Posy's heart rate was returning to its usual slug-like pace. 'Thanks for all your support there, Very.'

Verity looked entirely unrepentant. In fact, she even waved a hand too, in a fair approximation of Sebastian's jaunty farewell. 'I like to pick my own battles,' she said. 'Anyway, it looked like you had things under control.' She folded her arms. 'So that's your big idea: a bookshop that only sells romance?'

Posy nodded. 'Honestly, you can't be any more surprised than I am. It's *not* a bad idea, though, is it? A one-stop shop for all your romantic fiction needs.' She bit her lip. 'I need to figure out the details. Properly. With a flip chart and everything, but until I do, can you keep it between us?'

'We're only going to sell romance novels? Nothing else?' Verity's voice was flatter than Holland. She looked around the shop. 'That's hardly going to fill the entire shop, is it? I mean, I understand about going niche, but isn't that a bit too niche?'

'It's not. It's really not. People love romantic novels. Here, in the main room, we could have new releases, bestsellers and contemporary fiction. Plus all the classics: *Bridget Jones*, Jackie

Collins and chicklit — though I have *major* problems with that term. *Major*.' Posy moved through the shop, into the room on the left. Now that she'd started to think about it, it was all so obvious. 'We could have classics in here: Jane Austen, the Brontës, poetry, plays and then in the next room — '

Verity held up her hand. 'Enough!'

Posy turned to her with a troubled expression. 'You don't think it's a good idea? But you love romance novels, Very! I know exactly what you buy with your staff discount, and even Nina says — '

'Nina will be in soon. Tom's coming in this afternoon. We're going to close an hour early and you're going to talk us through this plan.' Verity still didn't sound as if she thought it was a good plan, but Posy tried not to take it personally. That was Verity's way. She'd once brushed past Benedict Cumberbatch in the Midnight Bell and didn't so much as flicker an eyelash, but then she'd had to go to the toilet and breathe into a paper bag because she was hyperventilating. 'I'll let you have some money out of petty cash so you can go and buy a flip chart,' Verity added kindly. 'After you've put the kettle on. And changed out of your pyjamas. What is that on them anyway? Looks like little piles of poo.'

'They're Christmas puddings! Can't you see the sprigs of holly?' Posy tugged at the offending garment that she was never, *ever* going to wear again. '*You* put the kettle on. I'm going to have a shower.'

4

By five o'clock that afternoon, Posy was coasting a wave of anxiety as she battled with her flip chart and the stand it was meant to clip to.

Technically, she was the boss now so what she said went, but she didn't *feel* like the boss. Although Nina and Verity were the same age as her, Posy had always felt like an underling. Still did, but now she had three employees; three people who were relying on Posy to keep paying their wages so they could afford rent, utilities, food and maybe a cheeky glass of wine and an occasional trip to the cinema.

Posy swore under her breath each time the flip chart refused to cooperate with her plans. How could she hope to take over an ailing bookshop and turn it into a successful, flourishing business when she couldn't operate a flip-chart stand?

'You have to do it like this,' said a voice behind her, and Sam relieved himself of the burden of his bulging schoolbag simply by dropping it on the floor so he could help her. Within seconds he had the flip chart firmly attached and was shuffling out of the back office. 'I only got a B for my rap in iambic pentameter, Pose. You'll have to do better next time.'

Sam was walking with strange pincer-like movements and showing even more sock than he had a couple of days ago. Posy made a mental note to take him shopping that weekend for new shoes and trousers. Maybe she could also buy some herbal supplements that would stop Sam growing at such an alarming, expensive rate. Because it wasn't only the Bookends staff relying on Posy's vision, it was Sam too. The shop was as much his legacy as it was hers, so it was up to Posy not to screw this up.

On cue, she heard the shop door close, then the key turn in the lock and Nina and Tom, followed by Little Sophie, the Saturday girl, and finally Verity trooped into the back office. They came with a hot beverage apiece and cake. It was quite hard to launch into her exciting, revolutionary plans for Bookends when people were tussling over a box of Mr Kipling's French Fancies.

'So, right, OK. Welcome to the new and improved Bookends,' Posy said with a jerky gesture as she revealed an inept drawing of the outside of the shop rendered in blue and green marker pen. 'A one-stop shop for all your romantic fiction needs.'

Everyone but Verity, who'd already heard the headlines, stopped fighting over who was going to get stuck with a pink French Fancy and looked up at Posy. This was good; she had their attention, though they didn't need to stare quite so hard, and Tom didn't need to look as if Posy had started to speak in tongues.

'What is romantic fiction?' Posy mused. It was a rhetorical question, so she ignored Little Sophie's hand, which had shot up. 'It can be high literature, like Shakespeare's *Romeo and Juliet* or Austen's *Pride and Prejudice*. It can be

69

commercial fiction like *One Day* or *Bridget Jones's Diary*. It could be a bodice-ripper or a bonkbuster. It could be a novel about a woman in charge of her own destiny who opens a small cake shop in a delightful village or . . . '

'Hang on! Back up!' Tom, who'd got stuck with the pink French Fancy, reared back in his chair. 'We're only going to sell chicklit? Ow! Don't hit me!'

Nina already had her hand poised to strike again. 'Nothing wrong with chicklit,' she announced. 'The only thing wrong with it is that novels primarily written for women about women by women are sneeringly and dismissively called 'chicklit' as if they have absolutely no merit.'

'I didn't mean it like that.' Tom made a big show of rubbing his head. 'I meant: are you seriously going to get rid of the children's room and the self-help section? The cookery books? The thrillers? You're going to stop selling them?'

'We never get any children in the shop these days,' Posy explained. 'Only in the school holidays when they want to have a go on the rolling ladder. And how many self-help books have we sold recently? Or any other kind of book, for that matter? We can try and be like all the other bookshops in the area, or we can do one thing and do it really well. We could become famous for selling romantic fiction; a destination bookshop. Just think of all those people coming to London for the day who'll make a point of coming to our shop because they know that we stock the largest collection of romantic fiction in

70

London? In the whole country!'

'Steady on, Posy,' said Sam, popping his head around the doorway. Posy suddenly found it hard to breathe but it was less nerves and more that Sam had slathered himself in a noxious man scent probably called something like Axe or Blade or Gunslinger because he'd realised Sophie was on the premises. How Posy longed for those innocent days when Sophie and Sam had been nothing more than mates, before their hormones kicked in. 'Does this mean that the publishers' sales reps won't give me free graphic novels any more?'

Then he realised he must sound incredibly whiny in front of Sophie, who was refusing to make eye contact with Sam and staring intently at the glittery polish on her fingernails instead.

'I'm sure they will,' Posy said firmly, 'when they see how many romance novels we're selling.'

'So how would the shop be planned out?' Verity asked. She had a big notepad on her lap and had been diligently making notes. 'Weren't you saying something about keeping the main room for contemporaries, popular fiction and new releases?'

'Yes! Yes, I was!' Posy nodded and she flipped over the flip chart once more to show the new layout of the shop. Even if she did say so herself, it had a much better flow once she'd reconfigured some of the more randomly placed bookcases. 'Then to the right, a Regency room, then a historical room, and the smallest room at the end can be for paranormal, fantasy and um, erotica. Sam and Sophie, you are never to go in

71

there unless accompanied by a responsible adult, right?'

Sam groaned like he was in pain and Sophie gave Posy a slightly pitying look, because whatever depravities might lurk in the pages of erotic romance novels, they couldn't begin to compare to the filth she could access on her home computer.

'To the left of the main room will be the Classics room, for Jane Austen, the Brontës, that kind of thing, along with plays and poetry. Then the next room will be Young Adult — Sophie, I thought you could help me with that. And the last room will be non-fiction and a foreign language section.' Posy exhaled. 'And that's the highlights.'

'What about the tearooms? Are you going to have books in there too?' Nina asked. She'd been nodding and giving Posy encouraging smiles all the way through her speech.

This was all moving too fast. 'I hadn't thought that far ahead,' Posy said, though she didn't have to think too hard about it. The tearoom had been her mother's domain. There was simply no way Posy could entertain the idea of taking it over, repainting and reorganising the space so that any lingering traces of Angharad Morland would disappear. 'There's more than enough work to do in the shop without worrying about the tearoom too.'

Nina didn't seem inclined to let the matter drop. 'But maybe at some point in the future, you could employ someone to run it so — '

'No,' Verity said emphatically, so Posy didn't

have to. 'We'll charge someone rent — that way you have guaranteed money coming in and they can sort out all the health and safety shenanigans. We'll have enough to do, as it is. Let's revisit the tearoom at a later date. What's on the next page, Posy?'

Posy's palms were still clammy, making it hard to find purchase on the flip chart and move on to the website portion of her plan. Although actually the page simply said, 'MAKE A BETTER WEBSITE.'

'Yeah, I'll sort that out for you,' Sam offered diffidently, as if he could knock one up overnight, though surely there was more to it than that? 'Might be hard to put our entire catalogue online, but we could offer a selection of books . . .'

'Yeah! Like our top fifty bestsellers and . . . and we could have a book of the month too,' Sophie said, leaning forwards on her chair eagerly. 'Maybe offer a discount on that one.'

'If we're going to have a book of the month, then why not have a book group?' Nina suggested. 'They could meet one evening a month. And if we were going to open the tearoom again — which I really implore you to think about, because it means there'll be a never-ending supply of cake in the shop — we'll also have onsite catering, then we could host book launches and author visits. Signings too. Though I suppose we could do that anyway.'

'And if you're going to have a proper website, then you need to be on Instagram and Tumblr,' Sophie insisted. 'Like, otherwise what's the point? I can set up and run the shop's Twitter account too and we can link it all back to the website, right, Sammy?'

Sam swept his fringe out of his eyes again. 'Yeah, I guess. Got to be multi-platform. We'll want paying though, won't we, Soph? Say, ten per cent of everything you make on the website.'

Posy folded her arms. 'How about you reimburse me for all the food and clothing and video games that I've bought you over the last seven years?'

'Just so you know, there are strict child labour laws in this country.' Sam folded his arms too and stuck out his chin for good measure.

Posy didn't want to ground him or send him back upstairs in front of Sophie, especially when he was the only person she knew who could build a website. 'Eight point five per cent. Final offer.'

'Are the pair of you trying to bankrupt us? If you want paying, Sam, then you have to go through me. I do the payroll and I might be prepared to consider three per cent — after costs,' Verity said. She was getting that antsy look that came over her when she'd done a full day's work and was still being expected to interact with other people. Posy could tell Verity was reaching the end of all reason, but before she did . . .

'Actually, the other big thing I wanted to discuss with all of you is the name of the shop.'

Tom had sunk down low on his chair so his chin rested on his chest, but now he found the strength to raise his head. 'What's wrong with the name of the shop? It's an institution, Bookends is.'

'It *was* — and that's the problem,' Posy said. It was a theme she'd kept coming back to after hours of mentally going around in circles. 'It *was* an institution, but most of the people who came to Bookends because of its history, its atmosphere, its reputation, were contemporaries of Lavinia, and they're dwindling fast. Without them, Bookends is one more struggling bookshop. If we're going to specialise in romantic fiction, we need a name for the shop which reflects that.'

'So, did you have a name in mind?' Tom asked. He was still slumped, still oozing the absolute opposite of enthusiasm.

'I did.' Posy gestured at the flip chart in the manner of a game-show hostess presenting a top-of-the-range fridge freezer to a delighted TV audience. 'Can I get a drum roll, please?'

She got a half-hearted stomping of feet as she turned the page over and was greeted with silence. Worse than silence. A collective, *what the . . . ?* look on all five faces.

Posy put her hands on her hips. 'What do you think? Yes, it's a bit out there, but it's memorable, right?'

' 'Reader, I Married Him',' Tom read it out loud like he'd only recently learned to speak English. 'No. No, right?' He turned to Nina, sitting on his left. 'Come on. I can't be the only one who thinks Posy's been huffing spray mount again.'

'That was only the one time and it was an

accident,' Posy protested. 'You're on my side, Nina! You love the Brontës! It's from *Jane Eyre*!'

'Oh my God, spoilers!' shrieked Sophie, but then she giggled and smiled at Sam, who tried to smile back but decided he'd be better off hiding his face behind his fringe. Sometimes Posy longed to knock their heads together.

'I know it's from *Jane Eyre* but I'm sorry, Posy, I love you loads, but that is a terrible name for a shop,' Nina said. 'Not every romance novel ends with a trip down the aisle. Hello! We're living in the twenty-first century.'

'You think a romantic fiction bookshop is a terrible idea?' Posy had to cling on to the flip chart stand for support. She thought she'd found the answer to all their problems, but now that she stopped to think about it, Verity hadn't expressed an opinion for or against the scheme and as for Sebastian . . . he'd made his feelings on the subject only too clear.

She was all out of ideas. This was it. Go big on romance or go home. Or else let Sebastian have the shop and God knows what he'd do with it. He had no respect for what Bookends represented. All those rooms, all those shelves that had held books that took their readers to magical lands and beautiful truths, the reading nook, the weathered floorboards that had been trodden by so many customers coming in for a story . . .

'Shit, Posy! Are you crying?' Nina scrambled to her feet so she could enfold Posy in her arms and press her against her amazing breasts, which admittedly always felt quite comforting.

'I'm not crying,' Posy said, but her words were muffled by Nina's chest and she was kind of crying. There had been a couple of tears and a throb in her throat. It was pre-crying.

'It's a crappy name, not a crappy idea,' Nina insisted as she stroked Posy's back rhythmically. 'It is a good idea, isn't it? Who doesn't love a bit of romance? Reading about it is the closest I get to it. Most times I'm lucky if I can find a guy who'll buy me dinner, and then it's only because he thinks I'm going to let him come home with me and see me naked.'

'God, Nina, there are children present!'

Posy couldn't see Tom because she was still face down in Nina's cleavage, but he sounded strained.

'I'm not a child,' she heard Sam snap.

'Do guys really expect you to get naked just because they bought you dinner?' That was Sophie. 'A really expensive dinner or, like, a cheeky Nando's?'

They were getting off-topic. Posy freed herself from Nina's embrace and sniffed. Then she looked plaintively at Verity, because Verity was Bookends' designated adult.

'I think your idea has possibilities, as long as we can achieve it on a budget of, well, zero pounds and nought pence.' Verity pressed one fist to her right temple as if she were reaching the limits of her endurance. 'But that name, I can't even say it out loud.'

If Verity was on board, then it only left Tom, who wasn't exactly swinging from the light fitting with glee. Though the light fitting, like

77

everything else in the shop, was past the first flush of youth and could barely take the weight of an eco bulb and a paper shade. 'What about it, Tom? Could you bear to sell nothing but romantic fiction if I promise not to paint the shop pink? I know you're doing a PhD in English Literature, but would it be a massive step down?'

'It's not solely on English Literature. It's more nuanced than that,' Tom said, because the topic of Tom's PhD thesis was a mystery to them all. Whenever Posy asked Tom about it he started using long, fancy words like epistemology and neorealism, and so Posy remained clueless. It was probably for the best. 'Anyway, I'm not wholly *against* the idea of romantic fiction. But I am *not* working in a shop called Reader, I Married Him. Can you imagine what it would be like having to answer the phone?'

'Hello, you're through to Reader, I Married Him, what can I help you with today?' Sam parroted, then looked at Sophie, who rewarded him with a smile.

'OK, I get the message,' Posy said in a resigned tone. 'What do we call the shop then?'

'The Love Shack?' Nina suggested. 'Though that sounds like we sell marital aids. What about Meet Cute? That's one of my favourite bits of a good love story.'

'What's a meet cute?' Sophie asked. Which ruled that out because not everybody knew what it meant. 'Couldn't we just call it Love Story?'

'Too vague,' Verity said. 'Come on, people — think! Why do people like romantic fiction?'

They sat in deafening silence for the time it took the clock on the wall to do a complete circuit then hit the minute mark with a sticky-sounding click.

Posy tried to think what it was about romantic novels that had her forsaking housework, TV, and going out on actual dates so she could find some real-life romance. 'Better a night in with a good book, than a night out with some lame guy who can't be bothered to put on a clean shirt,' she was fond of saying.

Was it the sparky heroines who didn't give up on love, no matter how many times they'd had their hearts broken? Was it the hero with his dashing good looks and sardonic wit, who might be nursing a broken heart too? The sizzling first kiss? The lingering looks? The attraction that couldn't be denied? It was all of those things that kept Posy coming back, but above all else, it was the happy ending. It was the hero and heroine walking off the page and into the sunset hand in hand. You might not get your own happy ending, Posy knew that only too well, but a good romance always finished with a happy ending, and if it didn't then Posy felt cheated. There had even been a couple of occasions when she'd flung a book across the room in disgust.

'It's the happy ending,' she said out loud. 'Everyone wants a happy ending.'

'Happy Endings?' mused Verity. 'Possibly.'

'Oh no. No. No. No.' Nina looked horrified. 'You can't call it Happy Endings. It sounds like a knocking shop masquerading as a massage parlour.'

'Does it? Why?' Both Sophie and Sam looked confused. From under Sam's fringe, Posy could almost hear the cogs whirring, then light dawned. 'Oh! I get it! Yeah, can't call the shop Happy Endings. I'd get rinsed at school.'

'God, why does everything have some smutty other meaning?' Posy lamented. 'Happy Ever Afters should be a beautiful thing, not some sordid double entendre. This is precisely why we need more romance in the world and not . . . Oh! That's it! Happy Ever After! It's perfect. It is perfect, isn't it?'

'A Happy Ever After guaranteed, or your money back!' Nina exclaimed. 'We could have that as our slogan.'

'Except we might have to issue a lot of refunds to people who bought copies of *Wuthering Heights* or *The Great Gatsby*,' Tom said, but he was smiling. 'I can cope with working in a shop called Happy Every After. Just about.'

'Happy Ever After, then. That's the name of the shop,' Verity said, as she started gathering up her things. 'All those in favour, raise their hand.' She looked around. 'That includes you, Tom.' Tom raised his right hand and gave Verity the middle finger of the other one. 'Great. We're unanimous. I really have to go now. I wasn't planning on staying late tonight.'

She was out the door with her coat hanging half on, half off, because when Verity decided she'd had enough, there was no weapon forged that could stop her.

'Happy Ever After. I like it,' Nina said. She looked around. 'So, pub, everyone?'

Sam nodded. 'Yeah, I'll have a vodka and tonic, if you're buying.'

'You will have no such thing because you aren't going to the pub — and neither are you, Sophie. The two of you are going upstairs and you can start on your homework until Sophie's dad comes to pick her up,' Posy said and really Sam should be thanking her instead of glaring, because now he and Sophie could bond over the Hundred Years War and what a bitch she was.

The two of them, grumbling all the way, stomped up the stairs as Posy followed Tom and Nina through the shop so she could lock the door behind them.

She watched them hurry across the courtyard. It was raining. Nina shrieked as she skidded over the cobbles. Tom took her arm and they ran around the corner.

Upstairs, she heard a door slam and the sound of music suddenly blaring out, but down here all was still and calm.

'Happy Ever After,' she whispered under her breath as she straightened display tables, plumped cushions and did a very lacklustre job of mopping the floors, because they couldn't afford a cleaner and it was usually Verity's job as she said it was the only way to ensure that it was done properly. 'Happy Ever After.'

No matter how many times she said those three words, they never lost their meaning. Their intent. Their promise.

'Happy Ever After.' She stood in the centre of the room, next to the main display table, her hand resting on the photo of Lavinia and Perry.

'Do you like your new name?'

Maybe Posy had been waiting for a sign, some acknowledgment from a higher power that she was doing the right thing for herself, for Sam, and for Bookends. Giving the shop a happy ever after too.

The shop stayed silent but Posy felt the same comforting glow that always came over her when she was alone among the books and decided that that was all the answer she needed.

5

It was all very well having a new name for the shop and a unique selling point, but Posy still wasn't sure how to get her plans from flip chart to reality.

Luckily, Verity and Nina were fired up and full of can-do spirit when they burst into the shop the next morning. Or rather, Verity sidled in, not being one for bursting, waved at Posy who was going through a box of new deliveries and said, 'I've had a think about it overnight and I'm completely on board with Happy Ever After. In fact, I'm very excited about it.' Verity shook her fists like they were cheerleader pompoms. 'See? This is me being excited. Now I've got to do the VAT returns, but later in the week, I think we should come up with an action plan. Maybe a spreadsheet too. And definitely a schedule. What fun!'

It didn't exactly sound like fun, but a moment later Nina burst — literally this time — through the door.

'I have paint samples!' she cried, holding up a fistful of colour charts. 'And I spoke to Claude, my tattoo artist, and he said that he'd design a logo for us. For free. I've given him so much money over the years that I always used to joke he should give me frequent-flier miles.'

'Paint samples?' Posy queried. 'Are we going to paint then?'

'I think we should. It is rather dark and well, woody in here, isn't it?'

It was, and in between dealing with the odd customer, two tourists who couldn't find the British Museum even though it was a massive building heavily signposted and only five minutes away, and many browsers who were more interested in sheltering from the leaden February skies and the seeping drizzle than buying books, Posy and Nina spent a very enjoyable morning debating colour schemes.

They decided on a light but warm grey for the shelves and a smudgy pink for accents. 'I did promise Tom I wouldn't paint the shop pink, but it's only a highlight colour,' Posy said as she held up the swatch. 'It's not a girly pink.'

'It's a clover pink. I had my hair that colour during my gothic Lolita phase,' Nina said. 'Now, shall we have a bash at coming up with a shop layout?'

As they pondered the 'flow' of the shop and how many bookcases they'd have to cull to achieve it, Posy wondered if she should speak to Sebastian, give him a heads-up. Not that she needed his permission to make sweeping changes to what belonged to her legally. Maybe she'd be better off hiring a lawyer, a kindly, avuncular lawyer, who could write Sebastian a letter telling him that. A kindly, avuncular lawyer who charged very reasonably for his time, Posy thought.

They were in the main room now, Nina chattering happily away about how to make the shop more welcoming 'Do you think there is anything in that Feng Shui? Have we got any books on it?' as Posy imagined Sebastian's lip-curling derision when he spotted the splashes of her clover pink accent colour dotted around the shop.

'Sebastian!' she muttered contemptuously.

'Yeah, what is he doing out there?' Nina asked. 'And who's that guy he's with? Do you think he's fit?'

'What? Is who fit? Sebastian? Can hardly see him at the gym lifting weights. The only bit of his body that ever gets a workout is his tongue,' Posy said as she crossed over to the window where Nina was watching Sebastian and another man on the opposite side of the yard.

'You saucy mare!' Nina nudged Posy and treated her to a theatrical wink. 'How would you know what he gets up to with his tongue? Something you need to tell your Aunty Nina about?'

'*What?*' Posy looked at her friend in confusion then wished she hadn't as Nina did something obscene with her own tongue so Posy could see the underside of her piercing, which always made her feel slightly vomitous. 'I didn't mean like that! His tongue has been nowhere about my person. As if! I meant his mouth! Not like that either. That he never stops talking and usually the content of his conversation consists mostly of unmitigated rudeness.'

'Protesting a little too much there, aren't you?' Nina teased.

They'd been standing at the window while carrying on this conversation, so it was inevitable that Sebastian spotted them. He looked past the other man, who was gesticulating wildly, then raised his hand in greeting.

No, that would have been too polite. What Sebastian was in fact doing was beckoning Posy with an imperious finger.

'I wonder what he wants,' said Posy, making absolutely no effort to find out. A moment later the beckoning turned into a clicking of Sebastian's fingers, as if he were summoning an underperforming lackey.

'So rude, but I'd better go out and talk to him,' Posy muttered without enthusiasm.

'Keep away from his tongue!' Nina cheerfully called after her as Posy squared her shoulders against the bitter February wind and opened the door.

'Morland! Over here! Haven't got all day,' was Sebastian's peremptory greeting.

Posy shuffled across the courtyard, thankful that unlike their last meeting, this time she was fully dressed in bra, jeans, jumper and cardigan, unadorned with anything that could be mistaken for piles of poo. 'And hello to you too!' she said as soon as she was near enough not to have to bellow. 'What's up?'

'Brocklehurst, this is Morland, quasi-owner of the bookshop,' Sebastian said to his companion even as Posy turned on him.

'There's nothing quasi about it. I am the actual owner,' Posy said furiously.

'I told you she was uppity,' Sebastian sighed. 'Morland, this is Brocklehurst. We were at Eton together.'

'Hello, I'm Piers,' said the other man. 'And I refuse to call a beautiful woman by her surname.'

'Posy.' She held out her hand but instead of shaking it Piers Brocklehurst raised it to his lips in a practised move so he could kiss the back of it. 'Nice to meet you.'

It wasn't exactly . . . nice. In fact, Posy longed to rub the back of her hand against her jeans. There was something about the smooth gesture, an oily quality to Piers' patter, the failure of his easy smile to reach his eyes, which remained flat and rather dead, that spooked Posy. In fact, Piers sent shivers rippling down her spine, in spite of the fact he was textbook good-looking, albeit in an ex-public schoolboy kind of way. He was tall, with blond hair slicked back from his ruddy face, and muscles that rippled beneath his blue pinstripe suit. The man wouldn't have looked out of place in an aftershave ad, smirking to camera as an unseen woman ran a caressing hand down his chest, but he wasn't Posy's type. She already had one extremely irritating ex-public schoolboy in her life — she didn't need any more.

'No, really, the pleasure's all mine,' Piers murmured throatily, and that flat, dead gaze of his rested on Posy's hips, breasts, face and then looked beyond her to the bookshop as if there was nothing there to hold his interest.

'That's quite enough of that,' Sebastian snapped, coming to stand between Posy and Piers. 'Posy only likes men in soppy romance novels, so you're on a hiding to nothing there.

Now about the bookshop, Morland, Brockle-hurst has been talking about redeveloping the site, maybe building a boutique hotel here.' Sebastian gestured at the row of boarded-up shops. 'And where the bookshop is, he was saying that we should put up a fancy apartment block, with concierge, basement gym, swimming pool and — '

'Do you ever listen to a single word I say?' Obviously not. 'Bookends is mine for at least two years and, as I tried to tell you the last time I saw you, it's going to be the only bookshop in the country dedicated to romantic fiction.' Posy finished with relish because she'd shocked Sebastian into silence.

Annoyingly, Sebastian still looked handsome even with his mouth hanging half open in a gorm-less fashion. 'Are you mad?' he asked hoarsely.

'Quite sane,' Posy assured him as Piers mut-tered something under his breath that suggested he too doubted Posy's claims to sanity. 'And as I was saying, I'm the owner of Bookends for at least the next two years.'

'More like two months if you insist on going through with some *ridiculous* scheme to turn it into a lavender-scented palace crammed wall to wall with bodice-rippers. Two months for the business to fail horribly and the bailiffs to turn up on your doorstep,' Sebastian summed up with obvious pleasure.

Posy felt shivers run down her spine as if Sebastian's words, aside from being hurtful on about a hundred different levels, were a prophecy.

'It won't come to that,' she insisted, fingers crossed behind her back to be on the safe side.

'Of course it won't,' Piers said, like it was any of his business. 'Why don't you leave this to me, Thorndyke?' he suggested, slipping an arm around Posy's shoulders — an arm under which she immediately stiffened like an angry cat. As Piers registered this, his dead eyes suddenly came to life, flashing with annoyance that his obvious charms weren't working. 'Look, Posy, I'm sure you mean well but it's clear you don't know anything about how to run a business. You're never going to get the footfall you need tucked away down this dingy alley.'

'It's not an alley, it's a mews,' Posy countered and she couldn't stand Piers' arm around her for even another second so she shook her shoulders to dislodge him. His eyes flashed again. 'Originally there were stables here. And we do get footfall — or we did and we can again. There used to be signs for the mews all down Rochester Street — and there will be again. Why don't you do up the empty shops and rent them out?' Posy turned back to Sebastian in the vain hope that she could win him round. 'Do you remember when old Mr Jessop had the tea and coffee merchants? How he'd sell broken biscuits by weight and roast coffee beans on Monday and Wednesday afternoons and the whole area would smell wonderful?'

'I always thought it smelt of burnt toast,' Sebastian said crushingly. 'Though of course there was the time he caught me shoplifting broken biscuits.' He smiled wickedly, even reaching his eyes, which gleamed with memories of past wrongdoings. 'Took my ear between thumb and forefinger and marched me across the mews to Bookends and wouldn't let go until Lavinia promised to thrash me soundly.'

'Which I'm guessing she didn't,' Posy said.

'Of course she didn't.' Sebastian rolled his eyes at the very suggestion, but his voice had softened at the mention of his grandmother.

'I can't believe that you're considering bulldozing the mews and putting up some ugly buildings in its place.' Posy clasped her hands together in an imploring manner.

'They wouldn't be ugly,' Piers said. 'I work with an architect who specialises in cutting-edge design.'

Posy ignored him. 'You could rent out the shops to independent businesses and you'd still make some profit. OK, not as much as a hotel and flats, but you already have loads of money, Sebastian, why do you need even more of it?'

'Morland. Dear, simple Morland.' Sebastian shook his head in a patronising way, which made Posy grind her teeth so hard she feared for her back molars. 'You have absolutely no idea how capitalism works, do you?'

'I do understand how it works because, unlike you, I didn't get kicked out of university. But that doesn't mean I agree with capitalism. I mean, it's all right in moderation . . .'

At this, both Sebastian and Piers made a synchronised scoffing noise, which they'd probably learned at Eton. Realising that the discussion was veering off course, Posy abandoned her attempt to educate them on the dangers of excessive capitalism. 'Anyway,' she said, a note of desperation creeping in. 'Anyway, you can't just barge in here, even if you do own the place, and decide to tear it all down. There are laws against that kind of thing! You have to apply for change of use for a building. And I'm pretty sure that you can't exceed the footprint of the existing buildings so — '

'Someone's watched a couple of property programmes, have they?' Piers sneered. Posy had thought it impossible that there could be anyone on the planet more patronising than Sebastian, but Piers was doing a very good job of proving her wrong. 'No need to worry your pretty head about that. An envelope of cash to the right person at the council planning department and we could demolish the entire alley and no one would bat an eyelash.'

'I would! Sebastian, really! What would Lavinia say?' Posy knew that deep down, deep *deep* down, Sebastian had a better nature — or at least, she thought he did — and she needed to appeal to it. 'The mews, Bookends, all the things your grandmother adored — why would you want to get rid of them?'

'They're just *things, places*, Morland.' Sebastian stood back and surveyed the cobbled yard. 'You can't live in the past for ever. Lavinia realised that she'd let things stay the same for too long. When things stay the same, they stagnate and fester and then drastic measures are needed.'

He made it sound as if the mews and her

91

beloved Bookends were some monstrous carbuncle that must be removed as soon as was humanly possible.

'Nothing drastic needs to be done,' Posy protested. 'All it needs is a bit of overhauling, rejigging. It's amazing the difference a fresh coat of paint can make.'

'You needn't worry, Morland. I wouldn't have you out on your ear,' Sebastian said in what he must have imagined was a comforting manner. 'You could have one of the fancy new flats, to own outright — because I know that's what Lavinia would have wanted. And if you're still set on this dreary business of bookselling, you could get a job in a bookshop, if you must . . .'

For one moment, a nano-moment, Posy entertained the idea of owning a fancy new flat and a stress-free job at a big chain bookshop. But only for that fleeting moment and then she was thinking of how every inch of Bookends meant something to her. It was where her heart was. Her haven. Her happy place. And if Bookends was gone, flattened to the ground, if Posy and Sam didn't live and laugh and love in the same place that their parents lived and laughed and loved, then the memories of her parents would fade and dissipate like the dust from the rubble.

Posy glanced back at the shop and saw Nina still peering out of the window, though unashamedly gawping would have been a more accurate description. This wasn't only about her and Sam. It was about the Bookends staff too. Until she'd come to Bookends, Nina had never managed to survive the probationary period of

92

her previous three jobs. And as for Verity! Introverted Verity, where else would she find a job with people who didn't mind if she never ever answered the phone?

' . . . very secure location. We're talking about a gated community. Keep out the riff-raff,' Piers was saying. Posy realised that she'd tuned him out completely. It was odd. He was one of those people that, the more you looked at them, the less attractive they became. There was something quite feral about his smile. 'And you needn't worry about the neighbours. The other flats will be snapped up by foreign corporations as an investment and no one will ever live in them, so you'll have the gym and the . . . '

She had heard enough! Her mouth opened on a gasp of sheer outrage. 'It's not even going to be affordable housing? It's people like you who are sucking the soul out of London. Killing our community spirit,' she said, wagging a finger at first Piers, then Sebastian, who sighed as if Posy was being wilful on purpose.

But she wasn't. It was Piers and his ilk who were responsible for driving all the character out of an area and replacing it with multi-million pound housing developments for the wealthy, and estate agents to sell the flats in the multi-million pound housing developments, and maybe a couple of coffee shops owned by corporations that didn't pay their tax. In fact, it was people like Piers who were responsible for the signs that had gone up locally declaring that the areas formerly and delightfully known as Bloomsbury, Fitzrovia and Clerkenwell were henceforth to be known collectively as Midtown. Over Posy's dead body.

Speaking of which . . . Posy put her hands on her hips and her best fight face on. 'I'm not listening to another word of this,' she insisted. 'This land, the shop, was gifted to your great-grandmother Agatha, in the hope it would distract her from being a Suffragette.'

'Are you going somewhere with this?' Sebastian asked, ostentatiously lifting his bespoke cuff to look at his watch, while Piers stared at Posy as if he'd quite like to demolish her along with the empty shops of Rochester Mews.

'Yes! Agatha got sent to Holloway Prison for chaining herself to the railings of Buckingham Palace and I will chain myself to Bookends if that's what it takes to stop you smashing it to smithereens.' Posy hoped that she'd never have to make good on that threat, but if it came to bull-dozers and wrecking balls in the mews, then by God, she'd do it!

Sebastian didn't seem too convinced. 'No disrespect to my great-grandmother, but you're the poster child for why women should never have got the vote, Morland,' Sebastian said, brushing down the front of his suit jacket as if Posy had unleashed a tidal wave of spittle during her impassioned rant, which she hadn't. Or she hoped she hadn't. 'Since you got the vote, you've all got ideas above your station.'

'Yeah, there's only two things a woman's good for,' Piers sneered. 'Or one thing, if you can afford your own private chef, which I can.'

'Oh my God — ' Posy began, so furiously that

94

she could barely choke out the words. Fortunately, she was silenced by a thump on her shoulder.

'What's the only other thing women are good for besides cooking, then?' asked Nina in her most sultry voice from behind Posy. 'Is it being generally amazing?'

Piers' mouth hung open as he took in the vision that was Nina. As for Sebastian: well, he'd never stared at Posy like that. Not even when she wasn't wearing a bra, but then Nina was built like Bettie Page, though Bettie Page had never been covered in tattoos, had a pierced nose and lip, or hair of a shade that Nina described as 'washed-up mermaid'.

Piers smiled so ingratiatingly he looked like a hyena in a flashy suit. 'Maybe I could tell you over drinks?' he suggested, brusquely sidestepping Posy so he could get closer to Nina, his eyes roaming her curves, showcased in her retro little black dress. 'I'm Piers, and you . . . you're gorgeous. I bet you get that all the time.'

Posy pulled a face at the exact same moment that Sebastian pulled a face. At least they could agree that Piers' chat-up lines were as vile as his plans to turn London into a desolate high-spec wasteland and that the only person who'd be foolish enough to fall for them would be . . .

'Nina — and only some of the time.' Nina, who had the worst taste in men of any woman that Posy had ever met, was smiling at Piers and batting her eyelashes. 'Posy, there's some woman on the phone who wants to know if you might be able to track down an out-of-print novel for her.'

'Well, that's sure to keep the bailiffs away,' Sebastian said dryly and it seemed they were done agreeing with each other. Normal service resumed. 'Anyway, Morland, I'd say it's been a pleasure, but that would be a lie. I'll be in touch.'

'I absolutely won't be looking forward to it,' Posy snapped. Next time she saw Sebastian it would have to be just the two of them so she could talk some sense into him without an interfering audience. It would be the hardest thing she'd ever done. 'Come on, Nina, we've got work to do, books to sell . . .'

Nina was still rapt under Piers' lascivious gaze. 'Just so you know, I don't put out on a first date,' she was saying.

'Yeah, well, third date is industry standard, unless there's champagne involved,' Piers said, his gaze lingering on Nina's breasts. 'So, these tattoos of yours, how far do they go down?'

'That's for me to know and you to find out,' Nina said.

Posy couldn't quite believe her eyes, and even Sebastian murmured 'bloody hell' under his breath, when Piers stuck a business card into Nina's cleavage.

'Call me,' he said.

'Well, aren't you a cocky one?' Nina purred.

Posy couldn't bear it any longer. Once Nina started with what she called banter and what Posy called smut and innuendo, it never ended well. It ended with Nina going out with yet another man who wasn't fit to kiss the hems of Nina's wiggle dresses, and Nina getting her heart broken. Again.

'I can and will dock your pay, young lady, if you don't go back to the shop right now,' Posy said in a very un-Posylike way.

'All right, all right, keep your hair on,' Nina muttered, but she let Posy tug her back to the shop.

'To be continued, Morland!' Sebastian shouted after them.

Posy raised her hand in acknowledgement and hustled Nina through the door. 'If you go on a date with that Piers, I will sack you,' she warned Nina.

'That would never stand at an employment tribunal,' Nina said. She hurried back to her spot at the window, Posy close behind her. 'He is quite handsome, in a *Wolf of Wall Street* kind of way.'

'He is appalling. How can you not see that?' Posy asked wearily, because they had been down this well-trodden path many times before.

'Oh no, I think Piers is different,' Nina insisted.

They watched the two men walk along the row of disused shops, Piers pausing to gesture wildly with his hands again as if he were describing his grandiose plans to eradicate every last bit of character and history from the spot where they stood. Sebastian was uncharacteristically still and silent until he rocked back on the heels of his handmade shoes and said something to Piers, which made the other man's mouth hang open.

Sebastian walked off, leaving Piers standing there. Sebastian turned as he reached the entrance to the mews to look back at the shop, his eyes searching for and finding Posy at her spot in the window. He lifted his hand, gave her a mocking salute then was gone.

Finally, Posy could begin to breathe again.

6

The nasty showdown with Sebastian and the pernicious Piers only strengthened Posy's resolve. This was no bad thing, because her resolve was usually weak in the extreme. If she started the week with a diet, she hardly ever made it to Monday lunchtime before diving headfirst into a packet of biscuits. And when she and Nina had decided to do a Dry January, Nina had gone all the way to February without a drop touching her lips whereas Posy had spectacularly fallen off the wagon on the third of January when she discovered that Sam hadn't done any of the homework he'd been set for the Christmas holidays.

As she'd watched Sebastian and Piers depart, Posy's resolve had been so strong it was as if it had been forged from titanium. And yet the next day as she sat behind the till with a new notebook on the counter next to her, opened to the first page where she'd written 'Happy Ever After', she could feel it wavering.

It was one thing to have an idea, a bullet-proof, recession-proof plan to transform Bookends back into the palace of stories and dreams that it used to be, but she had no real idea of how to make those three words she'd written into a reality. It was going to take more than wafting about with paint charts. Perhaps she really wasn't the right woman for the job.

Posy sighed. In Lavinia's letter not once had

she mentioned leaving Bookends to the tender mercies of someone who wasn't Posy. On the contrary. *'Because you, my dear, of all people know what a magical place a bookshop can be and that everyone needs a little magic in their lives,'* Lavinia had written.

Lavinia had put her faith in Posy. She'd bequeathed Bookends to her and Posy couldn't let her down. She didn't doubt that, if she did, Lavinia would find a way to come back and haunt her. She'd leave ghostly messages on mirrors that said soul-destroying things like 'I'm not angry, I'm just very disappointed with you, young lady.' 'I expected better from you, Posy.' Alive or dead, Posy didn't doubt Lavinia's ability with a crushing put-down.

Ghost-Lavinia would shelve books out of order, Jane Austen cosying up to Wilbur Smith, Jackie Collins next to George Orwell. Word would get around that the shop was haunted and then no one would buy it.

Not even Sebastian would want it. Posy could only imagine what Ghost-Lavinia might do to her grandson if she got wind of his plans for the mews. She'd start with his suits, Posy decided. The thought of Sebastian coming home from a hard day of being rude to people and womanising only to find all his suits covered in ghostly green ectoplasm made Posy laugh out loud, drawing a perplexed frown from the man who'd just come up to the counter to pay for a book.

'I'm so sorry,' Posy murmured as Nina bustled out from the back office where she'd been logging new stock to serve him.

'How you getting on with the plans for the shop?' Nina asked frostily. Clearly she was still annoyed with Posy for behaving like an over-protective Victorian mama and dragging her away from Piers Brocklehurst the day before, even though Posy had been doing Nina a favour — when even Sebastian thought a man was behaving abominably then it was time to rethink your taste in men.

Posy was saved from having to explain this to Nina, or confess that the plans for the shop consisted of three words written in her notebook, by her phone beeping.

It was a text from an unknown number.

Come round to Lavinia's now.

It had to be from Sebastian as if he could immediately sense when a woman was thinking about him, however uncharitable those thoughts might be. Posy didn't know how he'd got her number.

Is it important? I'm at work.

Yes. Far more important than waiting in vain for a customer who might actually buy some books.

RUDE, SEBASTIAN! VERY RUDE!

Not as rude as using shouty caps lock. Stop wasting time and get over here.

101

It was probably better to talk to Sebastian face-to-face. Tell him a few home truths. Then again, if he came to the shop at least there'd be witnesses to tell the court that Posy had only brained Sebastian with *The Complete Works of Shakespeare* in the face of extreme provocation.

Her phone buzzed again.

Are you on your way? Hurry up!

Lavinia's house was situated in a pretty garden square off Gower Street, the white stucco houses studded with blue plaques proclaiming that anyone who was anyone from legendary explorers to Victorian government ministers, Pre-Raphaelite artists and literary hostesses had once lived there.

Posy always thought that Lavinia's front door, painted a sunny yellow, was a glorious sight even on the greyest day, especially as Lavinia was always waiting behind it ready with tea and cake and good cheer.

Not today, and not just because the memory of Lavinia was still an aching wound, but because today the door was already flung open.

There was a removal van parked outside and Mariana, swathed in black lace, her official mourning period obviously still in full force, was supervising two men as they loaded Lavinia's dining room table into the back of the lorry. 'Please be careful, darlings, that was designed by Charles Rennie Mackintosh.'

Then Mariana, from her doorstep eyrie, caught sight of Posy, who was watching this tableau with dismay. Of course, Mariana and

102

Sebastian couldn't keep Lavinia's house intact as some kind of museum to its former inhabitant but it still felt as if it were far, far too soon.

'Posy! Darling girl!' Mariana held out her arms and Posy had no choice but to be swept into her *Fracas*-scented clutch. 'Kiss kiss,' Mariana murmured as she brushed the air above Posy's cheeks. 'Just taking a few bits and bobs,' she explained, though the lorry was piled high and stacked deep. 'Mummy inherited them from Granny Aggy, so it's only right and fitting they pass to me. Though, I don't want to sound churlish, they're simply never going to work in the chateau. Still, these things are sent to try us.'

Posy nodded. 'They are.' She gestured at the house behind them. 'Is Sebastian in there?'

'Yes, my darling little viper's in the sitting room. Such a ghastly boy.' Mariana put a hand to her bosom. 'Just as well I love him so.'

Holding her breath, Posy stepped into the hall. Immediately, she could see that Lavinia's house was already a shadow of its glorious, eclectic former self. There were gaps, darker patches on the walls, where furniture and paintings had once been — even Lavinia's lovely Tiffany lamps had been removed. No doubt they were on the lorry, which was now pulling away from the kerb.

With heavy feet and heavier heart, Posy climbed the stairs to the first-floor sitting room. Not just in dread of having to talk to the ghastly viper but because the last time she was here Lavinia had been sitting in her armchair by the huge picture windows that opened out on to a little Juliet balcony. Though somewhat scraped and bruised from falling off her bike a couple of days earlier, and a little fragile, a little preoccupied with the past, Lavinia hadn't seemed like a woman who'd be dead within the week.

But then, as Posy was leaving, Lavinia had taken her hand and held it to her papery soft cheek. 'Dearest Posy, don't look so anxious,' she'd said. 'Everything will turn out fine, you'll see.'

Nervously Posy pushed open the sitting room door, but before she could step into the room an exceedingly querulous voice rang out.

'God, you took your time! I told you it was an emergency. Mariana's gone and she's taken most of the good stuff with her.'

Sebastian was standing by the pretty tiled fireplace, one hand resting on the mantelpiece like he was posing for a menswear editorial. Today's suit was herringbone tweed with a pink fleck to it, picked up by his pink shirt and accessories. It should have looked ridiculous — it would have on anyone else — but even ridiculous looked good on Sebastian. Damn him!

Still, Sebastian's beauty was no match for his obnoxiousness. 'What did you want me to do?' Posy asked. 'Form a human barricade across the front door?'

'Hardly, but it's your tough luck. There's nothing much left for you to pick over now,' Sebastian said, his hands spread wide to indicate the room, though it looked as if Mariana's trolley dash hadn't extended this far.

'There must be things that you want to keep,' Posy said.

'Not really.' Sebastian picked up a brass figurine from the mantelpiece. 'What am I going to do with all this? Most of it is art nouveau. I hate art nouveau.'

'But Lavinia loved these things, and you loved Lavinia . . .'

'Yes, but loving Lavinia means she's in here.' He tapped the breast pocket of his suit right where his heart should be and just as Posy felt herself soften, he took his hand away and said, 'Doesn't mean I have to give houseroom to that sofa. It hurts just to look at it.'

It was a perfectly nice sofa, covered in a William Morris pink and green floral fabric. 'I'd love it for the shop, if you don't want it. We could do with a few more reading areas.'

'It's not a library, Morland. The last thing you need is customers who linger without buying anything, but you can have the sofa, and the armchairs too. Now what else do you want?'

Then he grabbed her by the hand, as if they were hand-holding buddies, and yanked Posy from one room to another, ignoring her protests that it was in bad taste to pick over Lavinia's things like they were first through the door at a Black Friday sale.

It was the books that did for Posy in the end. She called dibs on Lavinia's collection of Georgette Heyers, all first edition hardbacks with their original dust jackets. She also couldn't resist a complete set of Angela Thirkell's Barsetshire novels and was just stacking up some Nancy Mitfords when she admitted to Sebastian that she already had them all 'but these editions are so pretty,' and he pulled her away.

'That's enough,' he said sternly. 'I'm staging an intervention.'

'You might as well ask me to stop breathing,' Posy complained.

Sebastian rolled his eyes to the heavens. 'One day you'll be buried alive under the weight of all those books and it will be weeks before anyone discovers you.'

After that, Sebastian was absolutely intent on keeping her away from the bookshelves, hissing and swiping at Posy each time she tried to reach for a book. She gave it up as a bad job when he accidentally (or so he said) grabbed hold of her right breast in the melee.

'Well, at least you're wearing a bra this time,' he said, peering at the area in question. 'I don't know why you're clutching it like that,' he added as Posy pressed both hands to her chest as if she could cancel out his touch. 'I barely got a feel. It was a glancing blow.'

'You are impossible!' Posy said, and Sebastian grinned as though she'd paid him a huge compliment.

She added Lavinia's lovely primrose yellow tea set to her hoard, along with a couple of recipe books, and then stood outside Lavinia's bedroom as Sebastian strode to the wardrobe.

This was too much. It felt like trespassing.

'Here, take some dresses.' Sebastian turned back to her with armfuls of beautiful bias-cut evening dresses made of silk as fragile as tissue paper.

'Oh God, I could never get into any of them,'

106

Posy said, aghast. Unlike Lavinia and Mariana, who were both tiny, Posy came from sturdy Welsh peasant stock.

Sebastian looked at her breasts *again*, then her hips, making Posy regret every single one of the cheese crackers she'd eaten straight out of the box last night. 'True,' he said. 'Your hips. Are those what you call child-bearing?'

Posy bristled. Actually bristled. She was sure that every hair on her body was in a state of bristledom.

'Let's add all my body parts to the long list of things that are none of your business,' she snapped, but it was like talking to a breezeblock.

'And you might as well take the TV,' he said, tossing the dresses onto the bed. 'I only bought it for Lavinia a few weeks ago. After she had her fall.'

Posy kept forgetting that, despite the fact Sebastian was rude, unspeakably rude, he'd been devoted to Lavinia. Each day that Posy had come to see Lavinia after her accident, stopping on the way to buy out-of-season strawberries, or cinnamon buns from lovely Stefan who ran the deli, anything that might tempt Lavinia's appetite, Lavinia would mention that Sebastian had been in the night before. Her face had always lit up when she spoke about him, no matter how exasperated she sounded as she regaled Posy with his latest antics.

'Lavinia always said it was just as well that she only had one grandchild because she could never have loved the others the way she loved you,' Posy told him.

'Did she?' Sebastian turned to stare out of the window, arms folded. 'I don't think that's strictly true. She always said that she considered you and your brother to be honorary grandchildren, and that the pair of you had much better manners than I did.'

Usually Sebastian was a bit of a sloucher, as if the effort of holding himself straight was too much of a bore, but now his shoulders were so stiff that Posy's ached in sympathy. For a moment she contemplated going over to him and placing a comforting hand against the rigid line of his spine.

She stayed where she was though. 'We, Sam and I, always thought of Lavinia and Peregrine as our honorary grandparents.'

'Don't you have grandparents of your own?' Sebastian asked, still gazing out of the window as if the sight of the rain-soaked garden was absolutely riveting.

'Well, my dad's parents live in Wales, in a small town in the Vale of Glamorgan. We have a couple of aunts and uncles up there too, so we try to visit in the school holidays. My mum's family are Welsh too, but she was an only child . . . My grandfather, her dad, had had a heart attack and my parents were coming back from seeing him in hospital when they had the accident. He died shortly afterwards and my grandma was already showing signs of dementia, but after all that had happened, well, she deteriorated and now she's in a home . . . ' Posy spluttered out the last few words, then stopped. Those few months had been horrible, heart-breaking; a catalogue of catastrophes and grief. And then Peregrine had left them and now Lavinia, so it was no wonder that tears were streaming down her face.

She sniffed and wiped her eyes with the back of her hand, then realised that Sebastian had turned away from the window and was looking at her in horror, even though it couldn't be the first time he'd been in the presence of a weeping woman. It had probably happened an awful lot — with Sebastian responsible for ninety-seven per cent of the tears shed.

'Stop it! Stop crying immediately, Morland.' He reached for his pocket square then stopped himself. 'I'm not going to lend you a hankie because you'll only get snot all over it. Stop it right away! Now, these things of Lavinia's — you're not to lock them away and never use them.'

Sebastian's last edict shocked the next sob away. 'Rude! You really are the rudest man in London. Have you no filter?'

He shrugged. 'Filters are for the weak and the dull. Now, shall we talk about the shop?'

Posy sniffed long and hard to dispel the tears. 'Yes! Let's talk about the shop. I'm only going to say this once, so listen carefully. There is absolutely no way I am giving up the shop just so that you can parcel it together with the rest of the mews and go into partnership with some sharky property developer, who just happens to be one of your old school chums, and has no moral compass and worships at the altar of low investment and high returns.'

Sebastian assumed a bemused expression that

Posy wasn't buying for a second. 'So, you'd be all right with it if I found another property developer, one who was less evil, that I hadn't gone to school with?'

If he was deliberately trying to wind her up then he was doing a very good job of it. 'No! No property developers. No dice. And while we're on the subject, please think carefully about *why* Lavinia left you the mews.' Posy willed herself to calm the hell down because her voice was becoming very squeaky and it felt as if the tears were rallying for an encore performance. 'Maybe, like you said, things can't stay the same, they have to move forward, but there are enough soulless apartment buildings, fancy boutique hotels and Michelin-starred restaurants in London already. I swear I will never, ever forgive you if you raze Rochester Mews to the ground to make room for some more.'

'You wouldn't forgive me?' Sebastian leaned against Lavinia's art deco wardrobe and folded his arms. 'Not ever?'

'Not ever,' Posy confirmed. 'And stop being so flippant. I'm deadly serious.'

'No, Morland, what you are is completely overreacting,' Sebastian said wearily, as if he found Posy's squeaky-voiced sincerity unduly taxing. 'I have no plans to raze the mews to the ground, as you so melodramatically put it. All I'm doing is exploring my options and throwing the odious Brocklehurst a bone so he'll stop pestering me with investment opportunities.' Sebastian threw his head back in annoyance. 'Some people don't understand the meaning of

110

the word no, do they?'

Posy stared at him incredulously. 'They absolutely don't. In fact, I know someone just like that and . . . '

'Anyway, I couldn't flog the mews or demolish its sad collection of buildings even if I wanted to,' Sebastian continued blithely. 'It turns out — and no one could be more surprised than me — the place is Grade Two listed.'

'Really?' Posy was definitely more surprised than Sebastian. She loved the mews and its ramshackle and empty shops, but they had absolutely no historic merit that she could see. 'Why on earth would they be Grade Two listed?'

'Who knows? Who cares? Too boring. Now, let's talk about Bookends, shall we?'

'There's nothing to talk about. I've already told you: we're going big on romance. All the staff are in complete agreement and that's that.'

As far as Posy was concerned, the discussion was over so she walked out of the room. She also wanted to wipe her runny nose on the back of her hand without Sebastian lambasting her for her slovenly ways.

'I can't let you do this, Morland! The fortunes of the shop should not rest on the whims of a bunch of sad old women who can't get a man so they're forced to read about it in the saccharine pages of a romantic novel instead.'

Posy had been hurrying down the stairs but she came to such an abrupt halt that Sebastian went cannoning into her and had to grab her around the waist so they didn't both plunge to their deaths. That's what he'd claim, but it just seemed like another sly attempt to cop a feel.

'Get off me!' Posy dug her nails into Sebastian's grabby hands until he released her with a yelp. 'God, if we were at the shop, I would totally write you up in the sexual harassment book.'

'You really need to work on your threats.'

Posy raced down the last few stairs so she could shout at Sebastian without the risk of personal injury.

'Never mind that! How dare you say that about our customers? All sorts of women read romantic fiction. All ages! And, newsflash: some of them are happily married. Imagine that! And even if they aren't, there's nothing wrong with believing in romance, believing that two people are meant for each other.'

'Ridiculous! All romantic fiction does is foster completely unrealistic expectations in the minds of impressionable women. How long have you been single? I'll tell you: too long. And all because you think every man should be held up to some impossibly high standard and that . . . '

'I date! I go on dates,' Posy insisted because she did. Once a month. She and Nina had a pact that they would go on one date once a month, in the hope that the one date would lead to more dates. That said, Nina tended to average at least ten first dates a month while Posy struggled to find one. It wasn't her fault that the pickings were slim. No matter which dating site Posy chose, and no matter how much she tried to exert some quality control, she invariably spent two hours a month in the company of a man who made nothing stir inside her. Not the faintest fluttering. Not so much as a gossamer-light breeze ghosting around the parts of her that had lain dormant since her last boyfriend, Alex, had made his excuses and left.

When she and Alex had started going out at university, after their eyes met across a crowded room during a very dull lecture on *Beowulf* halfway through their first term at Queen Mary's College, Posy had been a different girl. The kind of girl who could down a pint of lager in ten seconds and finish up with a delicate ladylike burp. She was always the last to leave a party, usually in a shopping trolley stolen from the local supermarket. She was ten pounds lighter and giggled approximately fifty-seven per cent more, and she was infinitely more loveable, more dateable, more fun than she was now.

Alex had thought so anyway. He was studying Medieval History, Posy was studying English Literature and they were made for each other. Took day-trips to obscure museums and ancient monuments. Had big nights out with their group of friends and lived together in their final year in a small studio flat in Whitechapel.

It was a cliché, but it didn't feel like a cliché when Posy told her friends that without Alex she didn't feel complete. Didn't feel right unless his hand was in hers. Hadn't been able to sleep without him spooning her. They could spend hours in the pub yammering about everything from Beat poets to why the BBC should replace the cast of *EastEnders* with pugs. But then they could spend hours not saying a word, happy just to be in each other's company.

Posy had memorised Alex's every freckle, every smile, even his every unkind word — because they did argue sometimes. Then they'd always make up and, God, yes, she missed the sex. Not just THE sex, but sex with Alex, with someone who loved and cared about her and also knew that there was no way that she was going to come without prodigious amounts of digital stimulation.

But then she'd stopped being that kind of girl who partied as hard as she loved, and all their vague plans for a future had to be rewritten because now Posy hardly giggled at all. Plus she came with an added Sam and none of it was what Alex had signed up for.

'I love you, Posy, you know I do, but you're not the you that I fell in love with,' Alex had told her one night, six weeks, five days and three hours after her parents had been killed. He'd come home from his temporary summer job at Hampton Court Palace to find Posy lying on the living room floor, crying with her fist in her mouth so Sam wouldn't hear.

Alex had pulled her off the floor, washed her face, tucked her into bed and then had broken up with her very gently and very kindly.

'It's not the right time for us,' he'd said as he'd wrapped her in his arms and stroked her hot, tear-swollen face. 'There's a museum in York that's asked me along for an interview and, if things were normal, I mean, different, we could do a long-distance thing for a year or two, but things are different. Maybe a couple of years from now, you'll be in a better place . . .'

'A couple of years from now my parents will still be dead and I'll still have a little brother who needs me,' Posy had told him in a dull voice, because Sam was the most important person in her life now. Not Alex.

They'd talked around it for hours, for days, for weeks it seemed, but it was over and it was a relief when Alex landed the job in York. They'd promised to keep in touch but sooner, not even later, the awkward phone calls and the emails petered out. Now Alex was simply a name that popped up on Posy's Facebook newsfeed a couple of times a week. He'd emigrated to Sydney, not that they had any medieval history in Sydney, where he was assistant manager of a wholefood restaurant and was going out with an ethereal-looking redhead called Phaedra, who was an environmental campaigner. Posy couldn't imagine that, if she and Alex happened to bump into each other, they'd find any common ground.

Still, Posy knew the difference between being in love and reading about being in love in a book. And she dated once a month, to keep her hand in even if her heart wasn't, so Sebastian could bloody well shut up.

'I date,' she repeated forcefully. 'But I'd much rather be single than lower myself to use your HookApp or whatever you call it.'

'It's HookUpp, with two p's.' Sebastian came slowly down the stairs, eyes fixed on Posy, who huffed.

'Like anyone is ever going to form a

meaningful relationship based on mutual admiration, trust and passion by swiping up or down on someone's picture based on their geographic location and whether they conform to some narrow definition of attractiveness,' she said with icy disdain.

Sebastian had reached the bottom step now so he could loom over Posy and smirk in that smug way that made her blood pressure start the long climb upwards. 'Not everyone wants a meaningful relationship based on mutual admiration, trust and passion.' He parroted her words back at her with glee. 'Some people, Morland, just want to get laid.'

'Good for them! Meanwhile I will be selling romantic fiction for the vast numbers of people who want to read it. And unless you can come up with a better plan for the shop, I don't want to hear another word out of you. Is that clear?'

'Ma'am! Yes, ma'am.' Sebastian clicked the heels of his handmade leather brogues and saluted smartly. 'By the way, you seem to know an awful lot about my app for someone who has such a low opinion of it.'

Posy closed her eyes. She couldn't do it any more. Deal with Sebastian. She would probably cry again. And she would definitely shout at him and then, when he continued to smirk and loom and make smartarse remarks, she'd snatch up Lavinia's poker from the fireplace in the hall and use it to pierce holes in him.

Far better to leave now and close the door behind her so firmly that it might even be classed as slamming it.

That done, she stomped her way through the streets of Bloomsbury, which were no longer bathed in sunshine as they had been when she left the shop, but lashed by torrents of rain. The inclement weather was probably Sebastian's fault too, Posy decided. Each raindrop stoked the fiery flames of her temper so that by the time she flung open the door of Bookends in a way that would have had Sebastian suing for copyright, she was in a fury. Fuming. Seething.

'He's not just the rudest man in London, he's the rudest man in Britain,' she told Nina and the two Pac-A-Mac-ed ladies she was talking to. 'The rudest man in the whole bloody world.'

'So, you had a nice chat with Sebastian, then?' Nina asked. 'Also, do you know when Eloisa James's next book is out?'

'If by chat you mean he made several personal and unkind remarks and put his hands on my breasts on two separate occasions, then yes, we had a lovely chat.' Posy had to put her hands on her own breasts then, to wipe away Sebastian's phantom touch. It was no wonder the two Pac A Macs were staring at her like she was spewing black ectoplasm out of her ears. 'I'm sorry, what must you think of me? Eloisa James. Nothing out for a while, but have you read any Courtney Milan? Her *Brothers Sinister* series is very good. Not available in the UK, but we have some on our US import shelves, if you're interested.'

By the time Posy had sold them three books apiece and had a lively discussion about tropes in Regency romances ('Why is it the heroes always have a matching set of high-stepping grey

117

horses? Must be the Regency equivalent of a sports car!') her blood pressure was out of the danger zone.

It threatened to rise again when Verity presented her with a provisional timeline for transforming Bookends into Happy Ever After. It featured all sorts of onerous tasks like dismantling each room one at a time for repainting and restocking, returning unwanted stock to the publishers while at the same time wooing said publishers for discounted romantic fiction, promo items and author visits.

'You want us to be ready to relaunch by the end of July? That's only five months away!'

'Ideally we should relaunch at least a month before then to take advantage of the start of the tourist season and the school holidays, but there's so much to do.' Verity peered over her shoulder at the list that Posy knew would haunt her every waking hour. It would probably cut into her sleeping hours too and give her quite a few nightmares about never-ending bookshelves curiously resistant to fresh coats of paint and books turned into slabs of cheese. 'We'll all chip in to help. I don't mind doing the grunt work, as long as I don't have to do anything that involves talking to complete strangers.'

'Not even on the phone? Not even for the greater good?' Posy asked in dismay. She got that Verity was an introvert in an extrovert's world and that the happiest day of her life was when the self-service checkouts were installed in the big Sainsbury's opposite Holborn tube, but it was very hard to have an assistant manager who greeted a ringing telephone with the words, 'What fresh hell is this?'

'I don't mind emailing people. I love emailing people,' Verity said brightly. 'It will be fine. Is this also a good time to tell you that the bank called?'

'Really not,' said Posy, deciding this would be a good time to hide away upstairs with the box of cheese crackers that she hadn't completely decimated the night before.

The three sheets of paper that Verity had given Posy seemed to taunt her, so she turned them over, but then she felt guilty.

Posy switched on her laptop and thought about doing something useful, like emailing her favourite sales reps or drafting a letter to the bank, but instead she thought back to Sebastian being absolutely impossible. Not that his behaviour today was any more impossible than usual.

Except, today he'd accused her of being some lovelorn, dried-up old hag, smitten with the smouldering heroes in romantic fiction because she couldn't get her jollies on with a real man.

Posy pulled up a blank document and instead of any one of a number of worky things she ought to have been getting on with, she found her fingers pounding over the keys on something else entirely.

119

Ravished by the Rake

Sebastian Thorndyke, third Earl of Bloomsbury, scourge of The Ton, and the wickedest man in London, strode into the hall of a modest townhouse on the east side of Holborn.

'No need to announce me,' he declared in the dark treacle voice that had been the ruin of many a young debutante persuaded to dally down dark paths in the Vauxhall Pleasure Gardens while her ever vigilant mama was distracted. He tossed gloves and cane at Thomas, the footman, who manfully tried to block the earl's passage.

'Sir, I must insist that you wait here.'

'Insist, do you? Well, in that case . . .'

The earl pushed the faithful family retainer to one side and proceeded up the stairs to the first floor, Thomas tottering after him.

'Sir, my lady is not at home. And young Master Samuel is at school in Wales where . . .'

'Hate to call a man a liar, but I rather think she is,' said Thorndyke as he flung open the door of the drawing room, startling the young woman who was sat at her writing desk. 'Egads, sir, you are a liar! My lady is decidedly at home.'

'Goodness, my lord, I would have thought that even you would know the difference between being at home and being at home to callers,' said the calm and dignified young

120

woman as she turned back to the letter she was writing. 'Thomas, it would seem that the earl is staying and will surely be in need of some refreshment. It must be quite deleterious to one's health to charge about London demanding audiences with people, regardless of their feelings on the matter. Maybe some tea?' (Yeah! Suck on that, Sebastian!)

'Enough, Miss Morland! I grow increasingly impatient — '

'I would have it that you already are impatient. It's certainly not a state of being that you attain to. You are a master of impatience.'

And Posy Morland, daughter of the late Mr and Mrs Morland, booksellers to the gentry, turned once more to her correspondence, though lesser men had turned their backs on Sebastian Thorndyke and lived to regret it.

Lord Thorndyke gazed on the bowed head of Miss Morland. Silky auburn tendrils of hair escaped the lace cap she wore, which he found a dreadful affectation. True she was twenty-eight and should have long been married were it not for her harridan-like ways (he'd been on the sharp edge of her tongue on more occasions that he cared to recall), but she wasn't such a spinster that she had to take up the lace cap and the sour countenance quite yet. She was wearing a drab grey day dress, a white fichu tucked into the modest neckline, which framed the delicate lines of a neck he was of a good mind to snap. But he had other plans for Miss Morland. The shrew needed taking down a peg or two, and he was just the man to do it.

121

Once her letter was written and blotted, Posy Morland set aside paper and pen. A moment later Little Sophie brought in the tea tray and stood in the centre of the room, eyes wide and fearful at the sight of the earl lounging on his chair, his booted foot resting on the table as if he were supping ale at the lowliest tavern and not in polite company.

It was whispered in other drawing rooms that Thorndyke's valet wasn't allowed to retire for the night until he'd spent an hour blacking and polishing his master's Hessian boots. It was also rumoured that one evening Thorndyke had dragged the poor man from his bed and beat him with his riding crop when he'd discovered a smudge on the leather.

'Kindly remove your boots from my table. You are not in a gaming hall now,' Posy said grandly, rising from her chair so she could take the tray from Little Sophie, who was trembling so hard it seemed entirely possible that the tray might fall from her grasp and take the Morlands' good china with it. 'That will be all, Sophie.'

The maid bobbed, then scurried from the room. Posy placed the tray on the table and sat on the chair opposite Thorndyke. She arranged her skirts just so, then picked up the heavy silver teapot.

'Would you care for a cup of tea, my lord?' Posy enquired, though she rather hoped he would decline as their precious stock of tea was sadly diminished and there weren't the funds to replenish such luxuries. Indeed, she'd spent the morning writing to the grocer, the butcher and linen merchant, begging them to extend the Morlands' line of credit.

'Believe me, madam, you do not wish to know what I care for — but I will tell you nevertheless.' Thorndyke leaned forwards, his dark eyes dancing with mischief, his smile cruel. 'It is but a small matter of fifty guineas that I loaned to your late father. If you will discharge the debt, then I will gladly be on my way.'

He withdrew a letter from the pocket of his clawback coat, cut from superfine as black as his heart, and brandished it at Posy, who felt quite unable to breathe. She placed an unsteady hand on her breast where her heart fluttered like a trapped bird.

'Sir . . . my lord . . . I beg of you,' she implored. 'Our circumstances have become most unfavourable of late, but there is a small annuity settled on my brother Samuel when he comes of age. Will you show us some mercy until then?'

'No, Miss Morland, I will not. Just as you have never shown me any mercy with your viperous tongue and your cold disregard.' He rose to his feet, his figure lean, face haughty. 'Fifty guineas by the end of the month or I'll see you and your brother in debtors' prison.'

'You can't!' she gasped.

He grasped her chin with one gloved hand and raised her downcast head so Posy could see the devilish merriment that animated his chiselled features.

'Oh, but I can and I will,' he said softly, then straightened up, bowed low and took his leave.

7

Two days later, after a morning spent with Lavinia's lawyer, during which Posy had been required to sign so many different pieces of paper that by the end of it her signature looked like a hieroglyphic for water carrier, Posy was busy doing inventory at the shop.

Verity had told her to make three lists: books that could stay under the new regime, books to be returned to the publishers, and books that they'd have to sell in a massive Everything Must Go sale. Unfortunately, the plan had become derailed as soon as Posy found a copy of Shirley Conran's *Lace* on the top shelf in the main room. She hadn't read it in years and was now clinging to the top rung of the rolling ladder, rereading the goldfish scene. It couldn't be hygienic, Posy thought to herself, or very pleasant for the goldfish . . . and then she felt the ladder give a lurch and she squealed and dropped the book.

'What are you doing up there?'

Posy shut her eyes and gave a silent growl. Then she opened her eyes again and looked down to see Sebastian standing below her, the book clutched in his hand, open on the very page that she'd been reading.

He glanced down and sucked in a breath. 'Do *what* with a goldfish? Should you really be selling such smutty books?'

'It's a modern classic, actually,' Posy said.

Sebastian pulled a face. 'Think I'll give it a miss.' He raised his head and smiled. 'You know, it's just as well you're not wearing a skirt or I'd be able to see right up it.'

Posy was wearing jeans, thank God. As she started to hurriedly descend the ladder she felt Sebastian's hands grasp her hips, which made a change from him putting his hands on her breasts. His hands were large, his fingers long, but not as large as her arse. Posy didn't think she'd ever been so aware of that part of her body, or how unflattering it must look as it loomed ever nearer to Sebastian's face.

'I'm perfectly capable of getting down a ladder by myself. Been doing it for years,' she said. 'Unhand me!'

Great! Now she was talking like the Posy in the bizarre Regency romance that she'd found herself writing the other night, which she blamed on PMS. Or eating too much cheese. Or temporary insanity. Or some heady combination of all three.

'I'm unhanding you now,' Sebastian said. 'I told you she was chippy.'

Posy looked behind her to see that Sebastian had brought reinforcements with him: two men in blue overalls hefting a huge TV through the shop. 'Not meant to touch the young ladies without asking first, boss,' one of them said, winking at Posy, who was still mid-descent.

'What is that?' she asked.

'It's a television, Morland. Have you never seen one before?' Sebastian was all wide-eyed innocence, which didn't suit him at all. 'The stairs to the left of the office, then you can dump it in the living room, if you can find a spare patch of floor.'

'I know what it is, why is it going through my shop?'

Posy felt the floor firm beneath her feet as she jumped off the ladder and barred the TV's passage.

'It's the one I bought Lavinia. Don't be boring about this, Morland. I don't need the TV. I already have a massive one and I don't need an entertainment system or a PlayStation either.'

'You got Lavinia a PlayStation?' Nina asked, who'd apparently been standing behind the counter all this time, like some kind of stealth eavesdropping ninja. 'Why would you do that?'

Sebastian sighed dramatically as if the answer was obvious. 'To improve her cognitive functions and her visual-motor ability, of course. What a silly question. Anyway, weren't you the girl who was rather taken with Brocklehurst? Were you dropped on your head as a baby?'

'Not as far as I know. And FYI, Piers and I were flirting. He was being charming — you might want to try that sometime. So, now we've cleared that up, I've got a bone to pick with you.' Nina came out from behind the counter and advanced on Sebastian, who suddenly didn't look quite as self-possessed as usual. 'I downloaded your stupid dating app and every man that I've tried to hook up with has been a complete waste of make-up. One guy said he was a DJ, but he turned out to be a fishmonger and

126

he didn't even take a shower before he showed up expecting to get into my pants.'

'Well, um, when you download the app, you automatically agree to our terms and conditions, which state quite clearly that we can't be held personally responsible for the calibre of loser that you may hook up with. Naturally my lawyers threw in a few 'henceforth's and an 'indemnification' or two to make it all sound suitably legal. So, did he get into your pants?'

'Sebastian, you can't ask someone that!' Posy exclaimed as he turned to her with a genuinely bewildered expression.

'Why not? She was the one who brought up her pants,' he pointed out. 'So, did he, then?' He turned back to Nina, unflappable Nina, who didn't seem to mind that Sebastian and the two schleppers he'd brought with him, who were currently lingering by the New Releases shelves, were so interested in her pants.

'He did not,' Nina said with some relish. 'Girl's got to have some standards. Neither did the bloke who turned up half an hour late because he said he had to take his little sister's hamster to the vet. Seriously, I mean it, you need to have a better dickhead filter on that app.'

'I always wash up after work and I don't have a little sister or a hamster,' said the TV-lugger Posy had mentally christened Cocky Young 'Un. He had a roll-up behind one ear, a pencil behind the other, manly forearms, a crew-cut and a shit-eating grin.

Just Nina's type. And he had to be an improvement on Piers Brocklehurst.

Nina must have thought so too. She took out her phone; he took out his. They found each other on Sebastian's vile app then they both swiped upwards, while Sebastian looked on like a proud papa. 'So, I'll message you, yeah?' Cocky Young 'Un said to Nina, who smiled.

'Cool. Maybe I'll message you back.'

Posy's top lip curled so hard she wondered if it would ever uncurl. Where was the romance? Where were two strangers locking eyes across a crowded room, that spark of recognition, of something deep and magical, of two hearts finding each other? No hearts had been involved, just a lot of talk about Nina's pants. There was no difference between modern dating and doing an online supermarket shop. At least if you did an online supermarket shop and they didn't have your item in stock they substituted it for something more expensive.

'All right, Romeo, that's enough,' said Cocky Young 'Un's colleague, whom Posy had mentally christened Grumpy Old 'Un. 'Guv, we're gonna leave the telly down here 'til the young lady can make up her mind. Now where do you want the sofa and chairs?'

'In the tearoom on the right for now. It'll be easier if I unlock the front door, instead of you bringing it through the shop,' Posy said brightly, because the sooner they were done, the sooner Sebastian would be on his merry way. 'I'll get the keys.'

'Don't be stupid, Morland,' Sebastian barked, shouldering her out of the way. 'Take the sofa and chairs that are currently in the living room

128

and put them in the tearoom and you can have Lavinia's sofa and chairs upstairs. You'll be much more comfortable. I sat on your sofa last time I was here and I was almost sodomised by a loose spring.'

There *was* a loose spring; she and Sam knew to avoid it, but still it was their rogue spring and their sofa, and it didn't need Sebastian coming in and trying to take over everything: her life, the shop, even her choice of seating.

'Well, that's very kind of you, but it's better to leave them down here. There's too much stuff in the way to start rearranging the furniture upstairs . . . '

Posy walked over to the counter, her back to Sebastian so she could grimace and roll her eyes at Nina to her heart's content, their disagreement over Piers forgotten, as she fumbled under the counter for the keys to the tearoom. No sooner had she got them than Sebastian was right there, in her personal space, so he could snatch the keys and refuse to give them back, even when Posy tried to stamp on his foot.

'Take it upstairs, boys. You'll have to fight your way through the books, but it can't be helped.'

'Sebastian, you can't keep coming in here and issuing orders like you own the place. You don't. I do,' Posy said, trying oh so very hard to keep her voice calm and modulated but she couldn't help but clutch at his arm. Beneath the soft, fine wool of his jacket sleeve, she felt his muscles twitch frantically as she made contact.

'Now, we've talked about this before,' Sebastian said gently, as he prised her fingers

129

free from his arm. 'You must never, ever touch the suit.'

'You are impossible,' she told him, while Cocky Young 'Un and Grumpy Old 'Un crunched their way up the stairs accompanied by muttered exclamations of 'Bleeding hell!' and 'He wasn't joking about the books.'

'And why is it, since Lavinia's been gone, that you're always *here*? Haven't you got other people you could be annoying?'

Sebastian stuck out his bottom lip in an audacious pout. 'That's a very churlish attitude when I've decided that since you're so determined, against my better judgement, to keep the bookshop, I should lend you my wealth of expertise.'

Posy didn't have so much of a sinking feeling as a feeling like all her internal organs had suddenly plummeted to the centre of the earth. 'Oh,' she said with a sideways look at Nina.

'So, Sebastian, do you have much experience of book-selling?' Nina asked sweetly. 'Did you work here in the school holidays, back in the day?'

'As if!' Posy snorted. 'Far too busy locking me in the coal-hole.'

'That was one time, Morland. I only did it to stop you mooning over me. She had a terrible crush on me *back in the day*,' he added for Nina's benefit, who grinned.

'Yeah, 'terrible' being the operative word.' Posy shuddered at the memory of her childhood infatuation.

'Anyway, I've realised that if we're to make a go of this bookshop, then we need to go niche,'

130

Sebastian announced proudly, as if he'd come up with that concept all by himself.

'Yes, I did mention that,' Posy reminded him. 'It's why I'm going to relaunch Bookends as a room — '

'A crime bookshop!' Sebastian said quickly, with a pointed glare at Posy. 'Please stop interrupting. So rude. Anyway, I've been doing some research. Well, I got some interns on it. That's where the money is: crime. At any one time half the bestseller list is made up of crime novels. It's perfect. Brilliant!' He peered at Posy, who couldn't decide on stony-faced or furious as a suitable facial expression. 'You look constipated. What's the problem?'

Where to begin? 'For one thing, I don't like crime fiction.'

'Why not? It's fantastic. There's murder, intrigue, suspense, sex, heroes and villains, untraceable poisons. What's not to like?' He strode over to the counter, where Nina was stifling a yawn. 'You like crime, don't you?'

Nina shook her head. 'Nah. By the time I've found out who's done it, I'm bored. Besides, there used to be a crime bookshop on the Charing Cross Road and it went out of business.'

Sebastian, undaunted, tossed his curls back. 'Well, they were probably very bad at selling books and we're not. We're going to be fantastic.'

'Honestly, do you hear when people are disagreeing with you or does your brain automatically block the words out?' Posy asked, genuinely curious. 'We're not doing crime. We're doing romance.'

'Romance, shomance.' Sebastian took Posy's hand, though she tried to tug it free, and pulled her to the middle of the shop. 'Now, we'll have new releases and bestsellers in here.'

'Is it just me or are you getting the déjà-vu thing too?' Nina asked.

Posy shook her head. There was nothing else for it but to wait for Sebastian to run out of steam.

'Through here will be our classic murder mystery room,' he said, dragging Posy to the first room on the right. 'Agatha Christie, Conan Doyle and so on. Then through there we'll have Scandi crime. Oh! And graphic novels. On the left, we'll have real crime — who doesn't love a serial killer?'

'Quite a lot of people,' Posy said. 'The families of their victims, any decent law-abiding citizens . . .'

'Boring. Also, we should sell book-related bits and pieces: branded tote bags, mugs, stationery. It's cheap as chips to buy it wholesale, cheaper than chips, and you wouldn't believe the mark-up on it.'

That was actually a good idea. Never mind serial killers, who didn't love a tote bag? Maybe some scented candles, book-related greetings cards, wrapping paper . . . They could even offer a gift-wrapping service. Posy made a mental note to look up gift-wrapping tutorials on the internet because all her presents looked as though they'd been wrapped by a five-year-old without opposable thumbs.

Then she realised that Sebastian was still

yammering away. 'Obviously we should think about changing the name of the shop. I did a quick straw poll at the office to see what people thought of the name Bookends. Most of them didn't know what a bookend was. We should probably have a brainstorm with your staff, but what do you think about The Bloody Dagger?'

'I'll make sure I've wiped it clean long before the police find it next to your lifeless body,' Posy said blankly.

'There you go! You're getting into the spirit of things,' Sebastian said, because he was made out of Kevlar or some other impenetrable material, which made it impossible for him to get a clue, take a hint or pick up on social cues. 'So, we're agreed: crime bookshop, yup?'

He was never going to leave. He was going to stay until they agreed to relaunch as a crime bookshop and stock a whole load of grisly novels and taut psychological thrillers, all with dark covers. And Posy shouldn't generalise because she hated it when people made assumptions about romantic fiction, but it seemed that every crime novel she'd ever picked up featured huge amounts of death and creeping menace. And an emotionally scarred ex-police officer tormented by the death of a loved one at the hands of a vengeful serial killer they'd put away for a ten stretch who'd then been acquitted on a technicality. Now *that* was boring *and* depressing, but there was no point telling Sebastian that. He wouldn't listen.

What would Lavinia do? Posy asked herself, as she had so often these last few days.

133

Lavinia had always told her that no one ever said no to Sebastian. 'Mariana certainly didn't, or any of his nannies, even Eton tried and failed. Perry and I should have been firmer with him, but he was our only grandchild so we did rather indulge him and now he simply doesn't respond to no.'

Then she wouldn't say no, Posy decided. She turned her attention back to Sebastian, who was waiting for her reply. 'Crime bookshop,' he repeated. 'You and me, in it together?'

'Fine, whatever,' Posy said diffidently because that wasn't yes and it wasn't no. It was a grey middle ground that would never stand up in a court of law. 'I'm sick to death of talking about it. Are we done now?'

It wasn't a yes, it really wasn't but Sebastian slowly turned, caught in a shaft of fading sunlight, and beamed at her as if she'd screamed to the heavens, 'Yes! Yes! A thousand times yes!'

God, it was a good smile. Sebastian always looked pretty when he scowled, but when he smiled he looked beautiful, but also goofy and boyish so that Posy couldn't help but smile back. 'Ha!' he said. 'I knew you wouldn't be able to resist me.'

'Actually, it's very easy to resist you,' Posy told him, but now that he thought he'd got his own way, Sebastian was too busy taking Posy in his arms and waltzing her around the main display table to listen. It was quite nice to be held by someone, especially someone who towered over her so she felt like a delicate slip of a girl and he did smell lovely. It was quite the moment they were having, until Posy trod on Sebastian's foot.

'Did you do that on purpose?' Posy was saved from having to reply by an ominous crash from upstairs followed by, 'It's OK, missus. Nothing broken, just bent a few of your books.' Then the shop bell tinkled and Sam walked in, followed by his best friend, Pants.

'All right?' Sam grunted, and would have carried on through the shop and straight up the stairs except Pants lingered, because Nina was still behind the counter and Pants saw Sam home from school every Thursday solely so he could gaze upon Nina. Nina, the light of his life, his one true love. Nina.

'How are you doing, Pants?' Nina asked him kindly, because Pants made people want to be kind to him. He was short, rotund, ginger and even his parents called him Pants.

'Oh, can't complain, though it's quite nippy for this time of year,' Pants said, rocking back on his heels, because the other thing about Pants was that he was a middle-aged man trapped in a fifteen-year-old's body. He continued to stare at Nina while she smiled gamely, then he hoisted his school bag higher and started backing away. 'Well, must be off. This maths homework isn't going to do itself,' he said, and then he was gone.

'Sorry,' Sam said to Nina. 'Every Thursday he says he's not going to come back with me and then he changes his mind halfway through Geography.'

'Oh, it's fine. I think Pants is my longest-lasting relationship.' Nina's shoulders slumped. 'Well, until he hits his growth spurt and starts

135

chasing after younger women.'

'Yup, true that,' Sam agreed. He hadn't noticed Sebastian yet, though Sebastian had noticed him and was looking Sam over from head to toe and side to side with the most peculiar expression on his face.

'You should go upstairs,' Posy said quickly. 'I bet you've got loads of homework. Just so you know, there are two men up there delivering a sofa that we absolutely don't need . . . '

'We do. Every time I sit down on ours, I forget about the loose spring and it pokes me in the arse.'

'Well, you should be more careful,' Posy said. 'Go upstairs and make sure they haven't broken anything.'

Sam pulled a face. 'So bossy.'

'She is, isn't she?' Sebastian was never going to stay silent for long. 'I'm Sebastian, who the hell are you?'

Sam reared back slightly and Posy had no choice but to introduce them. 'This is Sebastian, Lavinia's grandson. You don't remember him? Though I suppose he usually comes in to bother us when you're at school. He's also very rude, so don't take anything he says personally. Sebastian, this is Sam, my little brother.'

'Not little brother, Posy. Younger brother. I'm much taller than you are.'

The two of them, Sam and Sebastian, looked at each other. If Sebastian said anything about Sam's spots or his light sprouting of facial hair, which Posy had been meaning to speak to him about, or the three centimetres of sock

136

protruding from his trousers, she would kill him. Painfully. Very, very painfully.

Sebastian didn't. 'This isn't Sam,' he said. 'Sam is a small child. About yay high.' He held his hand to his breast pocket.

'I haven't been yay high since I was, like, six.'

It was Sam's turn to stare Sebastian down. It was a bit like watching stags in that split second before they locked horns, while David Attenborough provided a play-by-play.

Then Sebastian shrugged and Posy unclenched. 'Hey, Sam. Lovely to meet you. Would you like a PlayStation, a state-of-the-art home entertainment system and a forty-six-inch screen plasma television? Your sister said I should take them all back.'

'Why would you say that?' Sam shot her a positively demonic look. 'Our telly is crap. We can barely get Freeview on it.'

Posy knew when she was beaten. 'If we keep them — if — you're only allowed one hour telly or PlayStation a night, two hours on weekends, and you have to do your homework first. Do you promise?'

'Fine, whatever.'

Sebastian looked at Sam again. 'You'd better help the guys lug it all upstairs. My suits aren't cut for lugging. Have you got biscuits? Your sister didn't so much as offer me a cup of tea. You ought to have a word with her.'

'She's probably eaten all the biscuits,' Sam said disloyally, the little git, and then they were gone and Nina turned the full weight of her most withering stare on Posy, who duly withered.

137

'What? What did I do?'

'We're becoming a *crime bookshop*?' If ever the *Downton Abbey* folk needed a stand-in for the Dowager Countess, Nina was good to go.

'Of course we're not.'

Now it was Verity's turn to come barrelling out of the back office where she'd been skulking the entire time. 'But you told him we were. I heard you. This is the worst thing ever.'

'It will be awful.' Nina sounded close to tears. 'A crime bookshop. We'll have loads of panty-sniffing psychopaths coming in to buy books on Ted Bundy, and then they'll follow us home, kill us horribly and fashion our skin into onesies.'

'You're both completely overreacting,' Posy protested. 'Anyway, I didn't agree to turn Bookends into a crime bookshop. I said, 'Fine, whatever,' which isn't even a bit like saying yes. He wasn't going to shut up about it so I had to say something and 'no' wasn't registering. Anyway, he's got the attention span of a fruit fly. He'll have forgotten all about it in a week and we'll be left in peace while he invents some shady app that lets you cheat on your spouse without them ever finding out.'

Verity remained sceptical. 'Are you sure about this?'

'I have never been more sure about anything in my life. Though, to give Sebastian credit for the first and last time, and we're never to mention it again, that was a genius idea about selling postcards and mugs and tote bags.'

Nina clapped her hands together. 'I know! I

love tote bags! We can design our own bags with quotes from our favourite novels.'

'But only the ones whose authors have been dead for longer than seventy years so we don't have to pay copyright fees,' Posy noted, because she was totally getting the hang of this business owner thing. By the end of the year, she'd probably be hanging out at the Small Business Owners annual conference and swapping digits with other successful small business owners and arranging breakfast meetings.

Eventually Cocky Young 'Un and Grumpy Old 'Un left, although not before knocking over a display of books about London, which Posy had put together to tempt any tourists who might wander into the shop. Then Nina and Verity closed up and went home too and yet Sebastian was *still* upstairs with Sam.

As Posy climbed the stairs, she could hear the low murmur of conversation coming from the lounge and when she pushed open the door, Sam and Sebastian were looking at something on the computer.

For one heart-stopping moment, Posy thought it might be porn, but as she got nearer, she saw the shop's rudimentary website up on the screen. Sebastian and Sam hadn't heard her come in because they were talking about databases and style sheets and properties panels and weird acronyms that weren't even words.

Posy knew that Sebastian was a digital entrepreneur and made scads of money from his apps and websites and whatnot, but she'd always assumed that he just came up with vague ideas for his techy bits and bobs and had a team of minions that did the heavy lifting. Or the heavy coding. Whatever. But as he talked to Sam about something called a CSS, without one single snarky comment or outright insult, his fingers flying over the keyboard, Posy was forced to admit that she might have been wrong.

And Sam! Her little Sam. Her baby brother, whom she knew everything about, was holding up his end of the conversation. Nodding, shoving Sebastian out of the way so he could do something that made the screen go black then flickery green type appear as he talked excitedly about hyperlink presentation modules.

Sam was a person in his own right, with his own stuff going on, his own likes and dislikes, passions and ambitions, and soon he wouldn't need her getting on his case about anything. Which was good, it meant that Posy had done right by Sam, had in some small way stepped into their parents' shoes and now Posy could start living her own life. So why did the thought of it make her feel so sad?

'I hope this means that you don't have any homework,' Posy said, just to remind herself that Sam still needed her, but she knew immediately it was the wrong thing to say because Sam turned around with a wounded look and Sebastian snorted.

'God, your sister is one hell of a buzzkill,' he said. 'And stubborn too. How do you stand it?'

'She's all right. About some things anyway,' Sam said, with a lot less enthusiasm than Posy would have liked. 'Like, she doesn't ever shout at me to make my bed. She says it will only get messy again as soon as I get back into it . . . So, did you want to stay for dinner?'

'Hello! I'm standing right here,' Posy reminded them. She couldn't bear it if Sebastian stayed for dinner. He'd want to talk more about the crime bookshop that was never, ever going to happen, and it was only pasta and pesto for dinner with whatever green leafy stuff was left in the fridge, because Posy hadn't had time to get to the shops.

They had pasta and pesto for dinner at least twice a week.

'I would love to stay for dinner, but your sister's housekeeping skills are lacking and I'd hate to die of botulism,' Sebastian said as he stood up and rolled his shoulders. 'Lovely to meet you, Sam. You're my favourite Morland. Number one with a bullet. I'll get Rob to email you about the website.'

Sam didn't seem to notice that Sebastian was sucking all the air out of the room simply by existing and had just insulted his sister on at least three counts. In fact, Sam didn't even look up from the computer. 'Cool. See you soon then.'

Posy led Sebastian out through the darkened shop. Taking a deep breath, she decided to cut him some slack — though he'd been high-handed and domineering, he had had some good ideas.

'I'm very excited about the tote bags,' she told him as she unlocked the door. 'And it's really kind of you to help Sam with the website.'

Instead of walking through the door, away into the night to forget all about his plans for a crime

141

fiction empire as soon as the first shiny bauble caught his eye, Sebastian paused in the doorway and put his hand on Posy's forehead. His hand was cool and her forehead was hot because she was frazzled and it was probably warm enough now to go without her thermal vest.

'I think you must be coming down with something, Morland,' Sebastian said in a voice so concerned that it bordered on parody. 'You just thanked me without any trace of sarcasm. Really, I'm quite touched.'

'Cherish this feeling, because I can't see it lasting,' Posy said, and she pushed him out the door while he squawked about his precious suit. 'Thanks so much for all the business advice. If I need any more help, I'll give you a call.'

Sebastian started to say something but Posy never heard what it was because she shut the door, turned the key and slid the bolts across. When Sebastian still made no sign of moving, she waved him away with a shooing motion and drew the blind.

Ravished by the Rake

The rain started to fall as Posy Morland trudged across the hunting lands known as Marylebone Park.

She had been visiting her dear friend Verity Love, a rector's daughter, in the parish of Camden where they had performed acts of charity; visiting the sick and reading to the children at the local poor school.

But now the fading afternoon light darkened further as the clouds closed over her head and the heavens did truly open. Soon her thin muslin gown was soaked quite through; her shawl and bonnet no protection from the cruel elements.

~~Kind of like that bit in Pride and Prejudice when Mrs Bennet wouldn't let Jane take the carriage to Netherfield Park in the hope she'd get caught in the rain and have to throw herself on the mercy of Mr Bingley.~~

What with the thunder rolling and the rain heaving down, it took Posy quite some time to isolate the sound of hooves and by then a horse and rider had loomed out of the darkness. She bit down a scream and hoped that the shadow of the trees would shield her. The hunting lands were notorious haunts of highwaymen, cutthroats and worse.

There was a sudden jagged streak of lightning

and the horse reared up in panic. Posy caught sight of the rider as he cursed and struggled to keep his mount under control. Saw the grim, forbidding lines of his face before they were blunted by the dim light again and she started to run, though the ground was waterlogged, the thin soles of her boots no match for the mud, her skirts sodden.

She could hear the horse behind her, fancied she could feel its hot breath kiss the back of her neck, and she tried to quicken her pace but instead stumbled, hands outstretched to break her fall.

'Miss Morland! You impossible little fool!' shouted a familiar, sardonic voice. The rider was leaning down so he could scoop her up (NB: is this physically possible? Maybe if he'd been working out and I'd lost two stone?) and she landed in the saddle with an ungainly thump and a squeak as she jarred every bone in her body. 'You'll catch your death out here, or risk meeting a man less charitable than I.'

She was soaked through and shivering so it was hard to talk through chattering teeth. 'I wager it would be hard to find a man less charitable than you even if I found myself in the most disreputable tavern in all of London!'

Sebastian Thorndyke laughed throatily. 'Maybe I should leave you to fend for yourself and pity the poor man who chances upon such a shrew.' But then he settled himself in the saddle as the powerful beast shifted beneath them, opening his great coat so he could press Posy back against the hard, unyielding wall of his chest. As he

144

wrapped the soft, damp wool around her, he added: 'Then again, maybe I won't. If something untoward should happen to you, there would be little chance of recovering the fifty guineas you owe me.'

'You are absolutely insufferable,' Posy told him as he urged his horse into a gentle canter, but truth be told, she was grateful not to be left on the rain-soaked hunting grounds to find her own way back to Bloomsbury. Not that she would ever admit that to Thorndyke, not when he just laughed and held her tighter.

8

Posy always had the utmost admiration for anyone with the talent and the determination to write a book. Especially to *finish* writing a book, but now her own dreadful, florid attempts to write in a genre that she loved, which should have come easily to her, gave her a whole new respect for authors.

She had wanted to be a writer ever since she could remember. The summer that her parents . . . the summer of the car crash, she'd been accepted on the MA course in Creative Writing at the University of East Anglia to start the following October. Apart from marrying Ryan Gosling, it had been her life's ambition to gain a place on the same MA course that had honed the talents of Tracy Chevalier, Ian McEwan, Kazuo Ishiguro and just about every other literary novelist who'd ever won a prize. Posy had even considered taking up her place and relocating Sam to Norwich (though her grand-parents had said that they'd be happy to have Sam in Wales with them and Lavinia and Perry had also offered him a home during term time) but she and Sam had both lost so much that abandoning their home, their familiar London life and each other, would have been a step too far.

It didn't mean that Posy had given up on her dreams of becoming a novelist. On the computer were no less than nine of her attempts to write the Great British Novel. Unfortunately, none of them were good attempts, which was why she'd abandoned them. One was called *The Crocus Throat*, though Posy couldn't imagine what she'd been thinking of when she'd decided it would be a good idea to write a stream-of-consciousness narrative novel or even if crocuses had throats.

But this . . . this *thing: Ravished by the Rake*. It was deeply, deeply troubling. Not troubling enough to delete it, because Posy could always do a find-and-replace on the names (once she'd had a proper crack at rewriting and editing it and maybe allowing someone else to read it; perhaps Verity, if she swore her to absolute secrecy) but troubling enough that she saved it on to a thumb drive so Sam wouldn't find it.

Still, was it any wonder that she was writing ridiculous fanfic about Sebastian when he was the only man she came into contact with on a regular basis? Apart from Tom, and he didn't count. He was her work buddy, her employee now, and though he was *quite* attractive in a young academic kind of way with his cardigans and his quiff and his vague but stern manner — he could hand-sell books to middle-aged women like books were a black market commodity in the former Eastern Bloc — Posy didn't like to think of him in a sexual way. Oh dear God, no.

She really needed to banish all thoughts of Sebastian from her mind, her fevered imagination and her hard drive. She needed a man as a matter of some urgency. Though finding a decent, dateable man was like trying to find a Stephanie Laurens novel that she hadn't read yet. Posy hadn't been on a date for weeks and the recent messages she'd had from the dating sites (she was signed up to five at the last count) had all been very subpar.

On her profile, Posy had listed her interests as long walks, visits to art galleries and the theatre as well as curling up on the sofa with a bottle of wine and a good film. Though, to be honest, only the last one was truly applicable, but if she had more free time, she was sure that she'd be hoofing all over London to attend all sorts of cultural events.

The trouble was, Posy knew she could never form a meaningful attachment with a man who messaged her: 'hi darling how r u?' She could never love a man who spurned capital letters and rudimentary grammar. The same went for the numerous variations on 'wow! sexy pic. wanna hook up?' Besides, there was nothing remotely sexy about the black-and-white shot of Posy peering over a copy of *Jane Eyre*, or the photo of her taken at last year's Christmas party where she was sitting on the rolling ladder proudly wearing a reindeer jumper *and* glow-in-the-dark antlers.

But there wasn't time to worry about that now. Posy needed to find a man, and if the internet wasn't going to help, she'd just have to do things the old-fashioned way.

'Please can we go out on Saturday night?' she asked Nina and Verity as they came through the door on Wednesday morning, before they'd even had a chance to take their coats off or argue about whose turn it was to make tea. 'I need to talk to a man who isn't bloody Sebastian Thorndyke.'

'What about Tom?' Verity asked.

'Tom doesn't count,' Nina and Posy both said in unison.

'Could you imagine going on a date with Tom?' Posy added.

'Especially if he decided to wear that polka-dot bow tie that he breaks out on special occasions,' Nina said. 'And my God, he'd be hard work. I've been to the pub with Tom more times than I can count and I still don't know what he's writing his thesis on or who he lives with or any other personal information. I'm working on this theory that he's in the Witness Protection Programme.'

'Or he's secretly married with five kids and he only comes to the shop for a bit of peace and quiet,' Verity suggested and while this was all very entertaining, it was getting off the subject as far as Posy was concerned.

'Can we focus here? I need to go out and drink my bodyweight in alcohol so I can flirt with men, they don't even have to be that good-looking, and forget about the shop and Sebastian for a few hours. Please can we do that?'

'We can do that,' Nina agreed. 'Three words: hot Swedish men. Another three words: cold Swedish vodka. We just bumped into lovely Stefan from the deli and he's invited us to his birthday party next Saturday. Said he's got friends visiting from Sweden. Even Verity said she'd come.'

Verity was in the kitchen making tea but she stuck her head out of the door so she could pull a face at Nina. 'I do go out socially sometimes,' she said. 'But I'll have to leave work early on Saturday, Posy, so I can go home and have a disco nap first.'

'I have to take Sam clothes-shopping on Saturday,' Posy said, which was another reason why she needed to go out on Saturday night, because clothes shopping with Sam was always an ordeal and she deserved a reward after, hence the need for a lot of alcohol. 'I'll be back around three if I haven't murdered him first, so you can leave then.'

Maybe, now that she was in charge, Posy should be stricter and establish boundaries, but Nina and Verity, Tom too, had been her friends long before they became employees. She didn't doubt that, when she really needed them, especially as they got nearer to relaunching in July, they'd come through for her.

'By the way, I went through the books last night,' Verity said, which proved Posy's point. Only a true friend would spend her Tuesday evening going through her friend's accounts, especially when *Masterchef* was on. 'Now, I don't want to cause panic, or maybe we should panic a bit, but you really should have a chat with Lavinia's accountant. And I think we're going to have to move the relaunch forward. Do you want tea or coffee?'

'Tea, please,' Posy said, distracted. 'Forward,

150

not back? I thought the end of July was pushing it.'

Nina melted away with a horrified look and a murmur about chasing some outstanding orders as if the word 'accountant' had put the wind up her.

'We're barely breaking even,' said Verity. 'The shop's been so quiet lately, and if we leave it much longer, we'll be in the red and you'll have to see if you can get an emergency overdraft.' She put a mug of tea down in front of Posy. 'Sorry. Hate to hit you with this first thing.'

'Oh God, it's not your fault.' Posy sighed and wrapped her fingers around the mug as if she could leach some of its warmth to heat up her heart, which was gripped in an icy chokehold. 'Um, should I get an emergency overdraft?'

'I don't think so, unless you want to get clobbered with fees and charges.'

It was then that Posy knew the shop must be in a bad way, because Verity enveloped her in a quick, perfunctory but very sincere hug despite the fact Verity was the least huggy person Posy knew.

'I think it's time to bring in the big guns, Posy,' Verity said, picking up her own mug.

Posy could feel her skin grow clammy. 'You don't mean what I think you mean . . . ?'

'Afraid so.' Verity nodded grimly. 'A wall planner, a variety of coloured gel pens and stickers, and several packets of biscuits.'

'Oh, say it isn't so!' The last time they'd needed to call on the services of a wall planner and stickers had been when they were organising a week of events for Bookends centenary. Posy

151

remembered now, with a pang, that was the last time they'd strung fairy lights from the trees in the courtyard. The big one hundredth birthday party bash had spilled outside and it had been like the old days. But then they'd toasted to absent friends and Posy had retreated back inside the shop to be with her ghosts; her mother, her father except Lavinia had got there first and was sitting forlornly on one of the sofas.

'How I miss Perry,' she'd said when she glanced up to find Posy hovering in the shop doorway, not wanting to intrude. 'I don't think I'll ever get used to him not being here.'

'I'm sorry,' Posy had said and she hoped those two words conveyed that she had some small understanding of the measure of Lavinia's grief. 'Do you want to be alone, because I can go if . . .'

Lavinia had shaken her head. 'You can stay if you promise to be very, very quiet.'

So Posy had sat down next to Lavinia, taken the older woman's hand, stroked her papery soft skin, and neither of them had said a word, because words didn't need to be said.

But before that, there had been a wall planner and so many arguments over which stickers to use and how long each task added to the planner might take that Lavinia had got as cross as Posy had ever seen her and told Posy and Verity (who'd only started at Bookends the month before) that she'd knock their heads together if they didn't stop.

And yet now Verity thought that a wall planner was exactly what was needed.

152

'It's the only way,' Verity pleaded. 'Come on, you know it makes sense.'

Posy put up a spirited defence, but Verity was having none of it. She despatched Posy to the nearest stationery shop for supplies and to lovely Stefan's deli for sweet treats to keep their energy levels up, because Verity refused to leave the back office. 'I have stuff to do and I'm not emotionally equipped to deal with the general public or even lovely Stefan today.'

'You feel like that every day,' Posy groused, but she did as she was told. For someone so introverted, Verity was exceedingly good at getting her own way. Once she was outside, though, Posy was pleased of the chance to clear her head before being sequestered in the back office for the rest of the day.

They started their wall planner scheduling with the best intentions, designating coloured stickers for different aspects of the relaunch: green for stock, blue for redecorating and so on. Verity, because she was able to write in teeny tiny letters, wrote every single task down on the chart, no matter how mundane.

It all began to go pear-shaped when Tom, who was meant to be working that afternoon, phoned in sick, though he didn't sound sick so much as hungover. When you'd worked with someone for over three years you got to know the difference, though short of demanding a doctor's note there wasn't much Posy could do about it.

'Don't suppose you can cover the lunchtime rush then go home an hour early to make up for it?' Posy asked Nina.

'No, I can't! I have plans,' Nina snapped, as if Posy was the most tyrannical of employers, which she didn't think she was. 'I have a life outside this shop, you know.'

The reason for Nina's defensive behaviour strolled into Bookends at five to one. Piers Brocklehurst, bold as brass, in his too-loud pinstripe suit and a pink shirt (much more garish than Sebastian's pink shirt) which clashed with his florid complexion.

'Really?' Posy raised her eyebrows at Nina, who was frantically gathering jacket and bag so she wouldn't have to suffer Posy's scrutiny for a moment longer than was absolutely necessary. 'Him? What about the other guy? The one who came round with Sebastian that you HookApped with?'

'HookUpp, not HookApp! And what about him? I like to have more than one string to my beaux, you know that. I'm too young to be tied down,' Nina hissed while Piers strode around as if he owned the place, eyes assessing their square footage as if were calculating how much he could flog it for.

'We meet again, Miss Morland,' he said, not bothering to hide his disdain. 'You heard from Thorndyke lately? He's a hard chap to get hold of.'

If only that were true, Posy thought to herself, and Sebastian really was an elusive creature instead of a nuisance who burst into the shop on practically a daily basis. 'Oh? So he hasn't told you that we're Grade Two listed then?' Posy enquired sweetly. 'Not just us but the whole Mews.'

'On what planet are you Grade Two listed?'

'Enough of that,' Nina said sharply as she came out from behind the counter in a cloud of Chanel No. 5. 'I'm sure we can think of more exciting things to talk about than Bookends.'

Posy put a hand to her heart, as though she'd been stabbed. And in a way she had, but Nina gave a firm shake of her head as if to say 'Not now.'

'So, what do you fancy for lunch? Something hot and spicy?' Piers pretended to lunge at Nina, who giggled and skidded away from him on the four-inch heels that she hadn't been wearing that morning.

'Oh, you naughty boy,' she cooed huskily, and they left, Nina still giggling as Piers put a hand on her bottom to steer her out the door.

'Oh, Nina,' Posy said out loud as the door closed behind them. 'You have the worst taste in men.'

'The absolute worst,' came the echo from the back office where Verity was still waiting. 'Come on, let's get this done.'

It was very hard to get it done when people would insist on coming into the shop on their lunch break to buy books. Since Verity absolutely refused to take a turn behind the till, it was left to Posy to man the shop for almost two hours until Nina finally came back from lunch.

She turned up shortly before three with her red lipstick smudged and her hair, currently lilac, a birds' nest rather than the beehive it had been before lunch.

'Sorry, sorry,' she muttered as she came

through the door and saw the queue of people waiting to pay and Posy doing battle with a stubborn new till roll. 'I should have told you about Piers and I should have been back an hour ago. I'll totally work late.'

'There's not much point,' Posy said in a tight voice because she didn't want to argue in front of the customers. There was already a lot of collective muttering about how long it was taking her to change the till roll. 'It's not like we're going to stay open an hour later, is it?'

'I suppose not,' Nina said meekly. 'I'll go and make tea, shall I?'

By the time Nina was settled at the counter with a mug of tea and her comfy Converse back on, Sam was home from school and in a chatty mood for once and it was gone five when Posy was able to rejoin Verity in the back office.

Then she really wished she hadn't. 'Very!' Posy gasped. 'What have you done?'

Verity clutched her hair. 'I might have gone a bit overboard on the stickers.'

'You think?'

The period from the beginning of March through to the start of July, when they were meant to reopen as Happy Ever After, were obscured by a sea of stickers. There were stickers on stickers. There were colours of stickers that Posy didn't even remember buying.

'What do the purple stickers represent?' she asked. 'And the gold?'

'I don't even know any more,' Verity admitted. 'And also I've realised that I should have added the stickers *after* a task's been completed, not

156

before. A whole afternoon wasted.'

'Not wasted. I mean, it's good to see . . . Wow! Just how much stuff we have to do in a few short weeks.'

This was Verity's cue to leap in with a stirring pep talk. Except stirring pep talks weren't Verity's thing. 'Shall we take some money out of petty cash and buy a bottle of wine?' was the best she could offer.

'God, yes!'

Thirty minutes later they were halfway down a bottle of very cheap, very acidic Cabernet Sauvignon while Nina provided a reproachful running commentary as she closed up the shop. 'It's OK, I didn't want any wine,' she called out. 'I'll just sweep the floor, shall I?'

Posy and Verity ignored her as they tried to peel off the stickers one by one, though the stickers proved very resistant. It was as if the stickers were a metaphor for . . . something. It didn't bode well for a successful relaunch if they couldn't even master a wall chart between them.

'What's wrong with us? We both have university degrees,' Posy muttered.

'Maybe it would be easier if we did a spreadsheet on the computer?' Verity mused, but Posy was saved from having to reply by the shop door being opened so violently that it crashed back on its hinges.

There was only one person who entered a building like that.

'Hello, Tattoo Girl, why the glum face? No! No need to answer, I'm not really that interested. Is Morland around?'

157

Posy prayed that Nina would make up for her earlier misdemeanours by lying for her. No such luck.

'Yup, she's in the back office,' Nina informed Sebastian cheerfully.

It was time to have a chat with Nina about her attitude. On second thoughts, Posy would rather wrestle spreadsheets.

She barely had time to arrange her features into a less scowly configuration before Sebastian burst into the office. He immediately took up every centimetre of spare space as Posy and Verity both shrank back on their chairs, which they'd pulled out from behind the big old-fashioned desk in the centre of the room so they could sit in front of their wall planner and gaze at it in dismay.

'There you are! You look sulky too. What is it with you women?' Sebastian didn't look sulky, but inordinately pleased with himself. 'Is this a hormonal thing? Have your cycles . . . '

'Please don't finish that sentence,' Posy begged. She lolled back on the swivel chair. 'What are you doing here? *Again.*'

'I needed to measure things. Across the yard,' Sebastian said, a flimsy excuse if ever Posy had heard one. 'Also I wanted to try out my new digital tape measure. It works off a laser.'

Boys and their toys. 'Does it?' Posy asked, not that she cared. 'Oh my God, are you pointing that thing at my breasts?'

Sebastian hastily tucked it away in his pocket. 'Of course not. Honestly, Morland, you're quite obsessed with the idea that I'm obsessed with

158

your breasts, which I'm not.' He did shoot them a sideways glance though, perhaps to check that they were still there. Posy folded her arms. 'Anyway, now that I'm here, I thought we could discuss our crime bookshop. Shall we call in Tattoo Girl so we can have that brainstorm?'

'I have a name!' Nina yelled from the shop, while Verity leaned over in her chair so she could bang her forehead gently against the wall.

Posy pinched the bridge of her nose. 'Since when did it become *our* bookshop? It's mine,' she began, then realised she didn't have the energy to do this now. 'Not going to specialise in crime either,' she couldn't resist adding though.

'Now, we've been through this,' Sebastian said. 'It was decided. You know it makes sense.'

'It makes no sense. I was only humouring you, you must realise that.' Posy and Verity exchanged glances. After four years they could convey all sorts of nuanced messages merely by a twitch of the lips or the faint arching of an eyebrow. This look said quite clearly, 'I cannot even deal with him right now' and 'Do you want me to kill him for you and make it look like an accident?' Posy shook her head and decided to try again. 'I'm reopening as a romance bookshop. Get used to it, Sebastian.'

Sebastian took hold of Posy's chair, stopping her swinging from left to right in a desultory fashion, so he could stare deep into her eyes. Up close, Posy could see that Sebastian, damn him, had a flawless complexion. Not a single open pore, not one solitary blackhead. It was the first time she'd been close enough to Sebastian to notice that his eyes weren't simply brown; his pupils were surrounded by flecks of green and his nearness was disturbing. 'I can't let you do that, Morland,' he said. 'Even I'm not that callous.'

Aesthetically pleasing he might be, but Sebastian was also incredibly annoying. It must have been God's way of redressing the balance. 'Is there some reason why you're all up in my face?' Posy pushed Sebastian away and he was about to say something, she knew he was, but then he caught sight of the wall planner and his eyes widened as he took a step back in alarm.

'My God, what is that? An explosion in a sticker factory?'

'It's our schedule,' Verity explained. 'For the shop reopening. You know, Posy, I think we're going to have to buy another wall planner and start again. You'll have to be in charge of the stickers though.'

'I'm going to have a bash at doing a spreadsheet tonight,' Posy said, levering herself up from the chair, which took a superhuman effort. 'It's impossible to try and do it during the day when I keep getting pulled away to help in the shop.'

'Oh, you can do spreadsheets?' Verity and Sebastian both asked with the same note of incredulity, which was incredibly hurtful.

'Of course I can!' Posy insisted. 'So it's about time I was left in peace to get on with it. Haven't you both got homes to go to?'

★ ★ ★

Later that evening, with the aid of Google and a fortifying cheese toastie, Posy attempted to master the art of spreadsheets, but it proved difficult with Sam around.

He sat next to Posy on the sofa to make sure that she didn't inflict any damage on the laptop that she'd bought with her own money although Sam seemed to think it belonged only to him.

'Do you really want to do that?' he'd ask every time Posy so much as right-clicked. 'Oh dear, I wouldn't do that if I were you.' And, 'Posy! What have I told you about eating and drinking while using the laptop? You're getting crumbs all over the keyboard.'

It was a relief to see that she had email, even if it was from Sebastian — and thankfully Sam didn't object to the way Posy navigated her inbox.

From: Sebastian@zingermedia.com
To: PosyMorland@bookends.net
Subject: Meet Pippa, project management guru, yours for a short time only

Dear Morland
Evening!

Hope you're enjoying the rare experience of sitting on your newly acquired sofa without getting poked. (By the springs, not by anything else before you slap me with a sexual harassment suit.)

Anyway, very excited about our joint venture, but it occurs to me after watching you in action earlier that (and you're not to get huffy about

161

this) you're better at taking orders than giving them.

Luckily, I'm great at giving orders. I'm also excellent at delegating, so I've asked Pippa, my director of project management, to come on board. She's absolutely terrifying but she's ace at, well, managing projects. Schedules, budgets, shouting at people. That sort of thing.

Her one downside is her love of inspirational quotes and business buzzwords, but if I can tolerate that, then you can too.

We'll both come by the afternoon after next for a quick brainstorm with the staff. You can close the shop early, can't you? It's not like there's hordes of desperate book buyers beating a path to your door.

Isn't it great when we work together instead of fighting, Morland?

Laters,
Sebastian

Posy idly noted that, unlike her potential internet suitors, Sebastian's use of capital letters and grammar was exemplary. However the thought was soon lost as she surfed a tsunami of absolute rage that had her biting her tongue as she took an angry lunge at her cheese toastie.

Then she was off the sofa (and it absolutely pained Posy to remember that she'd remarked to Sam only the night before that it was a relief to be able to collapse on the sofa without worrying about puncture wounds) so she could stand in the middle of the living room and actually flail her arms in fury. She could have kept it up for some time, but Sam was looking at her in alarm so she clamped her arms by her sides and sat down heavily.

Posy knew where her strengths lay and that was in hand-selling romantic novels. She was also good at creating eye-catching window displays, and more recently sourcing book-related gift items for the shop. Only yesterday, she'd found a candle maker up in Lancashire who had a whole range of scented candles with romantic names like Love, Bliss, and Joy, who did very competitive trade prices and, more importantly, had promised to send Posy some free samples.

Her strengths didn't lie in organisation and planning. And though Verity was great at doing the accounts and sending stern letters to people who owed them money, this morning all the colour had leeched from her face as she'd talked about moving up the relaunch date and emergency overdrafts. And who could blame Verity for being skittish? She'd never relaunched anything before. None of them had.

If they tried to do it themselves on such a short timeframe with absolutely no funds to invest, it would be like every single episode of *Grand Designs* Posy had ever seen. Cue hapless couple planning to build a huge carbon-neutral house over a slurry pit on a budget of five quid, and Kevin McCloud asking if they were using a project manager. The hapless couple, who had absolutely no experience of putting together even an IKEA flatpack, would insist that they were going to project manage the build themselves.

Then Kevin McCloud would laugh hollowly and for the next hour berate them for not having a project manager.

Posy didn't want a half-finished, half-arsed bookshop and an out-of-control budget, all because she'd turned down a project manager.

Sam had requisitioned the laptop while she was having her flailing episode, but Posy managed to prise his fingers free and take ownership of it again so she could reply to Sebastian's message.

To: Sebastian@zingermedia.com
From: PosyMorland@bookends.net

How much is this project management consultant going to cost? Is she on a day rate? Could we maybe have her for half a day, if she's not too expensive? Is she really that scary?

(This is me ignoring all your insults and trying to establish a more professional tone, by the way.)
Posy

For a digital entrepreneur and serial womaniser, Sebastian really wasn't very busy that evening because he emailed her back almost immediately.

From: Sebastian@zingermedia.com
To: PosyMorland@bookends.net

God, Morland, don't be so dense! I'm giving Pippa to you for as long as you need her, though she says that she'll mostly work off-site because she has dust allergies.

Yes, she really is that scary. Once she got so cross with me for going over the allotted time she'd set for a talking point in a meeting that she pulled my pocket square out of my suit and cut it. In front of me. With scissors.

Come to think of it, I'm sure you and Pippa will get along just fine.

Now stop bothering me with trivial enquiries. I'm a very important man.

Sebastian

Pippa sounded quite terrifying, but she also sounded exactly what Posy needed when she needed her most. Pippa could turn their problems into solutions.

First, there was the issue of Sebastian believing in his deluded way that they were opening a crime bookshop.

There was also the hurdle of the brainstorming session that Sebastian seemed to think they needed but that didn't have to be a big deal. They could just do what they'd done at the last brainstorm, only replace the word 'romance' with 'crime'. If that was what it took to acquire a project manager, then Posy was happy to go along with the charade.

Hopefully Pippa would be more involved with logistics and the bigger picture than asking awkward questions about how many crime novels Jilly Cooper had written.

And really, it was Sebastian's own fault for not listening no matter how many times Posy told

165

him that Bookends was to become the place to go for romantic novels.

He only had himself to blame.

9

To: all@bookends.net
From: PosyMorland@bookends.net
Subject: Brainstorm redux

Hi all

Can I just start off by saying excellent bookselling this week, everyone!

So, anyway we have to have another brainstorm tomorrow evening with the dreaded Sebastian. Though actually, I suppose he's not quite so dreaded as he's letting us borrow his project manager to help with the relaunch.

Her name's Pippa. Can you make her very welcome when she arrives? Can we also attempt to behave like professional booksellers so please don't turn up with French Fancies like you did last time? Or any other kind of baked goods.

One other small thing. As you know, Sebastian seems to think that we're turning Bookends into a crime bookshop. (Tom — Verity and Nina will fill you in on this.) Of course, we're not. We're so not. But can you pretend that we are, please? Just hit the high points of our last brainstorm, but don't mention anything to do with romance. Let's stick to lots of spontaneous and enthusiastic talk about book of the month, a book group, author visits, tote bags, etc.

Attendance at the brainstorm is mandatory, but afterwards we can go to the Midnight Bell to do the pub quiz and drink booze. So much booze. I have a feeling that we'll need it.

Go team!

Your loving pal and completely rational boss,

Posy xxx

At five the next day Posy meant to close the shop, but at quarter to five an entire coachload of ladies descended on them. They were in town from Shepton Mallet to see *Les Misérables* and had arrived in London early solely for the purpose of visiting Bookends.

'Read about your shop on a blog forum. Said you had one of the best romance sections in the South East, and I don't like buying things on the internet. Next thing you know someone in Kazakhstan has your credit card details and is using them to buy rocket launchers,' one of the ladies told Posy and she was sure she felt her heart swell with pride or that might have been because they kept sending her up the ladder to get books down from the top shelves.

As Posy was ringing up their purchases and Nina was trying to corral them into an orderly queue, Sebastian swept into the shop, followed by a woman in a chic grey dress, a fitted bright orange blazer and a turquoise necklace, so with one glance you could tell that she was put together and smart but also her own woman. It could only be Pippa, who also had the most bouncy hair and the most perfect white smile of anyone Posy had ever seen, apart from the Duchess of Cambridge. She looked as if she should be wearing a white lab coat and extolling the virtues of the latest technological advances in shampoo and tooth-paste, when she wasn't project managing and kicking Sebastian's arse.

'If you write your details in our book, I'll add you to our mailing list,' Posy said automatically to the woman she was serving, who'd just bought seven romances set in Paris because her husband refused to take her there for their anniversary. She lowered her voice to a furtive whisper as she saw Sebastian point her out to Pippa, who beamed at Posy and waved. 'We're relaunching in a couple of months as a specialist romance bookshop, so we'll have even more stock then.'

She watched as Sebastian ushered Pippa through to the first room on the left, his hand on her shoulder. 'Sorry, Pips, the whole place is a dust-trap. Hope it's not going to make your allergies flare up.'

It was the single nicest thing she'd heard Sebastian say to anyone since Lavinia had died, Posy thought as she greeted the next woman in line, who had six erotic novels hidden under a copy of *Great Expectations*.

'Books are a breeding ground for germs,' Posy heard Pippa say in a broad Yorkshire accent, which made her seem slightly less intimidating. Posy's favourite lecturer at Queen Mary's had been from Huddersfield so there was something about a Yorkshire accent that Posy always found instantly reassuring. 'Like dishes of bar nuts that have about fifty different traces of urine on them.'

Then again, maybe not.

169

'I don't think it's the books so much as the fact that Posy — the one behind the till with the shrewish expression and two pencils in her hair — is a complete slattern. You should see the flat upstairs. It's like an episode of *Extreme Hoarders*.'

Oh, she was going to kill him. Horribly. But first Posy had to be formally introduced to Pippa, who beamed again, murmured words of greeting then shook hands with the rest of the staff, with a firm and uncompromising grip. Pippa then made a short but heartfelt speech.

'I can't tell you how excited I am to be moving forward on this project with you all. We're going to be a great team. You need a team to make a dream come true.'

Posy didn't dare look at Nina or Tom, and Verity's head had disappeared into her neck so she looked like a very sad, very confused tortoise. She still hadn't raised her head half an hour later as the coach party departed *Les Mis*-wards, and the door was locked behind them, the staff gathered on the sofas. Sebastian lounged against the rolling ladder in another ridiculous suit with moss green accoutrements, Pippa tapped things into a handheld device, while Posy did battle with her flip chart and she talked about murder most foul.

'So yeah, that's what I was thinking we could call the 'crime' bookshop,' she said. Try as she might, Posy couldn't help but wrap imaginary quote marks around the word. 'Murder Most Foul. Any other suggestions?'

'I still like The Bloody Dagger,' Sebastian

piped up, but Posy wasn't even going to acknowledge his presence. Not after he'd called her a slattern. Besides, it had taken her *years* to perfect the art of a messy bun anchored into place with two pencils.

'Anybody else?' Posy looked pleadingly at Tom, who refused to meet her eye. She had a sneaking suspicion that he'd prefer to work in a bookshop that specialised in crime. It was far more manly than working in a bookshop that specialised in happy ever afters. 'Nina?'

Nina wouldn't let her down, but she just pulled a face like she was in a thousand agonies and looked at Verity sitting across from her for guidance. Verity shrugged.

'Um, well, er, Murder She Wrote?' Nina suggested. 'Though I suppose not every crime novel has a female author.'

Tom finally managed to raise his head and look Posy in the eye. 'What about Reader, I Murdered Him?' he drawled in a very challenging, unTom-like way.

Verity snorted and Nina sniggered; even Sam, who was there under duress and after much sighing and flouncing because he said it was wrong for Posy to lie when she was always telling him off for saying he'd done his homework when he hadn't, smirked from behind his fringe.

'Not funny, Tom,' Posy said sternly as Sebastian shot Tom a look of mild distaste.

'Is that some kind of bookseller in-joke?' he asked, with a disdainful arch of his eyebrow. 'I don't get it.'

'You wouldn't,' Pippa piped up. She'd been

171

silent up until now. 'It's a play on a line from *Jane Eyre*. It's a novel, Sebastian, written by a woman in the eighteen hundreds. There's no way in hell you've read it so let's move on with our lives, shall we?'

Posy thought that she might just have fallen in love with Pippa.

Pippa turned to Posy. 'Carry on,' she said. 'I'm really enthused about this.'

'Oh, shall we go with The Bloody Dagger for now.' Posy wasn't enthused. In fact, she was already bored with the entire farce. 'I'm sure we can come up with something better in the next few days and then I can get on with briefing Nina's tattoo artist to design the logo and we can order all the signage and stuff. Right?'

There was a murmur of agreement, though Pippa paused from whipping her fingers back and forth across her handheld device. 'You're having your logo, which you're going to use for all your branding, designed by a tattoo artist?' she asked, in the same way that Lady Bracknell might have enquired about a handbag. 'Are you sure that's a good idea?'

Nina was already shrugging out of her cardigan. 'He's an amazing tattoo artist,' she said huffily as she showed first her *Wuthering Heights* arm, then her *Alice in Wonderland* sleeve to Pippa. 'Also, he's not charging us anything, so there's that. Can we please get a move on because that important thing that we're going to starts in an hour? So, anyway, I think it would be a fantastic idea if we had a book group that met in the shop once a month.'

Posy nodded. 'That is a *great* idea.' She meant to sound perky but it was more manic than anything. 'Now here's a thing, this is just off the top of my head, but maybe the book group pick could be the featured book on the shop website.'

'Are you saying that we're going to relaunch the website at the same time as we relaunch the shop?' At last Nina was getting into the spirit of things. 'About time. Of course, we couldn't have the entire catalogue online, but maybe our top fifty bestsellers . . . ?'

'I'm loving this,' Pippa interjected. 'Let's talk more about the website now.'

'Sam, why don't you tell us about your exciting plans for the website.' To her own ears, Posy now sounded as if she were mere seconds away from a psychotic break.

'What? You mean I have to go through it all *again?* Don't worry about it, Posy. It's all in hand.' Sam sighed so hard that his fringe fluttered in the slipstream. 'Sophie's going to do the shop Twitter and Instagram accounts, maybe a Tumblr as well, and I don't know why she's not here. She's part of the staff too,' he added in an aggrieved voice.

'She's got a big history project due in tomorrow,' Posy explained and Sam instantly broke eye contact with her. 'Come to think of it, doesn't that mean that *you* have a big history project due in tomorrow?'

'That's in hand too,' Sam assured her, but he still wouldn't meet Posy's eyes.

Posy assumed her sternest expression, which made Nina snigger again. 'Are you sure about that?'

Sam glared at her, Posy glared back at him, each one daring the other to blink first, but it ended in a tie because they both blinked when Pippa clapped her hands.

'Let's move past this,' she advised them. 'No negative energy, guys, only positive thoughts about great suggestions we can action and expedite, OK? Tom, what have you got for us?'

Posy turned away from Sam with a look that said very clearly, I'm not done with you, to focus her attention on Tom, who was staring at the ceiling, eyes flickering, lips moving soundlessly as if he were trying to remember the script. 'Oh yeah,' he said at last. 'We could have a writer's group too, maybe author visits. What was the other thing, again?' Tom was making absolutely no attempt to appear spontaneous and enthusiastic. 'Tote bags.'

'Love it,' Pippa said. 'And what about, Verity? You've been very quiet.'

Verity's shoulders were touching her ears by this point. Posy's heart ached for her. This brainstorm was all Verity's worst fears realised. She swallowed convulsively, squeaked, 'Bookmarks,' then sank back down into the corner of the sofa and tried to make herself look as small as possible.

It was time to wrap this up before Posy lost the will to carry on, not just with the brainstorm, but with life itself. Also, Sebastian had been silent up to this point, but judging by the baleful looks he kept directing towards the sofas and the way he kept muttering under his breath, he wasn't going to stay silent for much longer. It

174

was a miracle he'd lasted this long — maybe Pippa had threatened to take the scissors to his suits. 'I think we're done here,' Posy said quickly. 'Pippa, I'll email you the relaunch schedule, and if it's not too much trouble maybe you could have a look at it and make sure we haven't forgotten anything? I'm sure we've taken up enough of your time this evening.'

'Time is life's most valuable resource,' Pippa said. 'But I value you, Posy, and what you're doing here, so I'm happy to spend my time helping you.'

Posy wasn't sure how to respond to that, or even what it meant so she just muttered her thanks while there was a flurry of activity from the sofas. After putting in an uncanny imperson-ation of sloths for the last hour, Tom, Nina and Verity were on their feet, coats on and heading for the door at a speed that was verging on superhuman.

'We'll see you at the thing,' Nina called over her shoulder as she fought with Tom to be first out of the shop, and then the three of them were running, actually running, across the courtyard as if they expected Posy to call them back to talk in depth about tote bags.

'Can I go to the 'thing'?' Sam asked. 'Because I genuinely have finished my history project, apart from some tiny bits I can do tomorrow, and I know loads of stuff about sport.'

It was setting a terrible example to let Sam go to a pub, especially on a school night and especially when Posy knew full well that the tiny bits of the history project that still had to be done were more likely to be huge bits. Then again, many was the time they'd taken a pasting in the Midnight Bell quiz because they hadn't managed to get a single answer right in the sports section and Posy couldn't face an argument with Sam. Not tonight.

'Yes, fine, go,' Posy said wearily, but Sam was already making his way to the door with his usual crab-like shuffle because he still needed new school shoes and Posy had yet to break it to him that they were going clothes shopping on Saturday.

And then there were three. Pippa was frowning over her screen and Sebastian's face was arranging itself from a sneer into a scowl and Posy closed her eyes and counted to five but she'd only got as far as two when . . .

'Sack them! Sack them all! Where on earth did you find them? Some community outreach programme for utterly useless, apathetic lay-abouts? Do you pay them actual money?' Sebastian clutched at thin air with his hands, looked up to the heavens then mopped his brow with his moss green pocket square. 'I never thought I'd say this but I think it's time to bring back National Service.'

'Oh, poor Sebastian,' Pippa said without a trace of sympathy. 'Have you been holding all that in for the last hour?'

'I've barely got started.' Sebastian was at Posy's side in three long strides then seized hold of her arms. 'You have to get rid of them! They have no work ethic!'

Posy unseized her arms. 'They have a great

work ethic!' she protested, because they all did in their own special and unique ways, none of which had been in evidence this evening. 'They just don't perform well in a brainstorm scenario to discuss a crime bookshop when none of them even like crime. We were meant to be relaunching as a romance bookshop,' she added for the benefit of Pippa, who was looking, with some consternation, at a discarded sweet wrapper lying on the floor. 'Sorry. Didn't have time to get out the broom before you arrived.'

'Ha! Like you'd even know what to do with a broom,' Sebastian scoffed.

'I can think of at least two things I could do with one,' Posy snapped back. 'So, normally, when they haven't been browbeaten into a scheme that they want no part of, they're very hard workers.'

'Browbeaten?' Pippa asked. 'So, they're not on board with Sebastian's plans to turn this into murder central?'

'Not really . . . '

'*Our* plans, Posy,' Sebastian reminded her in injured tones. 'You agreed that it was a fantastic idea. That there was a huge market for crime fiction and that it was sexy and you *loved* it when I talked about tote bags.'

'I did! I love the tote bags,' Posy said and right now she wished that there was a tote bag to hand so she could stick her head in it and not have to see Sebastian looking all earnest and sincere. The moss green shirt did wonderful things to his eyes.

'And you love the idea of a crime fiction

bookshop,' Sebastian persisted. 'Don't you?'

Posy started to form the word 'no', to confess everything. She could feel her tongue pressing against her front teeth in preparation for sounding out the n, but Sebastian didn't do no, like he didn't do off-the-rack or instant coffee. Besides, although she hadn't done any project managing yet, Pippa seemed like a woman who could do anything once she set her mind to it and Posy needed a woman like that in her life. And it had been a long day and she was tired and there was a huge glass of red wine at the Midnight Bell with her name on it. She didn't have time to say no.

'Fine, whatever,' she said, because that had worked out so well the last time she said it.

'I need full commitment from you, Posy. Ayn Rand once said, 'The question isn't who's going to let me, but who's going to stop me.'' Pippa had put her orange blazer back on and was standing by the door with her arms folded so she quite obviously wanted to leave too. Sebastian had been right about Pippa's love of inspirational quotes but it was best to get her on side, especially as she had magic Sebastian-wrangling abilities, which Posy hoped that Pippa might one day share.

'I'm absolutely on board with the plans for the relaunch,' Posy said firmly, which wasn't a lie when she hadn't specified which relaunch she was talking about. 'Shall we catch up early next week when you've had a proper look at our schedule? Verity says we have to be up and running by end of June, but I don't see how.'

'We'll talk about it next week,' Pippa promised and she sounded so calm and capable and utterly unruffled by the thought of an end of June relaunch that Posy hoped that Pippa could show her how to be unflappable too. 'Now, don't you have a 'thing' that you're meant to be at?'

'Yes! The thing!'

'What is this thing? Is it a bookshop thing?' Sebastian asked. 'Should I come too?'

'God no!' Posy exclaimed in horror as she started turning off lights. She'd deal with the sweet wrapper later. 'It's a bookseller thing. Very industry-focused. You'd be bored rigid.' She flapped her hands in Sebastian's direction. 'Come on, haven't you got somewhere that you'd rather be?'

'And deprive myself of the pleasure of your charming company, Morland?' Sebastian looked down his nose at her but stayed where he was.

'Right, well, I'm off,' Pippa said, opening the door. 'Sebastian! Your arse, move it!'

It was a miracle on the same level as the loaves and fishes, but Sebastian moved his arse. 'How come Sam's allowed to go to the boring bookseller thing and I'm not? And what does Sam knowing a lot about sport have to do with it?'

'I would explain but it's complicated. Boring and complicated,' Posy said as Sebastian finally stepped through the door so she could leave the shop too and lock the door. 'All this lingering about, Sebastian. Anyone would think that you liked being in my company.'

'I don't know why anyone would think that,'

179

Sebastian said haughtily, and Posy would have loved to stay and trade a few more insults but it was getting on for seven and she was in danger of missing the start of the quiz.

'I'm going to be late. So late. Must dash. Lovely to meet you, Pippa,' she said, and then because she could bear it no longer, Posy scurried away, picking up speed until she was running full pelt across the courtyard, around the corner and hurling herself through the door of the Midnight Bell before Sebastian had a chance to follow.

Ravished by the Rake

As Posy hurried up the imposing steps of Thornfield House, Lord Thorndyke's London residence, she felt dread settle over her like a fine mist of perfume.

She was shown into the library by his housekeeper, a capable, self-possessed woman who made her plain black dress look like the latest Paris fashions, called Pippa (note to self: Must find out Pippa's surname). The bodice of Posy's own modest grey walking dress felt uncomfortably tight, as if she were about to have a fit of the vapours.

But Posy Morland, orphan, guardian of her fifteen-year-old brother Samuel, and heiress to a series of bad debts, had never had a fit of the vapours in her life and she didn't intend to embark on such an endeavour at this juncture.

Instead, she took a couple of deep breaths, though the faint trace of cheroots lingered in the room, then gracefully comported herself to the nearest set of shelves.

Posy could never feel alone or scared in a room full of books. Her slender fingers caressed the worn leather spines. Who would have imagined that a rakehell, a rapscallion, a rogue such as Thorndyke would have such an extensive library?

No sooner had she pondered the question than the door was flung open and there he stood, dressed all in black, so he resembled an angel cast out of heaven. 'Miss Morland,' he said in dark, sonorous tones. 'An unexpected pleasure.'

'Lord Thorndyke,' Posy said evenly, though her heart trembled and her bosom fairly heaved. 'Forgive the intrusion, but I come to you with a proposition.'

'Indeed.' He seemed to suck the very air from the room with each long stride, until he was standing in front of Posy, cornered as she was by the shelves of books, which no longer seemed like friends but witnesses to her abject humiliation. Thorndyke looked down at her from his lofty height and Posy felt like a fox caught in a trap. 'A proposition, you say? How intriguing.'

'Not so intriguing, sir.' She scarce had room to open her reticule and pull out her treasure. 'I thought, that is, I hoped that you may be amenable to holding these items as a guarantee against the fifty guineas that you want so badly, though fifty guineas is naught but a drop in the ocean to you,' she finished on an angry breath.

'Now, now, my dear Miss Morland. If you want me amenable then you must conduct yourself in a more conciliatory manner,' Thorndyke drawled as he arched one devilish brow. He flicked an elegant, careless finger at the small muslin-wrapped package she clutched. 'I suggest you show your hand.'

With a sigh of weary capitulation, Posy

unwrapped the muslin to reveal a thin gold wedding band, a locket and a brooch set with garnets. 'They belonged to my late mother,' she explained. 'They're all I have of any value and I implore you, no, I beseech you, to take them as a sign of good faith that I will honour my father's debt. And if I haven't within twelve months, then they're yours to do with as you see fit.' And may Satan himself take you!

'What use do I have for these trifles, these mere baubles, when you have far greater riches to bargain with?' he enquired, and before Posy could ask him to explain himself for she knew not of any riches in her possession, he lowered his head so she could feel the kiss of his breath on her cheek. 'I propose to you, my sweet Miss Morland, that you warm my bed, lie in my arms, whenever I have use for you for those same twelve months and you may consider your debt discharged.'

Then as Posy stared up at his cruelly amused features, he suddenly enfolded her in his arms and proceeded to plunder the sweet lips that she'd opened only to protest his dastardly demands.

10

Posy barely slept at all for the rest of the week. How could she sleep when she was racked with self-loathing at the tawdry story that was pouring out of her every time she had a spare fifteen minutes in front of the computer?

And if Posy ever managed a fitful doze, she had to wrest herself out of dreams that involved Sebastian and herself locked in a passionate embrace while kitted out in full Regency regalia. She would come to with a panicked gasp, her whole body burning up as if she were going through an early menopause, and would spend the rest of the night trying in vain to get comfortable and to quiet that insistent voice in her head that wondered if Sebastian would be so masterful at kissing in real life.

On Saturday morning, sleep deprived and still deeply ashamed of herself, Posy was in no mood for an outing to Oxford Street. Quite frankly, she'd rather undergo a couple of root canals without any anaesthetic. Still, she was Sam's legal guardian and if she didn't buy him new school shoes soon, ones that he could actually walk in, social services might have to get involved.

Through trial and error and long, bitter experience, Posy had learned that when she needed to take Sam shopping for anything other than food and computer games, it was best not to give him advance notice.

Unless she sprang a stealth shopping trip on him at a moment's notice, Sam would start cultivating the symptoms of swine flu days beforehand, even volunteer for weekend school activities and generally wheedle and whine and do everything in his power to get out of a quick jaunt down Oxford Street.

So, once all the staff were present and correct, Posy grabbed Sam the moment he ambled downstairs to cast discreetly longing looks at Little Sophie and pollute the atmosphere with his most noxious body spray to date.

'Here's your coat,' she said, shoving Sam's anorak at him. 'We're going shopping.'

'To Sainsbury's?' Sam's eyes narrowed suspiciously. 'To buy food?'

'On the way back — after we've got new school shoes and trousers. How are you doing for underwear, by the way?'

Sam moaned like he'd just trapped his finger in the door. Too late, Posy looked around to see Sophie restocking the New Releases. 'It's all right,' Sophie said soothingly. 'I totally didn't hear anything about Sam's underwear.'

'You are so embarrassing,' Sam hissed. 'I'm not going anywhere with you. Not after what happened last time.'

'That was *your* fault.' The last time they'd gone shopping, at the height of the January sales, they'd almost come to blows about what constituted a suitable pair of school trousers. Sam had then refused to come into Gap with her and Posy had been forced to take her selection to the shop window and hold each garment up for

Sam's inspection. Unfortunately she'd set off the alarms and had been accused of shoplifting. Though, once she'd explained the situation, the Head of Security had been very sympathetic — he had a teenage son of his own — and marched Sam to the changing rooms then stood guard until a pair of trousers had been purchased. The whole debacle had taken *years* off Posy's life. 'Your trousers are too short, you can't walk in your shoes, ergo we're going shopping. End of discussion.'

They were already arguing and they weren't even within spitting distance of Oxford Street. It didn't bode well.

'I can walk in my shoes.' Sam took a couple of mincing steps. 'See!'

'That is not walking. That is barely shuffling.' Posy decided it was time to try a different approach. 'Look, I'm letting you have a sleepover with Pants tonight, so think of this as penance for being allowed to stay up all night playing Grand Theft Auto.'

Even through his fringe, Posy could see Sam roll his eyes. He badly needed a haircut too but clothes shopping *and* a trip to the barbers all in one day would really be pushing her luck. 'You're only letting me stay over at Pants' so you can go out and get drunk,' Sam said haughtily. 'And it's not a sleepover. We're not ten. We're hanging out then crashing.'

'Potato, potarto,' Posy sing-songed in a shrill voice as she heard the bell above the door jangle, though officially they weren't open for another ten minutes.

'Ah, Sam! How do you fancy escaping the petticoat dictatorship?' said a voice, and immediately Posy felt herself blush with the heat of a thousand fiery suns.

'Sebastian!' Sam cried gleefully and wriggled away from Posy, who had no choice but to turn around. She'd much rather have stayed where she was, in the corner with her back to the room like she was on a time-out, but she was a grown-up and sometimes grown-ups had to do things they didn't want to. Quite a lot of the time in fact.

Sebastian was dressed all in black, as he had been in the latest instalment of her novel. (Though it was hardly a novel. God knows what it was. The ravings of a woman who needed to get out more.) As a concession to the weekend, he was wearing black Converse and staring at Posy quizzically. 'Seen something you like, Morland?'

Was she gawping at him? She was! Gawping with her cheeks rosy red, her mouth hanging open. 'No. Not in the least.' She tried to remember his opening gambit. 'This is not a petticoat dictatorship. It's a democracy.'

'It's not,' Sam said. 'It's a totalitarian state is what it is.'

'Well, you'll just have to suck it up until you're eighteen, won't you?'

'Oh dear, have I wandered into the middle of a domestic? Just as well I've come to take you away from all this, Sam,' Sebastian said, producing two tickets from his breast pocket. 'Got passes for a Q & A with a panel of computer game industry experts at the ICA this morning. Fancy it?'

Sam was torn, Posy could tell. Not because he was secretly dying to spend the morning hoofing up and down Oxford Street. Instead, he cast one yearning look at an oblivious Sophie who was chatting to Nina behind the counter, but even Sophie couldn't compete with hanging out with his new god, Sebastian, at a computer games symposium.

He turned his cow eyes on Posy. 'Please.' He managed to stretch the word out over several syllables. 'Please, Posy, it will be educational and I promise I'll go shopping with you tomorrow, if you're not too hungover. I'll come into every shop you want and I won't give you any backchat.'

'Please, Posy, please let Sam come out and play,' Sebastian simpered. 'I promise I'll have him back before dark.'

Posy knew when she was beaten. 'Fine. Go. Do you need some money?'

'Stop fussing, Posy,' Sebastian said, his arm already around Sam's shoulders as he pulled him willingly towards the door. 'I'll take good care of Sam, you take good care of our bookshop.'

* * *

Posy spent the next few hours fretting that Sebastian had left Sam in the back of a taxi or abandoned him as soon as an attractive blonde crossed his path. Even so she managed to tick off at least ten items on her relaunch to-do list although there were still another hundred items to go, but Sebastian's crack about *their*

188

bookshop when it was *her* bookshop had spurred her into action.

By the time she'd finished writing copy for the new website, it was four o'clock and yet there was no sign of her baby brother who was gallivanting who knew where with the rudest and also the most irresponsible man in London.

'Where are you?' she texted Sam as she rushed out to buy a pair of tights that didn't have holes in them, because she'd suddenly remembered she was going out tonight and she was currently unshowered and with three-day-old hair.

'Back soon,' Sam texted in reply, along with a whole string of emoji, which might as well have been Urdu for all the sense they made to Posy.

It was almost six o'clock and Posy was on the verge of phoning the police to report Sam missing when he and Sebastian came barrelling through the back door.

Posy, freshly showered, in her black party frock and with foam rollers in her hair, stood at the top of the stairs with her hands on her hips. 'What time do you call this?' she demanded.

'Said I'd have him back before dark. Technically, sunset is at eighteen oh three so we're a bit early,' Sebastian informed her as he and Sam climbed the stairs.

Posy had plenty to say about that but then she caught a glimpse of Sam behind Sebastian and she decided it could wait, because she hadn't seen Sam smile like that in a long, long time. He was grinning from ear to ear, bouncing from step to step.

'Did you have a good time?' she asked him.

'Posy! It was the best day ever,' he said, then checked himself. 'Yeah, it was cool. You know, whatever.'

Sebastian brushed past her and the barely-there graze of his sleeve against her arm made Posy's face heat up again, though he was already in the living room, throwing his jacket over the back of the chair and sitting down. 'Put the kettle on, Morland. Let's see if your tea is as undrinkable as your coffee.'

'Make yourself at home, why don't you?' Posy muttered under her breath, and Sam grinned again. It was then that Posy noticed his face was no longer obscured by a curtain of hair.

She peered at Sam more intently. Her suspicions were correct: his chin was no longer covered in a light to medium dusting of fluff either. Sam suffered her scrutiny without saying anything, but he bit his lip as Posy's gaze travelled downwards to take in new jeans and a fancy pair of new trainers and several bright yellow Selfridges bags on the floor.

Now Posy's face was red for entirely different reasons. 'What have you been doing?' she asked in a tight voice. 'You moaned and moaned about going clothes shopping and now you and Sebastian have bought up most of Selfridges. Selfridges! How much money did he spend on you?'

'Posy, I know. Look, not here,' Sam whispered. 'In the kitchen.'

Once they were in the kitchen, door shut, bags on the table, Sam showed her the contents. A smart black suit, shirts and cardigans, a pair of heavy-soled brogues, all suitable for school but with price tags that made Posy want to cry. Then there were the grooming products: cleansers and moisturisers, a shaving kit and a bottle of Tom Ford aftershave. 'Sebastian said I should use it sparingly. That girls don't like it when you cover yourself in the stuff and he said that I should really work the geek thing too . . .'

'No.' Posy shook her head. 'It's going back. All of it. I hope you've got the receipts. How could you let him spend so much money on you?'

'I told him not to. I did! Again and again, but it's impossible to say no to him.' Posy could believe that only too well. 'He said that not having parents and stuff meant that I'd missed out on loads of birthday and Christmas presents, so he was just redressing the balance. He took me to a fancy barber's shop too and they showed me how to shave. I mean, you're great, Posy, but I was too embarrassed to ask you about *stuff*. Anyway, you always cut your legs when you shave them and shaving a face is much more complicated than doing your legs. Why have you gone red again? Oh God, you're not crying, are you?'

'Of course I'm not,' Posy said, but she was sniffling and a little misty-eyed.

When she'd had her first period at the age of fourteen, caught unawares as she was changing after a PE lesson, she'd hurried home to tell her mother. They'd talked about this day, a supply of sanitary products had already been purchased, but it was still a shock. Still felt terrifying, as if Posy had suddenly left the cosy confines of her

191

childhood but wasn't ready for the adult world.

Posy had cried in her mother's arms like the little girl that she still hadn't quite cast off and the following Saturday her mother had left Sam, then a baby who hadn't quite mastered the art of standing up unaided, with Lavinia and Perry, and they'd had a day out, just the two of them. Went to TopShop to buy make-up and M&S for pretty underwear, then to Patisserie Valerie for afternoon tea. Later, when they'd got back to Bookends, her father had organised a party with Lavinia and Perry and the girls from the shop, and Posy had had her first glass of champagne.

Her mother had turned something new and frightening into something to be celebrated. 'I can't wait to meet the woman you're going to become,' she'd told Posy, as they'd walked back to the shop, stomachs stuffed full of cakes. 'I know she'll be as smart and as funny and as kind as you are now. I also know that you can be anything and everything that you want to be. But I'll always be there for you, Posy. Even the most amazing women still feel scared and unsure sometimes. Still need kisses and cuddles from their mums.'

If their parents had lived, Sam and her father would have spent a similar day together. There probably wouldn't have been quite so much discussion about the merits of tampons over sanitary towels, but they'd have talked about the man he was going to become, the changes he was going through, how to close shave. Though Posy would do anything for Sam, there were some things she couldn't do and for some reason

192

Sebastian, of all people, had stepped up.

So Posy swallowed down her indignation and smiled. 'You had a good day then?'

'Yeah and I haven't even told you about the computer games thing we went to.' Sam stuffed all the designer clothes back into their bags without any consideration for their designer status. 'Though, you probably wouldn't understand half of it, but Pants will. Can I still go and hang out with Pants?'

''Course you can,' Posy said, because she was still planning to go out and drink cold Swedish vodka with hot Swedish men and because, right at this moment, Sam had a free pass — not that she was going to tell him that. 'I got you some munchies from Sainsbury's to take with you.'

It wasn't a ton of designer gear, only a selection of crisps, chocolate and Haribo, but Sam received it rapturously, even kissed her on his way out. Then Posy finally put the kettle on.

She took extra care with Sebastian's tea, making sure she dunked the bag until it was exactly the right colour, and added fresh milk rather than the milk that had been sitting in the fridge for a week. Not that her efforts were appreciated.

'My God, I thought you'd gone all the way to India for the tea,' he complained when Posy walked into the lounge with two mugs, one of which she handed to him. 'This isn't Earl Grey.'

'It's Tetley's,' Posy said evenly, and handed him five twenty-pound notes. 'I put this aside for Sam's new school clothes. I know it doesn't even begin to cover what you spent on him but — '

'Oh, Morland, don't be so boring,' Sebastian said, thrusting the notes back at her. She resolutely laid the notes on the table in front of him, but Sebastian ignored her as he settled back in the armchair and crossed his long legs, supremely at ease in her living room, in her life, with her little brother. 'Sam merely happened to mention that there was no way you'd be able to take him shopping tomorrow if you were hungover. Said you'd spend most of the day lying on the sofa watching the most appalling films and intermittently begging him to make you cups of tea and cheese on toast. So, I had to do something. He could hardly walk in those shoes.'

Sam had absolutely exaggerated her hangovers. They weren't *that* bad. But it was beside the point. Posy took a sip of tea. 'Well, anyway, thank you for taking him out today and for all the things you bought him, though you should have asked my permission first.'

'You were doing *so* well with the thank you speech and then you had to ruin it, didn't you?' Sebastian smirked over the rim of his mug and it made the other thing that Posy had to say much easier because he was acting like an utter dick again.

'I love Sam. You could take away the shop, you could burn all my books, trash every single thing I own and I'd get over it, but if you do anything to hurt him, Sebastian, I will hunt you down, I will visit every last torture I can think of on you, but I won't kill you. Not when I can make sure that every breath you take for the rest of your sorry life will cause you untold agony. Got that?'

That wiped the smirk off Sebastian's face. 'I'm not sure how we went from you thanking me to threatening to subject my poor, defenceless body to all manner of torture.'

'It's just a friendly warning. You can't decide that Sam's an amusing diversion then drop him when you get bored. He's not one of your women!' she added rashly and Sebastian didn't like that, because he stopped lounging, his posture suddenly becoming stiff and still, and there was a glint in his eye that hadn't been there before.

'And what do you know of my women?' he asked idly.

'Half of bloody London knows about your women,' Posy reminded him. 'You're in the *Evening Standard* all the time. There was that blonde whose husband named you in their divorce proceedings.'

'Oh, him! He was banging his secretary the whole time.'

'And that other blonde, the model, who sold her story to the papers about your sexual predilections.' Posy had to pause because Sebastian was smirking again and she was remembering what the blonde catwalk model had said about Sebastian's bedside manner. Or lack of it. *We made love five times in one night but I was forbidden to say a word.*

There wasn't enough tinted moisturiser in the world to spare Posy her blushes as she remembered the line, and if this was a scene from that sordid piece of Regency ridiculousness she was writing, this would be the part where Sebastian dragged her into his arms and said throatily, 'Not another word, Miss Morland.'

It should have been medically impossible for anyone's face to be as red as Posy's was, but Sebastian didn't appear to notice, because he leaned forwards, teacup on his knee, and said earnestly, 'Honestly, Morland, the prattle that came out of that woman's mouth. I feared for my sanity.' He shook his head as if he were ridding himself of the memory. 'Anyway, we were talking about Sam — and I like Sam. I like him a lot. I had no idea that there was more to fifteen-year-old boys than acne and chronic masturbation.'

Posy had no choice but to hide her face with her hands. If only there was another candidate to be a positive male role model for Sam. Or a male role model at least. Maybe she should try with Tom again, though the last time she'd asked him to have a friendly chat with Sam, they'd gone off to Starbucks and reappeared half an hour later, both of them ashen-faced. 'Never again,' Tom had said darkly.

'He wouldn't stop talking about genital warts and not getting girls pregnant, and you are *never* to leave me alone with him again,' Sam had complained, so maybe Tom wasn't the right man for the job. Posy decided to have a quiet word with lovely Stefan from the deli while they were out tonight. He was a much more suitable candidate. 'You're not to lead Sam astray,' she told Sebastian sternly. 'He's at a very impressionable age.'

'Oh. I had pencilled in a trip to an opium den for our next outing, but maybe that can wait until he's sixteen.' He raised his eyebrows at Posy and studied her curiously. 'Those things in your hair. What are they?'

She'd been laying down the law and all the time she'd had neon pink foam rollers in her hair. 'They're to give me tousled waves,' she said distractedly. 'I'm going out and there's going to be lots of vodka, thank God, because you drive me to drink.'

'I've driven women to much worse things than drink,' Sebastian said as he crossed his legs and jiggled one foot. 'One time I drove a woman to a very seedy club in Amsterdam. The things we saw.' He looked Posy up and down. 'Is that what you're wearing?'

She was wearing a loose-fitting, black lace shift dress, which hid a multitude of wobbly sins but showed off the least wobbly bit of her thighs. Posy was immediately on the defensive. 'Why? What's wrong with it?'

'Nothing's wrong with it.' Sebastian pulled a face. 'It's a bit short, isn't it?'

'Are you saying my legs are fat?' Posy looked down at the offending limbs. They hadn't looked fat before. Maybe a bit untoned, but she'd thought that her black opaque tights had taken care of that problem.

'I said your dress was a bit short. I didn't mention your legs,' Sebastian pointed out, though he was looking at them now as if he'd never seen a pair of legs before. Compared to the women he dated, all of them willowy and thin, her legs must look like second cousins to tree trunks. 'I mean, you don't want to give people — men — the wrong idea.'

'Wrong idea?'

'That you're up for it when you're not. Or you shouldn't be. What example is it going to set Sam if you're throwing yourself at men after too much vodka?' Sebastian sighed. 'At least you've managed to keep your other bits under wraps, I suppose.'

'Up for it? Throwing myself at men? My other bits?' Posy echoed in disbelief.

'This isn't much of a conversation if you simply keep repeating everything I say.' Sebastian leaned in to peer at her face. 'Are you sure you haven't already started on the vodka?'

'Oh my God.' It was hard to get the words out. 'Get out! Get out now!'

'What? What did I say?'

'What did you say? What didn't you say? Get out!' Posy was on her feet and tugging at Sebastian's hand, though he didn't respond well to being tugged but threaded his fingers through hers so that for one awkward moment they were almost holding hands, until Posy wrenched herself free. 'Come on! Shift it! I'm on a clock. I've got a lot of men to get through tonight, according to you. Assuming they're not repulsed by my thunder thighs, that is!'

'You're being irrational, Morland,' Sebastian said, but he was uncoiling himself from his chair and getting up. 'You're twisting everything I say. Maybe you do need to get laid, because you are incredibly uptight. But with one man,' he added hastily when Posy gave a bellow of pure rage, though she had never bellowed before in her life. 'Only one man and . . . '

'RUDE!' she shouted at him, snatching up his jacket from the back of the chair where he'd lovingly draped it and throwing it at him so it covered his hateful face. 'You are the rudest man I have ever met.'

'No need to take it out on my jacket,' Sebastian said, but at last he was going, even if it was with a martyred air about the whole proceedings. 'I don't suppose now's a good time to talk about the shop and — '

'No, it isn't! There will never be a good time to talk about the shop,' roared Posy, following Sebastian out of the room so she could shout at him as he took the stairs at great speed. 'You want to know something about the shop? My shop! It will never sell a single cr — '

She heard the shop door slam hard enough that she feared for the glass then Sebastian was out of earshot and couldn't hear Posy's passionate vow that as long as she had breath in her body, she would never run a specialist crime bookshop.

Ravished by the Rake

Posy had never known the touch of a man's hands on her body, his lips on hers. In truth, she had never even imagined such a passionate violation of her person, as she was an unwed, virtuous woman of eight and twenty from a reputable if impoverished family.

But now as Sebastian Thorndyke's lips crushed hers in a demanding kiss, his hands clasped around the enviably tiny curve of her waist, Posy Morland began to swoon. Her breasts swelled as if they wanted to burst free of her modest muslin gown and as she opened her mouth to protest, to try to take in air, Sebastian swept his tongue into the moist cavern. (NB: Maybe rethink 'moist.' And 'cavern'.) Posy whimpered in distress at the latest depravity that he wished to visit upon her.

'Damn you, woman,' he rasped, his mouth burning a path to her ear. 'Kiss me properly.'

She gasped in maidenly outrage and he kissed her harder, his tongue like a conquering army, one arm clamped around the feminine swell of her hips as he ground their bodies together.

'No! No! No!' With a strength the like of which she'd never possessed before, Posy tore herself free of Thorndyke's treacherous embrace. She placed a trembling hand on her bosom as if that alone would be enough to calm the frantic fluttering of her heart. 'You do me wrong, sir. I'm not some lowly tavern wench to be trifled with.'

Thorndyke looked at her with heavy-lidded eyes. 'I find I grow tired of tavern wenches, courtesans and other men's wives.' He tapped one finger against the lips that had ravished hers so cruelly. 'But I'll wager I won't grow tired of you, Miss Morland, not for many a long night, and that is why I intend to have you.'

11

Some women took up kickboxing. Some women did Ashtanga yoga. Or ran marathons. Took up guerrilla knitting, extreme baking, even basket weaving. Other women found lots of different ways to deal with their stress, but it seemed the only way Posy could deal with the stress, the utter pain in her arseness that was Sebastian, was to unleash her frustration with him on the page.

There was something deeply satisfying about turning him into the blackest scoundrel, the most villainous rogue, the er, most salacious seducer of innocent, well-bred ladies and even now, as she tried to cross Tottenham Court Road, Posy was already mentally drafting the next chapter of *Ravished by the Rake*.

She hadn't even had time to change out of the now-hated black dress. She'd been in such a rush, after several texts from Verity and Nina demanding to know where the hell she was, that Posy had done nothing more with her face than chuck some tinted moisturiser at it and apply mascara and lip-gloss with little enthusiasm or skill. She'd also left one of the foam rollers in her hair and had only realised when a man had stopped her on the street to tell her. It was now stuffed in her handbag and she wasn't sure that her hair was falling in tousled waves.

Posy wasn't sure about anything any more, except that she'd rather be prostrate on her sofa and halfway down a bottle of wine. Instead she was on her way to a party where she'd have to be witty and engaging in order to attract a man pleasing to the eye, who could maintain a conversation, with a view to going on a series of dates before they decided that they were in a relationship and then they could stay in and enjoy a bottle of wine together so that no one (especially Nina) would be able to judge her. Once you were one half of a couple, then staying in on a Saturday night was suddenly a valid lifestyle choice.

Sebastian would never dream of staying in on a Saturday night, Posy thought as she glared viciously at the traffic lights that had the temerity to still be on green when she wanted to cross the road. He'd be out with one of his women, or on a mission to find a new woman, all blonde and willowy and forbidden to speak, so he could do all manner of depraved things to her until another woman even blonder and willowier caught his interest.

'Bloody Sebastian, get out of my head,' Posy muttered as she hurled herself at the door of the Swedish café on Great Titchfield Street where lovely Stefan from the deli around the corner from Bookends was celebrating his birthday.

'Posy! At last! Come and give me a birthday hug,' Stefan demanded as Posy stood on the threshold of the café looking around for Nina and Verity but mostly scowling.

The scowl was instantly wiped off her face as six foot two inches of muscled Swede enveloped her in his arms. Posy had no choice but to hug

Stefan back, not that it was a chore. Stefan's hugs were consistently right up there in her top five of all-time best hugs.

'Happy Birthday,' she said, feeling rather bereft as Stefan released her. 'Sorry I'm late. Also sorry but I didn't have time to wrap your present.'

Stefan was going to properly celebrate his thirtieth birthday in New York for a long weekend with lovely Annika, his girlfriend, and so Posy had found a foodie guidebook that listed all the best places to eat and drink in the Tri-State area. She'd even paid for it. Cost price, but that was one of the perks of working in a bookshop.

'Nina and Verity are over there,' Stefan said, pointing at a table in the corner where Nina had a tall Scandinavian man on either side of her and was looking as if all her birthdays and Christmases and Easters had come at once. Even Verity, fortified by a disco nap and whatever was in her glass, was looking pretty chipper. 'And you have to meet my friend, Jens — I've been dying to get you two in the same room. Hey! Jens! Over here!'

Before Posy could adjust her settings from frazzled and annoyed to witty and engaging, a man detached himself from a nearby group of people and came over with a friendly smile on his face.

'Jens, this is Posy, who runs the bookshop round the corner from the deli. Posy, this is Jens who comes from a town in Sweden called Uppsala and teaches English.'

They shook hands. Jens wasn't quite as intimidating as some of Stefan's other male friends who were doing little to dispel the myth that all Swedish men looked like Vikings. Hot Vikings. He wasn't quite so tall and fair as most of the other men in the room. Posy didn't have to crane her neck to look in his eyes, which admittedly were as blue as the cool, clear waters of a fjord. He had light brown hair, which he was nervously running his fingers through, and he wasn't hot so much as warm. When Jens smiled at Posy, suddenly she didn't feel that she had to be witty or engaging, but could simply be herself.

'Stefan and Annika have told me so much about you, Posy,' he said. 'Is it true that you can quote the whole of *Pride and Prejudice* from memory?'

There were so many far worse things that Stefan and Annika could have shared with Jens, like Posy's preference for thickly spreading cream cheese over Stefan's delicious cinnamon buns. 'Maybe not the *whole* of it,' she admitted. 'That's my friend Verity's party trick, but I do find that there's an appropriate quote from *Pride and Prejudice* for most situations.'

'Oh, really.' Jens cocked his head, but not in an arrogant, run-his-eyes-up-and-down-Posy's-body-only-to-find-it-seriously-lacking kind of way but in a way that encouraged her to elaborate on her theory. 'Give me an example.'

'Well, when I find that someone's left a wad of chewing gum stuck to one of the shelves in the shop, which happens quite a lot, I usually say,

'Are the shades of Pemberley to be thus polluted?'' Posy explained and Jens laughed. Then Nina caught sight of Posy and waved and it seemed perfectly natural when Jens took her arm and steered her through the crowded room, found her a chair and offered to get her a drink.

Jens was lovely. Absolutely lovely. And it had nothing to do with the number of elderflower aquavit martinis Posy managed to guzzle down. He taught English in a secondary school in Portobello, which was no surprise because although he was Swedish he spoke English better than most English people Posy knew. They had a long chat about *Hamlet* and how William Shakespeare obviously hadn't known anything about Denmark, and then Jens tried to teach Posy some Swedish drinking songs, because he'd had rather a lot of martinis by then too.

It was very difficult for Posy to get her tongue around the hard Swedish vowels so they settled for shouting the words to their favourite ABBA songs at each other. Then at the end of the night, when they were all standing on the corner outside the restaurant, Jens asked for Posy's number.

'Because I will call you,' he said directly. 'I don't understand the English reserve. I like you and I want to get to know you better, without so much aquavit involved. Do you like me too?'

Posy was English and reserved but there had been an awful lot of aquavit involved so she was able to say without much blushing, 'Yeah, it would be nice to see you again.'

Jens nodded and smiled that warm smile of

his. 'We'll go on a proper date.'

He tapped her number into his phone then called it to make sure he hadn't missed a digit, and kissed her on the cheek before setting off with his friends to get a taxi back to Hackney.

Posy had insisted that Nina and Verity stay the night. Verity had no head for alcohol and was giggling every time she tried to speak, and Nina lived in Southfields, which was about as far from central London as you could get while still being in London. 'And when Sam gets back from Pants tomorrow, we can force him to make us tea and cheese toasties,' Posy said, not that either of them needed much convincing, when the ten-minute walk back to Bookends was far more enticing than taking the nightbus.

'A very successful evening, ladies,' Nina said with some satisfaction as she and Posy each took hold of one of Verity's arms to stop her veering off course. 'Verity, you got drunk and socialised, well done. And Posy, you got a phone number! See! You can't wait for the right man to suddenly appear on your doorstep, you have to go out into the wild and hunt him down.'

'That's what the internet is for,' Posy reminded her, though it was much less terrifying to go on a first date with someone you'd already met in real life than turning up to meet some stranger who looked ten years older, five inches shorter and three stone heavier than his profile picture.

Anyway, it was still only the first week of March and she already had a date, so Posy didn't have to worry about finding a stranger on a dating site to have a drink with this month. And Nina had pulled, because Nina always did, though being Nina she'd managed to find the seediest-looking man in the place and lock him down. He was a friend of a friend, covered in Death Metal tattoos and scowly of face; the one man at the party who didn't look as if he lived on a healthy diet of lingonberries, herrings and meatballs or swam in fjords and rode a bicycle around the pollution-free streets of Stockholm.

'Just my type,' Nina said when Verity commented on his surliness. 'You know how I love the surly ones. And didn't someone ask for your number, Very?'

'They did, but I think my boyfriend would have something to say about that.' Verity giggled. 'Peter Hardy, oceanographer — he's very possessive.'

'Are we ever going to meet him?' Posy asked but Verity merely shrugged as she always did when the subject of her boyfriend came up.

'Yeah, sure,' she mumbled. 'When he's not on the other side of the world graphing oceans. Anyway, Nina, aren't you seeing Piers? Didn't you say that he was going to take you up the Shard?'

Nina pretended to look shocked. 'Up the Shard?' she repeated. 'Now that's a euphemism if ever I heard one! And you a vicar's daughter too, Very. You should be ashamed of yourself!'

'You're still seeing him?' Posy tried to make her voice neutral. 'I didn't realise you were that keen.'

'Not that keen.' Nina held up her phone.

'Wouldn't be collecting other bloke's phone numbers if I was. But Piers did say he'd take me up the Oxo Tower, and I do like a bad boy, though I think Piers might be more evil than bad.'

'What do you mean by 'evil'?' Posy's voice was anything but neutral now. 'Because there's something about him that sends shivers down my spine. Not good shivers, but shivers as in something wicked this way comes.'

'Well, I've been on that one date with him and he spent the entire two hours staring at my boobs, which is entirely understandable, telling me all about the people he's screwed over in order to close a deal, and badgering me with questions about Bookends. That's when he wasn't lunging at me.' Nina wriggled her shoulders as if she was still trying to dislodge herself from a clinch with Piers. 'He said that his role model in life is Donald Trump.'

'You are not to see him again. I don't care if he wants to take you up the Shard or the Oxo Tower or upstairs at the Burger King on Tottenham Court Road,' Posy said. 'He is bad news, Nina. Seriously, if you keep on seeing him, we're going to have a problem. You could do so much better.'

'Yes, Mum,' Nina said, without any of her usual ferocity when her dating preferences were challenged. 'Anyway, let's not spoil the mood by talking about Piers. So, Jens seems nice. Like, you have so much in common.'

'He's really nice. But the only thing is, maybe he's a bit too nice. He agreed with *everything* I said. I wonder if that might get boring after a while. I mean, there's a reason people say that opposites attract, isn't there?'

'He agreed with everything you said?' Nina whistled. 'My God, what a creep!'

'Says the woman who only goes out with creeps,' Verity reminded her. 'Because Posy's right. I've only seen that Piers from a distance and he made my flesh crawl. You need to go cold turkey on the creeps.'

'They're not creeps, they're misunderstood.'

Nina was still listing the various ways each of her boyfriends had been misunderstood ('He didn't mean to shoplift that bottle of whisky, it fell into his pocket') when they reached Bookends.

Nina only shut up about the bad boyfriends she'd known and loved when her head hit Posy's pillow and she gave up talking in favour of snoring gently.

And it wasn't until the next morning when Posy was curled up in the armchair, swaddled in a blanket and pleading with Sam to make her a cup of tea, that she discovered the five twenty-pound notes she'd forced on Sebastian stuffed down the sofa cushions.

12

Since she'd thrown him out, Sebastian had obviously decided it would be wise not to darken the doorstep of Bookends for the foreseeable future, yet he still had a way of casting his long shadow over Posy and the shop.

Her stomach lurched every time she saw his name cc'd on the emails that went back and forth between Posy, Verity and Pippa, who'd decided that there was no good reason why the relaunch couldn't be moved up from the end of June to the first weekend in May. When Pippa had first mooted this crazy idea, Posy had thrown up a little in her mouth. Just a little. And no matter how many times Posy told her it was impossible, Pippa would email back a cheerful, 'Quitters never win and winners never quit!'

Yet Sebastian stayed silent behind his cc, which had to be killing him. It was killing Posy because now she was waiting for him to suddenly descend on the shop in person in a heady maelstrom of Savile Row suiting and snark, and with each day that he didn't descend, the more she fretted. It was as if the anticipation of Sebastian was slightly worse than the reality.

At least Sebastian hadn't got bored with Sam. They'd had another day out together — to see some specially curated *Doctor Who* episodes at the IMAX cinema — and Sebastian had offered Sam the opportunity to spend his work experience week at Zinger Media's Clerkenwell offices. Not that Sebastian's influence was entirely benign.

When Posy had steeled herself, after three dates with Jens, to tell Sam that she was seeing somebody, 'But it's not serious. Not at all. Not yet, but I thought you should know,' Sam hadn't been that interested. However when she'd told him what Jens did for a living, Sam had rolled his eyes and snapped, 'A teacher? Boring!' in a manner that was all too familiar.

Jens wasn't boring. He was great. Better than great. He wasn't quite as great as Verity's Peter Hardy, oceanographer, who was a paragon of boyfriendly behaviour, but Posy and Jens had been on three dates and he'd taken the news that Posy was primary caregiver to her fifteen-year-old brother on the chin. They'd also shared some really nice kisses, but he wasn't pushing Posy to have sex with him. Even though Nina said that it was industry standard to have sex after the third date, which was precisely why she'd kicked Piers to the kerb before their third date because, as well as being possibly evil, he was also quite clammy to the touch and she didn't want to have sex with him.

'Everyone knows the three dates rule. Five dates if there are extenuating circumstances,' Nina had amended, when she saw the panic-stricken look on Posy's face.

When you hadn't had sex for over two years (closer to three years, to be exact) then you needed more than three dates with someone, no matter how great they were, before you could entertain the *possibility* of letting them see you without your clothes on. Jens had been very understanding about that too. 'You'll know when the time's right,' he'd said, when Posy had brought up the subject by stuttering and stumbling around it but without ever really getting that close to the point.

'It's just I'm so busy with the relaunch and I haven't dated anyone in *ages*, not properly,' she'd persisted and Jens had leaned across the table in the Italian where they were having a quick dinner while Sam had football practice, and had kissed the babble right out of her mouth.

Jens even showed up bright and early on the first Saturday in April, the day of the great Bookends Everything Must Go! Sale, where Posy hoped to offload all the stock that couldn't be returned to the publishers. Verity had been quite adamant that they needed to do something to generate cash. She'd drawn up a list of all the money that was going out of the shop's bank account on essential things like wages and business rates as well as new stationery and tote bags, compared to all the money that was coming in, which was not very much at all. Posy had thrown up a little in her mouth then too, and grudgingly agreed to a fire sale.

It was the first truly warm day of the year. The kind of day that made you want to mothball your winter coat until October, bare your legs and turn your face towards the sun, which was valiantly shining down, so you could top up your vitamin D levels.

'We're going to have the sale outside,' Posy announced to the assembled troops: the staff, Jens, two teachers from the local primary school where Posy read with reluctant readers one morning a week, Pants and Pants's mum and dad, Yvonne and Gary.

There was a collective groan, which Posy chose to ignore. As Pippa reminded her constantly, if you want to achieve greatness, then you have to stop asking for permission.

Achieving greatness was all about delegating, as far as Posy could tell, and soon she had a slightly malcontent workforce lugging trestle tables out into the courtyard, pricing up the old stock and setting up a cake stall as a taster for the tearoom that would be restored and reopened at some far-off point in the future when Posy could find someone foolhardy enough to take it on. That was what she kept telling Pippa, who'd become quite fixated about opening the tearoom. But Posy knew that it would stay closed until she'd made her peace with someone taking over what would always be her mother's space. Posy couldn't see that happening any time soon.

Verity had emailed details of the sale to the Bookends mailing list, Sam and Pants had flyered the area and Sophie had done whatever it was she did on social media. There were posters up along Rochester Street and though Posy felt a lot like a party hostess worried that nobody would turn up, by ten o'clock a slow but steady stream of people started trickling into the courtyard.

By eleven there were a lot of determined browsers rifling through the boxes of books on each table, and by twelve they were absolutely swamped. Piers Brocklehurst was even in attendance, though he wasn't browsing so much as pawing Nina. He had his arms wrapped around her waist and was determinedly nuzzling her neck like he hadn't got the memo that he was dumped, while she looked quite bored with it all, though when he glanced up and saw Posy making 'throat-cutting' gestures at Nina, he stopped nuzzling in favour of glaring at Posy.

Still, Posy wasn't going to let a parasite like Piers harsh her mellow. As all the people milled about the courtyard, it was a faint glimmer of what the future might hold, Posy thought as she sent two little girls back to their parents with a complete set of Enid Blyton's *Malory Towers* series.

'Posy! Posy!' Posy blinked as her pleasant imaginings of staying open late on Thursdays during summer like the shops in Rochester Street, with customers spilling out into the fairy-light strewn courtyard to sit on the benches were interrupted by Pippa waving a hand in front of her face. 'Be present in the moment, Posy!'

'Oh, hi,' Posy said, a little flustered because she hadn't expected Pippa to turn up, especially when they were selling off their entire stock of crime novels, two pounds for paperbacks, five pounds for hardbacks. 'This is a surprise.'

'Thought I'd show my support,' Pippa said as she looked around. 'It seems to be going well.'

'It is, isn't it? Tom left some flyers around UCL and we've had loads of students come by to buy the academic textbooks that I thought we'd never shift,' Posy said, though Pippa didn't seem that interested in the nitty-gritty of shifting their old stock. That was because she was apparently something called a blue-sky thinker.

'Anyway, I did have an ulterior motive for coming by,' Pippa said and then she pinned Posy with a penetrating look that instantly made Posy fear the very worst: that Pippa knew Posy had been running a crime bookshop scam solely to secure her project management services and was about to rain retribution down on her head. In fact, Pippa's look was so intent and incisive that Posy suspected Pippa also knew that she'd surreptitiously scoffed one of the cupcakes that Pants's mum had baked without putting a pound coin in the kitty. 'It's a bit awkward.'

'What's a bit awkward?' Posy squeaked. It felt a lot like the time she'd been caught shoplifting pick'n'mix in the old Woolworths in Camden Town.

'The café,' Pippa said, waving at someone on the other side of the courtyard. 'Hope I'm not overstepping my remit . . . Mattie! Over here!'

A small, slim girl dressed in black cigarette pants, turtle-neck sweater and ballet flats detached herself from the huddle of people gathered around one of the tables and hurried over clutching a stack of cookery books.

'Mattie, this is Posy. I've told you all about her,' Pippa said, which didn't sound like a ringing endorsement. 'And Posy, this is Matilda,

216

one of my oldest friends who's recently back from Paris and just so happens to be looking for premises to open her own coffee shop. You might call it a coincidence, but I call it an opportunity and you know how I feel about opportunities.'

'That if you turn your back on an opportunity then you might as well have a sign pinned to your arse that says 'kick me',' Mattie said, with a fond but exasperated glance at Pippa as if the constant positive affirmations got her down too. She turned to Posy. 'Hi, I would shake hands, but I don't want to let go of these books. I already had an argument with a man who tried to snatch an old Florence Greenberg from me.'

'Hi,' Posy said, and though she didn't want a sign pinned to her arse that said 'kick me', she could only deal with one opportunity at a time. 'The tearoom, because it's a tearoom, not a coffee shop, well, it's not ready for anyone to take over. It'll need a lot of work. Huge amounts of work.'

'The only thing holding you back is you,' Pippa murmured. 'Not much difference between a tearoom and a coffee shop, and Mattie trained as a pastry chef in Paris, didn't you?'

Mattie nodded. 'I was also planning on serving savouries and sandwiches, and I know these guys in Paris who've sourced this wonderful coffee that I was going to import. But there'd definitely be tea. I can't function without a cup at regular intervals.'

Mattie had long black hair gathered up in a swingy ponytail. Underneath her blunt-cut fringe, her eyes were framed by sooty lashes and an insouciant flick of eyeliner. It wasn't hard to imagine Mattie gambolling down Parisian boulevards or cycling along the banks of the Seine on an old-fashioned bike with a cute little dog in her front basket.

'I'm sorry, I haven't had any time to think about the coffee shop or tearoom or whatever,' Posy said apologetically.

'Have you still got the old fixtures and fittings?' Mattie asked.

'Can't do any harm to have a look,' Pippa said with another steely look in Posy's direction, so she had no choice but to take them over to the tearoom, unlock the door and show them around.

There wasn't much to see. Just boxes upon boxes of old books, most of them unearthed from the coal-hole by Tom, that were being sold sight unseen to a dealer driving down from Birmingham on Monday. But if you could look past that, then you could see what the room had once been, what it might be.

'There's the original counter. I think it was put in in the Twenties. We've still got all the tables and chairs in the lean-to out the back. Bit of a mishmash of different eras,' Posy explained as Mattie slowly walked around. On first sight, Posy had cast her in Audrey Hepburn's role in *Funny Face*, now she decided that Mattie had none of Audrey Hepburn's *joie de vivre*. There was something sad and quiet about her as if she'd left her *joie de vivre* in Paris.

'Is there a kitchen?' Mattie asked, after she'd done three full circuits of the room.

'It's behind the counter and through that door.' Posy grimaced, because the kitchen was yet another overspill storage space full of display stands and boxes of promotional material for books long out of print. 'It hasn't been used as a kitchen for years, so I'm not sure if anything works and I suppose it would all have to be safety checked and you'd need to apply for a licence to serve food and drink and so, you know . . . ' Posy didn't want to see anyone weaving through the tables, dispensing tea and slabs of cakes, because one of her greatest fears was that then the memory of her mother doing those same things might diminish, fade away, until there was nothing left of her.

Mattie poked her head through the kitchen door, looked around then turned back to Posy. 'I like this place. It has a nice feel. But there's one thing you should know . . . '

If ever there was a more ominous sentence, then Posy had yet to hear it. 'What's that, then?'

Mattie's pretty face became quite stern. 'I don't do cupcakes. Never have. Never will,' she said challengingly. It wasn't what Posy had been expecting. In fact, it seemed rather random and quite unreasonable.

'What's wrong with cupcakes?' she asked, because there had been times in Posy's life when a Red Velvet cupcake from the Hummingbird Bakery on Wardour Street had been a bloody good friend to her.

'They fetishise feminine stereotypes. They're the culinary equivalent of a pair of pink stilettos,' Mattie said scathingly. 'They're a triumph of

219

buttercream over substance. If you want cupcakes, then let's call the whole thing off.'

Posy wasn't sure that the thing had ever been on. 'Well, I like cupcakes but I don't have a strong position on them,' she said.

'Let's move on. Mattie makes lots of other cakes,' Pippa said, like the facilitator that she was. 'New twists on old favourites. Her tangerine drizzle cake is out of this world, she even does a gluten-free version, and as for her white chocolate and passion cake brownies — Won-Der-Ful.'

Mattie nodded. 'I could bring you round some samples, if you like.'

Posy still wasn't ready to move on, but Pippa seemed very keen so she had to at least pay lip service to the idea. Besides, Posy never turned down free cake. 'That would be great.'

'And then we could talk about your footfall, because the shop . . . is it *only* going to sell crime novels? That's the thing I'm struggling with, to be honest with you.' Mattie frowned. 'And the name? The Bloody Dagger? I'm not sure that bloody daggers and cake work that well together.'

'We haven't one hundred per cent decided on a name,' Posy said vaguely, even though panic had suddenly seized hold of her. She knew she couldn't carry on with this crime bookshop charade for much longer, but the thought of having to come clean? Oh, no, not yet! Sebastian's reaction would be bad enough, he'd definitely throw things, but even worse, Pippa and now Mattie would think that she was a terrible person. And yet worse than that, Pippa would remove herself and her project managing skills and they'd be left floundering, so soon there might not be a bookshop of any description. 'It's still kind of up in the air.'

'Is it?' Pippa raised her eyebrows. 'I was pretty sure we had the name locked down because Sebastian said that, with Sam coming in next week, we could start work on the website. And I thought you said you'd put in an order at the printers for — '

'Oh, I'm sure Mattie doesn't want to hear about all this!' Posy scurried towards the door. 'Now I really must go and sell some books. It was lovely to meet you, Mattie. Let's get together soon. Must dash.'

Posy dashed until she was on the other side of the courtyard and could hide behind Jens and Tom, who she'd put on a table together so they could sell sports books and bond. 'Hello, you,' Jens said, and he smiled and put his arm around Posy.

It felt odd for someone, a man, to put his arm around her in full view of anyone who happened to glance their way.

She really had been single for too long.

'How's it going? You sold many books?' Posy rested her head on Jens' shoulder though she immediately wished that she hadn't because now her neck was at a very awkward angle.

'We sold all of the Wisden Cricketers' Almanacks,' Tom said, putting his own neck at an awkward angle as he stared at Posy like he couldn't quite believe that she was with a man either. None of her internet boyfriends had lasted beyond a lacklustre second date. 'Jens convinced a couple of geezers that they could sell first editions of Kenny Dalglish's autobiography for a fortune on eBay.'

'Seriously? Because we had five of them.'

Jens smiled modestly. 'They bought all five.'

She should probably kiss him for that, Posy thought, because it was a girlfriendly kind of thing to do, but she'd barely started to move in for the kill when a voice in her ear said, 'Morland, we need to talk.'

13

It was just like Sebastian to lull Posy into a sense of false security, to allow her to bask in his non-presence for two whole weeks, then suddenly reappear like a malevolent spirit who refused to be exorcised.

Posy pulled a face at Jens, who looked back at her in some confusion while Tom grinned knowingly, then she turned around. Sebastian was wearing a light grey suit with a white shirt and shades so dark she couldn't see his eyes for once. Nevertheless, she was sure there was an evil glint to them.

'What's up, Thorndyke?' She could do the surname thing too.

Sebastian's lips thinned for a second then he put a hand on her shoulder. 'I want to show you something,' he said and his fingers tightened as he tried to steer her away.

Posy planted her feet more firmly on the ground. 'It will have to wait,' she said firmly. 'I'm talking to my boyfriend.'

Jens' eyes widened because being straightfor-ward and not playing games didn't necessarily mean that you declared yourself boyfriend and girlfriend after only three dates. All the same, he showed willing and stuck out his hand for Sebastian to shake. 'Hi, I'm Jens.'

'Nobody has time for this,' Sebastian said wea-rily, ignoring Jens' outstretched hand, because he

223

really was unbelievably rude. 'Please come and find me, Morland, when you're done with these childish games.'

He stalked off. It didn't have the same flair as when he swept in and out of the shop, but it was still verging on a flounce.

'He said 'please',' Tom noted. 'I think that means he must be growing as a person.'

'Who is that?' Jens asked. 'And what is his problem?'

'The rudest man in London and he was over-indulged as a child,' Posy explained. 'I think that about covers it.'

It didn't even begin to cover the havoc that followed in Sebastian's wake. Posy decided to stay with Tom and Jens, not because she wanted to avoid Sebastian, but because Jens didn't know anyone and it would have been heartless to abandon him. Especially as Tom had gently rebuffed Jens' attempts at small talk with a 'Not really into football, mate.'

'Nobody knows what Tom's into,' Posy told Jens. 'We don't even know what he's writing his thesis on.'

'That's because it's too boring to talk about,' Tom said, as he always did, but it turned out that Jens had a couple of friends who were doing postgraduate studies at UCL too and Tom knew one of them.

While they talked, Posy kept an eye on Sebastian to make sure he wasn't causing any trouble. He seemed to be behaving himself, though he kept darting from table to table, talking to people browsing the books. Then he stopped in front of one couple, had a brief conversation with them, then started loading them up with books. Nina, who was manning that table, caught Posy's eye and shrugged.

'I'll be back in a minute,' she murmured, but Jens and Tom were discussing their mutual friend's hardline veganism and how he was a nightmare to have over for dinner, so they hardly noticed her slip away.

She circled the stall where Sebastian appeared to be haranguing her potential customers. 'Personally, I gave up after the first page, far too many long words, but if you're interested in Winston Churchill, then this is the best biography. And this is an excellent account of Rommel's desert campaign: Battle of El Alamein and all that stuff. Tattoo Girl, we got any books on the SOE?'

Sebastian was hand-selling? Books on military history? Had he suffered a major blow to the head on the way to Bookends?

'One of my stepfathers was *obsessed* with this stuff. Used to bore on about it for *hours*. Also had a large collection of Nazi memorabilia. Quite relieved when my mother caught him shagging the nanny and divorced him,' Sebastian said and by this time the man had a stack of books and the man's wife was staring suspiciously at her husband as if an interest in World War Two was destined to end in adultery and the divorce courts. Still, it wasn't Posy's place to interfere — not when the man was handing over his credit card.

Posy turned to make her escape, but it was too

late. 'There you are!' Sebastian had her in his sights and was striding over. It wasn't as if she could run away, hemmed in on all sides by trestle tables and browsing customers, so she stood with her arms folded and waited for him to reach her side. 'I need you to explain something to me.'

'You do?' Posy was intrigued, despite herself. 'Cause normally you barge in, making all sorts of assumptions, when if you just waited for an explanation — '

'Morland, you take so long to get to the point that if I waited for you to explain things, I'd be old and withered,' Sebastian said, then took hold of her arm and pulled her to the table nearest to their makeshift cake stall. 'What is the meaning of *this*?' he asked with a flourish.

'They're books, Sebastian,' Posy said. 'We sell them, people buy them. It's how our business works.'

'They're not just books, they're crime novels,' Sebastian said, picking up an Agatha Christie and waving it under Posy's nose. 'Why are you selling the crime novels in an Everything Must Go! sale? They're meant to be staying!'

Posy blinked. She wasn't good at thinking on her feet. 'Well, that's a very interesting point,' she said slowly, and Sebastian groaned as if he was in pain, which could easily be arranged.

'Tell me! Quickly! Now!'

'Um . . . ' Posy looked to Pants and his dad standing behind the table. They seemed as interested as Sebastian in hearing why she was hawking heavily reduced crime novels instead of selling them at the full RRP in a specialist crime bookshop, which only existed in Sebastian's imagination. Then she stared down at the dog-eared Agatha Christie and inspiration struck. 'Oh! Oh! It's old stock,' she said quickly. 'Very old stock. It's all tatty and the cover's creased and we want shiny, new editions in the new shop.'

'This one isn't tatty or creased,' Sebastian pointed out as he picked up a Martina Cole novel.

'Yeah, but it's an old edition. The latest one has a different cover,' Posy said, because she was on a roll now. In fact, she might as well go for broke. 'Look, Sebastian, I appreciate you trying to help — you and Pippa have been great with all the behind-the-scenes stuff — but you don't know anything about selling books and publishing trends and how sale or return works so . . .'

'It can't be that difficult if you've managed to master it,' Sebastian assured Posy. 'I've started subscribing to *The Bookseller*, in fact.'

'Well, in that case, you must be an expert by now,' Posy snapped. Panic should have taken hold of her again. There should have been icy fingers of fear slithering up and down her spine at the prospect of being found out, but she'd never been afraid of Sebastian — apart from that one time when he'd shut her in the coal-hole. When Posy was standing in front of him, it wasn't fear she felt. The feelings he aroused in her tended towards annoyance, irritation and teeth-grinding frustration.

Not that she was looking forward to Sebastian

finding out and having to deal with his inevitable tantrum, especially when there were so many people around.

Desperate to put it off for a bit longer, Posy tried to think of something conciliatory to say that would smooth things over, but he was working her very last nerve and the words that actually came out of her mouth were: 'Sebastian, you don't know what you're talking about.'

Sebastian huffed in indignation and Posy looked around desperately for a distraction. Then inspiration struck. 'Cake!' she said. 'Have some cake. What kind of cake do you like?'

'All kinds of cake, but stop trying to change the sub . . . Oh! Is that coffee and walnut?' Sebastian removed his shades to get a closer look and Pants's mum, who was in charge of the cake stall, put her hand on her heart as if the sight of Sebastian's dark eyes were causing it to beat erratically. 'I suppose it wouldn't hurt to have a slice.'

Yvonne cut Sebastian a piece of cake that was twice as big as any of the other slices she'd handed out. 'You look like you could do with fattening up.'

'It doesn't seem to matter what I eat, I never put on an ounce. Can you imagine what that's like?'

Both Posy and Yvonne shook their heads. 'I only have to *look* at a bar of Dairy Milk and it goes straight to my hips,' Yvonne sorrowfully declared.

'I wouldn't worry about it,' Sebastian said. 'Nice to have something to grab hold of, isn't it?'

Posy winced, but instead of taking offence Yvonne had just started to tell Sebastian about the time she'd put the whole family on a high-fibre diet when a breathy girlish voice behind them said, 'Baby, I know you told me to wait in the car, but you've been gone so long and I got bored.'

Before she turned around, Posy thought that the voice belonged to a small child. Possibly a goddaughter that she didn't know about, though why anyone would make Sebastian a godparent and expect him to renounce Satan, she couldn't imagine. Then Posy did turn around, and she saw that the voice didn't belong to a child.

It belonged to a goddess. An ethereal creature made entirely of sunbeams and spun sugar and fairy dust who was now draping herself around Sebastian, delicate limbs coiling about him, her silken golden head resting on his shoulder. The whole time, Sebastian wriggled and fidgeted as if this woman, this heavenly creature, was a coat that didn't quite fit, was too heavy now that the sun had come out.

Posy could do nothing but stare. The other girl had dewy, glowy skin, perfect silky blonde hair and a body that had all the grace of a gazelle and the allure of a Victoria's Secret model.

There was no way Posy — whose own beauty regime consisted of dabbing hopefully at her face with whatever skin gloop was on special offer in Superdrug and letting her hair air dry before scooping it up into a bun secured with two pencils — would ever come close to looking like this woman. They were poles apart, on different planets, Posy wasn't even sure they were the same species.

'Morland, this is Yasmin, my *girlfriend*,' Sebastian said smugly, because when it came to girlfriends, he'd won the lottery. 'She's a model.'

Posy had much better manners than Sebastian, so she shook hands with Yasmin, though it was the limpest handshake she'd ever experienced; like trying to grasp blancmange.

'Lovely to meet you,' she said.

'Oh, hi,' Yasmin said in her breathy, little-girl-lost voice. She sighed, shrugged a shoulder, then stood there barely looking at Posy, as if her beauty set her apart, raised her up to such a rarefied plane of existence that she found it impossible to interact with normal people. Or maybe the sight of Posy in jeans, holey cardigan and an old Harry Potter T-shirt was more reality than she could deal with, which was why she'd rather gaze at Sebastian. 'Baby, can we go now?'

'In a bit,' Sebastian said, disentangling himself from his *girlfriend* as if he was struggling to get himself out of a onesie and patted Yasmin's hand. 'Off you go. Look at the books.'

'Honestly, you can go, Sebastian,' Posy said, because now no one was interested in looking through the books — they were all staring at Yasmin. How would it feel to go through life with people stopping what they were doing so they could stare at your staggering beauty? The only time people had ever stopped to stare at Posy was during her student days when she'd left a nightclub loo with her skirt tucked into her knickers. 'Really, I don't mind. I'm sure we'll be

230

able to manage without you.'

'I doubt that.' Sebastian put his shades back on and gestured to the table at the far side of the courtyard. 'So, your *boyfriend?* Is it serious then? And what kind of a name is *Jens* anyway?'

'It's a Swedish name, because he's Swedish and he's really nice, super nice in fact, but we're taking things slowly and seeing where it goes — not that it's any business of yours,' Posy added as Sebastian smirked at the very idea of taking a relationship slowly. He probably had no truck with waiting for the obligatory three dates before he had sex with one of his girlfriends. Though Yasmin looked as if she would shatter into a million pieces of glitter if she engaged in any activity more vigorous than languidly wafting about, much as she was doing now.

'Sounds very boring to me,' Sebastian said. 'Well, I hope you have a very long, very boring life together.'

'We've been on three dates! It's not like we're getting married,' Posy said crossly, but she was speaking to the empty space where Sebastian had once stood because he'd caught up with Yasmin and was saying something to her that made her laugh. Though it looked more like a simper to Posy but then she mentally checked herself because she didn't want to be one of those women who thought unkind things about other women just because they were beautiful and absolutely perfect in every way.

Though maybe Yasmin wasn't quite as perfect as she appeared, because twenty minutes later, as Posy was lugging another box of books out of the shop so she could restock the stalls, Yasmin tugged on her sleeve. 'I want to buy these,' she whispered, indicating the five books she had tucked under her arm and generally acting as if she were buckling under their weight.

'Come into the shop,' Posy said, and Yasmin gratefully collapsed on one of the sofas as Posy bagged up her books: the hapless copy of *Men Are from Mars, Women Are from Venus* that Lavinia doubted they'd ever sell, three more self-help manuals and *Fifty Shades of Yay: How to Drive Your Man Wild between the Sheets*.

Even the most perfect-looking people were as unsure and doubtful as the imperfect-looking people, Posy decided as she took Yasmin's money and saw her out of the door.

'Take care of yourself,' Posy said, because now she felt guilty about unfairly judging Yasmin when they'd barely spoken. There was something fragile and vulnerable about Yasmin's beauty that made Posy want to wrap her up in cotton wool so she wouldn't come to any harm. That, and warn her off the likes of Sebastian. 'It was lovely to meet you. I hope we'll see you again soon.'

Yasmin waggled her fingers and smiled back at Posy. 'I love your shop. It has a really cosy vibe, such a shame it's only going to sell crime books. Yuk! I can't even watch *Law and Order* without having nightmares.'

Posy watched her drift back to Sebastian, than gave a start as she heard a step on the stairs. 'Who's there?' she asked sharply, her heart thudding erratically as Piers Brocklehurst came into view. 'What are you doing up there? That's

232

'off-limits.' She pointed to the door and the private sign that separated shop from non-shop. 'Can't you read?'

'All right, calm down, dear,' Piers said in a sneering way that made Posy feel anything but calm. It was different to the feelings of irritation that Sebastian roused in her. Though Posy would never admit it, most of the time she did enjoy sparring with him. Putting Sebastian firmly in his place was one of her joys in life but Piers . . . there was something, quite a lot of things actually, about him that she didn't trust. She remembered Nina theorising that he was evil and her skin was suddenly halfway to crawling. 'I was looking for the loo. It's hardly the crime of the century.'

It wasn't, but Posy didn't believe him. She longed to make him turn out his pockets but she knew that Piers would only laugh in her face.

'There's a bathroom on the left just before the tearoom,' she said bitingly. 'It's signposted quite clearly. But it's for customers only.'

'Fine. I'll buy a book,' Piers said and he took his time perusing the shelves because they both knew that he'd been poking about upstairs for nefarious reasons. If anything was missing . . . 'Here! I'll take this.'

This was a copy of Machiavelli's *The Prince*, because Piers' menace was as clichéd as his naff red jeans and loafers worn without socks. Tight-lipped and fuming, Posy rang up his purchase. 'That will be eleven pounds, ninety-nine pence,' she said and it went against everything she believed in not to say please too, but sneaky, possibly evil snoopers didn't deserve manners.

'Keep the change, darling,' Piers said, throwing a twenty-pound note down on the counter, and Posy clenched her fists until he sauntered out of the shop.

Yasmin and Sebastian left soon afterwards. 'Laters, Morland,' he threw over his shoulder, and Posy was glad to see the back of him, though she really did need to think long and hard about how she was going to broach the subject of The Bloody Dagger never happening.

It was something that occupied her mind for the rest of the day, in between selling large numbers of books, keeping an eye on Sam and Pants so they couldn't make any lightning forays on the cakes, and hanging out with Jens.

At six o'clock when the light was fading, the book buyers and browsers had vanished, and they were clearing up, Jens was still there. Posy thought he might have got bored and gone home hours ago but he was obligingly carrying the tables back into the café area and being generally helpful.

He was so kind and he had a knack for getting on with everyone, even Verity, who didn't do so well with people she didn't know and there was nothing wrong with having a long, boring life with someone, Posy told herself. Besides, just because life wasn't full of fast cars and stunning blondes, didn't mean it was boring.

'Pub,' Tom declared as Posy dropped the last box on the floor with a grateful sigh. 'Who's in? Very?'

'I would, but I'm seeing, y'know, Peter tonight,' Verity said as she became very interested in a dog-eared copy of *Moby Dick*.

'Bring him along. We're all dying to meet him,' Posy said, because Peter Hardy, oceanographer, was even more of a man of mystery than Tom was. At least Tom was always happy to go pubwards.

'I'd love to, but we hardly get any time together and he's off to Belize first thing in the morning,' Verity said. 'Maybe next time.'

Pants and his parents also begged off, but took Sam with them and then it was just Tom, Nina, Jens and Posy. 'Right, pub then,' Jens said decisively. 'I'll wait for Posy to lock up.'

'Oh, there's no need to do that,' Posy said. 'You go on ahead, I've got a couple of things to do first. I'll be fifteen minutes. Half an hour, tops.'

Jens looked quite crestfallen, which was rather validating, Posy thought as she raced upstairs and turned on her laptop.

Ravished by the Rake

There were so many people at Almack's that Posy feared she might faint.

Not just thronging the dancefloor. Even in the supper room debutantes were accompanied by their proud mamas, ever-vigilant chaperones and the more sedate members of the Ton who could be persuaded to spend the evening at Almack's rather than seeking their entertainment at rowdier routs or the Vauxhall Pleasure Gardens.

Posy had been lucky to secure an invitation under the auspices of Lady Jersey, who remembered the many kindnesses that the late Mrs Morland had shown her ailing husband. 'You may not be top drawer, my dear Posy, but you know how to comport yourself in polite company and, though you have left it rather late, you may well yet find a husband of means,' Lady Jersey had said when Posy explained the delicate predicament that she found herself in.

Now with her dance card full and having danced a second time with the dashing Swedish count who had monopolised her attentions so completely that he'd earned himself a gentle remonstration from Lady Jersey, Posy felt certain her fortunes could change.

Perhaps misfortune no longer had to be her constant companion. Lord knows, she had no need of a husband, was perfectly content not to be shackled to the yoke of matrimony, but beggars couldn't be choosers. Besides, if she could find a gentle man, one who cared more for the wellbeing of others than raising hell, then perhaps marriage might not be such an ordeal.

'Miss Morland, I believe the next dance is mine.' The Swedish count was by her side again. Posy relinquished her glass of ratafia to Mrs Pants (NB: MUST change her name — maybe she could be Madame Pantalon, French aristocrat who'd fled to London to escape the guillotine?), who'd agreed to be her chaperone for the evening, and shot the count a grateful smile.

They took their place, but the opening bars of a country dance were drowned out by a dark, insinuating voice in Posy's ear: 'I do believe that Miss Morland promised me this dance,' drawled Lord Sebastian Thorndyke, leaving the count no option but to gracefully withdraw and for Posy to smile up at Sebastian, though she longed to rap the sneer off his face with the sharp edge of her fan. Alas, to do so would ensure her banishment from polite society.

'Who on earth is that doughty fellow?' Thorndyke asked, bowing mockingly to Posy as they began the intricate steps of the dance.

'Count Jens of Uppsala is not in the least bit doughty,' Posy hissed as she and Thorndyke passed each other. 'He fences every day.'

'A milquetoast if ever I saw one. I'll wager he wouldn't be so keen to court you if he knew you'd enjoyed the attentions of another man.'

237

'Suffered, not enjoyed,' Posy reminded him in a trembling voice, because she did truly tremble when she remembered how Thorndyke had forced himself on her, devoured her with his cruel, demanding kisses.

'You suffered them well enough at the time. I recall you were quite out of sorts when I set you aside,' Sebastian said tauntingly as he crossed her path again, then bowed to the lady on his left.

'You black-hearted wretch!' Posy pressed her lips tight together and refused to look at Thorndyke for the duration of the dance. As soon as the music stopped and she rose from her low curtsey, she fled the ballroom.

Lifting up the skirts of her old-fashioned pale blue silk dress, she ran down a deserted corridor. Posy paused at the end, not sure if she should turn left or right, then she heard a firm but soft tread behind her.

'By all means make me chase you, Miss Morland. The hunt only quickens my blood,' he warned.

Posy gasped, turned right and tugged at the first door she came to. It was locked. So was the next one and the one after that.

The frantic pounding of her heart could not drown out the sound of his footsteps growing ever closer. Posy's fingers fumbled with the next doorknob, it turned and she flew into the room and tried to close the door behind her but Thorndyke was there, forcing the door open.

'I grow tired of these games, Miss Morland,' he told her. 'I'll not have you making cow eyes at other men, milksops all, when I mean to keep you for myself.'

Her nerveless fingers lost their grip and Thorndyke advanced towards her. His face in shadow, dark as his soul, as he reached for her, pulled her towards him as if she were as light as thistledown, as sylph-like as Yasmin Fairface, heiress to a fortune made from importing gulls' eggs, whom he'd danced four dances with that evening until her mother had dragged her away.

Then all thoughts of Yasmin, or even Count Jens of Uppsala, fled and all Posy could do was feel, as Thorndyke's lips descended on her and he pulled her soft curves up against his hard, unyielding body.

He kissed her so ardently that all reason left her and Posy found herself kissing him back, her fingers clutched in his devilish black curls.

It was only when his lips descended to the soft swell of her breasts above the daring neckline of her gown that Posy found her reason again and the strength to push him away.

'I will never, never be yours,' she told him breathlessly, and when she turned to leave, his mocking laughter followed in her wake.

14

Considering everything, it wasn't that much of a surprise when Jens gave Posy the 'let's be friends' speech as he walked her the hundred paces home from the Midnight Bell later that night.

Actually, it was quite a relief that Posy didn't have to worry about getting naked in front of Jens any time soon. She could cross that item off her to-do list. But she'd have to get naked with someone eventually, once she'd discovered exactly where she was going wrong with her forays into dating.

'Is it because I introduced you as my boyfriend too soon?' she asked, and Jens stilled her by putting his hand on her arm.

'No, of course it isn't. I don't care about that stuff,' he said. He tucked a strand of loose hair behind Posy's ear, which was pretty boyfriendly behaviour for someone who was letting her down gently. 'Look, to be honest, I don't think you're in the right headspace for a relationship. You've got a lot going on right now, you're very distracted, and our timing is all wrong.'

'So, maybe once the shop is relaunched, we could try again?' Posy suggested, even though she knew it wasn't what she wanted.

Posy really liked Jens, but it wasn't the sort of liking that turned into fancying the pants off him. In fact, it was hard to imagine that any man could rouse her to the sort of passion that would make her want to tear off his clothes. But she'd have been happy to do the other stuff with Jens: the long walks and the curling up on a sofa with a bottle of wine; the relationship stuff. Without passion though it didn't qualify as a real relationship. And if Posy couldn't make it work with Jens, who was lovely and super-super-nice, after three pretty good dates, then she was doomed to spinster-of-this-parish-dom.

She'd have to get a cat — and she didn't even like cats that much.

There was no time to brood about her relationship failings over what was left of the weekend because Sam decided this was as good a time as any to embark on an existential crisis. Though, more accurately, it was a wardrobe crisis.

'I haven't got a thing to wear!' he lamented when Posy went into his room on Sunday morning to see if he planned on getting out of bed before lunch. 'What am I meant to wear tomorrow when I start my work experience?'

'What about the new trousers and jacket you got the other week?' Posy asked, perching on the edge of Sam's bed as he pulled clothes out of his drawers and heaped them on the floor.

Posy hoped he wasn't expecting her to put them away again, because in that case he was going to be sorely disappointed.

Sam turned to her with an incredulous look on his face. 'I can't turn up wearing a suit. It's a tech firm. In Clerkenwell. Nobody will be wearing a suit.'

'Sebastian will,' Posy pointed out.

'That's different. He's the boss and he's Sebastian. Suits are his thing.' Sam waved a handful of material at her. 'Look! All my T-shirts have cartoons on them or you've stretched them out with your boobs. Don't even get me started on my jeans.'

Posy had been warned but couldn't help herself. 'What's wrong with your jeans? Didn't Sebastian buy you a fancy new pair the other week?'

'I'm saving them for best. All the others are too baggy, and all but one pair have elasticated waists.' Sam clutched at his hair and Posy thought that he might cry. 'We have to go out and buy me new clothes. Now. Please. Posy, don't make that face. Is your thirty per cent off Gap voucher still good?'

It was and she also had a coupon for Pizza Express. After the purchase of a pair of skinny jeans so skinny they made Posy's eyes water, and several long-sleeved tops in muted shades with absolutely no cartoon characters on them, which she was forbidden from borrowing, they celebrated their first ever argument-free clothes-shopping trip with pizza and Nutella doughballs.

Posy dared to hope that this marked a new chapter in their relationship and that they could enjoy many more future trips to buy clothes for Sam without it descending into sulks and setting off security alarms.

It never occurred to her that Sam, her baby brother, had only been buttering her up. She didn't suspect a thing, not even when they got home and he settled her on the sofa with a pot of tea and the new Sophie Kinsella.

Then Sam sat down on the edge of the coffee table so he could look Posy in the eye and said, 'You do realise I'm going to have to tell Sebastian that The Bloody Dagger is actually Happy Ever After?'

Posy slopped tea down her T-shirt in alarm. 'No, you don't! Why would you have to do that?'

'Because it's going to come out when we start building the website,' Sam explained. 'Otherwise you're going to be stuck with a website for a crime bookshop that doesn't exist.'

'But all the techy stuff is still the same, isn't it? And I wrote some fake copy for The Bloody Dagger . . . '

'Oh what a tangled web we weave when first we practise to deceive,' Sam intoned sorrowfully. 'That's Shakespeare, you know.'

'It's not Shakespeare. It's from Sir Walter Scott's poem *Marmion*, which you'd know if you ever paid attention in your English lessons,' Posy said tartly because Sam's marks for English were abysmal. 'Now, this isn't a big deal, Sam. Just let them make the website and then, y'know, we can cut and paste the Happy Ever After stuff on to it after it's done.'

'Cut and paste? You don't know anything about web design, do you? You're going to waste the web team's time and I don't want to double-cross Sebastian when he's been so cool. Anyway, you always say that it's wrong to lie.'

Posy really didn't know anything about web design so she decided to gloss over that detail and get to the point. 'It's not lying, Sam. It's being economical with the truth. You're going behind enemy lines, subverting from the inside . . .'

Sam stood up so he could stare down at his sister with a disapproving look. 'It's lying, Posy, and I won't do it.'

He managed to make it as far as the door before Posy launched herself at his retreating back. She wrapped her arms tight around him, pressed her face to his and opted for the deadliest weapon in her arsenal. Not that she was proud of what she was about to do, but desperate times and all that.

'Sam, the sweetest boy that I know,' she sang softly in his ear to the tune of Michael Jackson's *Ben*, as she had done ever since he was a baby. 'How I love to sit and watch you grow.'

'You are evil,' Sam pronounced as he wriggled to get free. 'You should be ashamed of yourself, Posy. And I've told you countless times that your rubbish version doesn't even scan.'

'When I am here you'll never be alone and you my baby bro will see you've got a big sis in me . . . ' Posy hugged Sam even tighter. No matter how annoying he was or how much he currently hero-worshipped Sebastian, she thought her heart might cave in with the weight of her love for him. That didn't mean she was about to let him grass her up, though. 'Do you want me to go on? Chorus, verse, refrain? You can join in if you like.'

'No!' With superhuman effort, Sam managed to escape her clutches. 'Fine! I won't say a word, but you're setting a very bad example as my legal guardian.'

'I know,' Posy agreed, as she flopped back on the sofa. 'Now, if you're going to the kitchen, can you bring in the HobNobs?'

★   ★   ★

Sam could never stay mad at Posy for too long, and he was so excited about his work experience that he all but skipped out of the shop the next morning with a cheery wave and a 'Yes, I've got my Oyster card, stop fussing.'

Posy spent the morning scrubbing down the walls and shelves in three of the anterooms, now clear of books, in preparation for painting them.

Then one of their lunchtime browsers turned out to be a reporter from *The Bookseller* who was very interested in Posy's plans for the shop and promised she'd ask her editor if she could write a piece about the relaunch.

That afternoon Posy had a meeting with the publisher of a huge romantic fiction list. They were surprisingly amenable to Happy Ever After hosting author events and wanted to bring in their marketing team to see how they might develop this new relationship. They also promised Posy some promotional items to support their latest releases, including yet more tote bags. The whole world loved a tote bag, although Verity had cut their own tote bag order by fifty per cent after a very passive-aggressive letter from the bank asking them to come in and meet with a business advisor to discuss their cash-flow issues. They'd never had letters from the bank before, only statements and invitations to take out credit cards.

As Posy walked back to the shop after her meeting, she was sure that she could feel something unfurling in her. It wasn't the usual fluttery panic at how much she had to do in a few short weeks; it was hope.

She was making plans — that wasn't anything new, her notebooks were full of plans, dreams and schemes — but these were plans that she was seeing through. For once, she was working towards a sharply defined future rather than simply getting to the end of each day.

Sam was similarly afflicted. He arrived home just after six with a dreamy look on his face. Posy had come back down to earth by then: scrubbing walls with sugar soap would do that to a girl.

'Did you have a good day?' she asked anxiously when he tracked her down to the furthest room on the left. 'If you hated it, you don't have to go back tomorr — '

'Oh, Posy, it was *amazing*.' Sam twirled around the bucket of sugar soap. 'Everyone has two monitors and they've got all the latest software. Software I didn't even know existed and in the break room there's a ping-pong table and a pinball machine and loads of food and you can have anything you want and you don't have to pay for it. They had these KitKats you can only get in Japan. I got you a salted caramel one.'

'Thank you. I'll have that for pudding tonight,' Posy said. She'd been squatting down to do the skirting boards and now she slowly stretched as she hoisted herself upright. 'Was everyone nice to you?'

'They were great. Everyone was great.' Sam's joy was almost trance-like, as if he'd spent the last six months with a religious cult who'd fed him huge amounts of psychotropic drugs, instead of one day with a boring tech company doing boring techy things. 'If you promise not to embarrass me, you could come with me tomorrow if you wanted.'

'That's sweet of you,' Posy said because she was touched that he'd want his nagging big sister hanging around. 'But I'm so busy here and I don't really get all that computer stuff.'

'They run computer literacy courses and coding workshops specifically designed for women,' Sam said. 'You should sign up, then you wouldn't have to ask me for help every five minutes.'

'I wouldn't have to ask you for help if you didn't keep changing the Wi-Fi password without telling me,' Posy said without rancour, because this was a discussion they'd had many times before.

'You're meant to change it every week, Morland,' said a voice from the doorway. 'So people can't hack into your router and steal all your data.'

He kept popping up like an evil genie. Posy resolved that this time she would remain calm and serene, no matter the provocation. 'I really don't think my data is worth stealing,' she said mildly.

'You see what I have to put up with?' Sam

asked Sebastian with a grin. He turned back to Posy. 'Sebastian gave me a lift home because — don't be mad — I've lost my Oyster card.'

Posy wasn't mad, or even that surprised, just resigned. 'Again? Really?'

Sam shrugged. 'It's probably at work somewhere.' He frowned. 'Unless I dropped it in the street.'

'I'm going to report you to the Mayor's Office,' Posy told him. 'That's the third one you've lost in the last year.'

'Naughty boy,' Sebastian said. 'Nothing but bread and water for you until you've paid your sister back.'

'He actually gets free bus travel but it's the principle of the thing,' Posy said, and Sam hung his head.

'Sorry,' he said in a small voice. 'I promise it won't happen again. What's for dinner?'

Posy gestured at her bucket and sponge. 'I haven't had time to think about dinner. Can you make do with toast and spaghetti hoops?'

Sam looked aghast at the prospect. Sometimes, not often, but occasionally, Posy envied Verity and Nina who had both told her that on nights when they didn't feel like cooking they could make do with anything from peanut butter and breadsticks to olives and fancy crackers left over from Christmas. But when you lived with a fifteen-year-old boy who was growing at a rate of knots, that wasn't ever an option.

Posy gave Sam a ten-pound note so he could get some fish and chips from No Plaice Like Home around the corner. 'And get some mushy peas too. You have to eat some green stuff,' she reminded him. She thought that Sebastian might leave too, but he was poking around in the bags of decorating supplies that had been delivered that morning.

'Thanks for bringing him home.' Posy owed him that. She actually owed him a lot more than that. 'And for giving him the chance to do work experience. And for, well, looking out for him.'

Sebastian smiled. 'But . . . ' he prompted. 'I know there's a but coming.'

'Actually there isn't.' Posy was as surprised as he was. 'It's a genuine, heartfelt thank you. While I'm on a roll, I should thank you for letting us have Pippa too.'

'You're not going to finish off with a few tart remarks about my sex life or my failings as a human being?'

Posy thought about it, then shook her head. 'No, not tonight. Don't get used to it though. I'm sure you'll do something quite soon that will make me rain vengeance down on you.'

'I'm counting on it.' Sebastian gingerly prodded her bucket with the tip of one highly polished brogue. 'Why are you washing the shelves? What's the point when they're going to be painted anyway?'

'I have to wash them first. Get rid of decades' worth of dust and grime.'

'I hate to do anything to jeopardise our *entente cordiale*, but I didn't think cleaning was your area, Morland,' Sebastian said carefully, which was a first. Posy didn't think he'd ever said anything carefully in his life.

She pulled a face. 'It's not. That is, I clean myself. Regularly. Daily. Sometimes twice daily, but I think you already know my position on housework.'

'Can't you get the decorators to do the scrubbing for you?' Sebastian asked.

'There's no money in the budget for decorators,' Posy said. Despite Sebastian's many faults, he was unstintingly generous and she could see his eyebrows shooting up, his mouth opening, hand reaching into the inner pocket of his suit jacket for his wallet. She headed him off: 'I don't mind doing it myself. It will be so satisfying when it's done, to know that I put all this hard work in. That I got my hands dirty and I sweated and broke nails and did irreparable damage to my lower back to make my dreams a reality.' She pulled a face. 'I'm beginning to understand what people mean when they say hard work is its own reward.'

Sebastian looked even more perplexed. 'Why isn't your *boyfriend* helping you?' He sniffed. 'Not very gentlemanly to expect you to do all the heavy lifting.'

'Do you do all Yasmin's heavy lifting then?' Posy asked, though from what she'd seen of Yasmin, lifting a teaspoon would unduly exert her.

'You seem very interested in my girlfriend,' Sebastian said.

'You were the one who mentioned my boyfriend first,' Posy countered, and they were back to glaring at each other again, which felt more natural than being calm and serene.

It was a relief when Sam came hurtling through the door with his fish and chips and expressed his amazement that Sebastian was still cluttering up the place.

'I was just going,' Sebastian insisted. 'I hope you and your bucket have a thrilling evening, Morland. And I'll see you tomorrow, Morland Junior.'

Then he stood there for ten very awkward seconds before he finally left.

Ravished by the Rake

The engagement between Count Jens of Uppsala and a pretty debutante who'd only been out for a mere handful of weeks was announced in The Times that morning.

Posy Morland experienced a pang of regret as she sipped her tea, trying to savour each last aromatic drop as there was no money left to purchase any more. The pretty debutante was in possession of a handsome dowry and Count Jens was in possession of a large estate in Uppsala that had fallen into a state of disrepair.

Ten thousand pounds a year could buy even the most steadfast man's affections, Posy thought as she adjusted her lace fichu, which was rubbing against the marks on her neck.

Marks left there by Sebastian Thorndyke as he'd feasted on her tender flesh.

Posy put down her teacup with a trembling hand (NB: check how many times you've used tremble already) as she remembered that night at Almack's. How Thorndyke had chased her, cornered her in a quiet side room. Then, when she'd tried to escape, he'd picked her up as if she weighed no more than a handful of feathers and thrown her down on a fainting couch.

'You mustn't,' Posy had said in a wavering voice, but Thorndyke shook his head.

'I must, for I will have no peace of mind until I do,' he said as he swooped down on her trembling wavering quivering body. 'How you torment me, intrigue me, possess me with thoughts of making you mine.'

He had kissed her then, more tenderly than she'd have thought possible, and she must have been possessed too for she kissed him back, their tongues duelling for dominance, then dancing together and all the while Sebastian's hands were busy unhooking the bodice of her dress.

Posy voiced not one word of dissent as Thorndyke bared her trembling heaving breasts to the moonlight and his hungry gaze. 'Damn you for being so beautiful,' he rasped before he bent his head and sucked one of the trembling (FFS) succulent morsels into his mouth.

By the time he was done, Posy was quite undone. Her flesh gleamed from his ministrations and she ached with a sweet, piercing agony, for Sebastian had lavished her pert breasts with his devotion but had not taken the necessary steps that would have satiated them both and left Posy utterly ruined.

Alas, he had already ruined her for all other men, she'd thought as she struggled to sit up and cover her brazen flesh with the chemise that Sebastian had tugged down in his passion.

Posy could not look at him, her cheeks aflame, now that other fires had ceased to burn. But Thorndyke had taken her chin in his hand so she could see the steely look on his face. 'Five guineas off your debt, Miss Morland,' he'd said cruelly. 'Only another forty-five to go.'

Oh yes, even without the marks of his possession marring her otherwise alabaster skin, Posy remembered it only too well.

She put down her teacup, rested her head in her hands and wept.

15

The next day involved a lot more sugar soap so it was a relief when Pippa dropped by while Posy was up to her elbows in grimy liquid.

'Did we have a meeting?' asked Posy when Pippa suddenly appeared in the furthest ante-room to the left, which Verity and Nina had been studiously avoiding in case Posy asked them to pick up a sponge and help.

Pippa sat down on the kick steps. 'No, no meeting.'

Posy scrubbed at a particularly stubborn spot in the corner of one of the bottom shelves where the dust had congealed into thick black gunk. 'I chased up the tote bag and mug people and they promised that, if they don't deliver by Monday, they'll knock ten per cent off.'

'That's not why I'm here. God, you lot are *obsessed* with tote bags.' Pippa hadn't pulled out any of her electronic devices but was staring hard at the back of Posy's head. Posy knew that without turning around because suddenly all her hair follicles were tingling unpleasantly. 'Can you look at me, Posy? I'm going to ask you a question and I want you to be honest with me.'

That was no incentive for Posy to put down her sponge and turn to face Pippa. 'Can't you just ask me anyway? Without audience participation.'

'Posy Morland, turn around immediately!'

Pippa snapped and Posy instantly swivelled around because it was a tone of voice that brooked no riposte. (Posy made a mental note to use the phrase 'brook no riposte' in her next instalment of Ravished by the Rake — not that she was going to be writing any more, but if she did . . .) 'Pay attention to me!'

'I'm paying attention,' Posy said. Pippa had a look on her face like she was all out of inspirational quotes and positive affirmations and was going to start swearing instead. 'What's the problem?'

'Obviously you are planning a relaunch, that much I can say for sure. But, honestly, are you rebranding Bookends as The Bloody Dagger, a specialist crime bookshop?'

Now it wasn't only the follicles on Posy's head that were tingling. Every hair on her body was standing to full attention. 'Um, what makes you think we aren't?'

Answering a question with another question was a textbook evasion tactic. Posy knew that and so did Pippa, because she narrowed her eyes and sucked in a breath. She twirled a lock of impossibly glossy, impossibly bouncy hair around one immaculately manicured finger. 'Lots of things,' Pippa said. 'Whenever anybody asks Sam for the final website artwork, he goes bright red and says that you've got it. Then you told Mattie that the name of the shop hadn't been finalised when it was agreed weeks ago. Whenever I email you links to crime fiction festivals as inspiration for pitching author events, you never reply. And a moment ago, when I asked Nina if we had enough books to stock a whole room dedicated to Scandinavian crime fiction, she said, and I quote, 'I'm buggered if I know.''

'Oh, you know what Nina's like,' Posy said weakly. 'Always with the jokes.'

'Nobody in this shop, including you, seems to have the slightest interest in crime. And Sebastian tells me you sold all the crime novels at the sale on Saturday.'

'Yeah, well, I explained to him then that they were old editions, and anyway he doesn't know —'

'Posy, I have a Masters degree in Non-Verbal Communication and you have been blinking rapidly, touching your hair and looking to the side every time you speak to me. Classic tells when someone's lying. So, yes or no: is this going to be a specialist crime bookshop in three weeks' time?'

Posy took her hands out of her hair and stared down at her feet. 'No,' she admitted. It didn't feel good to tell the truth. It felt like an industrial-sized can of worms had just been opened. 'We're reopening as Happy Ever After, a one-stop shop for all your romantic fiction needs.'

'I see.' Pippa knitted her fingers together then rested her chin on them. 'Actually, I don't see. Why don't you hit the headlines for me?'

It all came spilling out then in an ungainly gobbet of words, and now it did feel good to confess all her crimes even though Pippa's face remained impassive so it was impossible to tell what she was thinking.

'Sebastian was meant to have got bored of the whole thing by now,' Posy finished on a petulant note because really this was all Sebastian's fault. 'I'm sorry that I've lied to you and taken advantage of your project management skills under false pretences, but it all spiralled out of control.'

'I have to tell Sebastian,' Pippa said.

'Oh, please, don't.' Posy wasn't above begging. On the contrary, she felt entirely comfortable with begging. 'I've got so much to deal with without having to deal with him too.'

'Give me one good reason why I shouldn't.'

'Um, because . . . because, er, sisterhood?'

Pippa took a deep breath. 'Posy, he pays my wages.'

'Yes, I know that, but somehow you've mastered the art of saying no to him so that he listens to you. Whenever anyone else says no to him, he just doesn't hear it. I did try to tell him . . . ' Posy thought about it. ' . . . several times, although the last time we were in the middle of an argument and he ran away before I got to the important bit.'

Then there was nothing for it but to take Pippa into the office and show her the paint swatches, the calendar with all the author events pencilled in, the designs that Posy had signed off weeks ago, the boxes of stationery, bookmarks and carrier bags that had arrived on Friday. All the while Verity stared at her in horror.

'Everything all right?' she finally ventured when she couldn't stand the tension between Pippa and Posy a moment longer.

258

'I don't know,' Posy whimpered. 'Are you very angry with me, Pippa? I didn't mean to waste your time, but it wasn't really wasted because your revised schedule has been a godsend and your floor plan made much more sense than mine did. We're just going to be selling a different genre of book. That's not so bad, is it? It's still books and stationery and tote bags, but instead of being all murdery, they're a celebration of love. That's a good thing. Love. All we need is love. Love is all around.'

'You have to tell Sebastian,' Pippa said firmly, before Posy could rattle off any more song titles. 'Either you do it or I will.'

Of course Posy had to tell Sebastian what she'd done. Catalogue the sheer depth of her deception. Confess her wrongdoings. Own up to every brazen and barefaced lie. What was the worst that could happen? He might bill her for Pippa's services and for the web stuff, but that wasn't so bad in the grand scheme of things. Or, as executor of Lavinia's estate, could he take the shop away from Posy before her two years were up? Was there a clause on one of the many forms and letters she'd signed that gave Sebastian full control of Bookends in the event that Posy was found guilty of subterfuge? Surely, there couldn't be.

But Sebastian would be very angry. He'd say hateful things, which Posy could handle because she'd had a lifetime of Sebastian saying hateful things, but if he stopped coming around, then Sam would be dreadfully hurt and Posy wouldn't be able to handle that quite so easily.

Sam and Sir Walter Scott had been right with their talk of tangled webs.

'All right, I'll tell him,' Posy said. 'But you have to let me pick the right time.'

'There is no time.' Pippa was starting to sound quite stressed about it. 'As Paulo Coelho says, 'One day, you will wake up and there won't be any more time to do the things you've always wanted. Do it now.''

'You really do have one of those quotes for every occasion,' Posy said. 'How do you remember them all?'

'Not every occasion, but I do find them a powerful motivational tool,' Pippa insisted. She then pinned Posy with one of her penetrating looks, another powerful motivational tool. 'You can't keep taking advantage of Sebastian's good nature like this.'

Verity rolled her eyes so furiously that Posy thought she might be having a seizure. 'Since when does Sebastian have a good nature?'

'It's absolutely impossible to tell him something that he doesn't want to hear,' Posy added.

'I find it only too easy,' Pippa said, without the least bit of sympathy. 'I don't think anyone else at the office has a problem with it either. You have to be decisive, that's all. Give him no wriggle room. You make your point. Let him process it. Move on. Point. Process. Move. PPM.'

'PPM,' Posy and Verity repeated.

'PPM him by next Monday or I'll tell him, but it would be so much better if it came from you. OK?'

'Yes, but . . . ' Pippa was already gone and Posy had to follow her out into the shop. 'Pippa, hold on!'

'I can't. I've just PPM'ed you.' Pippa already had her hand on the door.

'Please, it's about your friend Mattie,' Posy shouted across the shop floor to the consternation of a middle-aged man in an anorak and bobble hat who was scanning what few self-help titles they had left on the shelf. Pippa paused and turned. 'She's emailed me a couple of times. Well, actually, she's emailed me every day for the last two weeks. I haven't reached a decision about the tearoom . . . '

'Posy! Please stop springing all these confessions on me! What do you mean you haven't decided yet?' Pippa demanded and she was sounding properly cross now.

'You have to make a decision very soon,' Verity chimed in, like a Greek chorus. 'And the decision needs to be yes. The tearoom is dead space. It's not earning any money standing there empty. We need to start earning money instead of just spending it.'

It seemed to Posy that no matter how hard she worked, the stress never lessened. With every passing day it seemed to increase until she could feel the weight of it pressing her down, squashing all her vital organs so it was hard to breathe.

'OK. OK,' Posy said, holding up her hands to ward off any more criticism. 'I'll seriously consider what I'm going to do about the tearoom.'

Pippa sighed heavily as if Posy's serious

261

considerations weren't enough. 'As Walt Disney said, 'The way to get started is to quit talking and begin doing.''

When Pippa started with the inspirational quotes, then Posy knew she was beaten. 'Fine! Yes! I'll do something with the tearoom. Do you think Mattie might decide that baked goods and romantic fiction would be a better combination than cake and crime, then? Could you sound her out? Please.'

'I suppose I could,' Pippa agreed. 'I'll set up another face-to-face.'

'Oooh! Could you ask her to bring cakes?' Nina chimed in from high up on the rolling ladder.

'Enough!' Pippa wrenched open the door. 'I'm PPM-ing the whole lot of you!'

Ravished by the Rake

He came to her, as she knew he would, by dead of night. Sleep had evaded her these hours past and so when she heard the rattle of stones at her window, it did not startle Posy out of slumber.

The pebbles skittered against the glass again and, afrit that Thorndyke (for it could be no one else) might break the window or rouse the household, Posy rose from her bed and peered out.

'What are you about, sir?' Posy hissed, but Thorndyke was already hoisting himself up the apple tree that grew close to the house, its branches almost touching the windows as Posy had had to dismiss the gardener last Michaelmas. 'Are you mad?'

'Ill met by moonlight, my dear Miss Morland,' Thorndyke said, his voice steady despite his exertions. 'How enchanting you look. So adorably dishevelled.'

Posy was sure she looked neither adorable nor enchanting enveloped in her voluminous, lawn cotton nightgown, with her hair loosely plaited.

'You must have taken complete leave of your senses if you imagine that I'll let you in,' she told him firmly, for only that past afternoon she'd taken her dear friend Verity into her confidence. Although she was a rector's daughter, Verity had not condemned her, nor judged her either, but she had warned Posy to be firm with Lord Thorndyke.

'Let no man put a price on your reputation or your heart,' Verity had said. 'Though indeed I do suspect that it's not the fifty guineas he longs to possess but your love, for that has much greater worth.'

Yet, Posy refused to believe that Thorndyke could or would love her. To love, one needed a pure heart and Thorndyke's was as black as the few measly lumps of coal that were all Posy could afford to burn of an evening.

'You'll let me in, Posy,' Thorndyke insisted. 'To your bedchamber and to that soft inviting place between your silken thighs. Now step aside from the window, dammit, woman!'

'I will not!' Posy stuck her head out of the window so she wouldn't have to shriek like a costermonger. (NB Do costermongers shriek? Must research.) 'You cannot toy with me, with my affections. I have no monetary means to repay my family's debt and, God help me, I will not debase myself any longer. Have me and Samuel cast out if you must, but I'd rather take my chances in debtors' prison than in your arms. Now leave me in peace.'

But as she reached out to close the window, to shut Thorndyke out, he leaned forwards and stole a kiss.

She ~~trembled~~ (No! Don't start that again!) shivered convulsively and Thorndyke took advantage of Posy's momentary distraction to jump from tree to window ledge.

'Will you have me break my neck, Miss Morland?' he enquired throatily. 'Will that make you happy?'

'I want no man's death, not even yours, on my conscience,' Posy said, and she stood aside so he could leap nimbly into her bedchamber. Then he stood before her, lean and strong and shockingly virile in his tight buckskin breeches and exquisitely cut coat of black superfine. 'But you will not have me. I will not be your whore, sir. Not even for five hundred guineas.'

'What nonsense!' Thorndyke scoffed as he gathered up a handful of her nightgown to draw her closer. 'You do both of us a disservice when such harsh words tumble out of your pretty mouth.'

'You must leave me in peace, my lord,' Posy said a little desperately as she felt the heat of him through the thin cotton, one of his hands clamping down on the curve of her hip.

'Why should you be left in peace when I am in torment?' Thorndyke asked with a desperation that matched her own, and she could not lift a finger to stop him, could not voice one protest as he ripped away her nightgown as easily as if it were fashioned from paper and left her standing there naked and trembling beautiful in her vulnerability. 'Lie with me, sweet Posy, lie with me and let me love you. Let me show you that, beneath my cruel, careless exterior, I can be kind . . . indulgent . . . biddable . . . yours.'

With every promise he took another kiss, shaping her curves to the granite of his body and *when Posy wound her fingers through his mid-night black curls, he swept her up in his arms and strode over to the bed.*

16

Posy thought about sending Sebastian an email. Or giving Sam a note written on her new Happy Ever After headed stationery to pass on.

But Sebastian would probably delete the email as soon as he saw who'd sent it then deny all knowledge of ever receiving it, and given Sam's ability to lose Oyster cards, his homework diary and keys with monotonous regularity, he couldn't be trusted as a reliable courier.

Posy would have to wait until the next time Sebastian descended on the shop then PPM him into the middle of next week. She could only hope it would prove more successful than her attempts to practise on fictional Sebastian. Dear God. He'd have her bent over the New Releases table before she could get to the point.

'Oh, I've got a point for you, Miss Morland,' Sebastian would say. As soon as she thought it, Posy blushed and, bloody hell, her hands were shaking as she applied her sponge to yet another grimy shelf. When this was over, and the shop was sugar soaped and painted, she never wanted to see another bucket or sponge as long as she lived.

She was saved by cake. Or, more accurately, by the arrival of Mattie carrying several pleasingly large Tupperware containers. 'Thought I'd drop by,' she said, placing her bounty on one of the empty shelves. 'Pippa said you'd be around and the pretty blue-haired woman said you were back here.'

'That's Nina,' Posy said. 'I'll introduce you to everyone properly later.' She nibbled at her ragged fingernail. 'I thought we should have a proper chat about the tearoom first. Though, to be honest, I'm still not entirely sure . . . it's just, I have so many other things to do . . . but Pippa was quite adamant that I make a decision about it, like, right now!'

Mattie nodded. 'I hear you! Love Pips to pieces but can you imagine what it's like going to dinner with her? You have to be ready to order within five minutes of getting the menu.' Today Mattie was wearing a baggy pair of dungarees over a long-sleeved black top and dirty tennis shoes, yet she managed to look charming and gamine. 'But I am really keen to take over the tearoom, if that helps your decision-making process. The space looked perfect, what I saw of it, but I wasn't feeling The Bloody Dagger. People who are into reading about serial killers probably aren't that excited about cake.'

'I think Agatha Christie and Dorothy L. Sayers fans would probably like cake,' Posy said — not that she'd given it much thought. 'Doesn't everyone like cake? It's a great leveller.'

'But this isn't going to be a crime bookshop, is it?' Mattie queried.

'God, no!' Posy said fervently. Her sugar soap solution was black by now and she was grateful for the distraction, so she showed Mattie around the shop and explained how it would look in a couple of weeks when it was painted grey, had a better flow, vintage display cabinets, and signage in a pretty pink cursive script.

Then they sat in the back office and Verity made tea while Mattie produced from the Tupperware containers her signature tangerine drizzle cake, two different kinds of brownies; salted caramel and pecan nut and white chocolate and passion fruit. There were also gruyere and red onion scones, miniature choux buns filled with cheese and chives, a three-layer apple and raspberry crumble cake, four different kinds of shortbread biscuits and . . .

'When can you open the café?' Nina asked around a mouthful of lavender shortbread. She was meant to be serving in the shop but kept darting into the office to sample Mattie's heavenly wares. 'Can you open it tomorrow?'

'I think tomorrow might be pushing it,' Posy said, and Mattie agreed.

'Have you got time for me to have a proper look at the tearoom?' she asked.

Posy showed her through the shop to the set of double doors that led to the tearoom, unlocked them and left Mattie to explore on her own. She returned to the shop just in time to hear the door close and catch a glimpse of Piers Brocklehurst, of all people, scurrying away.

Nina was nowhere to be seen, but Posy followed the sound of voices to the back door. She was about to step out into the backyard and demand to know what Piers had been doing in the shop and wasn't Nina meant to have dumped him already, when she heard Verity say, 'Do you think you should tell Posy?'

Nina made an unhappy sound. 'I don't want to worry her. She has so much on her plate right now, but it is kind of shady of him, isn't it?'

'Asking if you've got any dirt on Posy? It's the shadiest,' Verity said indignantly as Posy nodded her head in agreement. What on earth was going on? 'Anyway, Posy is dirt-free. Well, apart from the dirt upstairs. She leads a blameless life.'

'He didn't want interesting dirt either; he kept asking whether she owed back taxes or was violating health and safety rules. I shouldn't have told him that Posy didn't think we were right for each other when I dumped him, but it was easier than telling him that he kind of gave me the creeps. Maybe I should just shag him,' Nina mused. 'You know, take one for the team.'

Posy was horrified. She didn't even know where to direct her horror first. At Piers, who seemed intent on wreaking some kind of awful revenge on Posy for cockblocking him? Surely it couldn't be the first time that a friend of one of his hapless victims had staged an intervention? Or should she start with Nina, who, despite acknowledging what an odious, vile creature he was, was apparently thinking about having sex with him?

'Do not shag him,' Verity advised before Posy could barge in with her own tuppence worth. 'But let's keep this between ourselves for now. And next time that horrible man appears . . . well, I'd like to say that I'll deal with him, but I can't, Nina. I just can't. Maybe we could sic Tom on him.'

There was a moment's silence and then they

both laughed hysterically at the idea of Tom striding in to do battle on Nina's behalf. Posy, however, was not laughing. This was the last thing she needed, one more ball of stress to add to the pile. So instead of charging out there, guns blazing, to say that she'd deal with Piers, Posy fled to the comfort of her reading nook, though comfort was in short supply and it wasn't until Nina came back in and saw Posy's feet poking out and asked what she was doing in there, that Posy realised that she'd left Mattie on her own for quite some time.

When Posy walked back into the kitchen, she found Mattie kneeling on the floor, her head in the oven.

For one awful moment Posy feared the worst, but then she remembered that the oven had been disconnected ages ago and then Mattie emerged, scribbling something down in a notebook. 'This is a great space,' she said, but with a tiny frown. 'Is there a reason why you closed the tearoom? Is it the footfall? I noticed that there's a deli around the corner. Were they huge competition?'

'No, the tearoom was incredibly popular. Not just with people coming into the shop; it was always packed at lunchtime and Stefan — he owns the deli — he doesn't do eat-in, says it's too much bother, though he does sell sandwiches at lunchtime, but with a Scandinavian theme. Lots of rye bread. And fantastic cinnamon buns.' Her throat was throbbing, eyes prickling, though she had only talked about lovely Stefan so far.

Would she ever reach that final stage of grief, of acceptance, when she could say in an off-hand

271

fashion, 'Oh, my parents passed away seven years ago. Of course I still miss them, but time's a great healer.'

But it wasn't true. Time didn't heal. It made their absence hurt even more, made Posy determined to hang on to the pain, because if she started to feel better, to miss them less, then her memories of them — the sound of her mother's laugh, the honeysuckle scent of her perfume, the feel of her father's arms around her, the buttons of his waistcoat digging into her cheek — would fade, disperse, disappear and they'd be gone for ever.

'So why did you close up when it was such a money-spinner?' Mattie asked. 'It's odd. The place feels as if it shut down suddenly. There's a recipe book open on the worktop, cutlery in the sink drainer, and I had a look in the store cupboard and — '

'My mother . . .' She couldn't get the words out. Posy took a deep breath in, then exhaled. 'My father managed the shop and my mother . . . she ran the tearoom. They were . . . there was a crash on the motorway and . . . after, Lavinia, she owned the shop, took over the book side of things.' Posy swallowed. 'I think she planned to reopen the tearoom eventually, but it was all so sudden and painful, and it just got left.'

Mattie stayed where she was, leaning against the worktop. She didn't try to hug Posy, which was a relief, because Posy was sure that she'd have fallen apart and started sobbing on Mattie, which wouldn't be very professional. 'I'm sorry,'

Mattie said softly. 'I lost my father when I was twelve. It doesn't get any easier, does it?'

'It really doesn't.'

'I understand now. That it's too weird for you to have someone take over the space. I get it.' Mattie walked over to the door so she could cast her eyes over the tearoom again.

It would be weird to see Mattie where Posy could only see her mother, but as Posy considered it, she wondered whether it wasn't *too* weird. 'I know that it's time to move on, but knowing it and acting on it are two different things,' Posy said. 'Then again, it's so silly to leave the room gathering dust when it could be such a lovely place for people to sit and eat cake and talk about books.' When she thought about it like that, resurrecting the tearoom seemed like it might actually be a good idea. 'Though, if you did want to take it on, you'll probably have to deal with me being quite over-protective and banging on a lot about how we used to do things back in the day. Do you think you could put up with that?'

'I'd probably try to heal you with cake. That's what I usually do when people are sad.' Mattie looked around the room again. 'It's easily the nicest place I've seen. So friendly and light, yet cosy at the same time. But there's an awful lot to sort out: I haven't asked you about the rent or licences, and there's no way on earth it would be ready for the shop reopening, but if you're OK with it in principle, then I'd love to take over your tearoom,' Mattie said in a squeaky-voiced rush because it was obviously a huge step for her too.

'I think . . . I don't think it will ever feel like

the right thing to do, but you feel like the right person. Does that make sense?' Posy smiled. 'I reckon my mum would approve though, and also she'd be begging for your scone recipe. Shall we shake on it?'

Just before they did, Mattie paused. Posy was surprised to discover that she was dreading Mattie having second thoughts when she'd expected to be the one having second thoughts. 'Just so we're clear though, I really don't do cupcakes,' Mattie said.

'I can live with that,' Posy lied, because she was going to do everything in her power to persuade Mattie to have a change of heart.

'Strictly speaking, I don't do happy ever afters either, but let's not even go there,' Mattie said and they shook hands.

Then the handshake turned into a brief but heartfelt hug and Posy had a feeling that she hadn't just found a tenant but a friend too.

★ ★ ★

The warm glow of potential new friendship and the rush from all the cake she'd eaten lasted for the rest of the morning and gave Posy the motivation and the energy she needed to finish the last of the sugar soaping.

Then there was nothing left to do but prise open the first tin of paint. It felt like such a huge step. A no-turning-back kind of step and Posy wasn't sure she'd be able to paint anything neatly and steadily when she'd consumed so much sugar and was still shaky from coasting so many big, deep emotions.

Posy wandered back into the main shop to look for Nina, who could always be relied upon to come through with a rousing 'You go, girl!' speech. But before she could hunt Nina down, the bell jangled and Sebastian came through the door, phone clamped to his ear. Immediately and shamefully, the now-familiar fiery flush swept over her, mottling her skin and making Posy feel quite lightheaded as she remembered how the fictional Sebastian of the night before had climbed in through her bedroom window and had his wicked way with her.

'For God's sake, Brocklehurst, why are we still talking about this?' he snapped. Obviously, Piers had decided to spread his evil tidings far and wide that afternoon. 'I told you the site was Grade Two listed and even if it weren't, I have zero interest in going into business with you. Less than zero.'

Posy turned smartly on her heel. With Sebastian otherwise engaged, she had time to lock herself in the tearoom and when Sebastian came after her, she could shout what she had to say through the door.

It sounded like a plan. A really good plan.

'Oh, stop whining, Brocklehurst. No one likes a whiner. Laters. And not so fast, Morland! Where do you think you're going?' Sebastian said before she could take a step, leaving Posy no option but to turn around with a bright and insincere smile on her face.

'Sebastian! I didn't see you come in,' Posy said. He'd brought reinforcements in the shape of Grumpy Old 'Un and Cocky Young 'Un, which was good because now Posy would have witnesses. 'Actually I'm glad you're here because I need to talk to you about something.'

'Really?' Sebastian didn't sound that interested. He gazed around the main room, at all the empty spaces on the shelves, until his eyes rested on Nina who'd come through from the office and was now standing behind the counter pointedly ignoring Cocky Young 'Un, who obviously hadn't bothered to use Sebastian's nefarious app to hook up with her. 'Tattoo Girl, you're looking lovely as ever.'

Nina smoothed her hands down the front of her tight red wiggle dress as if she were brushing away crumbs, then looked up with a pleased smile. 'Yeah, I know. Pity some people haven't got the message,' she added, with another pistols-at-dawn look in the direction of Cocky Young 'Un, who suddenly felt the need to hide behind his older and burlier colleague.

'Anyway, shall we go somewhere we can talk?' Posy suggested, because there was no point in prolonging the agony. 'The office, perhaps?'

'Is it about the tearoom? That friend of Pippa's who doesn't do cupcakes? I hope you sent her packing,' Sebastian said. He rearranged his features into a lip-thinning, nostril-flaring, eye-narrowing sneer yet still managed to look pretty. 'Can't have a tearoom without cupcakes, though I prefer something a bit more rugged when it comes to patisserie.'

'I'm partial to a nice slice of Dundee cake myself,' Grumpy Old 'Un ventured. Posy shot him a vague smile, then turned back to the matter at hand.

'Apart from the cupcake veto, Mattie is the perfect choice to run the tearoom,' she told Sebastian with no small amount of satisfaction, even though she'd promised herself not to get confrontational. 'We shook on it.'

'Honestly, Morland, I can't leave you on your own for one moment without you making rash decisions. You'll have to unshake on it.'

'I will do no such thing,' Posy said, but he was gone, darting through the archway that led to the rooms she'd prepared for painting. Posy gestured for Grumpy and Cocky to come with her and darted after Sebastian. 'I wish you'd stay still long enough for me to have a conversation with you.'

'I didn't get where I am by standing still.' Sebastian crouched down to investigate the paint tins stacked against one wall. 'You should have told me you were getting paint. I can't expect you to pick up all the expenses — and why the devil have you got pink paint? Where's the red? And the black? You can't have pink in a crime bookshop called The Bloody Dagger.'

'Says the man lamenting the lack of cupcakes,' Posy sniped. 'Anyway, pink is only a base colour.'

Except it wasn't, it was an accent colour to be used sparingly but effectively.

'You don't want to be using pink as a base colour,' Grumpy Old 'Un said.

'Make a right pig's ear of it if you do,' Cocky Young 'Un piped up. Posy turned to glare at them.

'All right. OK. Sebastian, I need to tell you something.' She could do this. She *had* to do this. Though maybe it would be better coming from Pippa, who was sure to have some inspirational quotes at hand to ease Sebastian's pain. No, even if Pippa did do the deed, Sebastian would only come and hunt Posy down to shout at her, so she might as well cut out the middleman. 'So, the reason why I bought tins of pink paint is because this is my shop, also my tearoom, and maybe I should have been firmer about this from the start, but there will be no crime bookshop. There will, however, be a bookshop catering for readers of romantic fiction . . .'

'Oh God,' Sebastian groaned and actually collapsed on the floor with no thought at all for his expensive suit. 'Not this again. Somebody kill me now.'

'That could easily be arranged.' Posy stood over him, hands on her hips. She considered putting a foot on his chest to keep him there, prone and at her mercy, but that was probably going a little too far and would lead to nothing good and probably more fevered chapters of *Ravished by the Rake*. 'I shouldn't have carried this on for so long, but Happy Ever After — that's the name of my shop — is going ahead whether you like it or not. That's why I sold all the crime novels at the — '

'You do realise I can see right up your skirt, Morland? And while the view is enchanting, even if you are wearing those passion-killing woolly tights, I thought I'd better let you know before you go any further.' Sebastian then rested his hands behind his head as if he were planning to stay prostrate for quite some time.

Posy leapt away from him as if she'd been scalded. 'Rude! You are so rude!' She flapped her hands in frustration. 'Talking to you is like repeatedly banging my head against a wall.'

'Stop talking then,' Sebastian said helpfully. 'I hope you're not going to be so shrewish with Greg and Dave while they're slaving away.'

'Who are Greg and Dave?' Posy asked, and Grumpy Old 'Un took a step closer.

'Greg,' he said, and yanked his compadre forwards. 'This here is Dave. I see you washed everything down yourself.'

'Yeah,' Posy said, not sure exactly what was going on. 'Um, why?'

'Well, that means we can get straight on with sanding down the woodwork. Best to get that done before we start painting the walls. You wouldn't believe the mess,' Greg said sadly. 'Gets everywhere, the dust. You not got any plastic sheeting to put down?'

'Well, no, I didn't realise I'd need any,' Posy said. She shut her eyes, shook her head in an effort to clear it. 'What do you mean when you say that *you're* going to sand everything down and *you're* going to do the painting?'

'Don't be boring about this, Morland,' Sebastian drawled from his prone position on the floor. 'It's a pity that your sugar soaping frenzy didn't extend to the ceiling. Did you know that you've got dreadful cobwebs?'

'Have I?' She had. They were floating

gracefully down from the light fitting and the very tops of the shelves where Posy hadn't sugar soaped because she figured that nobody would see or care that she hadn't washed the tops of the shelves before she painted them. Then she remembered that cobwebs were not on the agenda. 'Sebastian, I'm doing the decorating myself. There's no money in the budget to hire people to do it.'

'Oh, budgets shmudgets. Greg and Dave are my facilities staff, but all my facilities are in top working order so you can have them for a week or so. It's much more exciting for them to paint *stuff*, than change the odd bulb or mend a dripping tap.'

'Don't they get a say?' Posy turned to Greg and Dave, who were inspecting her decorating supplies and muttering to each other as if they found her supplies severely wanting. 'Perhaps they'd rather not deal with my cobwebs.'

'Makes no difference to me,' Greg said. 'At least you don't play loud music here. Sometimes I can't hear myself think.'

'It's settled then,' Sebastian decided. 'No need to thank me, Morland. You're welcome.'

'It's not that I don't appreciate the offer, but I can't accept any more help from you until I'm absolutely certain that you understand that I'm going ahead with my plans for a romance bookshop. I've been lying to you *for weeks*, Sebastian.'

Posy peered down with a stricken fascination to see his reaction, but Sebastian remained recumbent, his eyes closed, then he gave a delicate snore. 'Somebody wake me up when

280

Morland's done ranting,' he said.

'That's no way to talk about the young lady,' Greg admonished, while Dave sniggered and earned himself a pained stare from Posy, who was going to make sure that Nina never went on one single solitary date with him. 'Not when she's trying to tell you something.'

'I hear the word 'romance' and it immediately sends me into a catatonic state,' Sebastian said.

'You certainly talk a lot for someone in a catatonic state,' Posy said dryly, and Dave sniggered again so maybe he wasn't that bad. 'There will never be a shop called The Bloody Dagger, Sebastian, and now that you know that, I don't mind if you decide to withdraw Greg and Dave's services. I can do the painting myself.'

'Don't be ridiculous,' Sebastian said, suddenly springing up in one fluid movement that would have played havoc with Posy's knees. 'Now, first of all we'll get rid of all this grey paint. And the pink! What were you thinking, Morland?'

Posy clenched her fists, her jaw, even her buttocks and flung her head back so she could plead for some divine intervention. 'God, give me strength!'

'What's God got to do with anything? Come on, let's make this brief because I really do have to dash.' Sebastian dashed. One moment he was standing there with a supercilious smile on his face, the next he was striding back into the main shop. 'Do keep up, people!'

Once again, Posy was forced to scurry after him. 'Sebastian, please, will you stop and listen to me!'

Sebastian whirled around and fixed her with a concerned look that didn't sit well on a face that was best suited to mocking. 'Yes, you're having jitters, second thoughts, all those sorts of things, but it will be fine. We'll open The Bloody Dagger to a rapturous reception, money will flow into your till and then you can show me your undying gratitude. I'll pencil that in for three months from now. And oh, by the way, Sam's fine. Surprised you never asked how he's getting on. Everyone in the office loves him and he's doing a fantastic job on the website with only the tiniest bit of supervision.'

'He is? And he's having a proper lunch every day, isn't he? Not just Japanese KitKats but vegetables — '

'Oh, that reminds me. Here, catch!' Sebastian drew something out of his pocket and threw it at Posy, who attempted to catch it but failed. A salted caramel KitKat landed at her feet. 'Typical!' Sebastian snorted, then he was striding around the perimeter of the room. 'Black paint. Lots of black paint. With touches of red for dramatic effect.' He shot a baleful look at the shelves. 'Such a pity there are so many books in the way. It's hard to know where to put the mural.'

Posy hardly dared ask. 'The mural?'

'The mural!' Sebastian confirmed. He turned to Dave. 'Where's the mural?'

'Right here, guv.' Cocky Young 'Un had been carrying a document tube, which he unscrewed with a considerable flourish to pull out something, which he then gently unfurled.

282

Posy struggled to make out what it was. Some kind of template or . . .

'A bloody dagger!' Sebastian announced with relish. 'I was thinking maybe the wall behind the counter would be the best place for it, what do you think, Morland? We're meant to be in this together, aren't we? Or, how do you feel about having it on the floor as you walk in? Obviously we'll paint the floorboards black first, it's a faff but can't be helped, and then as soon as people walk through the door, they'll be confronted by a knife positively dripping with blood.'

'No,' Posy muttered to herself. 'No. No. Hell no!'

'What was that, Morland?' Sebastian asked as he took the template from Cocky Young 'Un and placed it on the floor. 'Probably needs to be a bit bigger. We'll have to get this blown up. Do you have a photocopier?'

'Over my dead body!'

'No need to shout.' Sebastian looked quite hurt. 'It was a simple enough enquiry.' He looked around the assembled company, including a young girl who'd been rifling through their sale box but had decided that Sebastian was far better entertainment. 'Will somebody go and get this copied for me, then?'

'No! Nobody is going to get it copied for you,' Posy shouted. Shouted so loudly the back of her throat protested at its cruel treatment. She skidded across to where Sebastian was kneeling down, snatched up the template of the bloody dagger and ripped it in two. It made an awful sound. But Posy ripped the two pieces into four, then eight, which fluttered to the ground when she threw them away from her in disgust. 'There is going to be no bloody Bloody Dagger. There never was! We're opening a romance bookshop called Happy Ever After in less than three weeks and there is bugger all you can do about it. Do you hear me? Do you *actually* hear me, Sebastian?'

He had to have heard her because Posy was screaming now and it was funny really, because Posy had agonised over this moment. She'd rehearsed a hundred passionate yet panicked speeches where she defended her actions in the strongest possible terms, but never once had she envisaged that she'd end up turning into a demented harpy in an effort to get her point across. Already she was regretting it. Not the telling, Sebastian had needed to be told, but the screaming, the ripping of the template — and Posy was pretty sure that she'd stamped her foot several times as well.

Their one potential customer had fled, Nina was staring at Posy in horror, Verity had come out of the back office with a look of disbelief on her face, and Greg and Dave were staring at their feet, the floor, the walls, anywhere but at Posy and Sebastian, who was doing a convincing impersonation of a cartoon character who'd had an anvil dropped on his head.

Sebastian struggled to his feet, his usual elegance gone. 'Morland,' he said brokenly. Then he folded his arms, his head sunk so low that his chin was resting on his chest. 'Morland, you mean that all this time, you've been . . . but you

. . . I can't believe you've betrayed me.'

Posy was coming to her senses. Her rage began to fizzle out as shame washed over her. Yes, she'd had to be cruel to be kind and the volume of her shrieking had finally pierced Sebastian's skull when reason had failed, but she hadn't expected him to seem so . . . wounded.

'I think betrayed is a very emotive word, Sebastian,' Posy said carefully.

He raised troubled eyes to her. 'It's the only word that sums up how I feel.'

It was all coming back to Posy now. How a younger Sebastian had had his every whim indulged by his various nannies, Lavinia, Mariana, even her own younger self. It was the sorrowful look in his eyes, the pout, the way he clasped his hands together like he was praying for mercy that did it. Made you forgive him. Let him get his own way time after time.

But she wasn't that little girl any more. Besides, they wouldn't be having this horrible, awkward conversation if it weren't for Sebastian charging about doing whatever he wanted when he wanted and never taking into account anyone's feelings but his own. 'I did try to tell you. More than once,' Posy said, her tone not quite so conciliatory now. 'But as usual you only hear what you want to hear.'

'You didn't try very hard,' Sebastian flung at her. By now she'd have expected him to be shouting and flouncing around like he usually did, taking books off the shelves and waving them about as symbols of Posy's *betrayal*, but he wasn't doing any of those things, just standing there and looking at Posy as if she'd confessed to kicking puppy dogs for cheap thrills. 'But what about our crime bookshop?'

Posy glanced helplessly at Nina and Verity, who offered no help beyond shrugging back in unison. 'It was *your* crime bookshop, your wild idea. I wanted no part of it.'

'That's not true,' Sebastian said indignantly, his voice sharper now. 'You agreed.'

'No, I didn't,' Posy's voice was getting sharper too. 'I said, 'Fine, whatever.' That's not agreement. That's 'For God's sake, shut up!''

'All these weeks you were taking advantage of my good nature. Morland, you completely played me! We even had a brainstorm!' Posy winced and wanted to cover her ears with her hands because Sebastian roared the last word. 'Your staff were in on it too? Sam? Pippa? I'm the last person in London to find out.'

'Not the last person. Sam and the others were unwilling accomplices — '

'Very unwilling,' Nina piped up from the cheap seats.

Posy glared in her direction. *Et tu, Nina?* Then she turned her attention back to Sebastian, who was glowering now rather than pouting. It occurred to Posy that she'd never seen Sebastian angry before and she didn't much want to see him angry now. 'And Pippa didn't know but she suspected and forced a confession out of me. Said that we both needed to PPM. So, I've pointed out what's really going on, you're processing, now shall we move on?' she suggested hopefully. 'And for the record, I do

286

feel bad about it. Honestly. And I am sorry.'

'You have a very odd way of showing you're sorry.' Each word was like a chip of ice.

'I am sorry.' It wasn't a lie. Posy had never wanted to live a life of subterfuge. And though she'd expected Sebastian to be angry, she'd never imagined that she might hurt his feelings. His ego, his pride, yes, but not the gooey soft centre that lay beneath them. 'Please, Sebastian. Think about this calmly. I was quite clear from the very start that I was opening a romance bookshop, but you wouldn't listen. I know it was wrong of me, but I pretended to go along with your plans because I badly needed a project manager and there was no way we could have afforded one without — '

'No! No! NO!' Sebastian turned a full three hundred and sixty degrees then stabbed the air with his index finger. 'You've gone too far this time, Posy! Played me for a fool. An absolute fool — and Lavinia was an even bigger fool to leave the shop to you.'

'Leave Lavinia out of this!' It was Posy's turn to shout, to point a finger at Sebastian. 'And don't you dare talk about Lavinia like that!'

'Well, you don't have the first clue about how to run a successful business. Seriously, have you any idea how ridiculous your plans for the shop are? Why I didn't pay any attention to them? Romance! It's laughable. When are you going to start living in the real world, Posy? It's time to wake up!' Sebastian *was* angry now and it was horrible. Worse than horrible. He wasn't shouting, wasn't even gesturing — his hands were shoved tightly into his pockets — and he was doing what he always did best: saying hurtful things in that cutting voice. Made even more hurtful because they skirted the truth. Echoed all the doubts in Posy's head. 'This is the very last time I try to help you.'

'*Help* me? You call that helping? You're deluded!' Posy groaned in sheer frustration. 'None of this would ever have happened if you'd only listened to me! Oh, but the mighty Sebastian Thorndyke thinks he knows everything and has the right to ride roughshod over anything that gets in his way: my feelings, my plans, my shop. It's *my* shop, not yours! When will you realise that?'

She sounded like a petulant child; maybe that was why Sebastian scoffed. 'Not your shop for much longer,' he said nastily. 'I'm the executor of the estate. I have the power of veto . . . '

'No, you don't,' Posy said, but she was on shaky ground now. She'd had to sign so many forms and Lavinia's lawyer had asked if she wanted her own solicitor to look over them, but Posy had been sure that Lavinia, dear sweet Lavinia, would never do her wrong. Despite her best efforts to diligently read everything she was meant to sign, there had been so many forms, so many clauses, and she'd skipped breakfast and it was nearly lunchtime by the time it got to the last few pages, so Posy had given up being diligent. 'You're bluffing.'

'I am not bluffing,' Sebastian said coldly. 'If I think that the future of the shop is in jeopardy, then I can take control of it.'

'You know *nothing* about selling books! It's not even a little bit like your tawdry apps! It's not for you to say whether the shop's in danger. You're not qualified to make that call,' Posy protested hotly as icy fingers played an arpeggio up and down her spine.

'And neither are you,' Sebastian informed Posy.

The two of them stood there in the empty shop — Nina and Verity had fled to the safety of the back office while Greg and Dave had retreated to the furthest reaches of the furthest anteroom and were having a hushed conversation about primers.

Apart from that, it was so quiet that Posy could hear the thump of her heart and Sebastian's ragged inhalations as they faced each other, so close that they were practically nose-to-nose.

'You can't do this, Sebastian. Be reasonable for once in your life,' Posy said, and it was one more rash, wrong thing to say, because there was a glint in Sebastian's eyes that was nothing like the gleam where they were sparring with each other, bickering. It was colder, crueller, utterly without any humour.

He stepped away from her. 'My lawyer will be in touch,' he said, then stalked out of the shop.

Ravished by the Rake

Thorndyke lay with her until daybreak. He had taken her virtue, her dignity, everything she had to give, and in return he had turned her from anxious spinster to a woman, ripe and ready to be plucked again and again and again.

Now they lay there side by side, his magnificent body like marble hewn from the hands of Michelangelo himself, as they heard the household begin to stir.

'I must take my leave of you, Miss Morland,' Thorndyke said, his voice husky with spent passion. 'I trust my attentions . . . pleased you?'

Posy smiled, though truly there was little to smile about when she, an unmarried woman with responsibilities heaped heavy on her fragile shoulders had welcomed the most scandalous rake into her bed. For ultimately she had welcomed him, not just with lips and treacherous limbs, but with rapturous sighs and throaty moans of encouragement too. Her reputation had been the only currency she possessed for she had little in the way of coin, and now she no longer had that.

Yet still she smiled. 'My lord, since when have you ever had any regard for what pleases me?'

'Touché, Miss Morland,' Thorndyke told her, his dark eyes heavy and slumberous. (NB Can eyes be heavy? And slumberous? Wouldn't he just look like he was knackered?) *'But I'm not the kind of rogue who thinks only of his own pleasure. I trust I rose to the occasion? That you weren't disappointed?'*

In truth, as Thorndyke had schooled her in the art of lovemaking, he'd been the most tender, the most obliging of men, but as the sun slanted through the curtains that Posy had hastily drawn last night as Thorndyke began to disrobe, so the magic they'd experienced by flickering candlelight was already a fleeting memory.

'For once you didn't disappoint, as well you know. But the Ton, indeed all of London, know that you take your pleasure where you can find it, then move on to fresh sport,' Posy said sadly, though she knew it would be madness to expect anything more from Thorndyke. Certainly not his heart.

'But are your charms worth fifty guineas?' Thorndyke asked, and suddenly his eyes were as cold and as hard as the diamonds that Posy was sure that he possessed in abundance. 'I think not.'

'Sir! What do you mean?' Posy scrambled to cover the flesh that Thorndyke had worshipped for hours, but his hands closed around her wrists. 'Was I merely a game to you?'

'Aye! And one I tire of playing,' Thorndyke said with a cruel laugh. 'I had a ten-guinea wager with Sir Piers Brocklehurst that I could take you. Oh, come now. Wipe the frown from your face. I'm not a complete monster, I'll take the ten guineas off your debt.' He flung Posy away from him and rose from the bed as she cowered amid the crumpled linen that had borne witness to her ruination. 'Perhaps Piers might be willing to pay the rest in return for your favours, but I fear not. He likes fresher flowers.'

'How could you do this to me? After what we shared? The intimacies? The promises you made?'

'I made no promises to you, Miss Morland,' Thorndyke sneered as he dressed with a slow ease as if he were entirely comfortable. 'The only promise I made was to myself years ago, that I would not let a woman treat me the way you always have, with contempt, with damnable haughtiness as if it were I that was some lowly guttersnipe and not the other way round. If you were a man, I'd have challenged you to a duel for your insolence and disregard, but you are not a man so I sought my revenge as best as I could.'

'You blackguard! You scoundrel! Would that I were a man, I would dash your brains out with my bare hands!' Posy rose up on her knees, dragged her gaze away from the cruel curl of Thorndyke's lips to light on the tumbler sitting on the night-stand. She snatched it up and threw it at his damnable face.

Thorndyke caught the glass in one hand. 'Is that the best you can do? What a ridiculous excuse for a woman you are!' He laughed mirthlessly. 'Now, I must away. Retire to purer climes.'

'Go!' Posy screamed. 'And may Satan himself be at your heels!'

Thorndyke paused in tying his cravat — and how Posy wished that it were a garrotte. 'I fancy you'll be better acquainted with hell than I am, for it will be the debtors' prison for you if you don't pay off your debts.' He bowed mockingly. 'And now I must bid you farewell, madam,' he said, then leapt out of the window just as Little Sophie knocked on the door.

17

The day after their spectacular row, Posy had half expected Sebastian to burst into the shop and act as if nothing catastrophic had ever happened. 'Oh, Morland, as if I'd set all manner of legal nasties on you,' he'd drawl.

Posy would even have welcomed Sebastian banging on about The Bloody Dagger, but his silence was deafening. His absence palpable. He had been around an awful lot lately, most days in fact, and now he was gone. Probably marshalling an army of expensive lawyers to wrest control of the shop and evict Posy and Sam. It didn't bear thinking about.

Not that Sam seemed at all concerned about the uncertainty of their future. Nina had told Sophie all about the row when she'd popped in to pick up her wages. Sophie had then told Sam, who was more worried that Sebastian might call a halt to his work experience than the fate of the shop.

'Sebastian's in a terrible mood,' Sam had reported back the next day. 'He's shut himself in his office and when he does come out, everything's wrong from the taste of his coffee to the latest app he has in development. I told you it was wrong to lie to him,' he'd added piously, which was rich coming from Sam, who regularly lied about the state of his coursework, but even so, Posy knew that he was right.

Posy had emailed Pippa: 'I tried to PPM Sebastian

but it went horribly, horribly wrong. Sebastian's upset and furious. I'm upset and furious too, but also so sorry that I let things go so far. I know I've put you in an awkward situation, but could you try to explain my point of view?'

It was no use. Posy had received an out-of-office auto-reply informing her that Pippa wasn't responding to emails as she was in Vancouver taking part in a fully immersive global think-tank on the future of global think-tanks.

Anyway, there wasn't much time to worry about the Sebastian situation as Posy's life was pretty immersive too. Her days largely consisted of meetings with sales reps, publicists, marketeers and editors. It should have been thrilling, because Posy had never been the kind of person who had meetings before, but it wasn't thrilling. None of it. Especially the meeting she'd had with the business advisor at the bank, who'd looked over Verity's painstaking cashflow projections with a jaundiced eye, told them that as things stood the business couldn't survive another six months, then asked them if they wanted to extend their overdraft limit.

It was now mid-April. The skies over Bloomsbury were a glorious duck-egg blue and the trees that lined the squares had burst into pink and white blossoms, but for Posy the world was as grey and bleak as it had been in the days after Lavinia died.

She had the same sense of impending doom, a creeping menace, a feeling that all her endeavours were doomed. Sam had just come back from Wales, where he'd stayed with their grandparents for the bulk of the Easter holidays so he could drive them mad by starting every sentence with the words, 'Yeah, well, Sebastian says . . . ' Posy had fondly imagined that, without Sam around to cook and care for, she could easily get on with what needed to be done. And yet she hadn't managed to get so much as halfway there.

Posy tried to ignore the new and nagging voice in her head that told her in no uncertain terms that the shop wouldn't be ready to reopen as Happy Ever After in just over two weeks' time. Then it was two weeks. Then one week and six days. The countdown was on, the clock was ticking, and there was so much to do and Posy hadn't even started painting yet.

Mindful of the conversation she'd heard between Greg and Dave, Posy had done some judicious googling and confirmed that it was necessary to apply primer to the shelves before painting them. She had never fully appreciated how many shelves there were, let alone how much primer would be needed to cover them. And then she had to wait for each shelf to dry before she could start painting. And of course, Posy hadn't thought to buy the quick-dry primer. Sebastian was right, she was a ridiculous woman who couldn't do anything properly.

Then there were the vintage display cabinets that Posy had bought on eBay, even though Verity had said that they couldn't afford them. It now transpired that the cabinets had somehow disappeared halfway down the M1.

The outside of the shop still had to be painted

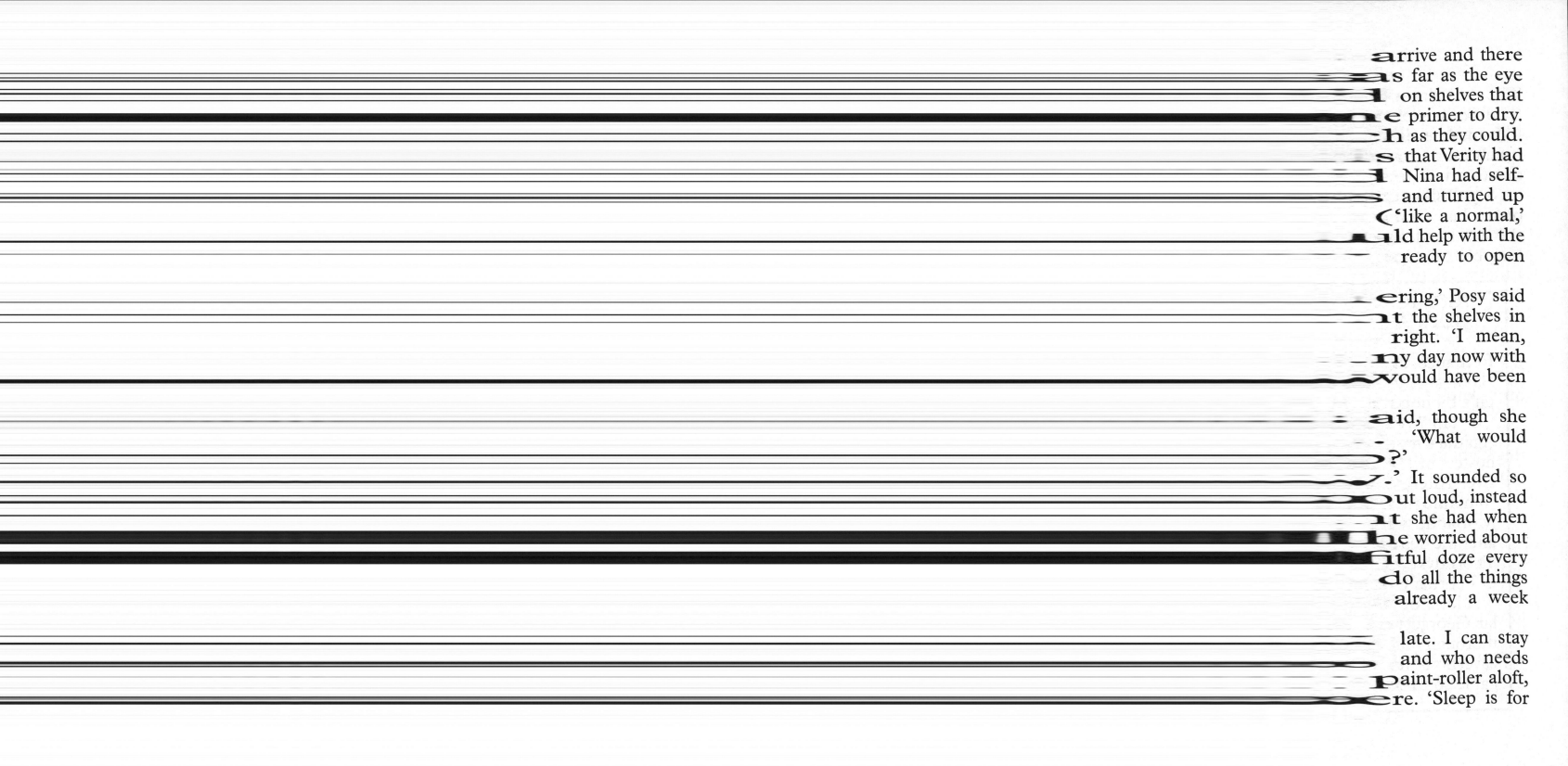

★

The next day the inte...
The Bookseller hit the...
   It made everything t...
much more terrifying.
of no return several w...
on a collision course ...
plans, her dreams, in ...
she was hurtling throu...
tangible to grip on to.

ICONIC LON...
GETS A NEW ...

Romance is in the...
Bloomsbury booksh...
tal's bibliophiles.
   From 7 May, the...
Agatha Drysdale, S...
hostess in 1912, will
Ever After, 'a one-s...
romantic fiction ne...
Morland, who was
after the death of Ag...
Thorndyke, Booken...
in February of this ...
   A lover of Regenc...
lar Georgette Heye...
thorough redesign of
cavernous interior ...
gable so that reader...

but it went horribly, horribly wrong. Sebastian's upset and furious. I'm upset and furious too, but also so sorry that I let things go so far. I know I've put you in an awkward situation, but could you try to explain my point of view?'

It was no use. Posy had received an out-of-office auto-reply informing her that Pippa wasn't responding to emails as she was in Vancouver taking part in a fully immersive global think-tank on the future of global think-tanks.

Anyway, there wasn't much time to worry about the Sebastian situation as Posy's life was pretty immersive too. Her days largely consisted of meetings with sales reps, publicists, marketeers and editors. It should have been thrilling, because Posy had never been the kind of person who had meetings before, but it wasn't thrilling. None of it. Especially the meeting she'd had with the business advisor at the bank, who'd looked over Verity's painstaking cashflow projections with a jaundiced eye, told them that as things stood the business couldn't survive another six months, then asked them if they wanted to extend their overdraft limit.

It was now mid-April. The skies over Bloomsbury were a glorious duck-egg blue and the trees that lined the squares had burst into pink and white blossoms, but for Posy the world was as grey and bleak as it had been in the days after Lavinia died.

She had the same sense of impending doom, a creeping menace, a feeling that all her endeavours were doomed. Sam had just come back from Wales, where he'd stayed with their grandparents for the bulk of the Easter holidays so he could drive them mad by starting every sentence with the words, 'Yeah, well, Sebastian says . . . ' Posy had fondly imagined that, without Sam around to cook and care for, she could easily get on with what needed to be done. And yet she hadn't managed to get so much as halfway there.

Posy tried to ignore the new and nagging voice in her head that told her in no uncertain terms that the shop wouldn't be ready to reopen as Happy Ever After in just over two weeks' time. Then it was two weeks. Then one week and six days. The countdown was on, the clock was ticking, and there was so much to do and Posy hadn't even started painting yet.

Mindful of the conversation she'd heard between Greg and Dave, Posy had done some judicious googling and confirmed that it was necessary to apply primer to the shelves before painting them. She had never fully appreciated how many shelves there were, let alone how much primer would be needed to cover them. And then she had to wait for each shelf to dry before she could start painting. And of course, Posy hadn't thought to buy the quick-dry primer. Sebastian was right, she was a ridiculous woman who couldn't do anything properly.

Then there were the vintage display cabinets that Posy had bought on eBay, even though Verity had said that they couldn't afford them. It now transpired that the cabinets had somehow disappeared halfway down the M1.

The outside of the shop still had to be painted

find their romantic fix, whether it's Jane Austen or Jackie Collins, YA or erotica. Happy Ever After will also have a larger online presence and carry a range of exclusive branded items including tote bags, stationery and specially commissioned scented candles. The relaunch will kick off with a week-long Festival of Romance, including author events, a bloggers' tea party and a champagne reception. The tearoom attached to the shop, which has been closed for several years, is also set to reopen before the end of the summer.

'All the greatest art and literature is inspired by love and I think, when times are hard, there is no better cure than reading a novel that will guarantee you a happy ever after,' Posy says. 'Although the shop will have a different name, a different owner and different stock, I still think of it as a family business. That's why I'm so happy that Sebastian, Lavinia's grandson (Sebastian Thorndyke, digital entrepreneur and creator of HookApp), is involved with the shop. He's been instrumental in developing the online side of the business, along with my younger brother, Sam.

'With Happy Ever After, the ethos of Bookends will live on; that we find our best friends, our best selves, in the pages of the books that we love the most.'

It was a very positive piece, though Posy wished that it had been spiked and never run. She could also have lived without the photograph of herself smiling gummily in one of the new Happy Ever After T-shirts she was insisting all the staff wore. Even Nina, who was very put out about the whole business and the effect it would have on her Fifties pin-up girl aesthetic.

As soon as the article went online, Posy was deluged with an avalanche of emails and phone calls from book editors, bloggers, friends who toiled away in other bookshops, and even literary luminaries that Posy had only ever gawped at from afar at industry parties. Not one single person took her to task for desecrating the memory of Bookends with her tawdry romance novels. 'I know Lavinia would be very, very proud of you, my dear,' one of Lavinia's friends, a publishing *grande dame*, had emailed Posy. 'I can't wait to visit Happy Ever After and buy my granddaughter her first Georgette Heyers.'

It should have spurred Posy on. She should have channelled her inner Pippa and reminded herself that quitters never win and winners never quit. That she owed it to the spirit of Bookends and the memory of Lavinia and her parents to push on through. But it didn't.

It was too late for that and time for a reality check. Posy stepped out of the back office, walked over to the door, locked it with icy cold hands then flipped the sign to closed.

Tom was behind the counter. 'It's only half four,' he said. 'Though I suppose we're not busy and we've hardly got any stock out to sell. Do you want me to grab a paint roller?'

Posy shook her head. Even that small movement was enough to dislodge a few tears that she'd been trying to hold back. She turned slightly so Tom couldn't see her wet cheeks. 'No. We're meeting on the sofas in five minutes.'

It actually took less than a minute for them to assemble with matching expressions of gravitas and for Posy to surreptitiously scrub at her face with a tissue. 'What's up, boss?' Nina asked. 'If you want me to work late again, I can. I'm meant to be meeting some random for a quick drink, but I don't mind bailing. Not at all.'

Posy shook her head again. This time she was determined to keep the tears reined in. 'No, you don't need to work late. None of you do, because even if you did, we're never going to be ready to reopen. We can't . . . I can't do this.' Posy could feel the throb in her throat, her head and heart pounding in unison and her eyes were smarting because the tears weren't that far off again. About two minutes away, she reckoned. 'The big relaunch: it's not going to happen on Monday.' Her voice caught on the last word.

'But it has to,' Verity breathed. 'We have a week's worth of events booked, and our finances are already stretched to breaking point as — '

'I know, but it's Friday afternoon. Even if we worked flat out all weekend, there's no way the shop will be finished. It's not just the painting; we haven't even started work outside and I've had to postpone the signwriter twice already. We haven't inventoried the new stock, never mind

shelved it. The display cabinets are still MIA
. . . It's a mess. The whole thing's an absolute
shambles. And what does it even matter when
Sebastian bloody Thorndyke could waltz in here
at any moment and take the shop away?'

'Maybe you could see a lawyer?' Tom said, like
Posy hadn't thought about that herself. It had
occurred to her, but any lawyer that she could
afford would be no match for the legions of
fancy lawyers Sebastian must keep on retainer.

'We could get the main room ready and do the
other rooms bit by bit,' Nina suggested in a weak
voice, because they all knew it was a half-arsed
solution to a full-blown problem.

'I'm sorry. I've let you all down. I'm a terrible
boss. I should never have agreed to take the shop
on.' Posy didn't get any further than that, not
because she was suddenly crying so hard that she
couldn't talk, but because she was also suddenly
enveloped in a group hug. Squashed against
Nina's bosoms, which had to be getting soggy
from the tears now flowing unchecked, her head
resting on Tom's shoulders, while Verity, who
didn't do group hugging, kept patting Posy's
back and saying, 'There, there.'

They left soon after that. Posy insisted. There
was nothing to be done and Sam was loitering in
Camden with a posse of school friends and
wouldn't be back until he'd run out of money
and was hungry, so Posy was on her own in the
empty shop.

Bookends. It had always been her happiest
place. Her safe haven. But all that had changed.
Now its lovely homely smell of books had been

302

eradicated by the overpowering, catch-in-the-back-of-the-throat stench of fresh paint. Its shelves were bare. Its nooks and crannies were obscured by boxes of books and stationery.

You always destroy the things you love. Posy had read that once somewhere and it was so true. In trying to turn Bookends into something new, she'd destroyed its spirit; that special and unique feeling it had always had so that whenever Posy had walked through the door, it felt as if she were home.

That wasn't all that had been lost. Posy couldn't believe how much she could miss someone who spent most of his time being an absolute thorn in her side. A Thorndyke in her side. Couldn't believe that she'd only just realised that she missed him . . .

Posy nearly jumped out of her skin as someone tapped on the door. She saw a tall figure and her heart salmon-leapt, then sank back to its usual place.

It was only Piers Brocklehurst. The very last person she wanted to see. Or, at least, one of the top five people Posy didn't want to see.

She unlocked the door. 'Nina's not here,' she said by way of a greeting. 'Anyway, I thought she'd dumped you.'

Piers smiled cagily. But then he did everything cagily. 'I'm not here to see Nina. It's more of a business call.'

Posy had been staring down at his Gucci loafers. There was something about a man who didn't wear socks with his shoes that squicked her out, but his words jolted her out of her reverie and she raised a troubled face to his.

'I thought you and Sebastian had called it quits.'

Piers' smile upgraded to something so sinister that it should have come with a parental advisory warning. 'Oh, I wouldn't say that exactly. In fact, Sebastian is why I'm here.'

It went from bad to worse to absolutely catastrophic. 'Sebastian sent you? I don't believe it!'

Posy had been expecting a notice to quit the premises from Sebastian's lawyers. Or, worse, a bunch of heavies turning up to evict her and Sam there and then, so they could change the locks and board the place up.

She'd half-hoped that Sebastian would come in person so she could try to reason with him. Not that reason and Sebastian were on speaking terms, which was obviously why he thought it was fine to send Piers around to do his dirty work.

'That man is something else!' Posy exclaimed. 'Can't even deliver the bad news in person.'

Piers' usually smug face momentarily assumed a discomfited expression, but then he shrugged. 'Thorndyke always was a deeply suspect sort.'

'I expected better from him,' Posy said, because there had still been that certainty deep in her gut that Sebastian would relent. See the error of his high-handed ways. So much for her gut feeling!

'Look, I know this is hideously awkward, but can I come in? Take a few measurements?' Piers was already in, sidling past Posy. 'It's all right, you'll hardly know I'm here.'

Then, as Posy stood there blinking, he was moving past the counter and into the back office.

'Oi!' She half-heartedly shouted then decided to . . . just not. Let Piers do his worst with his tape measure. What did it matter how long or wide things were when he and Sebastian planned to tear the whole building down anyway?

Except, wasn't it meant to be listed? And why was she letting this happen? To lose her home and her livelihood and the place where she had all the best memories of her parents and Lavinia . . .

Lavinia would never have stood for this, Posy thought, glancing at the photo of her and Perry on the central table. Neither would Posy's parents. And if she did stand for this, or rather did nothing and let Sebastian walk all over her, then she was letting them all down. Desecrating their memory. God, how ashamed they'd be if they could see her now. How disappointed they'd be that Posy let a little thing like a few unpainted bookshelves defeat her.

She'd been down for so long that it felt odd to feel something else. Something that flamed in her belly and made Posy clench her fists and her toes.

They could still relaunch on Monday. If Posy and the rest of the staff worked like dogs all weekend, they could get the main room and maybe the anterooms on the right done, and curtain off the left-hand side of the shop that led to the tearoom.

It wouldn't be the all-singing, all-dancing

grand reopening Posy had envisaged, but it would do. And as for Sebastian bloody Thorndyke, he wasn't taking her shop away. Posy shook her head decisively. She'd do another piece for *The Bookseller* denouncing Sebastian. Get the whole of literary London to join her cause. Start a petition, a Kickstarter, a campaign to keep the shop in the hands of the woman who loved it.

And if the worst came to the worst, then Posy would channel the shop's first owner, the honourable Agatha, and chain herself to the front door in true Suffragette style.

But first she had a shop to get ready for reopening on Monday morning.

'Piers?' As soon as she called his name, he popped his head through the archway on the right.

'What's up?' He knitted his brow together. 'You're very flushed. Has this come as a nasty shock? Well, time you found out what Thorndyke's really like.'

Posy would have sworn that she knew what Thorndyke was like. That underneath the bluster and the bravado, he wasn't that bad, just really, really irritating. And hadn't Nina said that Piers was actually more evil than bad? As Posy recalled Nina's pithy summing up of the man she'd been on two dates with, suddenly Piers' smile seemed quite snake-like and his slicked-back hair and dead eyes gave him the look of a cartoon villain. Posy felt a frisson of fear. And then she remembered that other nonsense, which she'd never got to the bottom of, about Piers trying to dig up some dirt on her . . .

She pushed the frisson of fear away. Verity might not be able to deal with Piers, but she could. 'You have to leave,' Posy said firmly. 'I don't care what Sebastian says, I'm not budging. Bookends is opening for business as Happy Ever After on Monday morning if it kills me.'

'No offence, but you don't look like you'll be ready to reopen on Monday as anything,' Piers said silkily.

Posy waved an airy hand about her. 'Pfffttt! Of course we will!' She put her hands on her hips. 'Now I don't mean to be rude but I've got loads to do, so I'm afraid I'm going to have to kick you out.' Posy hoped her smile would take the sting out of her words, not that she really cared either way.

She moved towards the door. Piers moved with her. 'I understand,' he said. 'I really do. Good on you for standing up to Thorndyke. About time someone did.'

'I know!' Posy agreed in a surprised voice, as she would never have imagined Piers to be an ally. Nevertheless, she followed him out of the door so she could be sure he was on his merry way. 'He's such a bully! Flouncing about, issuing orders, never listening to anything anyone says. Who does he think he is?'

'And those poncy suits of his,' Piers snorted. 'I don't get what women see in him.'

'Not this woman!'

'You know, you've got class, Posy. Not like Nina. All arse and no class, that one,' Piers said. And they'd been getting on so well too.

Posy gave Piers her most crushing look. 'That's an awful thing to say about any woman, but especially one of my clo — '

'What's down here?' Piers wasn't listening to her, which prompted a tiny pang as Posy thought of the other person who never listened to her. He pointed to the hatch, secured by two weather-beaten wooden doors, in front of the shop's big bay windows. 'Does that lead down to a cellar?'

'What?' Posy glanced to her left. 'Oh, that's the coal-hole. No! Don't unlatch the doors. There's nothing to see in there. Please, Piers! I said not to open it! What is it with you men who never listen?'

Piers had opened the hatch and was now peering into the black abyss of the coal-hole. 'There is something in there.'

Posy shuddered. 'Yeah — spiders. Come on, close the door now.'

'What's that thing in the corner? Something shiny?'

Against her better judgement, Posy crept closer to squint into the gloom. 'Probably an old display stand. Come away from — Ooooooof!'

A sudden push and Posy pitched forwards, hands outstretched, into the blackness. She landed on her hands and knees, the wind knocked right out of her, dust between her fingers, under her nails, in her mouth so she coughed frantically, cobwebs brushing against her face, her hair. She awkwardly pivoted around and tried to scramble to her feet but before she could ask Piers what the hell he was playing at, Posy had one brief glimpse of the gloating look of triumph on his face, then the doors slammed shut on her.

'Let me out!' Posy shouted, her words echoing back at her. 'This isn't funny, Piers!'

There was no reply.

The last time she'd been locked in the coal-hole, which only opened from the outside, she'd been small enough that she could stand upright, but Posy was too tall to do that now. Best she could manage was a stooped crouch. It really was a hole too — couldn't even give itself airs and pretend to be a room or a cellar — a small underground antechamber to store coal and, latterly, boxes of crap that Posy didn't know what else to do with.

The air was dank and damp, not that there was much air. Posy sat down, legs splayed in front of her. She couldn't see a thing, but from the smarting and stinging she could tell that she'd scraped her palms and knees, her jeans were torn, and there was a distinct possibility that she only had enough oxygen to last a few more minutes.

Then she felt something slither over her hand where it rested on the floor. Something slithery and spidery and when she strained her ears, she was sure she could hear the skittering of claws. Rat claws. She screamed then. It was a weedy, reedy scream because Posy had already had the wind knocked out of her when Piers pushed her to her doom.

Because, oh God, even if she didn't suffocate down here, she'd be eaten alive by spiders and rats. They'd find her bloodied, gnawed-on corpse days from now. Maybe the rats would go to town on her so hard that she'd have to be identified by her dental records. She squeezed her eyes shut so hard that she saw stars dance across her vision, closely followed by the heart-wrenching scenes that would ensue when the coal-hole doors were opened.

The grisly discovery. The forensic people, bringing out a pile of bones picked clean by the rats — all that remained of the person formerly known as Posy Morland. Sam having to be held back by Pants and Little Sophie as he tried to embrace what was left of his beloved sister. Nina and Verity, clutching each other for support and sobbing. Tom, a broken man, rocking helplessly to and fro. Sebastian clad all in black, his features harsh and unforgiving, vowing to the heavens that he would avenge Posy's death.

The stars danced away as Posy shook her head in disbelief. What was wrong with her? Writing *Ravished by the Rake* had ruined Posy. She'd become so melodramatic. No one, let alone Sebastian, was going to avenge her death.

Because Posy was going to choose life. Today was not the day that she was going to die from rat bites. Or from lack of oxygen. She had far too much to do for one thing.

By now, her eyes were adjusting to the darkness, able to make out indistinct shapes, and her gaze hit upon an old stool that had been consigned to the coal-hole after Sam's last-but-one growth spurt. It had metal legs. It would do.

Steeling herself and praying that she wouldn't come nose to nose with a rat, Posy got as upright as she could then hobbled over to the far corner, picked up the stool and scuttled back to the hatch doors. There were no sounds of life from outside. Not even the echo of Piers' mocking laughter.

'Let me out!' she tried one last time, but Piers was either long gone or doing God knows what to the shop. Tom had cheerfully told her about a Grade Two-listed pub in Oxford that had been burned to the ground by a property developer who'd had his plans to build a block of flats in its place turned down by the council. 'You let me out right this minute!'

All that wood! All the books! The shop would burn to the ground in seconds!

Posy took a deep breath, ignored the pain in her hands and knees, summoned up every ounce of strength that she possessed and swung the stool at the coal-hole doors as hard as she could.

They remained defiantly shut, no matter how hard and often Posy banged at them. Eventually she had to put the stool down so she could catch her breath and get the feeling back in her upper arms. She was just stretching her aching limbs when the doors were suddenly wrenched open and as Posy blinked rapidly, the light making her eyes water, she saw a familiar face gazing down at her.

'Morland! Thank God, you're all right!'

18

'Sebastian!' Posy gasped. 'What on earth are you doing here?'

'What does it look like I'm doing?' Sebastian snapped. He held out an imperious hand. 'Come on, I haven't got all day.'

Posy could have done without being rescued by Sebastian, of all people. She was quite capable of rescuing herself, but she grabbed hold of his hand and let him haul her out of the coal-hole into the fresh air with a very unflattering grunt like she was some kind of heffalump.

'How could you?' she demanded as soon as she was back on the blessed cobbles of Rochester Mews. 'How could you send that vile man to do your dirty work!'

'I didn't send anyone to do anything!'

'Then what was Piers doing here?'

There was a large bang from inside the shop and they both turned to see a tsunami of grey paint splatter across the window as if it had been tossed there by an angry sea, then slide inexorably down the glass so the inside of the shop was suddenly hidden from view.

'What the hell!'

'What the ever-loving hell!'

Posy closed her eyes, because she couldn't bear to look. Then she opened them again and no, this wasn't some awful living nightmare. It was really happening. Her hands flew to her face in horror. 'My shop! It's ruined! Why would he do something like that?'

'I have a pretty shrewd idea why!' Sebastian declared, his face almost as grey as the paint that dripped down the window to gather in a puddle on the wooden floor. 'Don't worry, Morland, I'm going to kill him!'

And with that, Sebastian dashed through the door into the shop, Posy staring after him. She'd said the shop was ruined, but she hadn't realised the half of it. It wasn't only the window. There was paint everywhere, except where it was supposed to be. Paint on the floor. Paint over the counter. The boxes of books. On the display table at the centre, the photo of Lavinia and Perry obscured — which of all the terrible things was the terrible thing that made Posy want to burst into tears.

The one thing not covered in paint was Sebastian as he came towards Posy, dragging a squirming, swearing Piers with him.

'Caught this wanker trying to escape out the back,' Sebastian panted, because Piers was struggling to free himself from the headlock that Sebastian had him in. 'Like the despicable coward that he is.'

Piers shouted something but it was muffled by Sebastian's arm against his windpipe.

'Look what you've done!' Posy couldn't even muster a shout. Her voice was a tiny, broken thing. 'What have I ever done to you?'

'Get off me, Thorndyke!' Piers twisted free of Sebastian's grip and stood there, loathsome and sweating. 'Nothing personal, Posy, except, actually it was personal because you told Nina to have nothing more to do with me after I'd taken her out for two very expensive meals and didn't get so much as a blow job to show for it.'

'You are disgusting!'

Piers preened as if it were a compliment. 'And as for you, Thorndyke. You haven't changed from the wretched little sneak who ratted me out and almost had me expelled from Eton. I was willing to let bygones be bygones, be the bigger man —'

'You know absolutely nothing about being the bigger man. It will come as no surprise to hear that Brocklehurst used to torture the lower boys who fagged for him,' Sebastian told Posy, fingers flexing and his hand back on Piers' windpipe.

'I have no idea what that means.' Posy glanced upwards. God, there was even paint on the ceiling. 'I thought you two had buried the hatchet. That you were going into business together to demolish Rochester Mews and turn it into a gated housing development for the filthy rich?'

'I was never going to do that!' Sebastian insisted furiously, as if he were offended at the very suggestion. 'I'm looking at various options for the mews and I was curious to see if Brocklehurst had changed for the better when he got in touch. Evidently not, as we can see.'

'Don't give me that. I drew up plans, told you who to pay off at the council.' Piers clenched his fists and threw Sebastian a look of such pure, unadulterated hatred that Posy felt something twist in her belly, as if Piers had plunged a knife into her guts. 'I had a member of the Saudi royal family all ready to sign on the dotted line for a five-million-pound penthouse apartment. Have you any idea how much sucking up I had to do? And then you decide to back out with some bullshit about the site being Grade Two listed? You're nothing but a pretentious wanker, defending the rights of people who are too lame to stick up for themselves.' Piers puffed out his chest. Posy was surprised that he didn't ping his horrible red braces while he was at it. 'Haven't you heard of survival of the fittest? I don't know why you're so keen on protecting Posy like some poncing knight on a white horse. Even you, Thorndyke, could do better.'

Sebastian paused to consider it for longer than was necessary because Posy obviously hadn't suffered enough for one day. Not that Posy needed protecting and it wasn't as if she was under any illusion that she was in the same league as the women Sebastian preferred, but still.

'Depends what you mean by better,' Sebastian conceded. 'But she's my Posy and you shut her in the coal-hole, which is so twenty years ago. And you've ruined the shop, which Posy loves, so now I'm going to ruin you.'

'Ha! I'd like to see you tr — ' Piers got no further because Sebastian charged at him, head down like an angry bull so they both went flying out of the door.

They rolled about on the cobbles for a bit then staggered to their feet. Piers shouted, 'En garde!' and then they both lunged at each other with an outstretched arm ending in a rigid fist.

Because they were posh boys. Their only knowledge of fighting came from fencing lessons at Eton. Posy rolled her eyes as Piers and Sebastian danced around each other, occasionally reaching out to try and jab, then retreating. There seemed little danger that they might actually hurt each other, which was a pity because Piers really deserved a good arsekicking.

'Pathetic!' she muttered. 'This isn't helping anyone.'

Then Piers somehow managed to manoeuvre his way around so that he had Sebastian against the shop window and was in a perfect position to pummel him mercilessly while Sebastian shouted inarticulately and tried to fend him off.

When Piers grabbed Sebastian by the lapels, Sebastian's shouts became clearer: 'Not the suit! Don't touch my suit!'

Posy had had enough and she wouldn't be responsible for her actions if they crashed through her window. She darted back into the shop, circling the small lake of grey paint on the floor, and ran to the back office where she picked up Verity's big, heavy Roget's Thesaurus that she always had to hand for when she was writing letters of complaint.

Then she ran outside again, where Piers still had Sebastian pinned to the shop front and was just about to take a swing at his face. Not Sebastian's beautiful face! Posy sent the book crashing between Piers' shoulder blades with all the force that she possessed. Which was a lot of force. She hauled boxes of books about for a living, after all.

It felt very satisfying, so Posy did it again.

'That's for my shop!' she shouted, as Piers cowered away from her and Sebastian was able to stagger free. 'And that's for trying to punch my Sebastian, and that's for putting your grubby hands on Sebastian's suit, and this one . . . this one is for Nina and this one is for my shop again, and this one is . . . '

'Enough! Get this mad bitch off me!' Piers was hunched over, his arms up to protect his face.

'Ugh! And that's for calling me a bitch!' Posy whacked Piers on the back with the Thesaurus one more time then Sebastian put a tentative hand on her arm.

'I come in peace, Morland!' he said, because it was obvious that Posy's blood was up and one wrong word, one black look, and he'd know the business end of the Thesaurus too. 'I hate to interrupt, I really do, but you should probably stop now.'

Posy stopped, after one more whack 'for pushing me in the coal-hole', then stood panting and paint-splashed. She could also tell from the way her cheeks felt as though they'd been put though a blast furnace that she was redder than she'd ever been in her life.

Piers took a step back. He was panting and when he straightened up, he winced. He was red-faced too but shot Posy the blackest look. 'I'm going to have you for assault.'

'Whatever!' Posy put her hands on her hips. 'I'm going to have you for criminal damage.'

'Assault, maybe even GBH, trumps criminal damage every time,' Piers said, and he was already pulling his phone out of the pocket of his stupid posh boy red jeans. Posy felt afraid. Very, very afraid.

'Probably does,' Sebastian said, brushing down the lapels of his suit. Posy didn't know how he'd managed it, but Sebastian didn't have a drop of paint on him, he looked as box fresh as ever. 'But in the time it takes you to call the police, I can have your bank accounts emptied and any unsavoury images on your computer emailed to your mother. Hacker friend of mine, you see. Lives in Mumbai. Lovely chap, but you don't want to get on the wrong side of him. How is your mother, by the way? Does she still live in Cheam?'

Piers stilled and then shoved his phone back in his jeans. 'Bastard!' he spat, but he was lumbering away at a sharp pace. 'Bitch!'

It almost killed Posy to let Piers have the last word, but everything she wanted to yell after him involved obscenities and several suggestions as to what he could do with various parts of his body, so she stayed silent and watched as Piers broke into a run as he turned the corner.

'Of course, I could have handled Brocklehurst all by myself, but who knew you had such a violent streak, Morland? I certainly won't be doing anything to incur your wrath ever again.'

'Can I have that in writing?'

'I never sign anything without my lawyer present.'

With Piers gone, Posy had only Sebastian to deal with.

Only Sebastian. Posy missed the carefree days

when Sebastian had been a very annoying, but mostly infrequent visitor. Since Lavinia's death, he was always underfoot, always making it impossible for Posy to sink back into her old inertia. Even in his absence, he'd continued to take centre stage in *Ravished by the Rake*. Which meant that Posy was constantly thinking about him. About the two of them, in all sorts of compromising positions, bodices getting ripped, mouths being plundered . . . She was glad it was dusky enough to hide her inevitable blushes, but not dusky enough to hide the carnage inside Bookends.

'I don't know where to start,' she said, mostly to herself because Sebastian was now uncharacteristically silent, probably because all his attention was focused on his phone. 'Maybe this is the universe's way of telling me to give up.' She sighed. 'You win. You can have the shop.'

There was a silence that stretched before them until Sebastian finally raised his head and looked around him. 'Sneaky plan there, Morland. Trying to stick me with this mess, but it's not going to work. Have you got any paper towels?'

As usual, Posy was struggling to follow. 'What?'

'Paper towels, absorbent rags, that kind of thing. Look, I've googled it.' Sebastian shoved his phone in Posy's face. 'It says here that it's imperative that we clean up as much of the paint as possible before it dries. Come on, Morland, time is of the essence.'

It really was. Posy didn't even have time to laugh when Sebastian climbed into the overalls that Nina had insisted on wearing so she wouldn't get paint on her jeans and T-shirts.

They were far too short on him — a good ten centimetres of leg protruded from the bottom.

Instead she gathered supplies and got to work. It was amazing what could be done with warm water, Fairy Liquid and pretty much every towel that Posy possessed.

Of course, there were casualties. The books that had been on the centre display table. One of the light fittings seemed to have shorted. And one box of books was ruined, but it was only one box of books, it could have been so much worse. They'd already had plastic sheeting down on the floor and over the sofas, on account of previous incidents of paint splattering when Posy had tracked grey matt emulsion into the main shop when she'd been called to deal with a customer.

They worked steadily for over an hour, Posy steeled the whole time for the inevitable sarcastic remarks from Sebastian. About how she could never do anything right, how she was a fool for letting Piers throw her into the coal-hole. But nothing. Deathly, intense silence.

At one point she asked him: 'Is the mews really Grade Two listed?'

'Of course it isn't! But I had to tell Brocklehurst something to get him off my back.' Sebastian became very interested in the slick of paint he was removing from the counter. 'And to allay your fears that I was going to turn the mews into a car park or some such. You're always determined to think the worst of me.'

'Yes, but . . . I don't *always* think the worst of you.'

Sebastian refused to be drawn in, though. It

was very disconcerting. As Posy mopped up the last of the paint from the blessedly empty shelves, she stole a look at Sebastian, who was wiping the paint off of the framed photograph of Lavinia and Perry. He did look rather out of sorts, his hair in disarray, but he'd been fighting and he was currently swathed in a white boiler suit from B&Q, which left even Sebastian sartorially challenged.

'I think we're done,' Posy said, at last. 'It's ironic, isn't it, that we've just had to clear spilt paint off shelves that needed to be painted anyway?'

Sebastian didn't reply, which was unprecedented. But it was the look on his face that gave Posy cause for alarm. His brow was furrowed, lips pushed out in a ferocious pout — when he wasn't opening his mouth then closing it again, as if all his words had deserted him.

'Are you all right?' Posy asked with some concern. 'Can I get you anything? Water? Tea? Do you want to sit down?'

'I'm not all right.' Sebastian slid down the nearest bookcase until his arse made contact with the now-clean floor. 'I'm far from all right.'

There couldn't be that much wrong with him if he was capable of acting like a drama queen, Posy thought to herself as she perched on the arm of the sofa across from where he was sprawled on the floor. 'So, what's up?'

'I think you know the answer to that already.' Sebastian folded his arms and his head sank so low that his chin was resting on his chest. 'I'm very confused, Morland.'

'Really? I'd say you're the least confused person I've ever met.' It was Posy's turn to frown. 'You're decisive. A man of action. I wouldn't ever describe you as confused.'

He raised troubled eyes to her. 'It's the only word that sums up how I feel after reading that *Bookseller* piece and — '

'You read *The Bookseller?*' Posy asked incredulously. 'Why would you do that?'

'I told you I'd subscribed.' Sebastian pinched the bridge of his nose. 'Sometimes, I think you don't listen to a word I say, Morland. It's very disheartening.'

Posy rolled her eyes. 'Right back at you.' She took a deep breath and moved from her perch to kneel in front of Sebastian. 'I don't want to argue with you any more. Proper arguing, where we don't speak for days and days; that was awful and I don't want it to happen again. But I really did try to tell you more than once that I was opening a specialist romance bookshop. I was quite clear about it. But I am sorry that I lied to you and pretended to go along with your plans for The Bloody Dagger just so I could take advantage of having a project manager. You have to believe me when I say I'm sorry, because I can't stand this awful silence between us.'

'I can't stand it either. And it is possible that I *might* have overreacted once you finally confessed, but I never dreamed that all that time you were . . . ' Sebastian shook his head as he found that, once again, his words were inadequate for the task at hand. 'You were . . . '

'A great fat liar?' Posy prompted.

'Machiavellian.' There was a hint of a smile playing around Sebastian's lips now. 'Duplicitous. Sneaky. I rather underestimated you, but you have to admit, Morland, The Bloody Dagger was an amazing idea,' Sebastian grumbled.

Clearly he wasn't about to let this go any time soon. 'I hate crime novels, Sebastian. I hate them.' Posy found herself taking Sebastian's hand and lacing her fingers through his to take the sting out of her words and Sebastian was obviously off his game, caught off guard, because he let her, though he watched her with wary eyes as if he doubted her intentions. 'They always start with a murder, a body, something awful happening, and I've had too many awful things happen in my life to want to read about them in my spare time. Do you understand?'

'I do,' he said quietly, and he leaned forwards, so for a moment their foreheads were touching and it seemed as if they were breathing in the same perfect rhythm. Posy couldn't have said how long they stayed like that until Sebastian broke the spell. 'But romance, Morland. Those books are preposterous,' he spluttered, but he hadn't let go of her. His thumb was rhythmically stroking the back of her hand, which was oddly soothing. 'They give women this false hope that one day they'll meet a knight in shining armour, when there's no such thing. It's an impossible ideal and you'll only be disappointed, if you insist on looking for a man that's like one of your romantic heroes.'

'I know real-life isn't like a romantic novel,' Posy said, and Sebastian's hand tightened around hers. 'My God, how I know that, but I still want to believe it's true. Maybe that's why I get a vicarious thrill from reading novels about two people overcoming all these obstacles, mostly of their own making, so they get to have their happy ever after. I know I should be getting myself out there and dating, but since my parents died, I've been stuck.'

Tears were suddenly streaming down her face. Sebastian delved into his overalls and pulled out his pocket square. With a gentleness that Posy wouldn't have believed he was capable of, he dried her eyes. 'Now blow your nose,' he instructed her.

'I don't want to get snot on your hand-kerchief,' Posy said, because he was right, life wasn't the least bit like a romantic novel. 'There's probably quite a bit of soot up my nostrils too from the *hours* I spent in the coal-hole.'

'I'd rather you ruined it than sat there with a runny nose,' Sebastian said. 'Not a good look, Morland. You're not a pretty crier, so I suggest you stop right now. And by the way, you weren't in the coal-hole for hours. I saw Brocklehurst push you in as I came into the Mews. You were down there for a minute. In fact, it barely qualified as a minute.'

'It was hours,' Posy protested. 'I stared death in the face. That takes longer than a minute.'

They were back on familiar ground. Posy glared at Sebastian who looked utterly unrepentant, then she snatched the hankie from him and blew her nose loudly and wetly and tried to ignore the horrified face Sebastian pulled when he caught sight of the streaks of black snot on his previously pristine pocket square.

'Thank you,' Posy said. He really was the most annoying man, but there was so much more to him that that. 'You know, I have been stuck, but these last few months I've felt like I'm finally getting unstuck, moving forward. And actually you're a huge part of that.'

'I am?'

'Of course you are!' Posy gestured at the shop. 'You might not believe in Happy Ever After . . . '

'The name alone makes me want to retch . . . '

'Oh, give it a rest, Sebastian! I couldn't have done all of this without you,' Posy told him, but Sebastian simply shrugged as if unmoved by her vote of confidence. 'If you hadn't been constantly badgering me and bombarding me, I'd never have got going. I'd have kept on making lists and fretting whenever Verity told me that we had no money.' She shuffled around so she was sitting next to Sebastian, because all that kneeling on a hard floor wasn't very comfortable. 'It feels like I've been sleepwalking for years, but you . . . you're like a really rude alarm clock: 'Morland, wake up, you lazy slut!' '

Sebastian huffed his annoyance. 'I don't sound like that — and I have *never* called you a slut.'

'You called me a slattern,' Posy reminded him. 'It's the same thing.'

'I'm sure it isn't. It just means your housekeeping skills are practically non-existent. You should think about getting a cleaner, Morland. It can't be good for you and Sam to have so much dust clogging up your lungs. Why are you smiling? I wasn't being funny.' He nudged her with a sharp elbow. 'I'm deadly serious.'

'I'm smiling because I've finally figured you out,' Posy said.

'I doubt that too. I'm an enigma, a puzzle, a mystery, a paradox — '

'Well, you certainly love the sound of your own voice. But you're right, you are a paradox. You say the meanest things, Sebastian. You say rude, hurtful things, but I've decided that they don't count for anything when the things you *do* are so kind, so thoughtful.'

'If you lapse into cliché and say actions speak louder than words, I will walk out or cry, I haven't decided which,' Sebastian said, but actions *did* speak louder than words and he didn't leave so Posy decided it was about time that they had a drink.

She went to get the emergency bottle of Pinot Grigio from the office fridge. Sebastian took a swig when she passed it to him and didn't even bitch about backwash. Though he did have a few choice things to say about the quality of any wine that came in a screw-top bottle.

Then, fortified by a good few gulps of Pinot Grigio, Posy said, 'Since Lavinia died, apart from when you've been insulting everything from my hair to my taste in literature, you've been there for me. You've helped me, loaned me staff, done all sorts of male bonding and techy things with Sam that I can't do, and you bought him a whole new wardrobe — though I'm still a bit cross about that. Even that whole business with

Lavinia's sofa was you trying to be nice.'

'I'm not nice, I'm the rudest man in London,' Sebastian said defensively. 'But I couldn't rest another minute knowing that you risked skewering an internal organ every time you sat down on your old sofa.'

'Which leads us on to these shenanigans with the shop,' Posy continued. 'I get that you thought you were trying to help, that you thought a specialist crime bookshop would be a better business model than a specialist romance bookshop . . . But, Sebastian, if there's one thing I know it's that you can't have a successful business unless you're passionate about it. And I am passionate about romance novels. I know the market, I know the readers. And if it does all go horribly wrong — it already *has* gone horribly wrong — then at least I believed in what I was doing. I went down with a fight.'

'It hasn't gone horribly wrong,' Sebastian said, as he took the bottle she was holding out to him. 'I won't ever let that happen. Even if it means I have to buy every last soppy, cloyingly sentimental book in the shop.'

'There you go again,' Posy pointed out. 'Rude and lovely in one sentence. I don't know how you do it.'

'Years of practice.' Sebastian checked himself. 'Anyway, I'm not lovely. I'm rude. Vile. Horrible. Seducer of virgins and happily married women. Architect of the moral decline of society: that last one was in the *Spectator*.'

'Oh, do shut up, Sebastian,' Posy said. 'Otherwise my next project will be rebranding

327

you as the Loveliest Man in London.'

'Don't go soft on me, Morland,' Sebastian drawled. Posy was getting rather misty-eyed. Although he drove her absolutely potty, she was rather fond of him. After quite a few gulps of Pinot Grigio, she was fonder still. In fact, she didn't think she'd ever felt quite so fond of him as she did in that moment. It was a relief when Sebastian broke the mood by struggling to his feet. Then he held out his hand. 'You might as well show me this shop of yours.'

Posy let Sebastian haul her up (though he winced with the effort, but insisted it was because of the after-effects of his fight with Piers) then she gave him the full, guided tour.

It was dark by now, so Posy turned on the rest of the lights and showed Sebastian into the furthest-flung ante-rooms on the right so he could see what the shelves looked like painted grey, rather than having grey paint flung at them, the names of each section picked out in clover pink. Showed him the boxes and boxes and boxes of books waiting to be shelved. Showed him photos of her vintage display cases, which were still MIA, and the actual stock that would go in them: the candles, cards, notebooks, mugs. Showed him the bookmarks that would be slipped into every book sold and the tote bags and T-shirts. Showed him the tiny bookcase that would house their only crime novels: Dorothy L. Sayers' Peter Wimsey and Harriet Vine novels, a handful by Margery Allingham and Ngaio Marsh, and a few other select titles. The display table that would always be dedicated to Lavinia's favourite books, and finally Posy led Sebastian to the doors to the café, which had been cleared out and prepared for painting.

Sebastian had stayed mostly silent the entire time and let Posy talk, though he hadn't been able to resist teasing her about her obsession with tote bags. Now he looked around the silent, empty shop and said quietly, 'Not bad. Not bad at all, Morland. I wish I could take more of the credit, but this is all down to you. This is your vision, probably why you insisted on buying those tatty old display cases when you could have got nice new ones, but it does have a certain charm.'

Coming from Sebastian, this was high praise. Posy didn't know what to do with it, so she ducked her head. 'Well, the thing is, it's not going to be finished before the grand opening on Monday. There's no way. I've accepted that, even if I'm not happy about it. If I put my shoulder to the wheel, forget about sleeping, I can get the main room and the rooms on the right done and stocked over the weekend, and everything else will just have to wait.'

Sebastian nodded, and thank God, he didn't make any smartarse remarks about how Posy went to pieces when he wasn't around to help. She'd have had to brain him with the wine bottle if that were the case, and just when they'd established a truce too.

Sebastian peered through the glass double doors that led through to the tearoom. 'What's happening in here?'

Posy pulled a face. 'Mattie hopes to open

329

before the end of the school holidays, but we need to get the kitchen up to spec first . . . '

'I haven't been in here since . . . well, since it was last open.' Sebastian hadn't touched her since he'd hauled her up off the floor, but now he took Posy's hand again. 'I keep expecting to see Angharad, your mother, suddenly bustle out of the kitchen with a plate of flapjacks.'

They both looked beyond the counter to the kitchen door, but it remained closed. 'So do I,' Posy sighed. 'But no matter how much I wish it, it's not going to happen.'

Sebastian gave her fingers a squeeze. 'Like you said, you can't stay asleep for ever. Lavinia always told me that you simply needed a little more time. It's been long enough now, Morland, you have to wake up.'

'Lately, I feel like I'm wide awake.'

'I never even told you why I came over today,' Sebastian said, his voice husky as if he were coming down with a cold, or more likely, had inhaled too many paint fumes. 'It was the piece in *The Bookseller*. Even though we were on no-speakers, you thanked me. Said I was family. I suppose you see me like an overbearing older brother.'

'Well, definitely the overbearing part,' Posy muttered, and she was glad that she was standing in a shadowy spot so he couldn't see the inevitable flush on her face. Sebastian wasn't the least bit like a brother to her. You didn't write Regency smut about men you considered to be an honorary brother. There was wrong, and then there was wrong, wrong, wrong with added bits of wrongness.

Posy steeled herself to look up at Sebastian and he looked down at her. He was silent again, which was always unnerving, and for the life of her, Posy couldn't think of a single thing to say. They were still holding hands and it was starting to feel awkward. Not exactly awkward but tense, even charged. Posy was suddenly, startlingly aware of her hand when before she'd never given much thought to it just being there on the end of her arm. Now she was terrified it might grow clammy or develop an involuntary twitch and she was on the verge of tugging herself free when Sebastian suddenly let go.

Then he cupped her face and, as her heart started to go pitter-patter, like a Regency lady of good character who'd never known the touch of a man, he pressed his lips to her forehead. 'This is ridiculous,' he said.

Posy felt inexplicably shy. 'It is, isn't it? I had no idea that you . . . that I . . . God, it really is ridiculous. Ludicrous, even.'

Sebastian ruffled her hair in a very big-brotherly and anti-climactic fashion before taking a hasty side-step away. 'I mean, now that we're friends again, honorary brother and sister and all that rot, there's no point in you only getting a half-finished website as well as a half-finished shop. I kept asking and asking Sam if he had the finished artwork. No wonder he was so shifty.' He gave Posy a disapproving look. 'I can't believe you dragged Sam into your subterfuge.'

The tension was broken. Although it seemed the tension had only been one-sided anyway and there was absolutely no reason why Posy should be disappointed. This was Sebastian and he wasn't the loving kind. He was the shag-them-and-leave-them kind. And, anyway, *this was Sebastian!* And she was Posy and they were like oil and water, or stripes and polka dots and a whole host of other things that didn't play well together. Also, he was very rude. He was now clicking his fingers in her face. 'Stay with me, Morland! Don't go back to sleep!'

'Stop it! You'll have my eye out,' Posy snapped. 'And for the record, Sam was appalled with all the subterfuge. I had to use extreme emotional blackmail to stop him from grassing me up.'

'Good. I'd hate to think that Sam was in league against me too,' Sebastian said. He clapped his hands together. 'So, that artwork? Are you going to give it to me sometime before the next Ice Age rolls by?'

'It's on one of those USB stick thingies,' Posy said. 'Upstairs. I'll go and get it.'

'Off you pop then,' Sebastian said. 'Judging by the state of your flat, will ten minutes be long enough for you to find it?'

'I know exactly where it is,' Posy said, but that was only because Sam had put his foot down and insisted that all thumb drives, USB cables and other computery things must have their own designated drawer.

'If you're not back in half an hour, I'll send up a search party,' Sebastian warned her.

As Posy marched up the stairs, she still wasn't sure how they'd moved so quickly from something to absolutely nothing.

19

After a frantic scrabble to find the thumb drive in the drawer of computer gizmos, Sebastian took it from her and left with a flippant, 'Don't go back to sleep now, Morland!'

Sleep was the last thing on Posy's mind. There was absolutely no way she was ready to snuggle down for the night when Sebastian had awoken all sorts of feelings in her. Feelings she'd wanted so desperately to have with someone like Jens, where there was every possibility that those feelings might be returned. She'd have to tamp them down somehow, as though she was putting out the dying embers of a bonfire, kicking earth over them to stop them smouldering. It was much safer that way.

Besides, sleep wasn't an option when Sam was cavorting around Camden Town where druggies and hoodies and all sorts of other reprobates roamed. Until he was home, unmugged and unharmed, Posy would have to wait up for him.

She was tempted to fire up her computer and dash off another chapter of *Ravished by the Rake*, but this evening had proved, beyond all shadow of a doubt, that no good could come of it. While she could give fictional Posy the ending she deserved, real-life Posy knew that there could be a world of pain and suffering lying in wait after the hero and heroine kissed, pledged their undying love then rode off into the sunset together.

So, as Posy walked back upstairs, she abandoned all thought of finding comfort in the pages of a book. Tonight there was no way that would provide the magic cure-all that it usually did. Instead, she took the key that hung on a hook in the kitchen and unlocked the door of her parents' room.

Posy hadn't been lying when she told Sebastian that she came in here all the time. But she only ever stayed long enough to run the vacuum over the floor, straighten up things that didn't need straightening because there was no one around to make a mess. Posy never lingered.

The room was just as her parents had left it, so that if they came back they could slot back into place as if they'd never left. Her mother's brushes, her make-up, the family photos in frames were still on the dressing table. The book her father had been reading, using an old postcard to mark his place, was still there on his nightstand.

Posy had turned off the radiator a long time ago and, though the day had been warm, the air in the room was cold and stale. She could no longer smell the honeysuckle sweetness of her mother's perfume, the old-fashioned powdery scent of her father's hair pomade.

She looked around for one long moment, then took a deep breath, set back her shoulders and vowed to do what she'd never had the courage to do before.

On the top shelf of the wardrobe were shoeboxes stuffed full of photos and birthday cards, Christmas cards, school reports, thank you letters. The old lined exercise books that her father had written his poems in: hundreds of pieces of paper and card, thousands and thousands of words that made up two lives.

Posy had hidden them up here, out of sight, never looked at them, tried not to think about them, but when Sam arrived home, a prompt five minutes before his curfew, he found her sitting cross-legged on the floor, surrounded by memories, and crying so hard that she shook from the force of her sobs.

'Posy! What are you doing in here?' At first she hardly heard him, then the panic in his voice, the shrill note that made him sound much younger than fifteen, punctured her grief and she tried to will the tears away, brushing furiously at her damp cheeks with shaking hands. 'Oh, please, don't cry.'

Sam was her baby brother. Posy looked after him. She took care of him. Made his health and happiness her number one priority. But tonight it was Sam who knelt down and took Posy in his arms, rocking her gently as he stroked her hair.

It seemed to take forever for her sobs to gradually turn to shuddering breaths. Sam scooched around so he was sitting alongside her, his arm around her shoulders. 'Are you all right now?' he asked anxiously.

Posy sniffed, then nodded. 'Yeah. Oh God, I'm so sorry. You shouldn't have had to see me like that.'

'It's OK. I don't mind,' Sam said unsteadily. 'Did something happen?' His gaze came to rest on the half-empty bottle of Pinot Grigio. 'Are you drunk?' he added, in a more accusing tone.

'Hardly! Sebastian came over earlier and drank some of that. I've only had about a glass. Maybe two glasses.' Posy felt calmer now, like she'd needed a really good weep to blast away the cobwebs.

'Did he say something to upset you?' Sam persisted. 'Because you don't ever come in here . . .'

'Well, I do . . .'

'Only to vacuum, and you're rubbish at vacuuming so it only takes you five minutes. And you've got all this stuff out.' Sam very gently touched the edge of a photo, then snatched his hand away like he'd been burnt. 'You never get this stuff out.' He touched the photo again. 'When was this taken?'

Posy picked up the picture so she could have a better look. 'It's the summer ball in their final year at Oxford, so that would have been, um, let me think . . . 1986.' Both of them looked so young, not much older than Sam; her father in a second-hand suit and pork-pie hat, her mother in a Fifties ballgown strewn with poppies. 'They were both twenty-one. Born a month apart. Did you know that? Mum in November, Dad in December.' A distant memory suddenly floated in front of her and Posy grabbed it with both hands. 'For one month every year, Dad would tease Mum that she was so much older than him and she'd get cross and say, 'Ian, it's only one bloody month!'' She shot Sam a look from under her lashes. 'Do you think you might go to Oxford? No pressure, but it would be nice to think that you were following in their footsteps.'

Sam bit his lip. No matter that for a short while their positions had been reversed, now he looked very young and unsure as he took the photo from Posy. 'Sometimes I worry that I'm forgetting what they looked like,' he said quietly. 'Cause, like, we don't have any pictures of them around. I mean, I know why we don't, because it would upset you, but sometimes it's hard to remember them.'

They shifted again so now it was Posy with her arm around Sam. She stroked his hair back from his face and then kissed his cheek. He was obviously feeling out of sorts, a bit adrift, because he let Posy fuss over him. 'I'm sorry,' she said. 'It's been too painful for me . . . this is the first time that I've looked at any of these things since I packed them away. If I didn't have any reminders of them, then I thought I wouldn't miss them so much, that I could just pretend that they weren't really gone, but I never stopped to think about how that might make you feel. Do you hate me for it?'

'Course I don't,' Sam said stoutly. 'And anyway I found these videos on YouTube of Dad reading his poetry. In one of them, you can just make out Mum standing by the side of the stage — but I don't like to watch it too often because it makes me feel sad and weird, and then I understand why you don't like to talk about them.'

That wasn't right. 'Don't I?' Posy frowned. 'I'm sure I do.'

'No, you don't, Pose.'

'How odd. I think about them all the time.' Posy leaned across to kiss Sam's cheek again. 'I'm sorry, Sam, I've tried my best but I've just been making it up as I go along. You know, if you want to talk about Mum and Dad, if there are things you want to know, don't ever think you have to keep quiet.'

Sam rested his head on Posy's shoulder. 'OK, as long as you promise it won't upset you. I don't like it when you cry. Proper crying. I can handle it when you cry because it's your special lady time.'

They grinned because the last time Posy had had her 'special lady time', she'd cried because the oven had started smoking and set off the fire alarm and she'd had to bash it with the broom to make it stop shrieking. Posy stirred through the pile of photos on the floor in front of her. 'I've bottled all this stuff up for too long. It's not doing either of us any good, is it? We should take a Sunday afternoon to go through all the photos together and pick out our favourites, put them in frames. Anytime you want to look through any of this, you know where the key is.' As she said the words, Posy realised how stupid they sounded. 'In fact, there's no reason to lock the door. It's so silly.'

'What about all their stuff? Clothes and things.' Sam brushed his fringe out of his eyes. 'Don't you think it's about time that we sorted through it?'

Posy waited for the pain to pierce through her, but there was only a dull throb. If she could bear a stranger, Mattie, in the tearoom, then she

338

could easily sort through a room whose occupants were long gone, not coming back to wear their clothes, finish the books they'd started to read. Sebastian had been right when he said that she'd turned her parents' bedroom into a shrine. She'd been so worried that she'd lose sight of them, but if she carried them with her, filled the flat with photos of their precious faces, shared all her stories with Sam, then they'd always be there.

'This is an awfully big room,' Posy noted as she looked around the space. It did seem bigger and emptier now she looked at it properly instead of seeing the two people who used to fill its space.

'It is, but it shouldn't take that long,' Sam said.

'It's bigger than both our rooms.' Posy winced as she levered herself up. She was stiff from sitting for so long. 'Your room is hardly big enough for a single bed and cupboard. You shouldn't have to do your homework all hunched up in a tiny gap on the floor.'

'I don't mind,' Sam said. 'Anyway, sometimes I go downstairs and use the office.'

Posy's mind was made up. There was nothing sad or painful about the idea she'd just had. In fact, it made perfect sense. 'You should move in here,' she said. 'You could have a proper desk by the window. We'll get you a new bed too, because it's not going to be long before your feet dangle off the end of yours, and you'll have loads of shelf space. You can have your friends over, instead of always having to go round to theirs.

What do you think?'

'But if it would make you feel sad, like you didn't want to come in here to say goodnight, then I can stay in my room.' Sam looked around. 'Though, this is much bigger. Could I paint the walls black?'

There was only so much that Posy could agree to. 'No, you couldn't,' she said aghast. 'Could you be any more emo? And I'm not doing this out of the goodness of my heart. I can use your old room to put my overflow books in. Might even turn it into a little reading nook.'

'I'm surprised you don't want to turn this room into a ginormous reading nook,' Sam grumbled. 'Force me out on to the streets, so you can have my room too and use it to store even more books in.'

Posy put a finger to her chin. 'There's an idea. How soon can you be gone?'

Sam huffed and rolled his eyes and when Posy caught him by the sleeve and pulled him up into a punishingly tight hug, he tried to wriggle free. 'I love you,' she told him fiercely. 'I love you so much. I will always try to do the right thing by you, even if I get it hideously wrong at times.'

'Now who's being emo?' Sam muttered, but for one second he hugged her back and whispered just as fiercely, 'I love you too, Pose. I don't know what my life would have been like if you'd decided you didn't want to be lumbered with me. And I know I can be a pain in the arse, but I do appreciate everything that you do. Now get off me!'

It might have been the wine, or her crying jag,

or maybe it was finally making peace with her grief or sheer exhaustion from too much painting and too much worrying, but Posy slept the sleep of the righteous.

★ ★ ★

Posy didn't know what had woken her up, but she was pretty sure she could hear a noise coming from the shop and when she stumbled downstairs, she was amazed to find it full of people.

That wasn't right. It wasn't opening time. It was still the middle of the night and she was in her pyjamas and . . .

'Mum? Dad?'

There were her parents. Much younger than Posy remembered them. Wearing the clothes they'd worn at that long-ago Oxford summer ball.

'Posy! There you are!' It was Lavinia and Perry, younger too, come to life from their photograph that sat on the centre display table.

There was another woman with them. In an old-fashioned dress with a bustle and a sash draped across her chest that said 'Votes for Women'.

'Agatha?' Posy gasped.

'That's the Honourable Agatha Cavanagh to you,' Agatha informed Posy icily. 'What have you been doing to my lovely shop?'

'Yes, Posy, what have you been doing? What a mess you've made!' Lavinia exclaimed, and Perry nodded his head in agreement and now Posy realised that her visitors were all covered in grey paint. 'How wrong I was about you!'

'You started off so well but you really are terrible at being a grown-up,' her father chimed in. 'It's a wonder that you've managed to keep Sam alive all this time.'

Her mother sighed. 'Which is more than can be said for Bookends. I always taught you that if something was worth doing, it was worth doing well — and yet you're going to reopen a shop that's only half-finished. Not even half-finished.'

It was lovely to see them all again. Close enough that Posy wanted to rush and hug them all, except Agatha, who looked very imposing, but they were all staring at her with such disappointment, such dismay.

'Well, yeah, I know the shop has looked better, but — '

'You should have left the shop to Sebastian, Lavinia,' Perry sniffed. 'He had such great plans for it. And Sebastian's a doer, not a ditherer. You do dither so, Posy.'

'I know I do,' Posy said. 'But I've been trying not to.'

'I cannot have my shop in such a state of disarray, and selling only the shallowest of books.' Agatha jabbed Posy with a Votes for Women placard that had suddenly materialised in her hand. 'Bookends becomes Happy Ever After over my dead body!'

'No disrespect, Agatha, but you kind of are already dead.' Posy twisted her hands. 'I'm sorry. I'm so sorry. I've been working so hard, but everything's gone wrong.'

'Posy! Posy! Posy!'

The five of them were moving closer to Posy and she wanted to cry. Wanted her parents to look at her with love and hold her and tell her that everything would be all right. Wanted Lavinia and Perry to be proud of her and for Agatha to be pleased that her legacy continued, but instead they just chanted her name, like they were getting ready with pitchforks and a bonfire.

'What?' The figures were coming closer and closer until Posy realised that they weren't her ghosts but a very much alive Sebastian. Five Sebastians!

'Wake up, Morland! I've been waiting forever for you to wake up!'

'I am awake! I'm wide awake!'

'No, you're not! Posy! Posy! Wake up! You have to wake up!' There were hands on her, dragging her away from the five exasperated Sebastians, and she opened her eyes to see one exasperated Sam, tugging at her bedclothes. 'About time! And you have the nerve to say that I sleep like the dead.'

Posy sat up. She must have been sleeping with her mouth open because it felt as if something had crawled in there during the night and expired. Talking of which: 'I had the most horrible dream.'

'Who even cares?!' Sam tugged at Posy's arm. 'You have to come downstairs now. You're not going to believe this.'

Posy swatted Sam away. 'Believe what?' She glanced at her alarm clock. 'It's eight already! I was going to get up extra early to do some painting.'

She flung back the covers and got out of bed

on wobbly legs, but before she could head for the bathroom, Sam had her wrist in an uncompromising grip and was hauling her to the stairs. 'No time for the bathroom,' he squeaked. 'There are people here to see you!'

Posy's heart lurched as she stumbled downstairs. What if Sebastian had had a change of heart? What if the bailiffs were at the door?

She stilled on the bottom step. She could hear lots of noise outside. Just how many bailiffs did it take to evict one woman and a teenage boy?

'Oh God,' she mumbled.

'Come on, Posy!' Sam growled and he yanked her down the last stair and around the corner into the shop. 'Look! Look at all the people!'

Through the shop window (and Posy noted a blob of grey paint that she'd missed) was a crowd of people in the mews who were all staring back at her. And when Posy moved towards the door on legs that were even more wobbly than when she'd got out of bed, they all surged forwards.

'Here!' Sam stuffed the shop key in Posy's hand. She was all fumbling fingers as she unlocked the door.

'What on earth . . . ?' she asked, because at the head of the queue was Grumpy Old 'Un and Cocky Young 'Un and three other men in paint-splattered coveralls with a ladder, a couple of buckets, a box full of rollers and brushes and various other decorating accoutrements.

'The guvnor sent us,' Greg said. 'Where do you want us to start?'

'I have no idea,' Posy said as more people

spilled into the shop. 'What's going on?'

'You're not the only one who can call an emergency staff meeting,' Nina said as she sauntered through the door. 'In fact we had one in the Midnight Bell last night.'

'It was actually more like a Council of War,' Verity said as she came in with her parents and two of her four sisters who were visiting for a long weekend. 'Pippa's always saying that it takes a village, so we asked the regulars if they were free today, called in a few favours . . . '

'Though Verity refused to do any of the calling,' Tom said, ushering in a gaggle of older teenagers. 'These are my undergraduate World War One poetry students. They'll do anything for extra credit.'

Still, more people streamed in. The parents of some of Posy's reluctant readers, Pants and Yvonne and Gary. Lovely Stefan from the deli. The Aussie bar staff from the Midnight Bell. Bringing up the rear, Posy could see Mattie, entirely obscured by a teetering stack of Tupperware, and Pippa, who had an iPad in one hand and a clipboard in the other.

'I can't believe it,' Posy breathed. She shuffled a full three hundred and sixty degrees to take it all in. All these people, friends, colleagues, neighbours, complete strangers. It was hard not to burst into tears; instead Posy contented herself with standing there opening and shutting her mouth because she'd lost all her words. 'I've been feeling like such a failure and now . . . all this.'

Pippa put an arm around Posy's shoulders. 'As

345

Maya Angelou once said, 'You may encounter many defeats, but you must not be defeated.' We might have lost a few battles, Posy, but we're going to win the war.' She smiled winningly. 'Do you mind if I organise people? Assign jobs. I took the liberty of rustling up a couple of task sheets on the way here.'

Posy nodded faintly. 'Yes, please. Knock yourself out.'

It seemed as if everyone had something to do, except Posy. Tom and Nina corralled his students and they started stocking the shelves that had already been painted. On the other side of the arch, the anterooms were being painted. Greg had already pulled Posy aside to compliment her 'on the lovely job you've done with the sanding and the priming'.

And in the main room, an army of people had cleared the shop — everything that could be carried out was sitting in the courtyard — and they were washing, sanding and priming the shelves.

It was incredible. Unbelievable. Miraculous. But perhaps the most incredible, unbelievable, miraculous moment of all was when Verity overheard the fraught conversation Posy was having with the courier company and snatched the phone from Posy's hand.

'You listen to me,' Verity barked in a way that had her father, a man of the cloth, pressing his hands and lips together in a silent prayer. 'If those display cabinets aren't here by three this afternoon, I am coming to your offices and I'm going to unleash hell on your sorry arses. Is that clear? Yes? Good! Because you really, really don't want me to come over there.'

The vintage display cabinets turned up at three on the dot as Posy finished briefing the signwriter and was preparing to leave the shop on a mercy errand for more tea, coffee, milk and biscuits, though Giorgio and Toni, who ran No Plaice Like Home, had brought round fish and chips for all the volunteers at lunchtime.

Now as she walked to Sainsbury's, three things occurred to Posy. The first was that Bookends would be transformed into Happy Ever After by the end of the day. The whole shop. All the anterooms. In one day. In fact, they were so ahead of schedule that Greg and Mattie were currently in the tearoom discussing what state the floor might be in underneath the cracked old linoleum. No half-arsed, half-done reopening on Monday morning.

The second thing was that the only person missing was Sebastian. Which was fine. It really was. Sebastian had sent over Pippa and Greg and Dave and assorted handymen, and he'd spent an hour yesterday mopping up spilled paint. But all day, Posy had been aware of his absence. Often she'd stop what she was doing to gaze around the shop, searching for a tall, lean man in a suit with impossibly dark hair only for her spirits to sink a little because he wasn't there.

And the other thing that occurred to Posy as she heard a woman hiss at her friend as she walked past, 'Oh my God, what is that girl wearing? And why are there turds all over it?' was that she was still wearing her pyjamas.

By five, it was all over. The last of the volunteers left with Posy's heartfelt thanks ringing in their ears and an invitation to the official launch party the following Saturday evening.

Posy was *still* in her pyjamas as she and Tom manoeuvred the sofas into place and Nina and Verity switched on the big industrial fan that would help to dry the last set of shelves overnight.

'OK, people,' Posy called out. 'Time you went home. And that's an order!'

'Pub?' Nina asked hopefully, as she always did at this time on a Saturday.

Posy shook her head. 'I'm so tired I don't think I could crawl the few metres to the Midnight Bell.'

'You do look done in,' Verity said. 'Have an early night. There isn't that much to do tomorrow, so you can have a lie-in. I wish I could,' she added sorrowfully, because her family responsibilities were weighing heavily and according to Verity her parents and her sisters 'never stop talking. As soon as one of them pauses for breath, someone else grabs the chatty baton and I can't hear myself think.' Now she closed her eyes and sighed. 'Just one more day of incessant prattle. I can do one day. It's only twenty-four hours and I'll be asleep for some of them.'

'If you like, Sam and I could join you for lunch tomorrow,' Posy offered as she held the door open. 'There's that pub in Islington, which

348

does a great Sunday roast. Text me.'

Nina stayed for another five minutes to plead the case for a swift glass of alcohol, but Posy stayed firm and, finally, she was able to lock the door and trudge upstairs.

Posy had imagined a very different weekend. One where she'd spend most of it up to her elbows in grey paint, occasionally pausing to have a little cry, so it was quite a novelty to have no plans for tonight, but plenty of options. A pile of new novels that she hadn't had time to start on. Three saved episodes of *Call the Midwife*. The rest of the bottle of Pinot Grigio in the fridge and a box of chocolate truffles from a grateful customer because Posy had managed to locate a vintage Florence Lawford novel the woman had been trying to track down for years.

It wasn't exactly rock 'n' roll but as Saturday nights went, Posy had had worse. And yet half an hour later, she found herself in front of the computer opening up a blank Microsoft Word document, because it turned out that she really needed a different kind of happy ever after to the one she'd been given today.

Ravished by the Rake

Despite everything he'd done; the indignities, the shame, the humiliation that he'd heaped on her, how Posy still ached for Lord Thorndyke. Hungered for his touch, longed for his smile, wondered if she'd imagined his tenderness.

But Posy would not go to him. He would turn her away. Cast her out. And she would not beg for his love and find herself beholden to him. Posy might not have much in the way of material possessions — indeed, it looked certain that the house would have to be sold to pay off their creditors, to keep her and Samuel from gaol — but she had her pride.

And so he came to her instead on one storm-swollen night when the wind howled and the rain lashed against the windows. All the servants were now gone, even Little Sophie, and when Posy heard the banging on the door, she had no choice but to answer it herself though she feared it would be another bailiff.

She struggled with the heavy key then with trepidation and fear in her heart, but when she finally opened the door it was to see Thorndyke standing there. His clothes were soaked through, his inky black curls dripping, a wild desperate look in his eyes. Before she could shut the door on him, he thrust one booted foot against it.

'No! Hear me out at least,' he said hoarsely.

'I'm sure, sir, there's nothing you could say that I would wish to hear.'

'That may be true, but I have to tell you that I love you. How I love you! I burn with it, ache with it, glory in it, and so I come to you and ask you to put me out of my misery. If you can't love me back, when I know I've given you no reason, then I'll leave this place, leave London, sequester myself at my country estate and never darken your doorstep again, though you will forever have my heart.'

Posy placed a hand on her breast where her own heart trembled. (NB: couldn't hurt to have another tremble after so long, surely?) 'Sir! Are you unwell?' she asked, for she could know no other reason that he would utter such things unless he was sick of a fever.

'Did you not hear what I said, woman? My love for you burns and scalds until I no longer know who I am. Certainly not a man worthy of your love. Could you love me just a little?'

'I could never . . . ' she started to say, but it was borne out of habit rather than her heart's truth. Could she live without this impossible man in her life? Indeed, it would be a dull, turgid existence.

He had taught her body how to sing and, without him, she would be mute once more.

'Perhaps, sir, I could love you,' she said. 'Perhaps I could love you very well indeed. Perhaps, my heart is already yours to do with what you — '

351

No! No! No! NONONONONONONONON-
ONO!!!!!!!

Enough! Enough of this, Posy told herself
sternly as she started to delete each line, each
word that she'd written.

This wasn't real. It was nothing more than
futile longing. Something she'd started writing
so she'd have a safe space to take out all her
frustrations on Sebastian without having to
resort to causing him actual bodily harm. But
somewhere along the way, it had turned into a
love story. An overblown, overwritten love story,
but a love story nevertheless.

Sebastian didn't deserve to be the object of
her hormone-drenched, period costume fantasies,
not when all he'd done since Lavinia had died
was try to help her. OK, help her and also be very
rude, but this was Sebastian and she'd written
florid Regency porn about him. Hadn't even changed
his name!

And why had the story taken such an alarming
turn anyway? Did she have feelings towards him?
Of course she did. She'd had feelings for him for
as long as she could remember. They ran the
gamut of the alphabet from A for annoying right
down to Z for er, zingy, which was the only way
to describe the exhilarating rush Posy got when
they were trading insults back and forth like a
long volley in a Wimbledon finals match.

Then there had been the moment last night
that had suddenly become fraught with a tension
that had never been present before. There had

also been handholding, a lot of handholding, and that moment when Sebastian had cupped her face and leaned towards her and Posy had thought he was going to kiss her. Her heart did a strange skippy, dippy thing as she remembered it. What would she have done if he had kissed her?

She didn't have to think about it for too long. She'd have kissed him back and then Sebastian would have thrust her away and said something scathing because it would all have been a cruel joke. At best, he felt sorry for her, considering her to be like an annoying little sister, and at worst, she couldn't ever begin to compete with his legions of other women. Not when her life was chaotic and messy and she had to fake being a grown-up. For all that she'd accomplished in these last few weeks, she still felt as if she were stuck, hadn't progressed emotionally from that twenty-one-year-old who had suddenly lost her parents one summer's night.

Why would any man, especially Sebastian, want to get involved with someone like that?

So it was time to put a stop to this. End it. Delete. Delete. Delete.

Posy opened the desk drawer where all the computery things lived and scrabbled frantically for the thumb drive. She wouldn't be able to have a moment's peace until she'd destroyed the evidence. But all the drives looked the same — they'd bought a job lot of them last time they'd gone to Costco — and by the time she finally found the one she was looking for and rammed it into the computer's USB hub, Posy

353

was sweating and yes, her hands were trembling.

There was no *Ravished by the Rake* on the drive but several InDesign files, containing the artwork Nina's tattooist had done for Happy Ever After. Which didn't mean anything because Sam had had to put the files on several different thumb drives to send to the stationery people and the tote bag people and the printers. It really didn't mean anything. So there was no reason for Posy to suddenly feel like she'd forgotten how to breathe.

'Bloody, bloody, bloody hell!' Posy muttered and then she didn't say anything as she went through every drive in the drawer.

Ravished by the Rake wasn't on any of them, so Posy tore through the flat, opening every drawer, rifling through all the little china pots and vintage tins that contained buttons and old keys and hair slides but no thumb drive.

Posy thought she might cry. Then she thought she might throw up because there was one very obvious and plausible reason why she couldn't find the thumb drive that contained all her sick, torrid fantasies about Sebastian.

She'd given it to the man himself.

Posy went straight to the fridge, yanked out the bottle of Pinot Grigio, poured what was left into a mug and gulped half of it down. You were meant to drink brandy when you'd had a shock but she'd never drunk brandy in her life so the Pinot Grigio would have to do.

She had another fruitless search for the thumb drive then she sat down on the stairs and wondered if she should phone Sebastian. It was

354

Saturday — he probably hadn't even had a chance to look at the thumb drive and she could pop over to his flat in Clerkenwell, exchange thumb drives and be on her way.

Nothing to see here. Move along.

She took her phone out of her back pocket, scrolled through her contacts until she came to Sebastian's number and stared at it.

But what if he had opened up the thumb drive, seen the file and his curiosity had got the better of him? Sebastian was terribly curious about everything, so what would happen then?

Dear God, it didn't bear thinking about.

Posy took another enthusiastic chug of her wine and put her head in her hands. It was a while until she became aware of a knocking sound. Someone was at the door. Maybe, hopefully, Nina who'd had a few in the Midnight Bell and needed reinforcements. Nina would know what to do.

Posy tripped down the stairs and into the shop, but the figure she could see through the glass wasn't Nina. It wasn't Nina at all.

20

Posy's hands were truly trembling like they'd never trembled before as she unlocked the door, though a part of her, a huge part, wanted to flee upstairs, jump into bed and pull the covers over her head.

'Oh hi, Sebastian,' Posy said once she got the door open. She cringed at the shrill note to her voice. 'What's up?'

He was dressed all in black with an intent look on his face as he stepped into the shop, then shut the door behind him and turned the key.

Posy leaned back against the display table and clutched the rim with her sweaty hands. 'Bit late for social calls, isn't it?' she asked.

Still, Sebastian said nothing, but stood looking at Posy with his head tilted to one side. He didn't seem angry, he didn't seem like he was about to laugh and poke ten shades of fun out of Posy and her ridiculous Regency romance either.

So maybe he hadn't read it and this really was a social call.

'I'm glad you stopped by,' Posy said a little desperately. 'I think I gave you the wrong thumb drive last night. I've got the right one upstairs. No need to look at the one you have, there's nothing important on it. Nothing important at all. Nothing that would interest you, but it's — '

'Ill met by moonlight, my dear Miss Morland,' Sebastian said, as he took a step closer to where

Posy stood, her eyes widening in alarm. 'How enchanting you look. So adorably dishevelled.'

Oh, no! No! No! No! NONONONONON-ONONONONONONO!!!!!!!

Posy attempted a carefree laugh and ended up choking while her heart thundered away like a marathon runner's on the approach to the twenty-six-mile marker. 'Have you been drinking?' she spluttered. He was still taking steps towards her. 'I think you should go, Sebastian. It is late and I'm really tired. Anyway, it's Saturday night. You must have a hot date.'

Sebastian continued moving closer and taking his sweet time about it. 'I find I grow tired of tavern wenches, courtesans and other men's wives.' And he must have memorised every awful word that she'd written because he tapped one finger against Posy's lips as she stared at him in horror and tried not to swoon. Not at Sebastian's nearness. But because even with an industrial fan whirring away in the corner, it was suddenly very hot in the shop. Posy was burning up. Oh God, he smelt so good. 'But I'll wager I won't grow tired of you.'

Posy sidestepped the table, one hand up to ward Sebastian off because he was smiling now and it was a smile as devilish as his Regency counterpart's. 'Please, Sebastian, you have to go now,' she said. But as she turned to flee, he caught hold of her arm and pulled her close enough that he could lean down and . . . was he kissing her cheek? He was, just the lightest brush of his lips and Posy couldn't have moved if she'd wanted to.

She did want to, she really did, but her legs didn't seem to have got the message.

'By all means make me chase you, Miss Morland. The hunt only quickens my blood,' Sebastian whispered in her ear, and he kissed Posy's burning, blushing cheek again — because he'd read her awful novel, realised that along the way she'd developed feelings for him and he thought it was a huge joke. He thought he could come here and mock her.

'Don't!' Posy tried to pull away, but his arms were around her waist now. 'This isn't funny! It's actually very hurtful. Please don't do this to me.'

Sebastian let his hands drop to his sides and Posy wanted him to say something, break character, tease her so she could come back with a few snappy one-liners herself — that was what they did. Then Sebastian took hold of her hand, drew it to his mouth and kissed her palm, while Posy stood there wary and mistrustful.

Sebastian frowned, maybe it was because her palm was very, very sweaty, which might have explained why he pressed a kiss to the corner of Posy's mouth instead. 'I must, for I will have no peace of mind until I do,' he said and softly kissed her again. 'How you torment me, intrigue me, possess me with thoughts of making you mine.'

'All right! That's enough,' Posy said, because it was. Without a thought for his suit, she pushed Sebastian away. 'I shouldn't have written what I did. In fact, I didn't write it. I was reading it for a friend of mine and I thought it would be funny to swap the names. Which was wrong. OK, I know it was wrong but — '

'Why should you be left in peace when I am in torment?' He sounded as if he meant it, which was the cruellest thing of all. Or maybe it was the way he was prowling towards her again, like a long, lean panther with a predatory glint in his eye.

'You've done some pretty shady things to me over the years,' Posy told him furiously, her hands on her hips. 'I think this is even worse than when you shut me in the coal-hole. You *are* an absolute rake!'

'Oh do shut up, Morland,' Sebastian said, suddenly dropping his facade. 'I'm genuinely trying to seduce you, so bloody well let yourself be seduced!'

He looked as shocked at his words as Posy did, but then her arms were suddenly around his neck because Posy realised that actually she would like to be seduced by Sebastian — she'd like it very much. 'Well, in that case, go on then,' she said. 'Bloody well seduce me!'

He did seduce her. Or rather he kissed her and she kissed him back. When it wasn't saying hurtful things, Sebastian's mouth was wonderful. Tender but demanding, playful but fierce and Posy didn't ever want to stop kissing him, even as they ricocheted off the shop fittings until they were stumbling to the stairs, still locked together in a frantic embrace.

There was an interlude as they lay sprawled uncomfortably on the stairs and tried to catch their breath, while Sebastian unbuttoned Posy's flower-sprigged blouse with shaking fingers. 'I'm trembling,' he told her with a sly smile. 'Quivering, wavering, but mostly trembling.'

'Shut up!' Posy said. 'I never want to hear you quote another word from *Ravished by the Rake*.'

'You'd better kiss me again, then,' Sebastian said, and so Posy did as she was told, although when they'd finally made it to her bed and were tugging at each other's clothes until they were skin on skin, he lowered his head to kiss the freckle just above her belly button and murmured, 'Contrary to popular belief, I do respond to the word no. So I'm asking you nicely, will you let me into that soft inviting place between your silken thighs, Morland?'

'You are a very, very bad man,' Posy said, as she wiggled under him in a way that made Sebastian clench his jaw. 'But seeing as how you're already halfway there, you might as well, I suppose.'

★ ★ ★

'That was good,' Sebastian said afterwards. 'Very good. What you lacked in experience, you made up for in enthusiasm, Morland.'

★ ★ ★

Posy felt as if she was floating on a cloud of euphoria, though she wasn't floating but lying in Sebastian's arms while he stroked her hair, occasionally backtracking when his fingers encountered a knot. 'Whereas you had both enthusiasm and experience,' she pointed out.

Then she didn't know what else to say. It had been a while, a long, long while since she'd entertained a gentleman caller, and she wasn't sure if they were meant to have a lengthy debrief about what they'd just done, which would then lead to a tense discussion about what would happen next. Which would then lead to an argument, which would only end with either Sebastian storming out or Posy throwing him out, and she didn't want that to happen. For one thing, she could barely move.

But it was going to get complicated, not to mention awkward, because they had a complicated and awkward past and oh God, she'd just had sex with Sebastian and now she was another name on the long list of women he'd bedded then dumped for a newer, shinier model.

Posy no longer felt euphoric, she was gripped by panic, but before she could force her cotton wool limbs to tense, Sebastian nuzzled a spot behind her ear and tightened his arms around her. 'Morland, I hate to kill the mood, but I'm absolutely parched. Do you think you could go and make me one of your undrinkable cups of tea?'

'If it's that undrinkable, why should I bother?' Posy snapped. Oddly, the snapping and the uncalled for dig about her exemplary tea-making skills didn't kill the mood, even when Posy had to grab her dressing gown and put it on under the covers because although they'd just made love, striding about naked was something she wasn't ready for. Snapping at each other and trading insults was what she and Sebastian did, and the fact that they were still doing it after *doing it* made Posy feel more at ease with the situation.

And because it was an auspicious occasion, she used the posh Clipper teabags, fresh full-fat milk and even arranged some HobNobs in a decorative pattern on a plate. Then she carried her laden tray back into the bedroom where Sebastian was lounging on her M&S floral bed linen and looking very comfortable with his surroundings.

'You were gone far too long,' he complained, and just as Posy was about to point out in her defence that even he had to wait for a kettle to boil, he assumed a sorrowful expression. 'I missed you terribly.'

'I was five minutes,' Posy protested as she handed Sebastian a mug and as their fingers brushed, it started off a little conflagration so that all Posy's nerve endings began to tingle from the tips of her toes right up to the top of her head, where it felt as if her hair was standing on end. Though, truthfully, her hair probably was standing on end after being tousled and tugged, and there had been one point where Posy had found herself upside down and half hanging out of bed.

'I've never met anyone who blushes as much as you do,' Sebastian noted as Posy quickly shed her dressing gown and dived back into bed. 'I suppose it's quite endearing now that I know that you blush all over. And I mean all over.'

Sebastian wasn't blushing because he was impervious to embarrassment, but his hair was also in a state of wild abandon and it was silly when they'd known each other so long, were lying in bed together, to suddenly feel so shy.

But this was outside of Posy's usual remit, whereas Sebastian must have been used to making post-coital chitchat and lounging about in beds that weren't his own. And those other women. None of them lasted very long and she and Sebastian weren't friends . . . and now Posy didn't even know what they were . . .

'You're thinking very loudly, Morland.' Sebastian put down his mug of tea so he could kiss Posy's shoulder. 'It's giving me a headache.'

'I hated it when we weren't speaking,' Posy blurted out. 'When you stopped coming round. And if this means that's going to happen again, because you really don't have a good track record when it comes to long-term relationships, then maybe it's better that we cut our losses now. Just agree that this was a moment of madness and that we're better off — '

'Getting married,' Sebastian interjected smoothly. 'Especially now that I've taken advantage of you. Isn't that the way it works in those awful romances of yours?'

'They're not awful,' Posy said. 'Well, the one I wrote was, but didn't I take advantage of you and . . . Hang on! Rewind! Did you just . . . Did you just *propose* to me?'

'Once again, Morland, I have to ask if you ever listen to a single word I say? You know, I quite liked being a Romantic Hero,' Sebastian decided as Posy tried to sit up. 'Please stop fidgeting. Though you should know that I don't have the upper body strength to lift you on to my horse. And I can't ride, but anyway, we'll still have to get married.'

It was the incentive Posy needed to succeed in freeing herself from Sebastian's arms so she could stare him in the eye. He didn't look as if he was joking. He looked deadly serious. 'Why on *earth* would we have to do that?' she asked.

Sebastian sat up and stuffed a couple of pillows behind him, then crossed his arms and sighed as though he couldn't understand why Posy was being so dense. 'Well, Lavinia adored you — though she adored me too, so she wasn't a particularly good judge of character. I did try to tell you this last night.'

'You did?' Posy frowned. 'I don't remember that at all.'

'Once again, I have to point out that you never listen to anything I say, do you?' Sebastian shook his head sadly. 'We were talking about your big sleep and how Lavinia kept telling me that you weren't ready to wake up. Let me ask you a question; why do you think she left me the mews and you the shop?'

'She said, in her letter, that she wanted us to be friends.' Posy smiled. 'She also said that I should give you a clip round the ear from time to time.' Then her expression became more serious. Whenever the topic of Sebastian had come up, Lavinia would shake her head and look exasperated but also tender at the same time and say things like 'He's such an impossible boy. Heart of gold, of course, but one would be hard pressed to find it when he hides it so well.' But then . . . 'She did say a couple of times that you needed the love of a good woman.'

'You weren't the only one to get a letter,' Sebastian said, and he twisted out from under the quilt to grope on the floor for his trousers. He returned with his wallet, which he opened and pulled out a folded sheet of cream paper. 'Here.'

Seeing Lavinia's navy blue handwriting still hurt a little. In the same way that Posy would occasionally find a list from Lavinia at the back of a drawer in the office or an old stock card and she'd be hit with the loss of Lavinia all over again.

Dear Sebastian

Darling, darling boy. How hard it is to say goodbye. Please never be in doubt of just how much I love you. And because I love you, I only want to see you happy — and I know that there's only one thing that will make you happy.

Posy.

She's not ready yet, Sebastian. She's still fast asleep. Still lost. But I know a way to make Posy find herself again and once she's found herself, then she'll find you.

That's not the only reason why I'm leaving Bookends to Posy, but it's one of the reasons. It's her home and I made a promise to her and Sam when their parents died, that it would always be their home. But I know the business is in a terrible mess and Posy must be the one to sort it out. I have every confidence that she'll transform Bookends' fortunes. Breathe life into it again. She needs to know that she's strong and that she can stand on her own two feet, and once she can do that, she'll be able to handle anything. Even you, my darling boy.

Obviously, I'm leaving the mews to you, which will be a clever way to bring you closer to Posy. Help her, by all means, Sebastian, but don't bully her. If things take a turn for the worse or the bailiffs are outside, then please offer her guidance and support, but give her the time and the space that she needs.

You'll both get there in the end and if you're even a fraction as happy as Perry and I were, then you'll have such golden years together.

I'm counting on it. Counting on you. Don't let me down, Sebastian.

I may not be around for much longer but I will never stop loving you.

Lavinia xxx

It was hard to read the last few lines because Posy's eyes were blurry with tears that trickled down her face, off the top of her nose and her chin, because Sebastian had been right the night before when he'd said that she wasn't a pretty crier.

'She really did love you, Sebastian,' Posy said, because that was clear even if she couldn't begin to make sense of everything else Lavinia had written to him.

'And she loved you too. Always said that if she were a betting woman she'd put money on the two of us ending up together,' Sebastian said softly. 'I'm only following Lavinia's last wishes, Morland.'

'You sure about that?' Posy asked. 'One of Lavinia's other last wishes was that you didn't bully me, but you managed to ignore that request.'

Sebastian pretended to choke on the sip of tea he'd just taken. 'That wasn't bullying. It was tough love. And a lot of the times that I tried to sweep in and save the day, you'd already saved it without me. You've become your own woman, Morland.' Sebastian gave Posy a sidelong glance with a hint of arched eyebrow that did things to parts of her that she was sure were still recovering. 'Just as Lavinia said you would.'

'It's still not even half a good reason to get married. *Married!*' Posy pulled the duvet over her head so she wouldn't have to look at Sebastian, who seemed to have inherited Lavinia's exasperated but tender expression.

'It's an excellent reason to get married. But I do have other reasons too. Would you like to hear them?' he asked solicitously.

'No,' Posy said from underneath the quilt.

'Sorry, can't hear you, Morland. Was that a yes? Well to start with, you're great with Sam, so it stands to reason that you'll be a good mother, though we probably shouldn't have children right away. Not until he's gone to university and you'll be what, thirty-one then so we'll need to get a move on. Two or four kids, I was thinking

— no odd numbers, someone will always feel sidelined. Certainly not one child, singular, I was a single child and look how I turned out.'

Posy pulled the duvet away so she could sit up and punch Sebastian on the arm. It wasn't a hard punch, but he made a big show of screwing up his face and rubbing the spot where she'd barely touched him. 'Are you really talking about the number of imaginary children we're going to have?'

'But we have to have children, otherwise it would be a waste of your childbearing hips! Also, for the record, you have fantastic tits.' And because they were right there, in front of him, Sebastian couldn't seem to stop himself from rubbing his thumb over one rosy nipple, which was distracting. Very distracting. 'You're not still going out with Count Jens of Uppsala, are you?'

'You are never going to stop quoting bits of that horrible book at me, are you?'

'Never. I have the whole thing committed to memory. And it's not horrible. It's a first draft. A work in progress. I found it rather gripping. Also, I liked Lord Sebastian Thorndyke. He was very thrusting and dynamic,' Sebastian remembered fondly, as he moved on to her other breast until Posy slapped his hands away and dragged the duvet up to cover her chest. 'Are you still seeing him, then?'

'We decided, or Jens decided, that we were better off as friends.' This wasn't going anywhere, it couldn't. They certainly weren't getting married, but . . . 'So, what about you and Yasmin, then?'

'I haven't seen Yasmin since the book sale. She sent me a text to say that I was too much for her.' Sebastian shifted around so he was lying on top of the covers with his head in her lap. 'It's your turn to stroke my hair now, Morland.' He waited until Posy was obeying orders and then sighed. 'You see, I'm not very good with women.'

Posy's hands paused from winding through Sebastian's curls. 'Sebastian, you've been out with *thousands* of women.'

'Don't stop and not thousands. Hundreds. Not even a hundred. I can get women, but then I don't have a clue what to do with them,' Sebastian said very quietly. 'I spent my childhood being fawned over by my grandparents and a succession of nannies, while each consecutive stepfather loathed me, then I was packed off to an all boys school where I happily hung out with the other geeks and played computer games until I couldn't see straight. When I was eighteen and went to university I suddenly had all these girls chasing after me, without any effort on my part, so I never bothered to make any effort. I'm not entirely sure that was a good game plan.'

'Sebastian, much as it pains me to say it, you're beautiful and rich and Lavinia was absolutely right: you have a kind heart when you bother to let people see it. So of course girls were going to be interested in you,' Posy said.

'I'm not beautiful,' Sebastian insisted. 'It's hardly manly.' Then he held up an arm. 'And I'm weedy. Thank God for a well-cut suit. You should see me in jeans and a T-shirt — I look like I've been on a year-long hunger protest.'

'I always thought you were beautiful,' Posy admitted. 'Until you locked me in the coal-hole.'

'Let it go, Morland,' Sebastian advised. 'I am terrible with women. For instance, when I really like a girl, really like her, instead of declaring my intentions, I end up insulting her. I'm a hopeless case.'

'Sebastian, you insult everybody!' Posy pointed out.

'Actually I don't. Yes, I'm tactless, but when I'm with you, I fall over my words and even when I'm trying to be nice, it tends to go horribly wrong. I will try harder in future though, I promise. Now, back to our wedding plans.'

Posy's heart had perked up. As if it could dare to dream again, but now she shut her eyes. 'There will be no wedding. We haven't even been on a date!'

'What's the point in dating? Dating is boring. We've known each other forever, so when you think about it, we've skipped the dating bit and moved right on to the part where we've already been married for years.'

'Sebastian, we argue all the time.'

'The snapping of courtship. Your parents used to argue. There was that time when Angharad didn't speak to Ian for three whole days because she was in the middle of making a cake and he took the recipe book she was using and sold it before she'd mixed in the dry ingredients,' Sebastian said. Posy didn't remember that at all, but she stored it away now to tell Sam. Sam! She couldn't even begin to think of what Sam would say about these new developments. 'And Lavinia

370

and Perry loved a good barney. He told me that they spent the first year they got married in one long, continuous fight, and that once she threw a whole roast chicken at him. I don't mind if you want to throw roast chickens at me.'

'Says the man who has a fit if I so much as touch his suit jacket.' Posy trapped a big, fat curl between her fingers. 'I do like touching your hair though — not that that's a good basis for a marriage. Not even close, so let's just talk about something else, all right?'

'Well, I don't fancy a long engagement. How do you feel about big weddings? Knowing you, you'll probably want the big poofy dress and the centrepieces and a choreographed first dance, but I reckon we could get married in the Registry Office in Euston one morning and be in Paris in time for dinner. We could take Sam along, if you wanted. In fact, where is Sam?'

'He's staying at Pants' house. Said the paint fumes were giving him a headache.'

'We should probably get dressed quite soon and mosey on over to Pants' house so I can formally ask Sam for his sister's hand. I wonder if we could get married on Monday if we got a special license? How long does it take to get a special license? Where's my phone? I'll google it.'

Posy screamed then. 'I'm not getting married. Are you mad? Why on earth would I get married to you?'

'Because I'm in love with you, Morland. Do keep up. Been besotted with you for quite a while now, though it took me some time to figure it out. It's why I've spent these last few weeks

371

trying to show you how much I care about you, and now that I've done that, we can spend the next sixty years arguing with each other, then having fantastic make-up sex. It will be great.'

'Shush. Stop it.' Posy placed a finger on Sebastian's lips to quieten him. 'We're not getting married. I might have feelings towards you, a crush, but I don't love you.'

Sebastian kissed the tip of her finger then took Posy's hand away from his mouth. 'Oh, don't you?' He didn't seem the least put out by her confession. 'I think you'll find that you do. There I was, worrying that you saw me as a substitute big brother — you even said as much last night . . .'

'You were the one who insisted that I saw you as an overbearing big brother,' Posy pointed out. 'But I only agreed about the overbearing part.'

'Well, it's a pity that you couldn't have been a bit more specific and we could have closed the deal last night,' Sebastian snapped, but then he smiled. 'I suppose I can forgive you when all this time you've been writing a *romance* novel with you and me as the star-crossed lovers, and you're always banging on about Happy Ever Afters so I bet you had one planned for Miss Morland and Lord Thorndyke.'

'Well, yes, but they're not real . . .' And then Posy recalled what she'd been writing an hour before; a happy ever after. Her heart and her fingers were way ahead of her. 'Perhaps. Perhaps I could love you, but that doesn't mean I'm getting married to you.'

'We are getting married.'

'We really are not.'

'Beg to differ, Morland.'

There was no telling him. Sebastian wouldn't listen once he'd got an idea in his head. So Posy said what she'd said the last time she'd found herself in this position.

'Fine, whatever.'

21

Posy had imagined this day for so long that she couldn't quite believe it was here.

She was surrounded by all the people she loved: Sam, her grandparents, aunts and uncles and cousins down from Wales, Nina, Verity, Tom, and yes, Sebastian, because it turned out she did love him too. Posy was finally getting her Happy Ever After.

There were other people milling about the room: Pants, Little Sophie, and their respective parents, most of the shopkeepers from Rochester Street, favoured customers.

Posy couldn't stop smiling even though her face ached with the unfamiliar stretching of her facial muscles. She didn't think she'd ever been as happy as she was in this moment, on this day, and suddenly she couldn't bear it any longer and she had to find a quiet spot to make sense of it all. No one should be allowed to be this happy. It just didn't seem fair.

'Why are you skulking in the corner? Sebastian is freaking out. Thinks you've done a runner.' Nina was suddenly right in front of her, squatting down so she could peer into the corner where Posy was hiding from the hubbub. 'It's all right. No one would blame you if you did a runner.'

'I'm a bit overwhelmed, that's all,' Posy admitted. 'It's all happened so quickly. Everything's changed and I haven't quite caught up with myself.'

'You have to be the change that you want to happen.' Nina was shouldered out of the way by Pippa. 'Come on, it's time to cut the cake, then speeches. You have got a speech ready, haven't you?'

Posy hadn't. She was just going to wing it. Try to give voice to what was in her heart, which was currently hammering against her breastbone. 'Not really but it will be fine. 'She gathered books like clouds and words poured down like rain,'' Posy quoted and Pippa frowned.

'Did Steve Jobs say that?' she asked.

'No, he didn't,' Posy laughed and she let Pippa haul her out of her hiding place and she smoothed down the skirt of her white dress as Nina herded her across the room, not letting her stop and speak to anyone, even though good cheer and congratulations followed in Posy's wake.

Nina didn't stop herding until they'd reached the table in the middle of the room where Sebastian and Sam were waiting for her. 'At last!' Sebastian cried, though Posy had only been gone ten minutes. 'I'm going to have you implanted with a tracking device.'

'I don't think that's legal,' Sam said. He thought about it for a moment. 'I also don't think it's a very husbandly thing to do.'

'It's not, is it? And I plan to be the best husband I can be,' Sebastian said grandly. 'I mean, I haven't once complained about the mess upstairs, have I?'

Posy rolled her eyes. 'That's only because you sent your cleaner over when you knew I'd be out, and anyway, I don't know why you keep going on about . . . '

'Ladies and gentlemen, can I have your attention?' Nina clapped her hands before Posy could set Sebastian straight on a few things. 'We're about to cut the cake and I know Posy would like to say a few words. And Sebastian would probably like to say a lot of words too.'

'True that,' Sam muttered and Sebastian gently cuffed the side of his head.

'Shut it, Morland Junior,' he admonished. 'And to think that you were my favourite Morland too.'

Someone had handed Posy a cake slice, which she used to prod Sebastian in the ribs until he mimed zipping his lips shut. Ah, if only . . .

Posy turned back to the assembled guests, a nervous smile pinned to her face. But then her smile softened as she looked past them to the shop. Her beautiful shop, painted that lovely smudgy grey and even Tom had agreed that the clover pink wasn't *too* pink.

Dotted about the shop, but not near the books because Posy had been adamant about that, candles glowed. The Happy Ever After candles that Posy had commissioned perfumed the air with the scent of honeysuckle in memory of her mother, roses for Lavinia, and somehow Elaine, the chandler, had managed to capture a hint of that musty smell of old books too.

In the vintage display cases that now took up one whole wall of the main room were mugs, stationery, T-shirts, Posy's beloved tote bags and necklaces and rings adorned with quotes from novels embossed on enamel, and all manner of other literary gifts.

And then there were the books.

The shelves were stacked deep with books, each one waiting for someone to buy them so together they could go on an adventure. Fall deeply in love. Maybe the words printed on the pages might be the words that the reader had heard for so long deep inside their souls but had never been able to say out loud. Each book promised its reader that, no matter what trials and torments life might throw up, there were still happy ever afters to be had.

Even if it was in a book, it still counted as a happy ever after.

'Speech! Speech! Speech!'

Posy was jolted out of her reverie to find every pair of eyes on her, while she stood there, mouth agape, brandishing the cake slice like it was a deadly weapon. Then she felt the warm slide of fingers against her own as Sebastian slipped his hand into hers.

'In your own time, Morland,' he murmured.

Posy breathed deep. She was among friends so there was no reason to feel scared. She just had to speak from her heart because her heart would never let her down.

'I'm going to keep it brief because I'd much rather get on with the cake cutting, then the cake eating,' she began, in a voice that was surprisingly squeaky. 'I'd like to thank you all for coming, because all of you helped to make my Happy Ever After come true. But I'd especially like to thank my amazing colleagues. How lucky

I am to get to work with my best friends every day: Nina, Verity, Tom and Little Sophie. Thank you for all your hard work.' Posy had to pause because people were clapping and she needed the oxygen. Then she turned to Sam, who mouthed no and shook his head. 'And thank you to my clever younger brother for building our website and agreeing to come along for the ride, and to Pippa for showing me how to PPM, but mostly I'd like to thank my parents for teaching me that I would never be alone if I loved books, and Lavinia, for believing in me and trusting me with her shop and lastly — '

'Can you wrap this up, Morland?' Sebastian whispered in her ear just as Posy was about to thank him for waking her from her seven-year sleep. 'It turns out that smart, successful women turn me on and I'm going to have to kiss you quite soon.'

He'd made her lose her flow and now all she could think about was kissing Sebastian. Posy had been thinking quite a lot about kissing Sebastian this last week, when she wasn't actually kissing Sebastian because she'd done an awful lot of that too.

'And I would thank Sebastian, but the praise would only go to his head.' Posy squeezed his hand and he returned the pressure until Posy needed her hand back to cut the beautiful red velvet cake that Mattie had made, iced then decorated with a quote from Jane Austen: 'I declare after all there is no enjoyment like reading!'

Posy's work here was done, but before she

could start handing out slices of cake, Sebastian put his arm around her. 'I'd like to say a few words too,' he said easily, though pressed against his side as she was, Posy could feel his heart thundering away. 'This shop has been in my family for a hundred years and I'd like to thank Morland for making it live again. I wanted to turn it into a crime bookshop, and I still think that would have been a game changer, but lately I've come to realise that romance isn't such a bad thing after all. And I think it's appropriate that Happy Ever After is a family-run bookshop that specialises in romance because Morland and I are getting married . . . '

'Oh God, we are *not* getting married,' Posy reminded him. 'I never said we were.'

'You said, 'Fine, whatever' — I ran it past my lawyer. He said that counts as a verbal agreement,' Sebastian informed Posy.

'You have no witnesses. And anyway a judge would absolutely overrule your lawyer, on the grounds that you're not of sound mind.'

'Don't be ridiculous. We both know we'd be married already if we didn't have to give twenty-eight days' notice first.' Sebastian raised his head to gaze out into the crowd. 'You're all invited by the way.'

'Maybe, at some point in the future, we *may* get married but no rational person gets married to someone who hasn't even taken them on a date,' Posy said, and she wished that they weren't talking about this *again* and not in front of so many people, whose eyes were flicking back and forth between her and Sebastian like this was much more fun than listening to any more speeches.

Though it was possible that they were just waiting for cake.

'We're getting married, Morland, and there's nothing you can do about it, except turn up on the day in question wearing a pretty dress and clutching a bouquet of flowers.'

'We are *not* getting married,' Posy repeated, louder this time for the benefit of those at the back of the room who might not have heard her the first time.

Sebastian was silent in the time it took her to cut the first slice of the cake, but as she transferred it to a paper plate, he stirred himself.

'We can't get the licence for another three weeks so I'll take you out on a couple of dates in the meantime,' he decided. '*Then* we can get married. Can't we?'

'I'll think about it,' Posy said and before he could say another word on the subject, she shoved the piece of cake in the direction of his mouth. 'But it's highly unlikely. Now shut up and eat some cake.'

And while Sebastian was otherwise engaged, Posy quickly raised her glass and asked everyone to join her 'in a toast to Happy Ever After and all who sail in her!'

As the words 'Happy Ever After' echoed around the shop, Posy shook her head. Married to Sebastian? Really? It was the most ridiculous thing she'd ever heard.

22

Reader, she married him.

Acknowledgements

Thank you to Rebecca Ritchie for ace agenting, Karolina Sutton, Lucy Morris, Melissa Pimental and all at Curtis Brown. Martha Ashby who knows a thing or two about romantic fiction, Kimberley Young, Charlotte Brabbin and the team at Harper Collins.

And much thanks to Eileen Coulter for patiently listening to me practically dictate the whole book to her as we tramped along the highways and byways of North London.

We do hope that you have enjoyed reading this large print book.

Did you know that all of our titles are available for purchase?

We publish a wide range of high quality large print books including:
Romances, Mysteries, Classics
General Fiction
Non Fiction and Westerns

Special interest titles available in large print are:
The Little Oxford Dictionary
Music Book
Song Book
Hymn Book
Service Book

Also available from us courtesy of Oxford University Press:
Young Readers' Dictionary
(large print edition)
Young Readers' Thesaurus
(large print edition)

For further information or a free brochure, please contact us at:
Ulverscroft Large Print Books Ltd.,
The Green, Bradgate Road, Anstey,
Leicester, LE7 7FU, England.
Tel: (00 44) **0116 236 4325**
Fax: (00 44) **0116 234 0205**

Other titles published by Ulverscroft:

MY HUSBAND THE STRANGER

Rebecca Done

When Molly married Alex Frazer, she knew it was for ever. Theirs would be the perfect future. However, after a night out with his twin brother, Graeme, a terrible injury leaves Alex with permanent brain damage. In a single moment, the man she married is transformed into someone new. Someone who has forgotten how to love her. And someone Molly isn't sure she can ever love again. The Alex she married no longer exists. Even with Graeme willing to help, Molly isn't sure that she can go on. How can she stay married to a man she doesn't know? Should she let the future she dreamed of slip through her fingers? And what really happened on the night that turned her husband into a stranger?

THE SECRET LIFE OF LUCY LOVECAKE

Pippa James

Daisy Delaney's life is pancake-flat. A talented baker and passionate lingerie specialist, she has wound up with no one to bake for and an unsuccessful career. But when she starts a delicious relationship with famous French author-chef Michel Amiel, everything begins to look a bit more exciting. That is, until Michel's bestselling cookbook is knocked off the top spot by newcomer Lucy Lovecake. His outdated recipes slide down the charts, while the popularity of Lucy Lovecake's new dating cookbook is rising like the perfect sponge. How can Daisy ever tell Michel that *she* is the mysterious Lucy Lovecake? And more importantly, does she even want to be with a difficult, egotistical, down-on-his-luck Frenchman just as her career is beginning to take off? Especially when she has some other very interesting offers . . .

A SECRET GARDEN

Katie Fforde

Lorna is a talented gardener and Philly is a plantswoman. Together they work on the grounds of a beautiful manor house in the Cotswolds. They enjoy their jobs and are surrounded by family and friends. But for them both, the door to true love remains resolutely closed. So when Lorna is introduced to Jack at a dinner party, and Lucien catches Philly's eye at the local market, it seems that dreams really can come true and happy endings lie just around the corner. But do they? Troublesome parents, the unexpected arrival of someone from Lorna's past, and the discovery of an old and secret garden mean their lives are about to become a lot more complicated . . .